Once Upon A WASTELAND

The Scripts

Season One

by

Brad Williams

For V – my muse, my North Star, and

my most steadfast supporter

Table of Contents

Introduction

On October 22, 2021, an audio fiction podcast premiered to little fanfare. Titled "Once Upon a Wasteland" and based on Bethesda Softworks' popular "Fallout" video game series, the show soft-launched with a prologue episode that set up the story that was to play out over the course of ten full-length episodes.

It received a total of five downloads that day. Since then, the show has been listened to more than half a million times by listeners in 183 countries across the globe, including Vatican City; I can't say for certain that Pope Leo is a fan, but I also can't say for certain that he's *not.*

In this book, you'll find the script for that prologue as well as for the ten episodes that followed along with some context and behind-the-scenes notes.

So how did this thing get started, anyway?

Once upon a time, 27 years after… no, wait. That's not it.

In February 2021, a creator named Lawrence McNamara posted a casting call for his Fallout-based audio drama – "The MODUS Files" – on Reddit. On a whim, I decided to submit an audition. I didn't expect to get the role that I auditioned for, given that it had been decades since I did any proper voice work. Much to my surprise and delight, however, I was cast as MODUS, a malevolent AI that played a central role in the story.

Over the next few months, Lawrence and I talked about storytelling. I had television writing experience, though it was of a similar vintage to my voice acting and narration experience, and he encouraged me to build some characters and their backstories.

One thing about me that differs from most other creators that I know is that I don't write for pleasure. That doesn't mean that I don't enjoy writing; quite the contrary, I *love* to write. What drives me to write, though, is the idea of moving people, and that makes it difficult for me to gin up the motivation to write anything that isn't intended for eventual public consumption.

I have friends who've self-published novels, and that's easier to do today than it's ever been. The biggest problem there is that I'm not a good writer of prose. I often say that I "think in screenplay." I've tried writing short stories and even novels, and to say that style isn't in my wheelhouse is, to be kind, an understatement. Before I got involved with Lawrence's show, though, I didn't know that it was possible to self-publish a scripted fiction project.

Lawrence eventually encouraged me to consider turning what I'd been sharing with him into an audio drama podcast like his and helped me do exactly that. He set me up with the Robots Radio Rocket Club, a service that helped new creators launch and promote their projects, and helped me build out the framework of what my show would eventually become.

Fallout 76, the most recent entry in the Fallout series, has a character named Odessa Valdez. It quickly became clear that Odessa was very popular among the player base, including a not-insignificant group of players who lamented that the character couldn't be "romanced" in the way other characters could be. I was among those players.

That's where the show's core concept came from – what if Odessa *could* be romanced? A simple idea, to be sure, but one that I felt had a great deal of narrative depth to explore.

But who would try to capture Odessa's heart? The natural candidate was Elizabeth Kirby, the character that I played in-game and whose backstory I built out in discussions with Lawrence. And with that, the two leads were set.

Odessa is a compelling character in the game, but her backstory isn't explored in much detail. That gave me a lot of room to work with; I just had to be sure to honor the backstory that *did* exist. That doesn't just mean not contradicting it – I had to ensure that anything that I came up with fit with what was already in black-letter lore.

The show's lore was starting to get a little unwieldy at that point, so I started writing a show bible. I put Beth and Odessa's backstories in there, along with ideas for supporting characters that we'd meet throughout the season – Odessa's boss, Paladin Rahmani; Beth's parents; Beth's best friend (and ex), Amanda; Odessa's pal, Knight Banks; and so on – as well as story beats that I wanted to work in as the season wore on.

And then I started to write. I wrote the first three episodes first, then the Prologue. I wasn't going to do any sort of prologue originally, but Tom from Robots Radio convinced me that it would be a good idea. He was right.

That's the story of how "Once Upon a Wasteland" started. What follows are the scripts for the Prologue and the ten episodes of the first season. I hope you enjoy them and maybe even take some lessons from them.

Season One
Prologue

by

D.K. Trueno

White Draft
17 October 2021

"ONCE UPON A WASTELAND: PROLOGUE"

FADE IN:

INT. ABANDONED HOUSE, NIGHT

We hear a keypad beep, and a heavy door opens. Two archaeologists-for-hire enter the room.

THE HISTORIAN
1 Well, that's good news. 1

THE ARCHAEOLOGIST
2 What is? 2

THE HISTORIAN
3 Since the keypad works, not only 3
does that mean that this place
still has power, but it means it's
the *right* place.
(beat)
4 Huh. Rad levels are pretty close to 4
normal in here. Must've really
locked things up tight.

THE ARCHAEOLOGIST
5 Yeah. Good thing, too, that 5
radstorm that's brewing looks like
a nasty one. We're probably going
to have to hunker down in here for
a while.
(beat)
6 I could've done without the Easter 6
egg hunt to get here, though.

THE HISTORIAN
7 Nobody's going to pay that many 7
caps for something that was going
to be easy. At least it was puzzles
and riddles and not, like, Super
Mutants riding Deathclaws or
something. I thought maybe it was
just because we had to come all the
way to Appalachia.

THE ARCHAEOLOGIST
8 Shine that flashlight over here. If 8
this place has power, maybe the
lights still work.

A switch flips.

THE ARCHAEOLOGIST (CONT'D)
9 That's better. 9

THE HISTORIAN
10 Holy shit. This place is *pristine*. 10
And judging by the dust, it's been
a hell of a long time since anybody
set foot in here. Wonder what
happened...

THE ARCHAEOLOGIST
11 Focus. Alright, there's a terminal, 11
but I don't see a door.

THE HISTORIAN
12 Try the password you decrypted and 12
see what happens. I really hope it
works.

THE ARCHAEOLOGIST
13 I'm charging her an extra 500 caps 13
if it doesn't. Her cipher key was
supposed to help us decode pretty
much everything.

THE HISTORIAN
14 Hang on, let me pull it up. 14

THE HISTORIAN taps at his Pip-Boy.

THE HISTORIAN (CONT'D)
15 Uh, let me spell it. K-I-R-S-C-H-E. 15
What does that even mean?

THE ARCHAEOLOGIST
16 It's German, you dolt. 16

THE HISTORIAN
17 Jeez, sorry. I guess I was busy 17
*writing the definitive account of
the first hundred years after the
war* and never quite got around to
learning a language that nobody
I've ever encountered speaks.

THE ARCHAEOLOGIST laughs.

THE ARCHAEOLOGIST
18 I was wondering how long it was 18
going to take for you to bring that
up.
(beat)
19 Alright, moment of truth... 19

THE ARCHAEOLOGIST clacks at the terminal keyboard. It beeps, and a bookcase - really a secret door - lumbers out of the way

THE HISTORIAN
20 Nice! 20

THE ARCHAEOLOGIST
21 Let's see what this old family treasure is all about. 21

THE HISTORIAN
22 Just remember, you're an archaeologist, not a Raider. 22

THE ARCHAEOLOGIST
23 How about you wait to see how much gold and jewelry is in here before you say that? 23

THE ARCHAEOLOGIST opens the door.

THE ARCHAEOLOGIST (CONT'D)
24 Huh. 24

THE HISTORIAN
25 What? 25

THE ARCHAEOLOGIST
26 Well... no gold, no jewels. 26

THE HISTORIAN
27 What is it? 27

THE ARCHAEOLOGIST
28 Holotapes, mostly. A lot of them. Some... books? Journals? Looks like sciency stuff. And a file cabinet. 28

THE HISTORIAN
29 Bring the holotapes out here, we might as well look through them. You know, to make sure we have the right "treasure." 29

THE ARCHAEOLOGIST
30 There are *boxes* of them. I'll grab... oh. 30

THE HISTORIAN
31 What? 31

THE ARCHAEOLOGIST
32 This one has a big "1" on it. I guess we can start with that one. See what's in there while I check out that file cabinet. 32

THE ARCHAEOLOGIST brings the box of holotapes into the main room and puts it on the table.

THE HISTORIAN begins to look through them as THE ARCHAEOLOGIST surveys the contents of the room again.

THE ARCHAEOLOGIST (CONT'D)
33 This is one hell of an archive. 33

THE ARCHAEOLOGIST opens a file cabinet.

34 34
35 This thing is filled with pictures. 35
(beat)
36 Whoa. 36

THE HISTORIAN
37 What, what is it? 37

THE ARCHAEOLOGIST
(enchanted)
38 She's beautiful. 38

THE HISTORIAN
39 Let me see! 39
(beat)
40 Wow. You weren't kidding. Who is she? 40

THE ARCHAEOLOGIST
41 The back of the picture says "Elizabeth Laurel Kirby, 2103." 41

THE HISTORIAN
42 That means this stuff is more than 200 years old! What else is in there? 42

THE ARCHAEOLOGIST
43 Uh... here she is with somebody else. Looks a little older here. 43

THE HISTORIAN
44 Husband? 44

THE ARCHAEOLOGIST
45 Uh, no. 45

THE HISTORIAN
46 Oh! Wow. She's beautiful, too. Does it say who *she* is? 46

THE ARCHAEOLOGIST
47 Uh... it says "Beth and Odessa, 2108." 47

THE HISTORIAN
48 Whoever Odessa is, it looks like 48
she’s pregnant.

THE ARCHAEOLOGIST
49 Yeah. 49

THE HISTORIAN
50 Anything in there on who she was? 50

THE ARCHAEOLOGIST
51 Uh... 51

THE ARCHAEOLOGIST shuffles through more files.

THE ARCHAEOLOGIST (CONT’D)
52 Wait, here’s a picture of her by 52
herself. It says... “Scribe Odessa
Valdez, 2104.”

THE HISTORIAN
53 So she was Brotherhood. 53

THE ARCHAEOLOGIST
54 Must’ve been. But... it looks like 54
most of what’s in these files are
just pictures... Chronological
order, but no real context. I
wonder if those holotapes have any
actual info on them.

THE HISTORIAN
55 Maybe. 55

THE ARCHAEOLOGIST and THE HISTORIAN step back into the main room.

THE ARCHAEOLOGIST
56 I don’t even know where to start. 56
There are so damn many of them. And
I don’t even know what half of the
labels on the boxes are describing.
“Scorched?” What the hell is
“Scorched?” “New Enclave” certainly
sounds interesting, though...

THE HISTORIAN
57 I think we should start with *this* 57
tape.

THE ARCHAEOLOGIST
58 Why that one? 58

THE HISTORIAN
59 Because the label says "start with 59
this tape."

THE ARCHAEOLOGIST
(chuckling)
60 Well, kudos to whoever put all this 60
together for helpfully labeling
everything.

THE ARCHAEOLOGIST inserts the holotape into the terminal and clacks at the keyboard.

THE ARCHAEOLOGIST (CONT'D)
61 Looks like it's all text. I guess 61
I'll start with the introduction.

THE ARCHAEOLOGIST reads from the screen.

THE ARCHAEOLOGIST (CONT'D)
(reading)
62 This is the story of a spy and a 62
Scribe. The story of their love,
and how it saved Appalachia from
the "Bringer of Light."

THE HISTORIAN
63 "Saved" Appalachia? I guess it 63
didn't take... sure doesn't look
"saved" now.

THE ARCHAEOLOGIST
64 Shush. 64
(beat)
65 Alright, here we go. 65
(goes back to reading)
66 Elizabeth Kirby - the spy - was 66
born on April 21, 2081 in Vault 76.
Her father, Andrew, was a British
intelligence officer and her
mother, Elise, was a German
diplomat.
(beat)
67 Odessa Valdez - the Scribe - was 67
born on July 17, 2075, in
California. Her parents were
officers in the United States Army,
and joined the Brotherhood of Steel
soon after it was formed by Roger
Maxson. The "Knights Valdez" raised
Odessa to be a Scribe, and she was
a very, very good one.

THE HISTORIAN
68 So she was there for the founding 68
of the Brotherhood, but how did she
make it all the way here?

THE ARCHAEOLOGIST
69 It says here that Maxson ordered an 69
expedition to Appalachia, and
another scribe was supposed to go,
but she couldn't handle the march.
Odessa volunteered to go in her
place.

THE HISTORIAN
70 Wait! She was part of the Lost 70
Expedition? The Brotherhood's been
trying to get the full story on
what happened to them for what, 150
years? I bet they'd give us a
truckload of caps for this stuff.

THE ARCHAEOLOGIST
71 Just remember, you're a historian, 71
not a Raider. And the last thing
you should want is all this stuff
sitting in a storage room at the
Citadel.

THE HISTORIAN
72 Smart-ass. Fine. 72

THE ARCHAEOLOGIST
73 Oh, this may also explain some 73
things.

THE HISTORIAN
74 What? 74

THE ARCHAEOLOGIST
75 It says that her fiancé was 75
supposed to go with her. Knight
Derek Hewitt.

THE HISTORIAN
76 Ahhh, now I get it. He must be the 76
reason she was pregnant in that
second picture.

THE ARCHAEOLOGIST
77 Maybe not. It says here that he 77
ended up not going.

THE HISTORIAN
78 What? Why? 78

THE ARCHAEOLOGIST

79 Wow. Whoever wrote this was *not* a fan. 79

(beat)

80 The long and the short of it is that at the last minute, he refused to go on the expedition and demanded that she stay, too. 80

THE HISTORIAN

81 Demanded? 81

THE ARCHAEOLOGIST

82 Yeah. Gave her an ultimatum and everything. Big fight, and the end result was that she stayed with the expedition and they broke things off. 82

THE HISTORIAN

83 Sounds like she made the right call. What an asshole. 83

THE ARCHAEOLOGIST

84 I mean, I'm an archaeologist and not a historian, but there are two sides to every story. The person who wrote this would definitely agree with you, though. 84

THE HISTORIAN

85 OK, that's the Scribe. What about the spy? 85

THE ARCHAEOLOGIST

86 Right, uh... Elizabeth. Had a fair number of nicknames. Most people called her Beth, her parents called her Lily or Schatzi... 86

THE ARCHAEOLOGIST chuckles.

THE ARCHAEOLOGIST (CONT'D)

87 ...and one person appears to have called her "Princess." 87

THE HISTORIAN

88 Interesting. 88

THE ARCHAEOLOGIST

89 Yeah, she really was. She had... man, a hell of a lot of special training in the Vault. 89

(MORE)

THE ARCHAEOLOGIST (CONT'D)
Intelligence, counter-intelligence, espionage, one-on-one combat training... mostly human intelligence, but some signal intelligence, too. And she was tall. Damn.

THE HISTORIAN
90 How tall? 90

THE ARCHAEOLOGIST
91 Look for yourself. 91

THE HISTORIAN
92 "Damn" is right. She must've been a 92
force of nature.

THE ARCHAEOLOGIST
93 It sounds like it. So, I guess 93
there was some kind of... Super Mutant business that Odessa and the Brotherhood handled, but it doesn't sound like Beth was involved in that. Sorry, I'm kind of skimming to get to the good stuff...
(beat)
94 Oh! Here we go. 94

THE HISTORIAN
95 What did you find? 95

THE ARCHAEOLOGIST
96 They ended up crossing paths when 96
they both stumbled onto a plot to take over Appalachia and started working together.

THE HISTORIAN
97 I guess that's the "saved 97
Appalachia" part. But...

THE ARCHAEOLOGIST
98 But what? 98

THE HISTORIAN
99 That's not what the intro led with. 99

THE ARCHAEOLOGIST
100 Oh... yeah, you're right. The love 100
story. I guess that's really what this whole thing is about. In fact...

THE ARCHAEOLOGIST clacks the keyboard.

THE ARCHAEOLOGIST (CONT'D)
101 Wow. There's a lot here about that. 101

THE HISTORIAN
102 You keep reading through that and see if there's anything else worth noting. I'm going to go look through some of those journals to see if they're all science and tech or if there's anything interesting in there. 102

THE ARCHAEOLOGIST
103 Alright. 103

THE HISTORIAN rustles through some books and papers as THE ARCHAEOLOGIST pokes at the keys to review the terminal entries.

THE HISTORIAN
104 Oh, hell yeah! 104

THE ARCHAEOLOGIST
105 What did you find? 105

THE HISTORIAN
106 There's a stasis case in here, and it's full of beer. 106
(beat)
107 "Old Possum?" "Blackwater Brew?" Never heard of those. Well, that radstorm doesn't sound like it's going to get better anytime soon, so I'm willing to give them a try. How about you? 107
(beat)
108 Hey. 108
(beat)
109 You okay? 109

THE ARCHAEOLOGIST
(emotional)
110 Oh, man... 110

THE HISTORIAN re-enters.

THE HISTORIAN
111 What is it? 111

THE ARCHAEOLOGIST
112 This... this is... a lot. 112

THE HISTORIAN
113 Are you *crying*? 113

THE ARCHAEOLOGIST
114 Shut up. 114

THE HISTORIAN laughs.

THE ARCHAEOLOGIST (CONT'D)
115 She was her North Star. 115

THE HISTORIAN
116 Hey, hey. Look, I found a manifest 116
of the holotapes. Most of them are
audio. Like... an oral history.

THE ARCHAEOLOGIST
117 Oooh! 117

THE HISTORIAN
118 Not that kind of oral history. 118

THE ARCHAEOLOGIST
119 Oh. 119

THE HISTORIAN
120 We might as well listen to some of 120
them. Easier than reading off a
terminal, at least. And those are
usually a little less dry.

THE ARCHAEOLOGIST
121 Says the guy who writes history 121
books for a living.

THE HISTORIAN laughs.

THE ARCHAEOLOGIST (CONT'D)
122 So where do you want to start? 122

THE HISTORIAN
123 How about at the beginning? This 123
looks like a set. 10 tapes, split
up into three groups - The Book of
Odessa, the Book of Amanda, and the
Book of Elizabeth.

THE ARCHAEOLOGIST
124 Who's Amanda? 124

THE HISTORIAN
125 I don't know. I guess we'll find 125
out. We have at least a few hours
to kill before that radstorm
passes. Might as well see if that
fireplace works, crack open a few
of these beers, and listen.

THE ARCHAEOLOGIST

126 And who knows? Maybe it's a good 126
story.

(beat)

127 Hand me one of those "Blackwater 127
Brews."

THE ARCHAEOLOGIST and THE HISTORIAN crack open a beer.

THE HISTORIAN

128 Here we go. 128

THE HISTORIAN inserts the first holotape into the terminal. A voice crackles over the terminal's speakers.

NARRATOR

129 Once upon a time, 27 years after 129
the bombs fell, there were two
people - a Vault Dweller and a
California Girl. They met, and
sparks flew. That's when things got
interesting.

(beat)

130 This is their story 130

FADE OUT.

CLOSING CREDITS *

NARRATOR *
131 “Once Upon a Wasteland: Prologue” 131 *
was produced and directed by Brad *
Williams and written by D.K. *
Trueno. *
*

Featuring Lawrence McNamara as the
Archaeologist and Brad Williams as
the Historian.

I’m your narrator, Ashley Sekhon. *
*

Beth and Odessa’s story will begin
with Episode 1: “Such Perfect *
Identity of Interests.” *

THE END

Season One
Part One: The Book of Odessa

Episode 1:
"Such Perfect Identity of Interests"

by

D.K. Trueno

Final
28 September 2021

"SUCH PERFECT IDENTITY OF INTERESTS"

INT. ABANDONED RESTAURANT - DAY

SCRIBE ODESSA VALDEZ types furiously at a terminal as KNIGHT ALAN BANKS and INITIATE GREGORY CARLSON watch a hastily barricaded door with their weapons ready. Weapons fire pops holes in the wooden wall, which shakes and strains as whoever or whatever is on the other side tries to break it down.

CARLSON
1 This wall's not going to hold! 1

BANKS
2 Then blast anything that comes 2
through!
(urgently)
3 How's it going over there, Valdez? 3

VALDEZ
4 Trying to concentrate, Alan... 4

A large chunk of wall flies across the room, nearly hitting CARLSON in the face.

CARLSON
5 Jeez! 5

BANKS
6 Do you want me to give it a try? 6

VALDEZ
7 You know you can't unlock a 7
terminal by punching it, right?

BANKS
8 That hurts, Valdez. 8

VALDEZ
9 Whatever those Super Mutants have 9
planned for us is going to hurt a
lot more if you don't let me do
this.

BANKS
10 Aye! 10

The action continues, with increasing ferocity and increasing cadence. VALDEZ mutters to herself occasionally as she continues to type.

Without warning, a previously unseen door flies open, and BETH KIRBY bolts into the room, stopping suddenly when she notices the three figures surrounding the terminal.

BANKS (CONT'D)
11 Whoa! Who the hell-- 11
(beat)
12 Stand down, civilian. 12

BETH ignores him and addresses VALDEZ.

BETH
13 Hey. 13

VALDEZ looks up.

BETH (CONT'D)
14 Use this holotape. 14

BETH tosses a holotape to VALDEZ.

VALDEZ hastily inserts the tape into the terminal and hits a few keys. A moment later, the large steel door next to the terminal opens, just as the top half of the barricaded door blows into a hundred pieces.

BANKS
15 We gotta go! 15

CARLSON
16 I hear that! 16

SUPER MUTANT
17 Die, little humans! Die! 17

Several Super Mutants fire into the room as the rest tear at the wooden door and rapidly disintegrating barricade.

VALDEZ, BANKS, CARLSON, and BETH rush through the steel door. BETH presses a button on the other side, and the door closes securely.

BETH
18 That should hold them for a while. 18
(beat)
19 Well, as long as they don't figure 19
out how to use that terminal.

VALDEZ
20 I grabbed the holotape. We're good. 20
Thank you, by the way.
(pause)
21 Oh... um, Scribe Odessa Valdez, 21
Brotherhood of Steel.

BETH
22 Elizabeth Kirby. Uh... 22
unaffiliated?
(MORE)

BETH (CONT'D)

(beat)

23 It's a pleasure to finally meet you 23
in the flesh, Scribe Valdez.
I've... heard a lot about you.

VALDEZ

24 You have? 24

BANKS

(interrupting)

25 Valdez! 25

(to BETH)

26 Let's cut the chit-chat. What are 26
you doing here, civilian? Other
than interfering with an official
Brotherhood operation, that is.

BETH

27 I literally just said my name, 27
Knight Mood Killer. And my
"interference" saved your asses.

VALDEZ

28 Thank you for that, Miss Kirby. 28
Knight Banks is just... a little on
edge.

BETH

29 I get it. Combat tends to have that 29
effect on people. And... call me
Beth. Please.

VALDEZ

30 OK... Beth. What *are* you doing 30
here? And where did you get that
holotape?

BANKS

31 We don't have time for this. And I 31
need you to stay focused.

(beat)

32 *On the mission.* 32

(pause)

33 Thank you, Miss Kirby. Your 33
assistance to the Brotherhood will
be noted in my report to Paladin
Rahmani.

BETH

(cheekily)

34 I'll tell you what, Scribe Valdez - 34
if we make it out of here alive,
you can... debrief me later.

VALDEZ
(flustered)
35 Oh! I... um... that would be very... um... enlightening... 35

BETH
36 And I'm coming with you, Knight. Your tactical assessment is correct; if you want to get what you came here for, you need to do it quickly. And that means you need me. 36

BANKS
37 The Brotherhood is more than capable of completing this mission without your help. 37

BETH
38 You three would be roasting on a spit right now without my help. Look, you can call it "fostering cooperation between the Brotherhood and the rest of Appalachia" in your report. But I'm coming with you. 38

VALDEZ
39 Alan, I should've been able to hack that terminal in 30 seconds, but I couldn't get into it without that holotape. I don't know what else we're going to run into down there, but I think we have a better chance at overcoming it with Miss Kirby... er, Beth's assistance. 39

BANKS
40 Fine. 40
(to BETH)
41 Just try to keep up. 41

BETH
(sarcastic)
42 I'll do my best, sir! After all, what would I do without a couple of big, strong men to protect me? 42

VALDEZ chuckles.

BANKS
43 Don't push it. 43

CARLSON
44 I like her. 44

BANKS
45 Alright, looks like there's only one way forward. I'll lead the way, Carlson, you take up the rear. Intel says this place is abandoned, but we don't need anything sneaking up on us. 45

CARLSON
46 Yes, sir! 46

BANKS
47 Valdez, you know what we're looking for, so keep your eyes peeled. 47
(beat)
48 Let's move out! 48

MUSICAL TRANSITION

INT. DEEPER INTO THE COMPLEX

BANKS unsuccessfully tries to open a door.

BANKS
49 It's locked. I don't see a terminal around anywhere... 49

CARLSON
50 Can we blast it open? 50

BANKS
51 We have that kind of ordnance back at Atlas, but a few grenades aren't going to do it. 51

CARLSON
52 I didn't see any exits along the way, so the only way out... 52

BANKS
53 ...is through a very angry group of Super Mutants. 53

CARLSON
54 Maybe they gave up and went away? 54

BANKS
55 That's not their style. If anything, they set up shop there and invited some of their friends. 55

SFX: Door opening

VALDEZ

56 Uh, guys? 56

BANKS

57 What the- How did you open it? 57

BETH

58 I picked the lock. 58

BANKS

59 So you're a criminal. 59

BETH

60 No, I am not a *criminal*. 60

(to VALDEZ)

61 Is he always like this? 61

(to BANKS)

62 I had specialized training while I was in the Vault. Part of that was getting into and out of places when people don't want me to do either or both of those things. 62

BANKS

63 A Vault Dweller. I should've guessed. 63

BETH

64 Born and raised. 64

VALDEZ

65 You were born in the Vault? 65

BETH

66 Yeah. About four years after the bombs fell. 66

VALDEZ

67 I'd love to talk to you about that... 67

BANKS

(mildly exasperated)

68 Can we please get back to the task at hand? 68

VALDEZ

69 Yes. Of course. Sorry. 69

BANKS

(to BETH)

70 *Please* stop distracting her. 70

BETH
71 Another of my many skills. 71

CARLSON surveys the room.

CARLSON
72 This place looks cleaned out. 72

VALDEZ
73 And recently. Alan, didn't you say 73
that it'd been abandoned for years?

BANKS
74 Intel indicated that nobody had 74
been down here in about ten years,
yeah.

VALDEZ
75 Someone's been here a lot more 75
recently than that. Look at the
dust around that terminal. And on
the floor.
(disappointed)
76 Almost all of the equipment is 76
gone. Someone beat us to it.

BETH
77 But not by much. This all looks 77
pretty fresh.

VALDEZ
78 I'll see if there's anything useful 78
on the terminal.

VALDEZ clacks away at the keyboard.

VALDEZ (CONT'D)
79 Well, at least this one was easier 79
to get into.
(pause)
80 There's still data here! But it 80
looks like it's heavily encrypted.
I guess whoever took the equipment
didn't have time to erase it.

BETH
81 Or figured it was useless without 81
the equipment itself.

VALDEZ
82 I'll copy the data onto a holotape 82
and see if I can decrypt it back at
Atlas. But it's like that terminal
back at the entrance...
(MORE)

VALDEZ (CONT'D)
I haven't seen encryption quite like this.
(beat, hopeful)
83 Is data decryption also something 83
they taught you in the Vault?

BETH
84 It wasn't, unfortunately. 84

VALDEZ
(disappointed)
85 Oh. 85

BETH
86 But I know a guy. 86

BANKS
87 Of course you do. 87

CARLSON
88 I think I found an exit! There's a 88
ladder here, and a hatch.

BANKS
89 Alright. Valdez, work on 89
transferring that data. Carlson, pop that hatch and see where it leads. I want to know if it's a dead end so we can prepare to blast our way out through the front door. I'm going to do some recon to make sure there isn't anything that we missed.

BANKS leaves. CARLSON opens the hatch and scampers through it, leaving BETH and VALDEZ alone.

VALDEZ continues to work at the terminal.

VALDEZ
90 So... about something you said back 90
there.

BETH
91 Hmm? 91

VALDEZ
92 You said that you'd heard a lot 92
about me. Did you mean that you'd heard a lot about the Brotherhood, and my name happened to come up, or...

BETH

93 Oh, no. It was about you, specifically. There's a lot of chatter about the Brotherhood, too, and about Paladin Rahmani and Knight Shin, but you come up so much that it really piqued my curiosity. I started to wonder if you were mythical. 93

VALDEZ

94 Oh. That's... concerning 94

BETH

95 I didn't really think you were mythical. 95

VALDEZ finishes her work on the terminal and begins the transfer.

VALDEZ

96 I mean that people are talking about me, individually. What kinds of things were they saying? 96

BETH

(stifling a laugh)

97 Mostly that they'd tried to pick you up, and failed. 97

VALDEZ

98 Ugh. Seriously? 98

BETH

99 It sounds like it happens a lot. 99

VALDEZ

100 It's like I was the first woman they'd ever seen. And the lines they use are the worst. 100

BETH

101 I can imagine. 101

VALDEZ

102 One guy said that his heart was beating too fast and asked if I could help with that. I didn't even think it was a line at first, I thought he was having an actual medical emergency. 102

BETH

103 He probably was. 103

VALDEZ

104 I tried to be polite. Paladin Rahmani is really focused on fostering good relations with people in Appalachia, and I didn't want to be rude. 104

BETH

105 I think you being rude would still be adorable. 105

VALDEZ

(flustered)

106 Oh! I... um... well, I don't even know how to respond to that. 106

BETH

107 Don't tell me that people flirting with you is a new thing. I can't believe that's true. 107

VALDEZ

108 It was... different in California. I didn't interact with people outside the Brotherhood that much, and everyone within the Brotherhood knew I was engaged, so... 108

BETH

109 Oh, you're engaged? 109

VALDEZ

110 I was. That... ended when I left on this expedition. 110

BETH

111 Oh. I'm sorry. 111

VALDEZ

112 Yeah. So was I. 112

(gathering herself)

113 Can we... change the subject? I don't even know why I'm going on like this to someone I just met... 113

BETH

114 People say I'm easy to talk to. 114

VALDEZ

115 I can see that. 115

(beat)

(MORE)

VALDEZ (CONT'D)
116 So, "Elizabeth Kirby, 116
Unaffiliated," now that you've met
the real me, how do I compare to
the mythical Odessa Valdez? You're
probably disappointed.

BETH
117 Oh, no! If anything, they didn't do 117
you justice.

VALDEZ
118 Now you're just teasing me. 118

BETH
119 I'm being serious! Maybe if I'd 119
spoken to a poet...

The terminal dings, indicating that the data transfer is complete.

VALDEZ
120 Saved by the bell... 120

BETH laughs.

BANKS clears his throat.

VALDEZ (CONT'D)
121 Alan! How long have you been 121
standing there?

BANKS
122 About... ten seconds? I apologize 122
for interrupting. I can do another
sweep...

BETH
(knowingly)
123 I have every confidence that you 123
did a very thorough job. Scribe
Valdez and I can continue our
conversation later.
(beat)
124 I hope we will, at least. 124

VALDEZ
(starry-eyed)
125 Me, too. 125

CARLSON drops down from the hatch, interrupting her reverie.

CARLSON
126 Good news. This tunnel leads 126
directly to an exit.
(MORE)

CARLSON (CONT'D)
It's chained on this side so people
can't get in from the other side,
but we'll be able to cut through it
without a problem.
(beat)
127 Did I miss something? 127

BANKS
(firmly)
128 No, Initiate Carlson, you did not. 128
Scribe Valdez and Miss Kirby were
exchanging intel while the
encrypted data was being
transferred to the holotape.

VALDEZ
129 And that transfer is complete, so 129
we're ready to head out.

BANKS
130 Carlson, you know the way, so you 130
lead. I'll bring up the rear. It
may have been quiet while you were
in there, but getting these two
back to Atlas safely is our top
priority right now.
(beat)
131 Let's move out! 131

MUSICAL TRANSITION

EXT. FORT ATLAS

SFX: WALLA

BANKS
132 We're going to head inside and let 132
Paladin Rahmani know what we found.

VALDEZ
133 I'll catch up, ok? 133

BANKS
134 Sure. Take your time. And good work 134
out there today. Be careful or
they're going to make you a Field
Scribe.

VALDEZ laughs.

BANKS and CARLSON leave.

BETH
135 So what's next? 135

VALDEZ
136 That depends on what's on that holotape... and whether I can decrypt it. 136

BETH
137 You'll crack it. You're The Mythical Odessa Valdez, remember? 137

VALDEZ laughs.

VALDEZ
138 Well, if I don't, do you think you can talk to your friend? 138

BETH
139 Of course! I'll give you a couple of days and then drop by to see how it's going? 139

VALDEZ
140 I'd like that. 140

BETH
141 See you soon, then. 141

VALDEZ
142 Try not to get into too much trouble between now and then, okay? 142

BETH
143 What fun would that be? 143

MUSIC OUTRO BEGINS

BANKS
(in the distance)
144 Valdez! You coming? 144

VALDEZ
145 I'd better go. 145

BETH
146 Go. Be awesome. 146

<u>END OF ACT ONE</u>

ACT TWO

INT. BETH'S RESIDENCE, MORNING

BETH is humming a tune while moving back and forth between a terminal and paper files.

CHARLES WATKINS enters.

CHARLES

147 Good morning, Elizabeth! 147

BETH

148 Good morning, Charles! 148

CHARLES

149 You're awfully cheerful this 149
morning.

BETH

150 What? I'm always delightful in the 150
morning.

CHARLES

151 Mmm hmm. 151

BETH

152 How's my dad? 152

CHARLES

153 Bored. 153

BETH laughs.

BETH

154 Mom isn't keeping him busy? 154

CHARLES

155 She's still tied up with that 155
Foundation mess.

BETH

156 "Mess" is a little strong. 156

CHARLES

157 Have you met Ward? 157

BETH

158 Point taken. I'll go see him today. 158
I have something he may be able to
help me with.

CHARLES

159 He'd love that. 159

BETH

160 I know. And I really could use his 160
help. I hit a dead end, and right
now my only lead is sitting at Fort
Atlas being decrypted.

CHARLES

161 You let the Brotherhood take the 161
equipment *and* the data?

BETH

162 That's the thing. There was no 162
equipment. Somebody got there
before us. From the looks of
things, before I even found out
about it.

CHARLES

163 Do you think it was the 163
Morningstar?

BETH

164 That's the most likely suspect at 164
this point, but it's not a
certainty. There are so many new
people wandering around Atlas, and
any one of them could be operating
undercover for the Morningstar, the
Raiders... hell, even Foundation.

CHARLES

165 Foundation? They don't strike me as 165
the cloak-and-dagger type.

BETH

166 Have you met Ward? 166

CHARLES laughs.

CHARLES

167 Point taken. You could always tag 167
along with your mother and see if
there are any shiny new brain
scanners sitting around.

BETH

168 I think I'm a little old for "Take 168
your daughter to work" day.

CHARLES
169 Come on, Elizabeth, you're 23. 169
You're not old. Like me.

BETH
170 True. 170

CHARLES
171 You weren't supposed to agree! 171

BETH laughs.

CHARLES (CONT'D)
172 Anything else interesting happen 172
with the operation? Or... anyone?

BETH
173 What's that supposed to mean? 173

CHARLES
174 I mean... you seemed pretty keen on 174
waiting until you could cross paths
with the Brotherhood on this, and
then you waited until they sent a
Scribe and not just a bunch of
dudes in power armor.

BETH
175 Getting in on this with the 175
Brotherhood made sense from the
moment I found out they had a lead
on that first lab. It's not ideal -
they were so loud that they drew a
bunch of Super Mutants to the
entrance and almost got themselves
killed - but it gets me the intel I
need faster, at the cost of some
equipment that they're not going to
have any idea how to use.

CHARLES
176 Mmm hmm. 176
(beat)
177 So what's she like? 177

BETH
178 You've been hanging around with my 178
father too long. You can read me
like a book, and I don't like it.

CHARLES laughs.

CHARLES
179 So? 179

BETH

180 She's... great? But God, I was such 180
a dork. I've done this, what,
dozens of times now? Go in, turn on
the charm, get what I need, get
out. Maybe get a new long-term
intel source out of the deal if
things work out just so.

CHARLES

181 Which they always do. 181

BETH

182 Well, almost always. But this 182
was... different.

CHARLES

183 Different how? 183

BETH

184 You know how it's supposed to work. 184
When you prep to meet a new contact
or resource for the first time, you
take all the intel you have and
kind of build a picture so you know
how to play it.

CHARLES

185 Right. 185

BETH

186 Well, roughly 85% of the intel I 186
have on her is how most of
Appalachia wants to get in her
uniform trousers.

CHARLES

187 Conservatively. 187

BETH

188 Conservatively! And that does *not* 188
help me get inside her head so I
can figure out how to play this.
Anyway, all I kept hearing was how
this Scribe Valdez was beautiful,
smart, funny, sweet...

CHARLES

189 I heard some other adjectives used. 189

BETH

190 I'm trying to be professional here, 190
Charles.

CHARLES laughs.

CHARLES
191 Of course. Go on. 191

BETH
192 I was... unprepared. 192

CHARLES
193 You? Unprepared? I refuse to believe that. 193

BETH
194 I had everything planned out. Pop into the room, toss her my skeleton key holotape to save the day, and do my thing. 194

CHARLES
195 And? 195

BETH
196 I froze. 196

CHARLES
197 You froze? 197

BETH
198 I froze. 198
(pause)
199 What are you grinning about? 199

CHARLES
200 I'm just trying to picture this scene. 200

BETH
201 There was a sunbeam shining on her, Charles. A *sunbeam.* 201

CHARLES laughs.

BETH (CONT'D)
202 Anyway, the Super Mutants blew a hole in the wall and almost took one of the guys' heads off, and that snapped me out of it. 202

CHARLES
203 Thank goodness. 203

BETH

204 But when we got to the lab, it was 204
cleaned out. At least the terminal
hadn't been wiped.

CHARLES

205 That's strange, isn't it? You'd 205
think that if whoever took the
equipment went to all that trouble
to cover their tracks at the
entrance, they'd take the time to
wipe the terminal, too.

BETH

206 Maybe it was... I don't know, 206
hubris? Figured that their
encryption was so strong that
nobody'd be able to crack it. And
maybe they were right. I guess I'll
find out when I go Atlas tomorrow
to check in.
(beat)
207 But... 207

CHARLES

208 But what? 208

BETH

209 I'm still debating whether I 209
actually want to do that.

CHARLES

210 Elizabeth! 210

BETH

211 I just... I keep replaying 211
yesterday over and over in my head,
and I'm worried that she's going to
be disappointed when I actually
show up... like, she was just being
polite and was hoping that was the
last she'd see of the awkward
weirdo who blundered into the
middle of her field mission,
because I'm the last person she'd
want to share intel or anything
else with.
(beat)
212 It's stupid, I know. 212

CHARLES

213 Elizabeth, look. It's really easy 213
to forget this given the business
we're in, but you're *human*.
(MORE)

CHARLES (CONT'D)
And you're having a very human reaction to meeting someone who clearly made a very strong first impression on you.

BETH
214 Yeah. And all I can think about is 214
what kind of first impression I made on her.

CHARLES
215 You engage with people in a way 215
that can't be taught - and believe me, I watched your father try. I've seen you use that as part of the job, and if this woman had the kind of effect on you that it seems like she has, I have no doubt that you were even more charming than you usually are.

BETH chuckles wryly.

BETH
216 Well, if nothing else, the skeleton 216
key made me useful.
(beat)
217 The skeleton key! I never got it 217
back from her!

CHARLES
218 She really did knock you off your 218
game, didn't she?

BETH
219 I guess I'm headed back to Atlas 219
after all. No way around it now.

CHARLES
220 None that I can see. Can't leave 220
that lying around. If the intel we have on her is correct, she's always laser-focused on the mission, so she might not have even noticed that she still has it.

BETH
221 That or she's already reverse 221
engineered it and everybody at Atlas has a copy. Either way, it probably means she hasn't given me a second thought. Fortunately.

MUSICAL TRANSITION

INT. FORT ATLAS, DAY

A computer trills in the background, hard at work decrypting data. VALDEZ is humming a cheerful tune as she clacks away at a terminal and shuffles papers.

A Brotherhood Initiate enters.

INITIATE #1
222 Scribe Valdez? 222

VALDEZ
(startled)
223 Oh! Um, yes, Initiate? 223

INITIATE #1
224 I'm sorry to interrupt. There's someone here to see you. 224

VALDEZ
(brightly)
225 She came a day early! 225

INITIATE #1
226 Excuse me? 226

VALDEZ
227 Sorry. I was... talking to myself. 227

INITIATE #1
(pause)
228 Um, okay. Do you want me to take you down to the lobby, or bring 'em up here? 228

VALDEZ
229 That's a good question, I hadn't thought about it... I don't want to come off as too aloof, you know? But I don't want to seem too eager, either. 229

VALDEZ knocks some miscellaneous equipment to the floor.

INITIATE #1
230 Are you alright, Scribe Valdez? I can... ask them to come back later if you're in the middle of something. 230

VALDEZ
231 No. No, I'm fine. 231
(resolute)
(MORE)

VALDEZ (CONT'D)
232 I'm fine and I will go down to the 232
lobby to meet her.

INITIATE #1
233 I... don't know what's happening 233
right now.
(beat)
234 Right this way? 234
(sotto)
235 I think? 235

VALDEZ and the INITIATE go down a flight of metal stairs to the lobby.

VALDEZ
236 Where is she? 236

INITIATE #1
237 Where is who? 237

VALDEZ
238 Beth. Um, Elizabeth Kirby. 238
Unaffiliated. Red hair, tall? I
thought you said she was here to
see me.

INITIATE #1
239 I'm sorry, Scribe Valdez, there's 239
no one like that here. But Mr.
Douglas has more technical data for
you!

VALDEZ
(extremely disappointed)
240 Oh. 240

DOUGLAS
(brightly)
241 Hi, Scribe Valdez! I found this in 241
Watoga this morning, and I wanted
to get it to you as fast as I
could.

VALDEZ tries to mask her disappointment, but fails.

VALDEZ
242 Thank you. You know, you can also 242
drop these off at Camp Venture. We
collect from that drop regularly,
and it's closer to Watoga.

DOUGLAS
243 And miss a chance to see your 243
pretty face? Never!
(MORE)

DOUGLAS (CONT'D)
(long, awkward pause)
244 So, um, Scribe Valdez... I... um... 244
can I call you Odessa?

VALDEZ
245 Scribe Valdez will be fine. 245

DOUGLAS
246 Heh. Of course. Right. 246
(gathering himself)
247 Hey, Scribe Valdez, crazy idea, I 247
was wondering if maybe you... um...
maybe wanted to... go to... you
know... food? Dinner, I mean?
Right, dinner, not food. How can
somebody go to "food?" There's also
lunch, if you like lunch... foods
better.
(trailing off)
248 Or, I guess... breakfast, too. 248
There are foods... of different
types... there...

VALDEZ
249 Mr. Douglas... 249

DOUGLAS
250 Kevin! Please, call me Kevin. 250

VALDEZ
251 Mr. Douglas, I'm flattered. I 251
really am. But I have to decline.
It's important that we keep our
relationship professional.

DOUGLAS
252 We have a relationship?! 252

VALDEZ sighs.

VALDEZ
253 Thank you again for the technical 253
data. Please feel free to drop it
off at Camp Venture whenever you
happen to find any in the future.

DOUGLAS
254 I'll always do whatever I can to 254
help, O...
(pause)
255 Scribe Valdez! And if you change 255
your mind...

VALDEZ

256 Initiate, please see Mr. Douglas to the exit and ensure that he receives appropriate compensation. 256

INITIATE #1

257 Of course, Scribe. Mr. Douglas, please come with me. 257

DOUGLAS

258 Oh, sure. Bye, Scribe Valdez! 258

KNIGHT BANKS enters.

BANKS

259 He seemed nice. I've got a good feeling about you two. 259

VALDEZ

260 Not now, Alan. 260

BANKS

261 What's wrong? You were the happiest person in Atlas this morning. It's a little weird to be that into decrypting data, I'll admit, but I'm not going to judge. 261

VALDEZ

262 It's nothing. And the decryption is going well. The file structure is pretty complex, but I was able to tweak the algorithm a few times overnight so it didn't stall. It keeps... adapting. 262

BANKS

263 I'm going to go ahead and assume that makes sense and say... good job? 263

VALDEZ

264 Okay, how about this - it's like the data knows I'm trying to decrypt it and keeps changing itself to stop me. 264

BANKS

265 Well, it was clearly encrypted by someone who never tried to win an argument with you, then. 265

VALDEZ

266 Flatterer. 266

BANKS

267 Do you want to grab some lunch 267
before you...

VALDEZ eyes BANKS as though she knows where this is going.

VALDEZ

268 Alan... 268

BANKS

269 269
270 tweak... 270

VALDEZ's glare becomes even more stern.

VALDEZ

271 *Alan...* 271

BANKS

272 272
273 ...your algorithm... again? 273

VALDEZ

274 Alan! Do you talk to Erika like 274
that?

BANKS laughs.

BANKS

275 I would never! 275
(beat)
276 Seriously, Erika is meeting me in 276
the mess in five. Come join us. You
need a break. The data can wait for
an hour.

VALDEZ

277 Half an hour. 277

BANKS

278 Fine, half an hour. But we're going 278
to keep checking on you today.

VALDEZ

279 Thanks, Alan. And I promise I'll 279
get a full night's sleep tonight.

BANKS

280 Just lock the door if you're 280
tweaking your algorithm.

END OF ACT TWO

ACT THREE

INT. FORT ATLAS, MORNING

BETH enters Fort Atlas and tentatively approaches an INITIATE.

BETH
281 Um... excuse me. 281

INITIATE #2
282 Yes, ma'am? 282

BETH
283 I'm here to see Scribe Valdez? 283

INITIATE #2
284 Oh, you have some technical data? 284
That's great! But Scribe Valdez left orders that she's not to be disturbed. You can just leave it with me and I'll be sure that she gets it.

BETH
285 Oh... er, no, I don't have any 285
technical data. She's expecting me. I mean, I think she's expecting me.

INITIATE #2
286 I'm sorry, ma'am, I'm under strict 286
orders not to let anyone interrupt her today.

BETH
287 Could you-- 287

INITIATE #2
(interrupting)
288 Or to interrupt her myself. If you 288
give me your name, when she's freed up I can let her know---

BETH
(slightly agitated)
289 She's expecting me, and she's 289
expecting me *today*.

INITIATE #2
290 Ma'am, it might be best if you just 290
left and came back at another time.

BANKS, who's been watching this exchange, finally intervenes.

BANKS
291 What's the problem here, Initiate? 291

INITIATE #2
292 Knight Banks! Well, sir, this... um... woman said that she needs to see Scribe Valdez, and I told her that she's in strict do-not-disturb mode right now. 292

BANKS
293 May I look at your orders readout, please? 293

INITIATE #2
294 Of course, sir. 294

Papers rustle as he hands them over.

BANKS
295 Well, it does indeed say that she's not to be disturbed for any reason. 295

INITIATE #2 sighs in relief.

BANKS (CONT'D)
296 But what's this here? 296

INITIATE #2
297 The list of exceptions. 297

BANKS
298 Read them for me, please. 298

INITIATE #2
299 Exceptions: Knight Alan Banks, Initiate Erika Hewsen, Paladin Leila Rahmani, and... 299

BANKS
300 And? 300

INITIATE #2
(deflated)
301 And someone named "Elizabeth Kirby." Is "unaffiliated" her last name? 301

BETH
302 No, it is not. 302

BANKS chuckles.

INITIATE #2
303 I'm sorry, sir, I saw the first 303
couple of names and just assumed it
was all Brotherhood personnel. And
I figured she was just one of the
Scribe's... fans, trying to get
some facetime with her.

BANKS
304 We don't "assume" in the 304
Brotherhood. When you get sloppy
like that, lives can be lost. And
have been lost.

INITIATE #2
305 I'm sorry, sir. And I'm sorry, 305
ma'am.

BANKS
306 Just make sure you use this as a 306
learning experience.

INITIATE #2
307 I will, sir. 307

BANKS
308 I'll escort Miss Kirby to Scribe 308
Valdez's lab.

BANKS and BETH ascend the stairs toward VALDEZ's lab.

BANKS (CONT'D)
309 She wasn't sure you were going to 309
show up.

BETH
310 Neither was I. 310

BANKS
311 Never doubted it for a second. 311
Besides, I would've tracked you
down anyway.

BETH
312 Oh, really? 312

BANKS
313 Valdez never got a proper chance to 313
debrief you.

BETH tries to stifle a laugh, but fails.

BETH
314 Good point. 314

BANKS
315 Here we are. 315

BANKS knocks on the door to VALDEZ's lab.

BANKS (CONT'D)
316 Stay here. 316

BETH
317 Don't you mean 317
(playfully mocking)
318 "stand down, civilian?" 318

BANKS chuckles.

BANKS
319 Just stay here. 319

VALDEZ opens the door.

VALDEZ
320 Alan, you don't need to keep checking on me. Erika's already been up here twice this morning and it's only... nine-hundred hours. 320

BANKS
321 Someone to see you, Scribe. 321

VALDEZ
322 Oh! Hi! 322
(flustered)
323 I'm... um... let me just clean this up a little... papers all over... 323

BETH
(slightly awkwardly)
324 Hi, Scribe Valdez. 324
325 325

BANKS
326 I'll... leave you to it. 326

VALDEZ
327 Thanks, Alan. 327

BETH
328 Yeah, thanks, Knight Banks. 328

BANKS leaves and closes the door.

INT. FORT ATLAS, VALDEZ'S LAB, DAY

BETH
329 You know, maybe he's not so bad 329
after all.

VALDEZ
330 Alan? Oh, he's a teddy bear. He's 330
been like a big brother to me from
the second he walked into Atlas.

BETH
331 I definitely get "big brother" 331
vibes from him.
(pause)
332 So... how goes the decryption? 332

VALDEZ
333 It's almost done! There's one file 333
that the system is still working
on.

BETH
334 That's great! I knew that 334
encryption was no match for you.
Find anything interesting?

VALDEZ
335 Well, the encryption itself was 335
interesting in and of itself. I've
never seen anything quite like it.

BETH
336 How so? 336

VALDEZ
337 Well, how familiar are you with 337
data encryption?

BETH
338 I've... dabbled in cryptography. 338

VALDEZ
339 The encryption was adaptive. 339

BETH
340 A rotating key? 340

VALDEZ
341 No! That's the crazy part! I wrote 341
an algorithm that should've
accounted for pretty much any
standard encryption method. Even
the... spicy ones.

BETH

342 Oooh, spicy encryption! I'm 342
intrigued!

VALDEZ

(excited)

343 This was really spicy. It's like it 343
analyzed my decryption algorithm on
the fly and adjusted so that the
data couldn't be decrypted further.

BETH

344 That *is* spicy. 344

VALDEZ

345 I tried to go at it manually, but 345
that would've taken forever. So I
wrote a multi-layered decryption
routine that mostly stayed a step
or two ahead of the encryption.

BETH

346 This is wild... 346

VALDEZ

347 Isn't it?! It was really 347
interesting and exciting to work
on, but... exhausting if I'm being
honest.

BETH

348 I'm sure. 348

VALDEZ

349 The good news is that there's only 349
one file left, but this one is...
different.

BETH

350 Different how? 350

VALDEZ

351 I'm getting nowhere with it. With 351
all the other data, even when the
process stalled I felt like I was
making progress. With this one,
though? It feels completely
impenetrable. Even the filename is
different.

BETH

352 What do you mean? 352

VALDEZ
353 All of the files I've decrypted 353
have functional filenames - dates,
a word or two indicating what's in
them. This one is... hang on.

VALDEZ types at the terminal.

VALDEZ (CONT'D)
354 It's "kersh." 354

BETH
355 "Kersh?" Can I take a look? 355

VALDEZ
356 Sure! 356

BETH
357 "Kirsche." 357

VALDEZ
(slowly)
358 "Kir-sche." 358

BETH
359 It's German. Means "cherry." 359
(pause)
360 My mom is German. I... picked up a 360
few words here and there.

VALDEZ
361 "Cherry." I still don't get it. 361

BETH
(concerned, but trying
to mask it)
362 Me either. 362

VALDEZ idly clacks at a keyboard.

VALDEZ
363 I'm kind of at a loss. And I have 363
to brief Paladin Rahmani on my
progress at 1300 hours.

BETH
364 You've been cooped up in here 364
staring at a terminal for what, 36
hours?

VALDEZ
365 Something like that, yeah. I did 365
get some sleep last night.
(MORE)

VALDEZ (CONT'D)
Alan threatened to sit on me if I didn't.

BETH
366 Well, since we got out of the 366
Vault, I've found that a nice walk really helps clear my mind and, you know... get a little distance from whatever wall I'm banging my head against.

VALDEZ
367 It's tempting. 367

BETH
368 I'm nothing if not a temptress. 368
(beat)
369 I'm sorry, that... came out wrong. 369
But I think a walk would do you some good. And... I could join you.
(getting flustered)
370 I mean, if you want to take a walk. 370
And if you'd want to take a walk with me. I mean, we could stay here and try to crack--

VALDEZ
(interrupting)
371 Beth. 371

BETH stops talking.

VALDEZ (CONT'D)
372 I think a walk to clear my head is 372
a great idea. And... I could use some company, too.

BETH
(relieved)
373 Great. Besides, I haven't had a 373
chance to explore the Savage Divide nearly as much as I want to. No better way to do that than with a guide!

VALDEZ
374 It's a really fascinating area! But 374
I've found that there's a lot that's fascinating in Appalachia

BETH
375 Yeah... I have, too. 375
(gathering herself)
(MORE)

BETH (CONT'D)
376 So... this is your neighborhood. 376
How should we proceed?

VALDEZ
377 I'll tell you what... how about we 377
just start walking and see where it
takes us?

BETH
378 I like that idea. 378

MUSICAL TRANSITION

EXT. FORT ATLAS, DAY

BETH and VALDEZ arrive back at Fort Atlas after a long walk. There is considerable commotion.

BETH
379 Whoa, what did we miss? 379

VALDEZ
380 Dammmit! I left my radio in the 380
lab. They're probably looking for
me.

KNIGHT BANKS rushes over.

BANKS
381 Where the hell did you two run off 381
to?

VALDEZ
382 Sorry! I'm so sorry, Alan, I left 382
my radio on my desk. I've been so
focused on this, and I'm so
close...

BANKS
383 One of the scout teams saw a wave 383
of Super Mutants that looked like
they were headed toward a
settlement a few miles from here.
We're on our way to try to bail
them out as much as we can, but
it's a pretty big group. Rahmani's
already on her way there, set to
arrive in ten.

BETH
384 What's with Super Mutants lately, 384
anyway? I mean, they're always a
pain in the ass, but they're really
riled up right now.

BANKS

385 Tell me about it. 385

BETH

386 I thought that it was you guys 386
doing the ol' Brotherhood Two-Step
that drew them to that restaurant,
but maybe not.

BANKS

387 I don't know. But we have to move 387
out, and now. I just wanted to let
you know what was going on, Valdez.
I'm glad you finally showed up.

VALDEZ

388 Do you need me to come with you? 388

BANKS

389 No. This is purely a military 389
engagement. We need you to stay
here and stay safe.

VALDEZ

390 Come on, Alan! I-- 390

BANKS

(interrupting)

391 Valdez, I would love to argue with 391
you about this, but I have to go
right now. You can talk about it
with Rahmani, because she gave me
explicit orders to make sure you
stayed here if you came back before
I left.

VALDEZ sighs.

VALDEZ

392 Fine. 392

BANKS

(shouting)

393 Let's move out! Ad victoriam! 393

BROTHERHOOD MEMBERS

(shouting)

394 Ad victoriam! 394

BANKS and his troops move out.

BETH

395 You okay? 395

VALDEZ

396 Yeah. I just feel... useless 396
sometimes.

BETH

397 Hey. Every piece of intel I've 397
reviewed about the Brotherhood in
Appalachia since you guys came back
is that you aren't just a critical
part of this team, you're its *soul*.
Without you, it's just another
faction trying to impose its will
on Appalachia.

VALDEZ

398 Come on. 398

BETH

399 I'm serious. And, in my objective, 399
professional opinion, everything
I've seen supports that intel.

VALDEZ

400 Thank you, Beth. You know, you 400
really have a way about you... you
just sort of... I don't know, make
me feel better... like everything's
going to be alright.

(beat)

401 I'm sorry for being so needy. I 401
barely know you and I'm leaning on
you like we've been best friends
for years.

BETH

402 You're not being needy. I know I've 402
only been out of the Vault for a
couple of years, but everyone I've
met in there or out here deals with
feeling that way sometimes.

(beat)

(sotto, reflective)

403 Well, almost everyone. 403

VALDEZ

404 Even you? 404

BETH

405 Are you kidding? I'm a basket case 405
most of the time.

VALDEZ
406 Are *you* kidding? It's like you 406
weren't even there when you walked
into that room and casually tossed
me that magic holotape and saved
our behinds.
(beat)
407 The holotape! I've been meaning to 407
give it back to you! I'm so sorry I
forgot - I was... kind of
distracted, I guess.

BETH
(knowingly)
408 Yeah... lots going on, I totally 408
understand. And hey, I forgot to
ask, so I was clearly distracted,
too.

BETH and VALDEZ share a silent look.

VALDEZ
409 Look, I, um... I really need to get 409
inside so I can monitor comms in
case they need me. And I need to
start analyzing the data I was able
to decrypt...

BETH
(interrupting)
410 Of course! I'll... um... take that 410
as my cue...

VALDEZ
(interrupting,
flustered)
411 Oh! No, I wasn't trying to get rid 411
of you! I mean, if you want to
leave, that's perfectly fine, of
course, I'm just saying if you
wanted to come inside with me...
(beat)
412 I'm sorry, I'm just... really bad 412
at this.

BETH
413 Odessa, I would like nothing more 413
than to come inside with you and
help you with whatever it is you
want to work on. Even if that just
means distracting you.

VALDEZ
414 You would? 414

BETH
415 I would. Besides, it would probably 415
irritate Knight Banks to no end if
he knew I was helping save his ass
again.

VALDEZ
416 Nah. He likes you. 416

BETH
417 Maybe he really is just a big teddy 417
bear. Shall we?

VALDEZ
418 Let's. 418

MUSICAL TRANSITION

INT. FORT ATLAS, DAY

BACKGROUND SFX - WALLA ACROSS RADIO

VALDEZ continues to type on keyboard

VALDEZ
419 I just don't get it. 419

BETH
420 Maybe it's... not possible to crack 420
it.

VALDEZ
421 Anything can be cracked. 421

BETH
422 What I mean is, what if it's just 422
there to waste your time and stop
you from concentrating on the rest
of the data?

VALDEZ
423 Hrm. Maybe... it would explain a 423
lot.

BETH
424 It's an outlier, regardless, at 424
least if the filename is any
indication.

VALDEZ
425 I'm just glad that we handled the 425
Super Mutant engagement without any
casualties.

BETH
426 That kind of thing goes a long way 426
with people out there. Good job.
(beat)
427 And if you want me to take that 427
holotape to my friend, the offer *
still stands.

VALDEZ
428 You know, I'm a Scribe, so it's 428
kind of my job to understand
things. But I still don't quite...
get you.

BETH
429 What do you mean? 429

VALDEZ
430 Well... it's like... when we met, 430
it was like something out of a
movie. If I wasn't there myself I
wouldn't have believed it.

BETH chuckles.

BETH
431 I do know how to make an entrance. 431

VALDEZ
432 I mean, look at it objectively - 432
we're about 30 seconds from getting
eaten by Super Mutants, I can't
hack into a terminal that's exactly
like the ones I've hacked a
thousand times, and all of a sudden
this tall, beautiful redhead
appears out of nowhere and saves
the day with a magic holotape.

BETH
433 Beautiful, eh? 433

VALDEZ
434 Even speaking objectively, well... 434
yeah.
(beat)
435 But... that's not the thing I keep 435
thinking about.

BETH
(mildly concerned)
436 What is? 436

VALDEZ
437 It was after that. In the lab. When 437
we were talking.

BETH
(quietly)
438 Yeah? 438

VALDEZ
439 I... well, it's just that we were 439
talking about things that... I'm
just not a person who talks about
that kind of stuff a lot. I mean,
Alan doesn't even know that I was
engaged before. But I was so
comfortable around you that just
sort of... flew out of my mouth
before I even realized it was
happening.

BETH
440 Is that... bad? 440

VALDEZ
441 I don't know yet, if I'm being 441
honest.

BETH
442 I understand. 442

VALDEZ
(mildly incredulous)
443 I really feel like you do. 443
(frustrated)
444 God, I hate feeling like this. The 444
core part of my job, the job of a
Scribe, is to gather information
and objectively interpret it,
right?

BETH
445 Right. 445

VALDEZ
446 Well, I can't seem to do that with 446
you, and it's frustrating.

BETH
447 Oh... 447

VALDEZ
448 But I'm not one to back down from a 448
challenge. And... you seem like
you'd be a fun one.

BETH
449 Well, I *have* been called 449
"challenging."

VALDEZ
450 I didn't mean it like that! 450

BETH
451 I know. I'm just teasing you. 451

VALDEZ
452 So you're a tease. I'll put that in 452
my notes.

BETH laughs.

KNIGHT BANKS knocks on the door and bursts in.

BANKS
(still amped up)
453 Valdez! 453

VALDEZ
454 Alan! You're back! 454

BANKS
455 Hell yeah I am. Kicked so much 455
Super Mutant ass I think my boots
are permanently green.

BETH
456 That's quite a visual... 456

BANKS
457 Hey, Kirbster. 457

BETH
458 Congratulations, I think that's the 458
most horrifying thing anyone's ever
called me.

BANKS laughs.

BANKS
459 Hey, everybody's coming back and 459
we're going to celebrate in the
mess. The settlers were so grateful
that we saved 'em that they gave us
a bunch of booze. You should join
us.

BETH
460 Um... thanks. I appreciate the 460
offer, I really do.
(MORE)

BETH (CONT'D)
But this was a Brotherhood victory
and the Brotherhood should
celebrate it.

BANKS
461 I get it. I promise I'll keep an 461
eye on Valdez. She parties pretty
hard.

VALDEZ laughs.

VALDEZ
462 That's me... the Brotherhood's 462
biggest party animal.

BETH
463 Now I know he's joking - no actual 463
"party animal" would use the term
"party animal."

VALDEZ
464 I'll join you guys in a few 464
minutes, okay? I want to give this
file one last shot.

BETH
465 Absolutely not. Let me take it with 465
me, I'll see if my friend can make
any headway.

VALDEZ
466 Really? 466

BETH
467 Really. You deserve to celebrate. 467

VALDEZ
468 You know what? I do. Thank you, 468
Beth. I've already moved the
decrypted stuff off to our
mainframe, so you can take the
original.

BETH
469 I'll let you know what I find. Have 469
fun!

VALDEZ
470 Alan will make sure of that. 470

BANKS
471 Erika will pitch in, too. 471

CLOSING MUSIC BEGINS, QUIETLY BUT INCREASING STEADILY IN VOLUME

BETH
472 Alright, you guys, I'll see you soon. 472
(beat)
473 Bye, Odessa. 473

VALDEZ
474 Bye, Beth. 474

There is a long pause.

BANKS
475 Um, guys? When you say goodbye you're supposed to... you know... part. 475

BETH
476 Right. I'll um... let you know what I find. 476

BETH leaves.

BANKS
477 Wow. 477

VALDEZ
478 Yeah. Wow. 478

CLOSING MUSIC REACHES FINAL VOLUME *

Once Upon A WASTELAND

Season One
Part One: The Book of Odessa

Episode 2:
"The Requisite Means"

by

D.K. Trueno

Final
16 October 2021

"THE REQUISITE MEANS"

EXT. RAIDER CAMP, MORNING

SFX - Walla

BETH KIRBY moves through a crowd at a Raider camp. She arrives at the door to a bar and knocks. The door opens.

TAVERN WORKER
1 We don't want any. 1

BETH
2 I'm here to see H.B. 2

TAVERN WORKER
3 She doesn't want any, either. 3

BETH
4 I don't think you have any idea how 4
wrong you are right now.

AMANDA
(from inside the bar)
5 Princess? 5

BETH
6 Yeah. Just kind of... hanging out 6
here...

AMANDA OTIS approaches the door and flings it open.

AMANDA
(to the worker)
7 Are you stupid? 7

TAVERN WORKER
8 Um... 8

AMANDA
9 I'll take that as a yes. Look, if 9
you want to keep this job -- forget
that, if you want to keep your head
attached to your body, be as
careful about who you turn away as
you are about who you let in.

TAVERN WORKER
10 I'm... uh... sorry, H.B. Won't 10
happen again.

AMANDA
11 You're god damn right it won't. 11

TAVERN WORKER
12 Um... right this way, Princess. 12

AMANDA
13 Hey. Only one person gets to call her that, and it's not you. 13

TAVERN WORKER
14 I'm sorry... again... 14

AMANDA
15 And she's not interested. 15

TAVERN WORKER
16 What? I didn't even... 16

AMANDA
17 Yes you did. Don't. 17
(pause)
18 Now. Stay out here and find something to do for the next... twenty minutes? Half-hour? 18
(beat)
19 If you walk in on us, I'm going to give you shaken-baby syndrome for grown-ups. Got it? 19

TAVERN WORKER
20 Um... yes, ma'am. 20

BETH and AMANDA enter the tavern and close the door behind them.

INT. RAIDER BAR

BETH
(laughing)
21 You were a little hard on him, weren't you? 21

AMANDA
22 He started eye-fucking you the second he opened the door. Don't tell me you didn't notice. 22

BETH
23 Of course I noticed. You're doing it too, by the way. 23

AMANDA laughs.

AMANDA

24 So what brings you here so early? 24
Want to break the "nooner and
lunch" routine? I have a crick in
my back that would probably help me
work out...

BETH

(interrupting)
25 Actually... I'm here on business. 25
I'm sorry.

AMANDA

26 Oh. 26
(feigning being upset)
27 I didn't want to bang anyway. I 27
have a new boyfriend, and he never
turns me down.

BETH

(laughing)
28 You're a terrible liar! 28

AMANDA

29 I am not! I'm an excellent liar! It 29
comes with the whole Raider thing.

BETH

30 Not to me you're not. 30

AMANDA

31 And why is it so unbelievable that 31
I have a new boyfriend? Just
because we broke up...

BETH

(interrupting)
32 ...several times... 32

AMANDA

33 ...several times, it doesn't mean 33
that I'm incapable of being in a
relationship.

BETH

34 That part's not unbelievable at 34
all. I mean, let's be honest here,
you're a catch.

AMANDA

35 Says the woman who caught-and- 35
released me.

BETH
36 We kind of released each other. 36

AMANDA
37 It was more of a... poorly 37
controlled explosion.

BETH
38 But the thing is, you'd never call 38
him your "boyfriend." Your nose
even curled a little bit when you
said it.

AMANDA
39 Remind me never to play poker with 39
you. Well, unless it's strip poker.
I think I have some cards behind
the bar...

BETH laughs.

AMANDA (CONT'D)
40 And wait a minute, I called *you* my 40
"girlfriend."

BETH
41 Among other things. 41

AMANDA
42 You loved being called those "other 42
things."

BETH
43 Still do. 43

There is a long, awkward pause.

AMANDA
44 Um... if we're going to talk 44
"business," we'd better start doing
it now. So...
(clears throat)
45 ...what's up? 45

BETH
(gathering herself.)
46 I, uh... I have a holotape with a 46
file that's got some kind of crazy
encryption on it.

AMANDA
47 Not exactly my wheelhouse, but I 47
can probably figure something out.

BETH

48 Here's the thing, though. The 48
encryption isn't the concerning
part. The file... it's named
"Kirsche."

AMANDA

49 Oh. Hrm. That *is* concerning. 49
Coincidence, maybe?

BETH

50 Maybe. But I really want to make 50
sure. It's a pretty big one, if it
is.

AMANDA

51 Yeah. And can I say how hilarious 51
it is that your nickname used to be
the German word for "cherry?"

BETH

52 You have. Several times. 52

AMANDA

53 And it never stops being funny. 53

BETH

54 Come on, you know damn well it was 54
because of my hair.

AMANDA

55 Mmm hmm. Sure it was. What's German 55
for "princess?"

BETH

56 "Prinzessin." 56

AMANDA

57 Doesn't really roll off the tongue. 57
How about "rope bunny?"

BETH

58 Amanda! 58

AMANDA

59 Am I still the only person who can 59
make you blush like that?

BETH

60 Yes. 60

AMANDA

61 Good. 61

BETH

62 So, here's the holotape. I had someone else working on it. 62

AMANDA

63 Whoa, whoa. This is a Brotherhood holotape. What's the Brotherhood of Steel doing with a file named after you? 63

BETH

64 Hey, let's not jump to conclusions, it isn't necessarily named after me. Could be a coincidence, remember? A big, weird coincidence. 64

AMANDA

65 Mmm hmm. How did you get this from the Brotherhood? Did you have to do anything... 65

BETH

(sotto)

66 Oh my God... 66

AMANDA

67 Sexy?! 67

AMANDA laughs.

BETH

68 You're terrible. 68

AMANDA

69 Well? Oooh, did you seduce Paladin Rahmani? Banging her would probably open up all kinds of intel, and you have a thing for authority figures. At least Knight Shin is gone, that guy was a *lot*. 69

BETH

70 Amanda. 70

AMANDA

71 I want all the details. Wait! I want to *roleplay* all the details. I know I have some Brotherhood uniforms somewhere at my place... 71

BETH

72 Amanda! I didn't seduce anybody to get the holotape. I was... 72

(MORE)

BETH (CONT'D)
kind of working with them and told them I had a friend who might be able to help decrypt that last file.

AMANDA
73 Boring! 73

BETH
74 Have I ever mentioned that you're terrible? 74

AMANDA
75 You have. 75

BETH
76 It was not boring at all, I'll have you know. 76

AMANDA
77 You're being coy. 77

BETH
78 It's not Brotherhood data on the holotape. It was in a hidden lab complex under an old restaurant in the Mire. I got a line on a Brotherhood operation to get some stuff out of that lab complex and figured I might as well let them do the heavy lifting. I got in first and waited until I could make a grand entrance. They almost got killed by Super Mutants before I had the chance. 78

AMANDA
79 That would've been disappointing. 79

BETH
80 Yeah. The real disappointing part, though, was that the place was cleaned out, except for a terminal that had a bunch of encrypted data on it. 80

AMANDA
81 You're still being coy and now you're trying to distract me from noticing. 81

BETH

82 And I went back to Atlas and offered to help the Scribe get at the data. 82

AMANDA

83 "The Scribe," huh? We wouldn't be talking about a certain smoking hot little brunette Scribe, would we? 83

BETH

84 Amanda! 84

AMANDA

85 Did you... debrief each other? 85

BETH

86 You're incorrigible. 86

AMANDA

87 Please tell me you used that line on her. I want to watch the shame wash over your face. 87

AMANDA laughs heartily, but lovingly.

BETH

88 ANYWAY! 88

AMANDA

89 Oh my God, I was joking, you didn't really, did you? 89

BETH

90 Can we move on, please? 90

AMANDA

91 Fine. 91

BETH

92 So I was hoping that you might be able to work your magic on that last file so I can figure out whether I need to be worried or, like, *really* worried. 92

AMANDA

93 Yeah... if someone's out there naming files after you, it's really weird. And not "fun" weird, more like... "creepy stalker" weird. 93

(pause)

94 It'll help if you can give me some context. 94

BETH
95 Well, I don't know much at this 95
point. The lead I was chasing has
something to do with some kind
of... neurological equipment and
research that was related to a
project before the war.

AMANDA
96 What was the project? 96

BETH
97 I don't know anything specific yet. 97
I'm hoping the other data that
Odessa decrypted can shed some
light on that part. But here's the
thing that concerns me - somebody,
and I don't know who yet, really
wants this stuff. And that implies
that there's a lot more to this
than just a regular old tech grab.
(pause)
98 What? 98

AMANDA
99 "Odessa?" 99

BETH
100 Ugh. 100

AMANDA
(singsong, teasing)
101 You like her... 101

BETH
102 Stop. 102

AMANDA
103 I love it when you pout like that, 103
Princess.

BETH
(frustrated)
104 Okay! Maybe I like her! Will you 104
please get off my back about it?!

AMANDA laughs.

AMANDA
105 Fine, fine! I'm all for it, 105
Princess. You're always more fun
when you're in the middle of one of
your little flings.
(pause)
(MORE)

AMANDA (CONT'D)
106 And, um... it's always fun when you 106
share.

BETH
107 I don't even know if *she* likes 107
me...

AMANDA
108 Look, I know I'm biased, but you're 108
basically impossible not to fall in
love with. And since when do you
act like this? The Beth Kirby I
know doesn't doubt herself,
especially when it comes to women.

BETH
109 I don't know. Maybe I'm sick or 109
something, I've been off my game
since I crossed paths with her.

AMANDA
110 You don't look sick to me. 110

BETH laughs.

BETH
111 That's... sweet? 111

AMANDA laughs.

AMANDA
112 Hey. Go get her. I want to hear all 112
about it.

BETH
113 Yes, ma'am. I was really worried 113
that you'd be mad.

AMANDA
114 Come on, why would I be mad? I 114
mean, if "the scribe" is as hot as
they say she is...

BETH
115 My God, Amanda, even in that frumpy 115
uniform...

AMANDA giggles.

AMANDA
116 And you're telling me you didn't 116
get her out of it yet?

BETH

117 Hey! 117

AMANDA

118 OK! Sorry, sorry, didn't mean to 118
trample on the purity of your
little crush, Princess.

BETH

119 Look, as of right now, she's my 119
best bet to get to the bottom of
this, and that's what I'm trying to
focus on.

AMANDA

120 You're the expert, but you might 120
want to figure out what "this" is.

BETH

121 All I know is that it's big. You've 121
been hearing about it for what,
months now? It's been like that
everywhere. The thing is, nobody
knows enough on their own for any
of it to make sense, so somebody's
got to be behind it and looking to
make a big play.
(beat)
122 I just don't know what that play is 122
yet.

AMANDA

123 I'll see what I can do with this 123
file. Maybe we'll at least be able
to figure out if the filename is a
coincidence or not.

BETH

124 I really hope it is. 124

AMANDA

125 Yeah. Me too. I worry about you 125
sometimes, Princess.

BETH

126 Only sometimes? 126

AMANDA

127 Fine. All the time. 127

BETH

128 That's better. 128

AMANDA

129 Alright, get out of here so I can get to work. I think we both know what's going to happen if you hang around while I work on this. 129

BETH

130 And that's a bad thing? 130

AMANDA

131 It is if you actually want me to accomplish anything. 131

BETH laughs.

BETH

132 OK. Fair enough. I need to check in with Odessa and see if there was anything useful in the data she decrypted. 132

AMANDA

133 Bye, Princess. 133

BETH

134 Bye, Amanda. 134

They kiss. Just a smooch.

END OF ACT ONE

ACT TWO

INT. FORT ATLAS, DAY

BETH KIRBY climbs the staircase to ODESSA VALDEZ's lab.

She knocks on the door, which opens moments later.

VALDEZ
135 Hi! 135

BETH
136 Hi! I... brought pastries. I wasn't 136
sure if you'd eaten yet, and my mom
is trying to teach my dad to bake,
so we had extra.

VALDEZ
137 Aww! 137

BETH
138 She's trying to keep him out of 138
trouble. This is the seventh hobby
she's tried, and she's running out
of ideas.

VALDEZ
139 I'm sure these are great, and... 139
thank you. It was really
thoughtful.

BETH
140 You may want to have Knight Banks 140
try one first to hedge your bets.

VALDEZ laughs and takes a bite.

VALDEZ
141 These are... actually really, 141
really good!

BETH
142 Mom's a good teacher. 142
(pause)
143 So now that I've bribed you, how's 143
the data analysis going?

VALDEZ
144 There's a lot to analyze, and it's 144
really fascinating stuff. A lot of
it is way above my head, though.

BETH

145 I find that difficult to believe. 145

VALDEZ

146 The general science and technology stuff I get. Even if I don't have enough information or background to fully grasp it, I can at least wrap my head around it to the point that I understand what they're trying to do. 146

BETH

147 But... 147

VALDEZ

148 But there's also a lot of neurology, psychology, psychiatry... This is some seriously heavy, involved stuff. I just... 148

BETH

149 What is it? 149

VALDEZ

150 I guess I just don't quite understand why it's getting this much attention. Pre-war, sure, I'd totally get it. But now? It's the kind of thing we'd be all over, but why are Raiders after it? And Blood Eagles? 150

BETH

151 It would probably help if you told me what you found. 151

VALDEZ

(flustered/embarrassed)

152 Oh... right... I'm sorry, I got ahead of myself. 152

BETH

(gently)

153 It's fine, Odessa. In your own time. 153

VALDEZ

154 From what I've been able to gather, there was a big research project that was intended to create a cure for dementia, Alzheimer's Disease, neurological trauma... 154

(MORE)

VALDEZ (CONT'D)
basically anything that locked away parts of a person's mind, especially memories. Memories seemed to be the key.

BETH
155 A noble idea. 155

VALDEZ
156 It is! It's... inspiringly noble. 156
It's the kind of thing that I hope we're able to work on at some point, when things get more... stable.

BETH
157 Does it say who was working on it? 157

VALDEZ
158 It does! When I said it was a "big" 158
project, I mean *huge*. It was an international effort - the US government along with some of its key allies were in on it, along with Vault-Tec.

BETH
159 Vault-Tec? 159

VALDEZ
160 Yeah. One common thread in most of 160
my research has been Vault-Tec. They had their hands in *everything* and...

BETH
161 And? 161

VALDEZ
162 And... not necessarily in a good 162
way. In fact, usually not in a good way. I'm sorry, I know they provided most of your training, I wasn't implying...

BETH
163 I know, Odessa. Trust me, I 163
understand Vault-Tec's dark side a lot better than I wish I did.

BETH takes a deep breath.

BETH (CONT'D)
164 So, Vault-Tec's got their 164
fingerprints all over this project,
which means there's probably a hell
of a lot more to it than just
helping people with dementia and
Alzheimer's. There's no good deed
with them without an angle.

VALDEZ
165 Well... maybe. Probably. But I can 165
see how that kind of tech would be
useful in a post-apocalyptic
environment.

BETH
166 How? 166

VALDEZ
167 Well, we've both seen that trying 167
to build... well anything even
resembling civilization is the kind
of thing that takes a massive
amount of effort from everyone.

BETH
168 I think I see where you're going 168
with this - looking at it from a
cold, Vault-Tec perspective, if
there's anything that can be done
to protect people from no longer
being able to contribute to that
effort, it's worth exploring.

VALDEZ
169 It's not really dissimilar to 169
building defenses against Scorched,
or Raiders, in a way.

BETH
170 Hmm. I mean, it does make sense, 170
but if that's the case, why haven't
we heard anything about it? You'd
think that there would be a team
from 76 out there curing people
left and right.

VALDEZ
171 From the research I've read through 171
so far, it sounds like they didn't
quite get to the point where it was
usable. There were... side-effects.
Even in cases where it mostly
worked. Things like...

VALDEZ checks her notes.

VALDEZ (CONT'D)
172 Um... insanity, emotional problems, 172
significant personality shifts...
sometimes it left them catatonic or
otherwise completely unresponsive.
Just... a whole lot of bad stuff.

BETH
173 But it sounds like they pressed on. 173

VALDEZ
174 They did. They kept trying to 174
refine the technology, but it was a
slow go. And then the bombs
dropped. That's where the logs end.

BETH
175 So this lab was only active *before* 175
the war. And it just sort of... sat
there for about 27 years, until
somebody decided to come grab
everything?

VALDEZ
176 And encrypt the data. 176

BETH
177 Wait, whoever took the equipment 177
encrypted the data? It wasn't the
original researchers?

VALDEZ
178 Yeah. That part really doesn't add 178
up, does it?

BETH
179 No. Assuming they copied it off 179
like you did, it would've been a
hell of a lot faster and easier to
just delete it, or even to destroy
everything they left behind.

VALDEZ
180 Maybe... a kind of off-site backup 180
in case anything happened to their
copy?

BETH
181 Maybe. But still... weird. 181

VALDEZ

182 Very. 182

(pause)

183 Oh! That reminds me! Did your friend have any luck with that other file? 183

BETH

184 I just dropped it off with her this morning. 184

VALDEZ

185 Her? 185

BETH

186 Hmm? 186

VALDEZ

187 You said you "knew a guy." 187

BETH

188 It was just a turn of phrase. Is that a problem? 188

VALDEZ

189 No, of course not. 189

BETH

190 Was there any mention of that file or that word anywhere else in the data? 190

VALDEZ

191 Nowhere. Since all the logs were in English and that filename was a German word, I tried to search for every possible iteration or variation I could think of. "Cherry" in dozens of different languages, different fruits, other German words... I came up empty. 191

BETH

192 Well, I guess our last hope is that there's something in that file. 192

VALDEZ

193 Oh! Another thing to add to the weirdness. That file was new. 193

BETH

194 New? 194

VALDEZ

195 Yeah. I was able to extract a 195
creation date from it... it was the
only thing I was able to actually
pull out of it. It was created
about six weeks ago. Everything
else on that terminal was from
before the war.

BETH

196 That's got to be when they cleaned 196
the place out.
(beat)
197 So they broke into the lab, took 197
the equipment, presumably also took
the data, but encrypted it rather
than deleting it and also added
another file.

VALDEZ

198 I just don't understand. I mean, 198
I've dealt with people here that
were unhinged, diabolical, ultra-
violent... but what they did
usually made sense, in a sick sort
of way.
(beat)
199 This? This doesn't make any sense. 199

BETH

200 It feels like they're playing a 200
game. Did you ever read about
serial killers?

VALDEZ

201 I've heard stories, but I never 201
really studied them.

BETH

202 Some of them played games with the 202
police. Like a "catch me if you
can" kind of thing. It wasn't
enough to kill people, their
satisfaction really came from
getting away with it and rubbing
everyone's nose in it. It was like
a... psychological imperative.

VALDEZ

203 You think that's what's happening 203
here?

BETH

204 I don't know. But at this point 204
it's the only thing that makes any
sense.

VALDEZ

205 If we can even call it "sense." 205

BETH

206 Yeah. Here's hoping they got sloppy 206
and put something in that file we
can use.

MUSICAL TRANSITION

EXT WHITESPRING RESORT, NIGHT

AMANDA OTIS walks through the grounds, keeping off the path to avoid the various robots making the rounds.

She hears a noise and wheels around, gun drawn. It's CINDY CONNER, an Enclave lieutenant.

CINDY

207 It's me, Angel! Don't shoot! 207

AMANDA chuckles wryly.

AMANDA

208 Sorry, Dollface. Can't be too 208
careful.

They kiss.

CINDY

209 I'm sorry I'm late... Colonel 209
Valeria wanted to go over a mission
briefing for a thing in Grafton
tomorrow morning and I thought she
was never going to leave.

AMANDA

210 It's okay... I don't mind waiting 210
for you.
(beat)
211 How early in the morning? 211

CINDY

212 0500. 212

AMANDA

213 I guess that means that you can't 213
come over...

CINDY

214 I'm sorry. I really wish I could. 214
The whole thing stinks. I... I miss
you.

AMANDA

215 I miss you, too. 215

CINDY

216 So what's up? Your message sounded 216
pretty urgent.

AMANDA

217 Um... I need a favor. 217

CINDY

(teasing)
218 Oh, so you didn't just want to see 218
me again?
(wary)
219 What kind of favor? 219

AMANDA

220 First of all, I always want to see 220
you, Dollface.
(beat)
221 But... I have a holotape with 221
encryption that's just been tying
me into knots, and I thought you
might be able to help.

CINDY

222 I mean... I'm really good with 222
computers, especially with all the
boring classes they've stuck me in,
but that's not really something I
know how to do...

AMANDA

223 Well, what I thought was... maybe 223
one of those fancy computers in
that bunker could probably cut
through it like butter.

CINDY

224 Hrm, I don't know... I could get 224
into sooooo much trouble...

AMANDA

225 I promise, I'll make it worth your 225
while.

CINDY

226 Give me the holotape and I'll see what I can do. 226

AMANDA gives CINDY the holotape.

CINDY (CONT'D)

227 Oh, no, Angel... this is a Brotherhood holotape! I don't know if I should, if the Colonel found out she'd be furious! 227

AMANDA

228 Ooooh, would she punish you?! 228

CINDY playfully shoves AMANDA.

CINDY

229 Stop it! 229

AMANDA

230 I'm joking! Mostly. She seems like she might be more into being punished anyway... 230

CINDY

231 I'm going to go ahead and not think about that, thanks. 231

(beat)

232 You're not going to let me say no, are you? 232

AMANDA

233 Nope. 233

CINDY

234 Well, in that case, I'll do everything I can to make that file readable. 234

AMANDA

235 That's all I can ask for. 235

CINDY

236 But no promises, okay? 236

AMANDA

237 Thanks, Dollface. 237

CINDY

238 So... I do have a little bit of time until I have to get back to the bunker... 238

MUSIC SWELLS

END OF ACT TWO

ACT THREE

INT. KIRBY RESIDENCE - DAY

BETH KIRBY types a six-digit code and opens the front door to her parents' residence.

BETH
239 Dad? You home? 239

CHARLES WATKINS enters.

CHARLES
240 Hey, kiddo. 240

BETH
241 Hey, Charles. Is my dad here? 241

CHARLES
242 Um... 242

BETH
243 Charles... 243

CHARLES
244 He, um... 244

BETH
245 Did he get captured again? 245

CHARLES sighs.

CHARLES
246 Yeah. 246

BETH
247 He needs to stop doing that. 247
They're going to catch on. Who is it this time?

CHARLES
248 Raiders. 248

BETH
249 UGH. Which group? 249

CHARLES
250 He didn't say. 250

BETH

251 He's been complaining that Amanda hasn't been over for dinner in a while, he probably did it so he could invite her. 251

CHARLES

252 That tracks. 252

BETH

253 He knows he can just walk into her bar at any time, right? Nobody's going to touch him. Hell, they'd probably buy him drinks all night. 253

CHARLES

254 That's not really your father's style. Well, the free drinks part is. 254

BETH laughs.

BETH

255 Do *you* remember anything about a project in the Vault about... memory, curing dementia, that kind of thing? 255

ANDREW KIRBY has silently entered and now speaks up.

ANDREW

256 That sounds like Project Mind's Eye. 256

BETH yelps in surprise. CHARLES laughs.

BETH

257 Where did you come from?! 257

ANDREW

258 Oh, just went out for a bit of a walk... 258

BETH

259 Mmm hmm. 259

ANDREW

260 At any rate, the project you've asked about... I'll help as much as I can, but I wasn't involved with it, even indirectly. 260

BETH

261 How did you know about it? Vault- 261
Tec compartmentalized *everything*.

ANDREW

262 One of my friends - Dr. Anthony 262
Flagler - was involved in it. He let something slip about it one day when we we'd had a bit of drink, and I thought it sounded fascinating.

BETH

263 And you got him to talk without 263
even realizing it.

ANDREW

264 Now, if I'd known that my daughter 264
would come to me for information about it twenty-five years later, I would've been rather more thorough.

BETH

265 I guess I'll forgive you. Given 265
that you didn't even have a daughter then and all.

ANDREW

266 I can tell you that it was 266
something they worked on right up until Reclamation Day, and the plan was to continue that here in Appalachia. They'd set up their laboratories so that they'd be able to survive anything short of a nuclear detonation directly on top of them.

BETH

267 Yeah. I saw one of them a few days 267
ago. Any tech that was in there got cleaned out, but other than that it looked like nobody had been in there since before the war.

ANDREW

268 Where was that lab? 268

BETH

269 In the Mire. Under an old 269
restaurant.

ANDREW

270 I believe there were five distinct locations. I don't know where most of them are, but I can tell you the location of one - the one that Tony was in charge of before the war, and where he was supposed to go after. 270

BETH

271 Similar setup? 271

ANDREW

272 Yes, in terms of reinforcements, radiation protection, that sort of thing. But it's under what was intended to be his home after the war rather than a restaurant. 272

BETH

273 Have you talked to him since we left the Vault? 273

ANDREW

274 Well... that's a bit of a sticky wicket. We didn't have a falling out or anything of that sort, but... he changed. 274

BETH

275 What do you mean... changed? 275

ANDREW

276 It started when we were in the Vault. He gradually stopped being the person I knew. He still had that in him, but he started having problems controlling his emotions, and he became more and more withdrawn. I always thought it was just a side-effect of being in a Vault for so long, but I wondered if the project had something to do with it as well. 276

BETH

277 So have you talked to him? 277

ANDREW

278 I've sought him out, but he's turned into a bit of a recluse. Won't even see me now. 278

(beat)

(MORE)

ANDREW (CONT'D)
279 Now it's your turn, Schatzi. What's 279
going on?

BETH
280 I'm still trying to figure that 280
out. All I know is that someone's making a big play for a bunch of technology and research that's in several secret locations in Appalachia. I finally got a lead on one, and glommed onto some Brotherhood muscle to get inside. But there was nothing there but dust and a bunch of encrypted data.

ANDREW
281 That certainly fits in with what I 281
know about the project. Who are the players?

BETH
282 That's the crazy part. There are 282
several groups in on the effort, but I can't tell if they're all working under one person or if they just found out about some valuable tech and are going after it because of FOMO.
(beat)
283 Have you heard anything about this? 283

ANDREW
284 I did hear some rumblings. Mostly 284
from the Blood Eagles, my goodness do they love to prattle on. But nothing specifically about what the technology was, and certainly nothing about any one person or group leading the effort.

BETH
285 So if they *are* working together, 285
they don't know it.

ANDREW
286 That's my read on it. If I'm being 286
honest, what I heard out there didn't seem like anything to be concerned about. But what you've learned changes that significantly.
(beat)
287 I'll get out there and see if I can 287
find anything out.

BETH

288 Dad, you're retired! 288

ANDREW

289 *Semi*-retired! And I was MI6, you 289
know...

BETH

290 Thirty-five years ago! 290

ANDREW

291 Moving to MI5 didn't soften me up 291
that much...

BETH

292 How about being a college professor 292
and living in a Vault for 25 years?

ANDREW

293 Oh, the "kindly professor" thing 293
has been absolutely invaluable.

BETH

294 I'm going to talk to mom about 294
finally finding you a hobby that
sticks.

ANDREW

295 I have hobbies! 295

BETH

296 Getting captured by different 296
factions just so you can see how
long it takes you to escape is not
a hobby.

ANDREW

297 Well... I did rather enjoy baking, 297
too.

BETH fails to stifle a laugh.

BETH

298 The pastries were wonderful, by the 298
way.

ANDREW

299 Thank you. 299
(beat)
300 Oh! By the way, Amanda will be 300
joining us for dinner this evening.
Will you be as well?

BETH

301 Well, if Amanda's coming, that means mom's making spaetzle, so I will make every effort to be here. 301

(beat)

302 I'm going to pay Dr. Flagler a visit. Maybe I can sweet-talk him into providing some intel about the project. If he's even still alive... 302

ANDREW

303 Just be careful. I haven't spoken to him in over a year, and I suspect that his... decline hasn't abated. I'll have Charles send his location to your Pip-Boy. 303

(beat)

304 And here. Take this. It might help. 304

ANDREW retrieves a bottle from a nearby cabinet.

BETH

305 Glenlivet? That's... wow. Are you sure? 305

ANDREW

306 Anything for my little girl. 306

BETH

307 Aww. Thank you, daddy. I promise to provide a full report on what I find. 307

(beat)

308 I just need to make one stop to... get something I need and I'll head right over. 308

MUSICAL TRANSITION

EXT. DOCTOR FLAGLER'S HOME, AFTERNOON

BETH

309 You're the scientist, Odessa, so you two will speak the same language. 309

VALDEZ

310 I'm not a neurologist, though. And the data I've analyzed is way over my head. 310

BETH

311 Not nearly as far as I'm sure it 311
would be over mine.
(beat)
312 You look great, by the way. 312

VALDEZ

313 Um, thanks... but I still don't 313
understand why I couldn't just wear
my uniform. And how did you have
something that fit me? We are *not*
the same size, and you're like a
foot taller than me.

BETH

314 I am *not* a foot taller than you. 314
(beat)
315 Six inches, tops. 315
(pause)
316 I thought it best that you not wear 316
a uniform because I don't know what
the good doctor's opinion of the
Brotherhood is... and my father
said that his mental state is...
fragile.

VALDEZ

317 Yeah. That's the part that has me 317
worried. I kind of wish we'd
brought Alan, or at least an
Initiate.

BETH

318 Hey, I'm pretty good in a fight, if 318
it comes to that. But it won't.

VALDEZ

319 OK. I trust you. 319

BETH

BETH takes a deep breath.

BETH (CONT'D)

320 Here goes... 320

BETH knocks on the door. There is no answer.

VALDEZ

321 Maybe he's not here? Or... 321

BETH

322 Let's not think that way. 322

BETH knocks again, this time more insistently. After a moment, we hear stirring.

FLAGLER opens the vassi on the door.

FLAGLER
323 Who the hell are you? It's not 323
delivery day.

BETH
324 I think we've met before. 324

FLAGLER pauses.

FLAGLER
325 There's only one person crazy 325
enough to haul a bottle of
Glenlivet all the way out here, and
you're not him.
(pause)
326 Wait. Lily? 326

BETH
327 Hi, Dr. Flagler. I'm surprised you 327
recognize me.

FLAGLER
328 I wouldn't have if you hadn't 328
brought the Glenlivet. It took me a
minute... putting two and two
together isn't quite as easy as it
used to be.
(beat)
329 Get in here! It's dangerous out 329
there.

BETH and VALDEZ enter the home, and FLAGLER shuts the door behind them.

FLAGLER (CONT'D)
330 I can't believe how much you've 330
grown. You're almost as tall as me!

BETH laughs.

BETH
331 I think you're safe. I'm about... 331
75% certain that I'm done growing.

FLAGLER
332 And who's your friend. Wait! Is 332
this Amanda?!

BETH tries to interrupt.

BETH
333 Um... 333

FLAGLER
334 I've heard so much about you from 334
Lily's dad!

VALDEZ
(whispering insistently)
335 Beth? 335

BETH
336 Dr. Anthony Flagler, please meet 336
Odessa Valdez. She's... a friend.

FLAGLER
337 Oh! Oh, I'm sorry, Miss Valdez, I 337
shouldn't have assumed.
(angry)
338 Goddammit, Tony, think! 338

BETH
339 Dr. Flagler, why don't we open that 339
bottle and talk a while?

FLAGLER
(calming down)
340 Yes... that's a good idea, Lily. 340
I'm... I'm sorry. My mind isn't
what it used to be. It's difficult
sometimes. I'm sure your father
told you about that. Wait... is
he... oh, no, that's why you're
here, and why you brought that
bottle!

BETH
341 Dr. Flagler, it's nothing like 341
that...

FLAGLER's voice begins to shake.

FLAGLER
342 I was such an ass to him last time 342
he was here! I tried to make him
understand, and he just wanted to
talk about nonsense! Who cares
about how things were back at VTU?
Who?!

BETH
(very calmly)
343 Odessa, would you please get some 343
glasses for us?
(MORE)

BETH (CONT'D)
The kitchen is that way, isn't it
Dr. Flagler? Through that door?
(beat)
344 Dr. Flagler, look at me. It's Lily. 344
Lily Kirby. My father is Andrew,
and my mother is Elise. They're
your friends, and they're both
fine. And you're fine, too.

FLAGLER pauses to gather himself.

FLAGLER
345 Thank you. I... the fog... it just 345
won't lift.

BETH
346 It's OK, Dr. Flagler. I understand. 346
Why is this happening?

FLAGLER speaks haltingly, every word and every thought behind it clearly a struggle.

FLAGLER
347 I suppose it doesn't matter now. 347
Keeping secrets for the "greater
good." At least I thought we were
trying to do good, but... but we
were doing more than that. We
didn't know. Some of us didn't
know. Not me, not until the end. I
figured it out. The system just
wouldn't do, would it? It had to be
wrong.

BETH
348 Dr. Flagler, do you remember 348
talking with Elise about where she
grew up?

FLAGLER
349 Yes... Elise... Elise is from 349
Munich. I spent a year very near
there when I was an
undergraduate... we talked quite a
bit about it. And that's where she
met your dad, isn't it?

BETH
350 That's right, doctor. Please go on. 350
Odessa has those glasses for us.
You remember Odessa, don't you?

FLAGLER
351 I do. Thank you, Odessa. 351

VALDEZ fills each of the three glasses. They drink.

FLAGLER (CONT'D)
352 That helps. 352

BETH
353 Doctor, Odessa is going to ask you some questions about the project. She's a scientist, just like you. Is that alright? 353

FLAGLER
354 Of course, Lily. What would you like to know, Miss Valdez? 354

VALDEZ
355 I've studied some of the pre-war research, and it's... well, it's truly fascinating. And it sounds like an incredibly noble effort - helping people who've lost access to their memories because of injury or disease... 355

FLAGLER
356 If that had been the real goal, I would agree. And I thought it was, for a long time. 356

VALDEZ
357 If that wasn't the goal, what was? 357

FLAGLER
358 Memory is a powerful thing. Nobody understands that better than I do right now... mine are betraying me. I tried. I did what I could to protect people, but in the end they were just too good at their jobs. They wanted to weaponize memories. 358

VALDEZ
359 How can you weaponize a memory? 359

FLAGLER
360 These people can weaponize anything. And even if they couldn't, they were certainly going to try. 360
(beat, struggling)
361 It was about... reading and writing. I had... paper, but I... I didn't have the pencil. 361
(MORE)

FLAGLER (CONT'D)
Not one that could do what they
wanted it to. Too sharp or not
sharp enough...

BETH
362 Doctor, can you look at me for a 362
moment?
(beat)
363 Let's take a drink. 363

BETH, VALDEZ, and FLAGLER drink.

BETH (CONT'D)
364 Now, I want you to think about the 364
time our theater club did that
production of "My Fair Lady." Do
you remember that?

FLAGLER
365 I... I don't know... 365

BETH
366 It's alright, I'll remind you. 366
There weren't enough boys, so I
played Henry Higgins. Casey - do
you remember Casey?

FLAGLER
367 I... I do. 367

BETH
368 Right! You're doing so well. Casey 368
played Eliza, and...

FLAGLER
(interrupting, happy)
369 And she couldn't do an English 369
accent to save her life!

FLAGLER laughs.

FLAGLER (CONT'D)
370 Oh, that was a sight, wasn't it? 370
But the two of you lit up the
stage.

BETH
371 We did, didn't we? 371

FLAGLER
372 Miss Valdez, I'm sorry. Where was 372
I?

VALDEZ

373 Reading and writing? 373

FLAGLER

374 Ah, yes! The part of the program that I originally worked on was rewriting pathways so inaccessible areas of the mind could be accessible. Kind of a... detour so that the information could get to its destination. 374

VALDEZ

375 I'm not a neuroscientist, but I think I remember reading that we still only use a small part of our brains' capacity, so there must be unused pathways that could be reprogrammed. 375

FLAGLER

376 There were! And we were making real progress in getting them to do what we needed them to. But what I eventually learned was that they were trying to extract memories directly from the brain, and also write those recorded memories to an unused portion. 376

VALDEZ

377 Ah! So in the event that an area of the brain was damaged but the memories were still readable, they could be rewritten to an undamaged area! 377

FLAGLER

378 Precisely! Oh, my dear, you're exceptionally perceptive. 378

(pause)

379 But, unfortunately, that was a cover story. As I said, they wanted to weaponize memories. And they wanted to do that by inserting altered, or outright false memories into people's minds. 379

VALDEZ

380 Could it also be used as an interrogation tool? Like, forcibly extracting information from people's minds? 380

FLAGLER

381 Oh, yes. That was the other part of their plan. This technology was going to be the basis of an entirely new type of human intelligence operation. Talk about being made more sinister and more protracted by the lights of perverted science... 381

VALDEZ

382 Do you still have your research here? I'd love to look at it. 382

FLAGLER

383 Well, my dear, I do still have my personal journals, and you're welcome to take them. I have no use for them anymore. But Vault-Tec took the centralized data when they took the equipment. 383

BETH

384 Vault-Tec took the equipment? When? 384

FLAGLER

385 About a month ago, I think? Time sort of... bleeds together these days. 385

BETH

386 Doctor, are you sure it was Vault-Tec? The only official Vault-Tec presence out here is the Overseer, at least as far as I know. 386

FLAGLER

387 I... well, I recognized them from the Vault, and they had credentials. But I suppose they could have just held onto the ones they had, and... oh, no. Oh, God! 387

BETH

388 It's alright, Doctor, it's alright... 388

FLAGLER

(agitated)

389 I... I just wanted it out of my sight. I tried to... fix myself. Recreate the experiments, write everything back. But it was already lost. 389

BETH

390 I understand, Doctor. Doctor, look 390
at me. It's Lily, and I'm here with
Odessa. You were just chatting with
her. Just a nice chat over some
drinks. Remember?

FLAGLER

391 I'm tired, Lily. I'm just... I'm 391
tired. Odessa, you can find my
journals and research materials
upstairs in my office. First door
on the left.

VALDEZ

392 I'll get them. Thank you very much, 392
Doctor.

FLAGLER

393 You're welcome, my dear. It was... 393
nice to talk to a fellow scientist
again. Thank you for that.

VALDEZ

394 It was my pleasure. 394

VALDEZ heads up the stairs.

FLAGLER

395 Can you do me a favor? 395

BETH

396 Of course. 396

FLAGLER

397 Can you tell your father that I'd 397
like it if he'd visit again? We can
empty the rest of this bottle of
Glenlivet together.

BETH

398 I think he'd like that. I'll tell 398
him as soon as I see him.

VALDEZ returns.

VALDEZ

399 All set! Thank you again, Doctor. 399
It was really wonderful to meet
you.

FLAGLER

400 You as well, Miss Valdez. Goodbye 400
for now. I hope we can chat again
sometime.

BETH and Valdez leave. FLAGLER closes and locks the door behind them.

VALDEZ

401 Are you okay? 401

BETH

(clearly not ok)

402 Yeah. 402

VALDEZ

403 Why did he call you Lily? 403

BETH clears her throat, gathering herself.

BETH

404 When I was ickle, I couldn't say 404
"Elizabeth." It sounded a bit like
"Lily," and it stuck. But only a
few people call me that. My
parents, a couple of their
friends...

VALDEZ

405 That's totally logical. Thanks for 405
explaining.

(beat)

406 I guess we should get back to Atlas 406
so I can start looking at this
stuff. It's going to be nice to
have some context... maybe we'll
finally figure out what this is all
about.

BETH

407 About that. 407

VALDEZ

408 What? 408

BETH

409 I was... well, I was thinking that 409
we could go to my place, instead. I
think it would be nice to
decompress a little.

(beat)

410 And... I'd really like to make 410
dinner for you.

VALDEZ
411 You... really? 411

BETH
412 Yeah. Really. What do you say? 412

VALDEZ
413 I'd like that. Today has been... a 413
lot.

BETH
414 It has. I'm a pretty good cook. And 414
if you don't like it, I have a lot
of booze, too.

VALDEZ laughs.

VALDEZ
415 You're a woman of many talents, 415
Elizabeth Kirby.

BETH
416 Thank you. Let's get out of here. 416

MUSICAL TRANSITION

INT. BETH'S HOME, NIGHT

Dinner is wrapping up, glasses and silverware clink.

VALDEZ
417 That was amazing, Beth. Thank you. 417

BETH
418 It was nice to cook for somebody 418
other than just me for once. Did
you really like it, or did I just
give you enough wine to mask the
taste?

VALDEZ laughs.

VALDEZ
419 Well, there *was* a lot of wine, but 419
it was excellent. Really. The,
um... company was better, though.

BETH
(turning on the charm)
420 You know, if you want, we could... 420
make this a regular thing. Dinner,
I mean.

BETH stands.

VALDEZ
(going with it)
421 We could... but, um... 421

BETH
422 What? 422

VALDEZ
423 Did you have anything in mind for 423
dessert?

VALDEZ stands.

BETH
424 I did, yeah. 424

BETH moves closer.

VALDEZ
425 One of those pastries? 425

BETH
426 No. 426

VALDEZ
427 Ice cream? 427

BETH
428 I was thinking of something... 428
hotter.

VALDEZ
429 I think that's exactly what I 429
need...

They kiss. Tentatively at first, then with increasing passion.

BETH
430 How was that? 430

VALDEZ
431 Sweet. 431

BETH
432 Would you like a second course? 432

VALDEZ
433 Yeah... 433

They kiss again. Mid-kiss, the door flies open.

AMANDA enters, out of breath.

AMANDA

434 Beth! I-- Oh, no. I am *so* sorry. 434

(beat)

435 Uh, I'm Amanda. I'm an... old friend of Beth's. 435

VALDEZ

436 *That's* Amanda?! 436

BETH

437 Odessa Valdez, Amanda Otis. 437

AMANDA

438 Oh... Oh! Look, um, I really am sorry I broke up... whatever this was about to turn into, but you need to see this. 438

BETH

439 See what? 439

AMANDA

440 Here. 440

VALDEZ

441 Is that my holotape? This is the friend you gave it to? Beth, what the hell is going on? 441

BETH

442 Odessa, I'll explain everything, I promise. Amanda, what's got you so fired up? 442

AMANDA

443 That file? It *is* about you. 443

BETH

444 Dammit. How do you know? 444

AMANDA

445 Look for yourself. 445

AMANDA loads the holotape into a terminal and clacks at the keys.

BETH

446 Oh, no. Oh, *no*. 446

VALDEZ

(more distraught than angry)

447 Beth, if you don't start explaining right now, I'm leaving. 447

BETH

448 You're right, you deserve to know. 448
I didn't want to say anything
unless I was sure. You remember the
name of that file?

VALDEZ

449 Of course I do. "Kirsche." German 449
word for "cherry." And?

BETH

450 And... Kirsche was a nickname I had 450
in the Vault.

VALDEZ scoffs.

VALDEZ

451 Why didn't you mention that? 451

BETH

452 I was hoping it was just a 452
coincidence...

AMANDA

453 A big, weird coincidence.... 453

BETH

454 But what you're looking at on the 454
screen is my full personnel file
from Vault 76. And when I say the
full file, I mean it - it even has
the redacted and compartmentalized
stuff.

AMANDA

455 I didn't read it, by the way. I 455
know that there are things in
there... well things that nobody
should see.

BETH

456 Thank you. But even that doesn't 456
matter now. We need to figure out
why that file was there, and why it
was encrypted differently than the
other data.

VALDEZ

457 If it was a Vault-Tec file, it 457
probably still had Vault-Tec
encryption on it. And not the
normal kind, some sort of... I
don't know... top-secret AI-based
encryption.

(MORE)

VALDEZ (CONT'D)
The kind of thing that even my
tools couldn't crack.
(beat)
458 Why could yours? 458

AMANDA
459 I... called in a favor. 459

VALDEZ
(conflicted, upset)
460 Beth, I... I feel like I'm on the 460
verge of either saying or doing
something I'm going to regret and I
don't want that to happen. I should
go.
(beat, gathering
herself)
461 I think we should talk about this 461
tomorrow, at Atlas.

BETH
(meekly)
462 OK. I'll... see you tomorrow. 462
Please be careful, it's late.

VALDEZ leaves.

BETH (CONT'D)
463 DAMMIT! 463

AMANDA
464 Shit, Princess, I'm so sorry. I 464
really fucked this up, didn't I?

BETH
(crushed)
465 It's not your fault. You did the 465
right thing. This couldn't wait.

AMANDA
466 Those sick fucks. 466

BETH
467 And I should've been more 467
forthcoming with her, too. I really
like her, Amanda.

AMANDA
468 I know, baby. 468

BETH
469 I guess there isn't much to do 469
until I talk to her tomorrow.
(MORE)

BETH (CONT'D)

I already know everything that's in
that file, and we already know that
it's not tied to anything in the
other data from that lab. I just...
(beat, trailing off)
470 I don't know... 470

OUTRO MUSIC BEGINS AND SWELLS

AMANDA

471 Do you need me to stay? 471

BETH

(softly)
472 Yeah. 472

CLOSING MUSIC REACHES FINAL VOLUME

END OF EPISODE 2

Once Upon A WASTELAND

Season One
Part One: The Book of Odessa

Episode 3:
"Checks and Limitations"

by

D.K. Trueno

FINAL
11 November 2021

"CHECKS AND LIMITATIONS"

INT. BETH'S HOUSE, MORNING

BETH is making breakfast, clanking pans and dishes.

AMANDA enters, groggy.

AMANDA
1 Ugh. 1

BETH
2 Oh, did I wake you? I'm sorry! I guess I was kind of in my own little world... trying to forget about last night. I guess I always default to cooking... 2

AMANDA
3 It's OK, Princess. I'm glad you got some sleep; you turned into a corpse the second your head hit the pillow. I just need to... get my bearings. I'm not used to being up this early. 3

BETH
4 I know. I really am sorry. At least I managed to get up without disturbing you. You slept on my arm, by the way. It seems to have been faster asleep than the rest of me, which is saying something. Took a good five minutes to get the feeling back below my elbow. 4

AMANDA laughs.

A kettle begins to whistle.

BETH (CONT'D)
5 Would you like some tea? 5

AMANDA
6 I still can't believe you don't keep coffee at your place. That's... unamerican. 6

BETH
7 Well, there hasn't really been an America since before I was born, so I think I'm safe. 7

AMANDA
8 Can you at least put a couple of shots of whiskey in it? 8

BETH
9 I thought that was implied. 9

AMANDA
10 You know me so well. 10

BETH pours and stirs the tea. Amanda takes a sip.

AMANDA (CONT'D)
11 That's better. 11
(beat)
12 So. Are you okay, Princess? 12

BETH
13 No. 13

AMANDA
14 I didn't think so. I had no idea you two were... together here. Should've guessed something was up when you didn't show up at dinner. 14

BETH
15 How was mom's spaetzle? 15

AMANDA
16 There's a plate of it waiting for you. 16

BETH
17 You couldn't have brought it with you last night? Might as well lean into the Kummerspeck. 17

AMANDA laughs.

AMANDA
18 Cummerwhat? 18

BETH laughs.

BETH
19 Kummerspeck. It means... uh... grief eating? Sorry, it's one of those German words that doesn't directly translate. 19

AMANDA
20 Unlike, say, *Seilhase*. 20

BETH

21 Amanda! You didn't ask my mother 21
the German word for "rope bunny,"
did you?!

AMANDA

22 I guess you'll find out when you 22
pick up your... uh... cummer...

BETH

23 Kummerspeck! 23

Beth laughs and sighs happily.

BETH (CONT'D)

24 How do you always know how to make 24
me feel better?

AMANDA

25 I'm just returning the favor. 25
(beat)
26 For the tea, I mean - it's exactly 26
what I needed this morning.

BETH

27 I think I need the rest of that 27
bottle in mine. I'm still...
processing what you found on that
holotape.

AMANDA

28 Full disclosure, I did read the 28
first paragraph of so of the...
um... compartmentalized stuff, but
I stopped as soon as I realized
what was going to be in there. You
told me enough about what they did
to you to know that I don't want to
know any more.

BETH

29 I just... seeing that on the 29
screen... I'd hoped that all of
that was going to be sealed up in
Vault 76 and the more distance I
got from it, the more I'd be able
to...

AMANDA

30 Make peace with it? 30

BETH

31 I'm never going to be at peace with 31
it.

(MORE)

BETH (CONT'D)
It's been two years since I left that Vault behind and I still have nightmares.

AMANDA
32 I considered skimming through it to 32
see if I could find any names. See if any of them were still alive. Make sure they'd... lack the necessary equipment to hurt anyone else.

BETH
33 Some things are better left at 33
rest.

AMANDA
34 Somebody disagrees. 34

BETH
35 And we need to find out who. 35

AMANDA
36 We? 36

BETH
37 I need your help, Amanda. And 37
Charles', and my parents'...

AMANDA
38 And Odessa's. 38

BETH
39 Yeah. I have no idea what I'm going 39
to walk into when I go to see her later.

AMANDA
40 She was pretty upset. And I can't 40
blame her.

BETH
41 It would be so much easier if she'd 41
acted unreasonably.

AMANDA
42 I have an idea! 42

BETH
43 Uh-oh. 43

AMANDA laughs.

AMANDA

44 Hey! 44

BETH

45 Alright, what's your idea? 45

AMANDA

46 You should bring her a present. 46

BETH

47 A present? 47

AMANDA

48 Yeah, a present. When you were 48
rambling last night before we went
to bed, you mentioned that she
seemed really happy when you
brought those pastries your dad
made.

BETH

49 I'll take your word for it. Last 49
night is still a little... foggy.

AMANDA

50 So, maybe if you brought her 50
something, it would start the
conversation off on a positive
note.
(beat)
51 What? 51

BETH

52 You seem very keen on helping me 52
smooth over last night's...
debacle.

AMANDA

53 It's like I said, you need her if 53
you're going to figure out what the
hell is going on. The Brotherhood
has resources we don't.
(beat)
54 And I don't like seeing you like I 54
saw you last night. I saw enough of
that when we were together, but I
was... we were just so deep into
it...

BETH

55 Yeah. We... both made a lot of 55
mistakes.
(beat)
(MORE)

BETH (CONT'D)
56 And I don't want to make the same 56
mistakes with her. Or different
ones, for that matter.

AMANDA
57 Did you really not tell her who you 57
were giving the holotape to?

BETH
58 I told her I was giving it to a 58
friend.

AMANDA
59 Come on, Beth. 59

BETH
60 What? Are we not friends? 60

AMANDA
61 You left out a *lot* of context. No 61
wonder she was pissed off. She's
not stupid.

BETH
62 What was I supposed to do? Tell her 62
that I wanted to give the tape to
my ex-girlfriend, who's a *Raider*,
and oh by the way we still have sex
now and again?

AMANDA
63 My point is that you were treating 63
her like... I don't know, an
intelligence asset or something.

BETH
64 That's what she *was* at that point. 64

AMANDA
65 Bullshit. Now you're starting to 65
piss *me* off. You know good and
goddamn well you didn't set up that
little encounter to get a new...
asset.

BETH groans.

BETH
66 Fine. Yes. I did it because I 66
wanted to meet her. Because I
wanted to see what all the fuss was
about.

AMANDA

67 And? 67

BETH

68 And no one's knocked me on my back foot since... gosh, I don't even know. 68

AMANDA clears her throat.

BETH laughs.

AMANDA

69 I can't decide if you're trying to get a rise out of me or not. 69

BETH

70 You didn't so much knock me on my back foot as tie me up and throw me into a pit. 70

AMANDA laughs.

AMANDA

71 That's a fair assessment. 71

BETH

72 But seriously, Amanda, I felt so... drawn to her. I mean, I barely know her, I get that, but she's just... 72

(beat)

73 I mean, when we were chatting, I got lost just... looking at her and listening to her voice. 73

AMANDA

74 She *does* have a nice voice. 74

BETH

75 You should hear it when she's not furious. 75

AMANDA

76 I'm sure I will at some point between now and the wedding. 76

BETH

(playfully)

77 Stop teasing me! 77

AMANDA

78 Look, Princess, let me give you 5 caps worth of free advice. You *just* met her. 78

(MORE)

AMANDA (CONT'D)
There's obviously a hell of a strong attraction there, given that you two were about to go at it on the kitchen table when I came in last night, but you said it yourself - you barely know each other. I was joking about the wedding thing, but it kind of feels like you're ready to pick out dresses.
(beat)
79 Just... let it breathe. 79
(beat)
80 Why are you looking at me like that? 80

BETH
81 When did you become such a... relationship expert? 81

AMANDA
82 I guess I've done some growing up since... us. 82

BETH
83 And now it's my turn, it seems. 83

AMANDA
84 So... after breakfast, how about you take a shower and then we'll pick out something nice for you to wear. Then we'll go through your tech stash to pick out that gift. 84

BETH
85 I'll stop to see my dad on the way to Atlas as well. If he's found anything out, that would be the best present of all. 85

MUSICAL TRANSITION

INT. FORT ATLAS, MORNING

VALDEZ is typing at her keyboard.

ALAN BANKS knocks tentatively, then enters.

BANKS
86 Valdez? Hey, it's Alan. You okay in there? 86 *
*

VALDEZ sighs.

VALDEZ
(sarcastic)
87 Never better. 87

BANKS
88 Uh... okay. Hey, I brought you some 88 *
coffee. You had a pretty late *
night, I figured maybe that was why *
you were so... grumpy?

VALDEZ
(mildly irritated) *
89 How do you know I had a late night? 89 *

BANKS
90 Erika isn't feeling well and I saw 90
you come in when I was getting her
some soup and crackers from the
mess. She gave whatever it was to *
me, too. I don't know what kind of *
crazy Wasteland concoction Dr. *
Hardy gave me for it, but I'm glad *
she started feeling better without *
it. *

VALDEZ *
91 You really sound terrible. I didn't 91 *
even recognize your voice. *

BANKS *
92 You think I *sound* bad? I feel like 92 *
I've aged 20 years in two days. *
(beat)
93 Look, talk to me, Valdez. What's 93 *
wrong? That doctor turn out to be a
wild goose chase or something?

VALDEZ
94 No, actually. Quite the contrary, 94
in fact. We had a very productive
conversation, and he gave me his
personal journals and notes. That's
what I've been going through this
morning.

BANKS
95 That was a lucky break, huh? 95

VALDEZ
96 Yeah, it was. He said that Vault- 96
Tec had come by and taken all of
his equipment and formal research,
but it was obviously *not* Vault-Tec.
(MORE)

VALDEZ (CONT'D)
He did say, though, that they had
Vault-Tec credentials and he
recognized them from the program,
so that may give us some insight
into who's behind this.
(beat)
97 How did you know that I went to see 97
him? I didn't see you here all day,
or the day before, for that matter.

BANKS chuckles.

BANKS
98 Am I really that invisible to you, 98
Valdez? Do I have to get up off my *
deathbed and bribe you with coffee *
to get you to notice me?

VALDEZ laughs.

VALDEZ
99 No, Alan... I guess I've just been 99
really focused. There's a *lot* to
all this, but I'm clearly missing a
big chunk of context.

BANKS
100 How do you mean? 100

VALDEZ
101 I was hoping that getting something 101
from the perspective of one of the
lead researchers might fill in some
blanks.

BANKS
102 But I'm guessing it didn't. 102

VALDEZ
103 It *kind of* did. I have a clearer 103
picture of what the project was all
about, and that picture wasn't
pretty.
(beat)
104 But I still don't understand why 104
it's suddenly become such a
priority for every bad actor in
Appalachia. Like, *I* can barely wrap
my head around the technology and
how it works, what's a Blood Eagle
going to do with it?

BANKS
105 Maybe they figure they'll be able 105
to sell it for a lot of caps?

VALDEZ
106 Maybe? But even that doesn't make 106
sense. It seems like there are much
easier ways to get things that are
a more reliable payday.

BANKS
107 So... the juice doesn't seem to be 107
worth the squeeze?

VALDEZ
108 It doesn't. But it's not like I 108
have any experience with black
markets, or access to the one
that's operating here, so I'm
really just speculating.

BANKS
109 And you don't... know anybody who 109
might have that kind of access?

VALDEZ sighs.

VALDEZ
110 I asked her to come by this 110
afternoon. We have a lot to
discuss.

BANKS
111 Why do I get the feeling that 111
there's more to that "discussion"
than black markets and brain
scanners?

VALDEZ sighs.

VALDEZ
112 Because there is. 112

BANKS
113 And I take it you don't want to 113
talk about it?

VALDEZ
114 Not really. I just... I guess I 114
made some assumptions that I
shouldn't have.

BANKS

115 Assumptions? That's really not like you, Valdez. You have your head screwed on straighter than anybody in this place, Rahmani included. And there's nobody here with better instincts. 115

VALDEZ

116 I mean, I'm a scientist. I'm supposed to deal with facts, not feelings. 116

BANKS

117 Well... 117

VALDEZ

118 Well what? 118

BANKS

119 You're a person, too, you know; you're more than just your job. I gotta be honest, sometimes I feel like you forget that. I see you open up sometimes, and it's really great to see that side of you. I just wish I saw it more, you know? 119

VALDEZ

120 Thanks, Alan. Look, I just... back in California, my life seemed pretty straightforward. I was *happy*. And then everything got turned upside down right before the expedition left, and everything that I thought was going to be a constant fell apart. 120

(beat)

121 I'd mostly managed to compartmentalize everything, and a big part of that was focusing on my work. And there's been a *lot* of work to do, so that made it easier. 121

BANKS

122 And then all that changed a few days ago. 122

VALDEZ

123 Yeah. Between this new threat... 123

BANKS
(interrupting)
124 What makes you so sure it's a 124
threat?

VALDEZ
125 Well... I'm not *sure*, but I think 125
it's smart to treat it as one until
we find out otherwise. Maybe we
should talk to Paladin Rahmani,
she's probably the best risk
assessor we have and she might give
us a little clarity there.

BANKS
126 Hmm... no, not yet. She's got 126
enough on her mind, and you're
right, this thing is too weird to
evaluate in a normal way.

VALDEZ
127 Dr. Flagler's notes are hard to 127
evaluate, too... in a normal way or
otherwise.

BANKS
128 What do you mean? 128

VALDEZ
129 They're all over the place. Some of 129
them are completely lucid, sober,
matter-of-fact. The kind of thing I
would write myself, you know?
(beat)
130 But others... it's like they're 130
written in code, but it's more
like... shorthand, I guess. But the
shorthand is almost
incomprehensible. I can practically
see his mental decline playing out
over the course of his journals,
and frankly, it's heartbreaking.

BANKS
131 It sounds like you need a break. 131

VALDEZ
132 I do, but I can't afford to take 132
one right now. There's one common
term he uses that keeps popping up,
and I'm trying to get a handle on
what he means.

BANKS

133 Maybe I can help you think through 133
it. Hit me.

VALDEZ

134 It's "North Star." 134

BANKS

135 Hmm. Well, uh... the North Star is 135
the brightest star in the sky, that
much I know. People have used it
for navigation for, what,
millennia?

VALDEZ

136 Yeah. And people have used it as a 136
metaphor for just as long.

BANKS

137 So he's probably using it as a 137
metaphor. But a metaphor for what?

VALDEZ

138 I don't know. I think that it would 138
be obvious if he was... of sound
mind, but he's not. Not close to
it, either. It's tragic. He's
clearly got a brilliant mind locked
inside there somewhere, he just
can't seem to get at it.
(beat)
139 He didn't start to use it until his 139
decline was really apparent. Maybe
that's a clue.

BANKS

140 You could always go back and ask. 140
You might catch him on a good day,
when he's more lucid.

VALDEZ

141 I don't even know if he has good 141
days, Alan. This wasn't caused by a
disease, it was caused by him going
in and tinkering with his mind. I
have no idea how it works. And all
I can really tell about that from
his notes is that it's really,
really bad.

BANKS

142 Might be worth a shot, though. 142

VALDEZ
143 I think it might be. But... 143

BANKS
144 But what? 144

VALDEZ
145 I don't think I can go over there 145
by myself. He seemed pretty
agitated, almost hostile when we
weren't the delivery person he
expected. He might remember me, but
he might not.
(beat)
146 I'd need to take Beth with me. 146
They've known each other since she
was a child, and I think that
connection was the only thing that
allowed him to focus as much as he
did.

BANKS
147 And that's a problem? Look, what's 147
going on with you two? Just from an
operational perspective, I'm not
going to ask anything about the
personal side of it, okay?

VALDEZ
148 Fine. She kept things from me, 148
Alan, and that... bothers me.

BANKS
149 Sure, I get that. It'd bother me, 149
too. What did she keep from you?

VALDEZ
150 Mostly a stuff about the last file 150
on that holotape. Remember how it
had a strange filename - "Kirsche" -
and she told me that it was a
German word that she recognized
because her mother was German?

BANKS
151 Yeah. "Cherry," right? 151

VALDEZ
152 Right. Well, it turns out "Kirsche" 152
was a nickname she had in the
Vault, because of her red hair.
(MORE)

VALDEZ (CONT'D)
She said she didn't mention that because she didn't want to raise any concerns unless the file turned out to be somehow related to her.

BANKS
153 Was it? I know she said her friend was going to try to decrypt it; did he have any luck? 153

VALDEZ
154 She. And yes, she did. Indirectly, I guess - she took it to someone else - who exactly I don't know - and that person got it decrypted. 154
(beat)
155 It turns out, the file wasn't just related to her, it was all about her - it was her full personnel file from Vault 76, including a lot of information that was supposed to be highly classified. 155

BANKS
156 Oh. This is getting... complicated. 156

VALDEZ
157 And there was no reason for it to be! That's what's so frustrating about it! It's like... it's like she was being secretive purely for the sake of being secretive. I trusted her by giving her that tape in the first place, and she didn't trust me enough to give me the whole story. 157

BANKS
158 Huh. That's strange. I wouldn't have expected her to be like that. I mean, you two seemed pretty open with each other when you were talking in that lab when you first met. 158

VALDEZ
159 I guess that's a big part of what makes it so frustrating. 159
(reflective)
160 Right from the minute she tossed me that holotape, we really seemed to... connect, I guess. Now I don't know what to think about... god, any of this. 160

BANKS

161 "Any of this?" Valdez, you don't have to tell me anything you're not comfortable with, but I'm your friend, and I'm worried about you. 161

VALDEZ

162 If I'm being honest, I'm a little worried about me, too. But right now, I think the only thing I can do is focus on this research and try to figure out what's going on. 162

MUSICAL TRANSITION

END OF ACT ONE

ACT TWO

INT. ANDREW KIRBY'S HOUSE, DAY

BETH rings the doorbell, and ANDREW answers.

BETH
163 Hello, daddy. 163

ANDREW
164 Well, hello, Lily, I was hoping 164
you'd stop by. I'm almost afraid to
ask, but... how is Tony?

BETH
165 He's... well, he's alive. But I 165
understand what you meant about his
decline. He was lucid one moment,
then spiraling the next. Odessa and
I managed to keep him mostly
centered, but it was a struggle.
(beat)
166 He wants you to visit again. 166

ANDREW
167 That's encouraging, at least. I'll 167
make it a point to do just that.
And soon.
(beat)
168 We missed you at dinner last night, 168
by the way.

BETH
169 I know, I'm sorry. Odessa and I 169
were both... drained after talking
with Dr. Flagler, and I thought it
would be best to just make her
dinner at my place and relax a bit.

ANDREW
170 You could've brought her over here! 170
We always have room for more. Oh,
but I suppose that could've been
awkward.

BETH
171 That would've been a moot point 171
anyway, since Amanda burst in just
as we were starting dessert.

ANDREW

172 She did say that she was meeting 172
her contact after dinner to
retrieve that holotape. Wouldn't
tell me who it was, and I couldn't
seem to figure it out, either.
(beat)
173 Must be losing my touch. 173

BETH

174 You're not. I can't figure it out, 174
either. But whoever it is, they
have access to some pretty powerful
decryption technology.

ANDREW

175 Indeed. Well, the reason I'd hoped 175
you'd stop by isn't so you can
retrieve your spaetzle. I have
information.

BETH

176 You do? That's brilliant! I have 176
some as well.

ANDREW

177 I thought so. Charles and I have 177
been working through our contacts.
(to Charles)
178 Charles, my boy, can you come in 178
here?

CHARLES

179 Elizabeth! So lovely to see you! I 179
promise that I did *not* eat your
spaetzle.

BETH

180 You'd better not have! I was 180
already gutted that I didn't get to
eat it right after mum made it!

ANDREW

181 Why don't we start with your news? 181

BETH

182 Sure. It may inform what you've 182
found out. Basically, that file
that Amanda's friend decrypted, the
one named after me... it was a full
copy of my Vault 76 personnel file.

ANDREW

183 When you say "full..." 183

BETH

184 I mean "full." 184

ANDREW

185 Even the compartmentalized files? 185

BETH

186 Yes. It had things even I didn't know had been recorded. School records, who my friends were, romantic relationships, very specific and very secret aspects of my training... it was very thorough. 186

CHARLES

187 That's troubling. All of that information should've stayed locked up in Vault 76. Even the Overseer didn't have access to some of the more sensitive compartmentalized information. 187

ANDREW

188 What's more troubling is that it was clearly put there by someone who knew that you'd be there when it was found. 188

BETH

189 I just realized... it's worse than that. 189

CHARLES

190 How do you mean? 190

BETH

191 Whoever put it there thought I'd be the one to find it. Remember, I specifically waited to go to that location until the Brotherhood sent Odessa. If I hadn't wanted to set up a situation where I could meet her, I would've gone in and found it myself before they'd even got wind of it. 191

ANDREW

192 And now they've been drawn into something that whoever's behind this intends to be personal. 192

CHARLES

193 This can't be just about her, can 193
it? I mean, no offense, Elizabeth, but this is a hell of a lot of effort just to... upset you, I suppose?

BETH

194 No offense taken, Charles, you're 194
right. This isn't about me, as such, but someone wants me to know about it. But why? I wasn't involved in this project at all; I didn't even know about it until everyone started chasing the tech.

ANDREW

195 I don't know why. And I'm afraid 195
the information we've gathered doesn't really shed any light on that side of things.

BETH

196 I guess we'll just have to hope 196
that whoever's doing this shows his cards at some point. Until then I'm going to have to be exceptionally careful.

CHARLES

197 Please do. This is a radically 197
different situation from what we thought it was.

ANDREW

198 I'm afraid, though, that you're 198
going to have to put that new level of care into practice right away.

CHARLES

199 The third lab was broken into and 199
looted several years ago, so the technology and research contained there has escaped our adversary thusfar.

ANDREW

200 But, based upon some conversations 200
with contacts, along with some chatter Amanda has picked up from patrons at The Spider's Web, we're fairly confident that we may know where it is.

BETH
201 I take it that it’s not in the 201
middle of Charleston with a bow on
it?

CHARLES
202 It is not. 202

ANDREW
203 Have you ever heard the name Craig 203
MacAllen?

BETH
204 I have. Amanda’s mentioned him 204
several times. Big underworld boss
from Pennsylvania, right?

CHARLES
205 Right. He and his sister Davina 205
took over the family business after
their parents died. They recently
expanded their operation here.

BETH
206 Makes sense. Lots of people to take 206
advantage of now.

CHARLES
207 Craig and Davina run a bit of a one- 207
stop shop in the Savage Divide.
Drugs, prostitution, weapons, that
sort of thing. The difference
between them and ordinary Raiders
or traders, though, is that they
cater specifically to high-end
clientele.

ANDREW
208 They offer... specialized services, 208
shall we say. Whatever a client’s
desires, no matter how depraved,
they generally find a way to
fulfill them. Bespoke weapons, high-
end drugs, um... exotic sexual
partners...

BETH
(agitated)
209 I hate them already. 209

ANDREW
210 Lily, I need you to stay focused. 210
(beat)
(MORE)

ANDREW (CONT'D)

211 At any rate, they recently began offering a new service, but they're keeping it very, very quiet. That's why we're one step ahead, for now. They've begun trafficking in experiences. 211

BETH

212 It sounds like they already do that. 212

ANDREW

213 Not like this. They're using technology that allows people to directly relive the experiences of *others*, via memories that had been recorded on some sort of high-capacity holotapes. 213

BETH

214 That definitely sounds like the sort of thing Project Mind's Eye could be used for. 214

CHARLES

215 We're not making any assumptions, but that certainly seems like the most likely possibility. Another, though, is that they simply heard about the technology and are luring people in with the intention of cheating them out of their caps. 215

BETH

216 An underworld boss certainly wouldn't be above that sort of thing. 216

CHARLES

217 But there's only one way, by our reckoning, to find out. You need to go undercover and find out what's going on. 217

BETH

218 That should be fun. What am I up against? 218

CHARLES

219 Well, it's a much more sophisticated operation than your typical Raider outfit. So you'll need to be on your toes more than usual. 219

ANDREW
220 You can do it yourself, if need be, 220
but it would be rather easier and
significantly safer with a partner.
Female, preferably.

BETH
221 Oh. Erm, can I take Amanda? She's 221
brilliant on operations like this.

CHARLES
222 I'm afraid not. Both Craig and 222
Davina know her, and it's likely
that some of the patrons at their
establishment will as well.

BETH
223 You want me to take *Odessa* 223
undercover with me?

ANDREW
224 Will that be a problem? I know 224
she's not a trained intelligence
operative like you, but she has the
kind of skillset that should fall
somewhere between "beneficial" and
"indispensable" given the nature of
the operation.

BETH
225 I'll ask her when I talk with her 225
at Atlas, but... we did not leave
things in a good place last night.

ANDREW
226 What happened? 226

BETH
227 I was... a bit too cagey with 227
information and it blew up in my
face when Amanda burst in. I hadn't
told her that Kirsche had been one
of my nicknames, and I didn't let
on at all about my relationship
with Amanda.

CHARLES
228 The latter bit makes sense. It 228
would be one thing if you were
still together, romantically, but
going into any sort of detail there
likely wouldn't have done anything
but introduce... unnecessary
complications.

BETH

229 I understand that, but... she 229
deserved to know.

ANDREW

230 I see. 230

CHARLES

231 We've backstopped undercover 231
identities for both of you, with
Amanda's assistance. You're a
wealthy couple from the
Northeastern part of Pennsylvania;
they're from the opposite corner,
so that should forestall any
uncomfortable conversations about
why they weren't aware of you
previously.

BETH

232 Names? 232

CHARLES

233 You're Alice Halstead and Miss 233
Valdez will be Courtney Fonseca.

BETH

234 What's our in? 234

CHARLES

235 I've taken care of getting your 235
names on the entry list. 15,000
caps each will get you through the
door.

BETH

236 15,000 caps? My goodness... 236

CHARLES

237 They have a special, very exclusive 237
tier, and that's the entry fee. You
need to be in that tier. Amanda's
arranged to have a couple of her
employees do the heavy lifting for
you. They'll leave as soon as the
exchange is complete to ensure
they're not recognized.
(beat)
238 Once you're in, Craig or Davina 238
will probably vet you. But I'm sure
you'll navigate that without issue.

BETH

239 As am I. How do I play it? 239

CHARLES

240 Their new endeavor seems to be 240
mostly centered around sex, so
steer the conversation in that
direction. They'll likely try to
get you to try a... romp with one
of their metahumans or something
like that, but try to get them to
volunteer the existence of the
"experience" we're looking for.

ANDREW

241 You'll have to be subtle about it, 241
of course.

BETH

242 Of course. 242

ANDREW

243 That's as much as I can help with, 243
I'm afraid. None of the people we
spoke with had even been near the
door to that area, so they were no
help in terms of what it looks
like, what kind of security is in
place, none of it.

BETH

244 We'll have to be nimble, and one of 244
us has never done anything like
this before.

ANDREW

245 You're making me wish I was forty 245
years younger. This would be
brilliant to watch play out.

BETH

246 I have to be honest, I'm not 246
comfortable putting her in harm's
way like this.

ANDREW

247 I understand. But I have every 247
confidence that you'll be an
outstanding teacher.

BETH

248 After all, mine was pretty good. In 248
fact... dad, can you take the lead
on getting her ready? I'll help, of
course.

ANDREW

249 I'd be happy to, dear, and it will 249
be very nice to finally meet her. I
promise not to embarrass you *too*
much.

(beat)

250 Now, Charles has prepared some 250
documentation for you two to
review. That may help.

BETH

251 I think it will. Thank you, 251
gentlemen. I guess I'm off to Fort
Atlas. Wish me luck! I'm going to
need it...

ANDREW

252 Good luck, Lily. 252

CHARLES

253 Good luck! 253

MUSICAL TRANSITION

INT. FORT ATLAS, DAY

BETH tentatively knocks on VALDEZ's door.

BETH

254 Um, Odessa? May I come in? 254

VALDEZ

255 Of course. Can you close the door? 255
We need to talk.

BETH

256 Yeah. I suppose we do. 256

BETH closes the door.

VALDEZ

257 About last night... 257

BETH

258 Yeah. I'm sorry about... all of it. 258
I never should've kept anything
from you. It was unfair.

VALDEZ

259 It was. And... it hurt. 259

BETH

260 The thing is, for nearly my entire 260
life, it's been "Semper Occultus."

VALDEZ
261 “Always Secret.” 261

BETH
262 Exactly. One of the most important tenets of my training was to be very careful about what information we revealed, lest it compromise an operation. 262

VALDEZ
263 And is that what this is? An operation? 263

BETH
264 No! And that’s why I’m gutted about how I’ve handled everything. That ends now. It will be “Semper Veritas” between us from here on out. 264

VALDEZ
265 I... hope that’s true. But I hope you understand that I can’t just take that at face value. 265

BETH
266 I do. And... I’m relieved that you’re even willing to talk about this. I thought you might just... have an Initiate at the entrance to tell me that you never wanted to see me again. 266

VALDEZ
267 I considered it. Well, not exactly. I felt you deserved to hear it directly from me and not an Initiate. 267
(beat)
268 But I need you to understand, that’s still on the table. 268

BETH
269 I understand. And I’m glad you changed your mind. 269

VALDEZ
270 I guess I’ll find out if I am, too. 270
(beat)
271 I... um... wanted to talk to you about... dessert. 271

BETH
(cautious)
272 What about it? 272

VALDEZ
273 What we were about to do... that 273
isn't normally the kind of thing I
rush into. I guess I should be glad
your friend interrupted.

BETH sighs.

BETH
274 I don't want anything to happen 274
between us that you're not
completely comfortable with. And if
Amanda's interruption stopped you
from doing something you feel you
would've regretted, then I should
be glad, too.

VALDEZ
275 That's just it. I don't know if I 275
would've regretted it. In the
moment, I wasn't conflicted about
it at all. I wanted it. A lot.

BETH
276 You certainly didn't seem 276
conflicted.

VALDEZ
277 I felt... free, I guess? Freer than 277
I have at any point since I left
California. The whole thing just
felt *right*.

BETH
278 And then, suddenly, it wasn't. 278

VALDEZ
279 Yeah. Very not right. 279

BETH
280 I want to make sure any lingering 280
questions get answered so we can
have a... bit of a fresh start, I
suppose.

VALDEZ
281 Who is Amanda to you? 281

BETH

282 I thought that would come up. I met 282
Amanda not long after I left the
Vault. We became involved fairly
quickly, but the relationship
was... toxic. We were not built to
be together in that way.
(beat)
283 So, after about six months of non- 283
stop fighting and making up, I
finally stormed out, vowed never to
speak to her again.

VALDEZ
(suspicious)
284 But that clearly didn't last. 284

BETH

285 A few months after that happened, I 285
got a freelance gig to track down a
missing Enclave lieutenant. When
Colonel Valeria gave me the
details, I got this sinking feeling
in the pit of my stomach. But, a
job is a job, so I went to Amanda's
bar to see if this missing
lieutenant was there.

VALDEZ

286 And? 286

BETH

287 She was. I collected her and sent 287
her back to the Enclave, and Amanda
and I began a reconciliation.

VALDEZ

288 I see. And I take it that you've 288
been back together since then?

BETH

289 Oh! Heavens no. We've never gotten 289
back together romantically. We've
managed to concentrate on the
aspects of our relationship that
did work. We're brilliant as
friends, but we understand that
we're terrible as a couple.
(beat)
290 But, in the interest of full 290
disclosure, we do sometimes serve
as a... bit of a relief valve for
each other.

VALDEZ
291 I'm a big girl, you don't need to 291
speak in euphemisms.

BETH
292 We still have sex. 292

VALDEZ
293 Hrm. And, um... have... 293

BETH
(interrupting)
294 That has not happened since you and 294
I met. Including last night. She
did stay with me, but just to make
sure I was alright.

VALDEZ
295 She sounds like a really good 295
friend.

BETH
296 She is. 296

VALDEZ
297 Thank you for telling me the truth. 297

BETH
298 You deserve it. 298
(beat)
299 I... um... brought you a present. 299

VALDEZ
300 A present? Why would you bring me a 300
present?

BETH
301 It was Amanda's idea. Something to 301
try to make up for how I'd behaved.

VALDEZ
302 Really, honesty is the only present 302
I need from you right now.

BETH
303 Oh... 303

VALDEZ
304 Um... what was it? 304

BETH
305 It was a specially engineered high- 305
capacity fusion core.
(MORE)

BETH (CONT'D)
It holds roughly 175% of the charge a normal one holds. I thought you might be interested in reverse engineering it so the Brotherhood could have longer stretches in their power armor without swapping cores. Might save some lives.

VALDEZ
306 That's... wow, that's really 306
thoughtful. Thank you, Beth.

BETH
307 It's my pleasure. And now I have 307
really good news. My father got a lead on where some of this brain tech is, and whoever's chasing it doesn't know about it yet.

VALDEZ
308 That's fantastic news! I can ask 308
Alan to get a team together and we can go there right now, before we get beaten to it again!

BETH
309 No, let's *not* do that. There are a 309
couple of factors at play. First, we believe there's a mole in the Brotherhood. We don't have any information on who it might be, but some information has gotten out there that only you guys had access to. I think that's one reason this group has stayed one step ahead of us.

VALDEZ
310 That can't be true! I need to tell 310
Paladin Rahmani...

BETH
311 No, this is something we need to 311
keep under wraps for now. The smart play is to wait it out and hope they make a mistake and reveal themselves. But until then, we have to be very careful about whom we share information with.

VALDEZ
(ruefully)
312 "Semper Occultus." 312

BETH

313 In some cases, that approach is 313
still justified.

VALDEZ

314 Alright, I'll go along with it, at 314
least for now. But at some point
we've at least got to loop Rahmani
in.

BETH

315 When we get a bit more clarity, I 315
agree.
(beat)
316 The other thing is that because of 316
the nature of who's holding the
tech, going in undercover will be
the best way to get our hands on
it. If we go in guns blazing, the
most likely outcome is that it will
either be rushed away to safety or
blown up in a firefight. Either
way, we lose access, and this is
the best shot we've had so far.

VALDEZ

317 That makes sense. So when are you 317
going undercover?

BETH

318 Um... I'm not going undercover. 318
We're going undercover.

VALDEZ

319 What?! Beth! I'm not an operative! 319
I'm not even a Field Scribe! How on
earth am I going to go undercover
without getting myself or both of
us killed?

BETH

320 You're not an operative, that's 320
true. But we need somebody who's
smart enough to know both what
we're looking for and what we're
looking at. And I need somebody I
can trust. There's only one person
who ticks all of those boxes.
(beat)
321 It's still early, so we have 321
several hours before we need to be
there. We'll stop by my father's
house and give you a crash course;
(MORE)

BETH (CONT'D)
he's the best teacher on the
planet.

VALDEZ
322 He'd better be... 322

BETH
323 And then we'll go to my place so we can pick out something to wear and get your hair and makeup sorted. This is a high-end establishment, and we're both going to need to look the part if we're going to have any success at pulling this off. 323

VALDEZ
324 Well... this is going to be exciting, if nothing else. 324

BETH
325 You're going to be brilliant, Odessa! Dad's provided some briefing materials that you can review on the way. 325

VALDEZ
326 So we're really doing this, aren't we? 326

BETH
327 We are. And we're going to make a brilliant team, you'll see. 327

VALDEZ
328 I guess we'd better get going. I hope your father has a lot of patience. 328

BETH
329 I'm his daughter. What do you think? 329

MUSICAL TRANSITION

END OF ACT TWO

ACT THREE

INT. BETH'S HOUSE, LATE AFTERNOON

VALDEZ
330 Your father is a great teacher. I actually feel like we might be able to pull this off. 330

BETH
331 He's the best, he really is. 331

VALDEZ
332 And your mom is adorable. 332

BETH giggles.

BETH
333 Alright, let's find something in this wardrobe for you.. I'm thinking... something black. 333

VALDEZ
334 You're the expert. I've been wearing Brotherhood uniforms almost exclusively for so long... I haven't picked out something because it looks nice since... well, since California. 334

BETH
335 You look fantastic no matter what you wear, so this will be easy. Oh, and I'll set out a bra and knickers for you as well. I'm guessing that Brotherhood underwear is... functional, but not stylish. Just let me know if I've guessed wrong on any sizes. 335

BETH enters the wardrobe closet.

SFX: PAN BETH HARD LEFT

VALDEZ
336 You did a good job with that when we visited Dr. Flagler. And it was nice; it made me feel like... more than just a Scribe, for once. 336

BETH
337 Oooh, this will work... 337

VALDEZ

338 I mean, don't get me wrong, I love being a Scribe and I'm proud of it. I just... I don't know. I haven't felt like a whole person since we left for Appalachia, and I want that back. Maybe that's part of why... dessert almost happened. 338

BETH re-enters.

SFX: PAN BETH BACK TO NORMAL

BETH

339 Well, if it helps, I've seen a lot more than "just a Scribe" since we met. You're... well, you're quite something, Odessa Valdez. 339

(beat)

340 I've put out the dress, and the rest. I do hope you like it; if you don't, please just say the word and I'll pick something else... or we could even pick something together, if you'd like... 340

VALDEZ

341 I'm sure it's lovely. 341

VALDEZ enters the wardrobe closet.

SFX: PAN VALDEZ HARD RIGHT

VALDEZ changes her clothes.

BETH

342 Was there anything about tonight that you want to go over? I have the briefing materials here with me, so we can talk anything through that you'd like. 342

VALDEZ

343 I think I'm pretty clear on everything, actually. I guess it's all going to come down to... how I react in the moment. 343

(beat)

344 Uh, Beth? 344

BETH

345 What is it? Do you hate it? 345

VALDEZ
346 Um... no... it's lovely. It's one 346
of the most... flattering things I
think I've ever worn.
(beat)
347 But I have a question. 347

BETH
348 Of course, what's up? 348

VALDEZ
349 Where's the rest of it? 349

BETH laughs.

VALDEZ leaves the wardrobe closet.

SFX: PAN VALDEZ BACK TO NORMAL

BETH
350 Oh my god... 350

VALDEZ
(mortified)
351 I know, I know! I'm sure you have 351
something a little more... I don't
know... maybe a sack?
(beat)
352 Beth? 352

BETH
353 I'm sorry, you... you took my 353
breath away.
(beat, gathering
herself)
354 If you're uncomfortable, I have a 354
shrug you can wear over the dress.
Or we can pick something else out
entirely. But you look... amazing
if that's your concern.

VALDEZ
(still embarrassed)
355 I... trust you, Beth. This is 355
just... a lot. Based on what your
dad and Charles said, this really
does seem like the best way to
finally get to something first.
We've been playing from behind
until now, and I want to do
whatever I can to change that.

BETH

356 It is the best way, Odessa. I 356
wouldn't put you in a position like
this if I wasn't utterly convinced
that was the case.

VALDEZ

357 Yeah... I believe you. 357
(beat)
358 Is it always like this? Knowing 358
you?

BETH

359 What do you mean? 359

VALDEZ

360 We've known each other for what, 360
less than a week? But it feels like
I've... *lived* more since I met you
than I have in months. Maybe years.

BETH

361 I guess I'm a bit of an... 361
experience sometimes. But I
promise, it's not always this much
of a... whirlwind, I guess.

VALDEZ
(chuckling)
362 That's comforting. 362

BETH

363 So, would you like that shrug? Or a 363
jacket? Or another dress entirely?

VALDEZ

364 You know what? I'm good. 364
(beat)
365 What are you going to wear? 365

BETH

366 Well, since you're wearing black, I 366
thought red would be a nice
compliment.

VALDEZ

367 You're the fashion expert... 367

BETH
(interrupting)
368 I am definitely *not* a fashion 368
expert. But I do think I have a
good eye.

VALDEZ

369 Well, regardless, I think whatever 369
you pick is going to look great.
(beat)
370 This dress is kind of growing on 370
me. It has a lot of "oomph."

BETH

371 Any "oomph" is all you, Odessa. 371

VALDEZ

372 You'd better get changed. We still 372
need to do hair and makeup, and
your father said that we had to be
there at 20 hundred hours sharp.

BETH

373 Yeah, this group is very big on 373
respect, and being late is
something they would consider *very*
disrespectful.

VALDEZ

(playfully)
374 Come on. I want to see this red 374
dress.

BETH

(playfully)
375 Yes, ma'am. 375

MUSICAL TRANSITION

EXT. ABANDONED BANK, NIGHT

NOTE: BETH SWITCHES BACK AND FORTH BETWEEN AN AMERICAN ACCENT AND HER NATURAL ONE IN THIS SCENE, AS NOTED

VALDEZ

376 This is it. Fascinating use for an 376
old bank, isn't it?

BETH

377 It is. I'll be interested to see 377
what they've done with the place.
Dad said that it's supposed to be
nothing like the Raider brothels
and gambling dens.
(beat)
378 Are you ready? 378

VALDEZ

379 No. But your dad got me as ready as 379
I'm ever going to be, so let's go.

BETH

380 You look great, and you're going to 380
do so well.

BETH and VALDEZ approach the bouncer.

BOUNCER

381 Yes? 381

BETH

(switches to American
accent)

382 I'm Alice Halstead and this is 382
Courtney Fonseca. We're expected.

The BOUNCER checks the list.

BOUNCER

383 Hmm... let's see... 383
(beat)
384 Yes, you are. I take it these two 384
guys are carrying your cover
charge?

BETH

385 Yes, they are. Boys? 385

The two RAIDERS give sacks of caps to the BOUNCER.

BOUNCER

386 I assume I don't have to count 386
them?

BETH laughs.

BETH

387 It's entirely up to you. 387

BOUNCER

388 This club is all about trust. So 388
I'm going to trust you. But
violating that trust is a very,
very bad idea. Do you understand?

BETH

389 We understand. 389

BOUNCER

390 Very good. Since you two are new to 390
the club and you're VIPs, Mr.
MacAllen is going to meet you
inside. Go to the bar and wait
there. I'll send word that you're
here.

(MORE)

BOUNCER (CONT'D)
(beat)
391 Being on-time is a good start. He 391
hates it when people are late.

VALDEZ
392 Thank you. 392

BETH and VALDEZ enter the club.

INT. CLUB, NIGHT

There is a lot of noise and happy chatting. Music plays in the background.

VALDEZ
393 That guy at the door wasn't like 393
any Raider I've ever met.

BETH
(reverting to natural
accent)
394 These guys are different. My dad 394
told me stories about the pre-war
mob. They were every bit as brutal
as Raiders are today, but they had
a rigid internal moral code that
they held fast to, and woe betide
anyone who violated it.

VALDEZ
395 Moral? I thought they were 395
criminals?

BETH
396 They were, and awful ones at that. 396
Murder, drug dealing, prostitution,
rigged gambling... you name it,
they were into it.

VALDEZ
397 That doesn't really help me 397
understand this "moral code."

BETH
398 It was really just a way to keep 398
everyone within the various
organizations in line. For everyone
to continue to operate with some
measure of impunity they had to do
so... well, if not cooperatively,
at least in a way that kept them
out of each other's way.

VALDEZ

399 I see. I'll keep that in mind tonight. And I'll try to keep quiet; I'll stick to the science once we get to that part. You can handle the spy work. 399

BETH

400 There's not an eye in this place that's not on us right now. Especially you. 400

VALDEZ

401 I thought undercover work was about blending in? 401

BETH

402 It's more about *fitting* in. When someone who looks like you comes to a place like this, it would seem off if you didn't flaunt your looks. So the smart play is to go completely in the opposite direction and... show off. 402

(switches to American accent)

403 Here comes the bartender. It's showtime. 403

A BARTENDER comes over.

BARTENDER

404 What can I get you ladies? Mr. MacAllen said that everything will be on the house. 404

VALDEZ

405 Something strong, please. 405

BARTENDER

406 Yes, ma'am, I think I know just the thing. And for you? 406

BETH

407 Make it two. 407

BARTENDER

408 I'll be right back. 408

VALDEZ

409 I thought something to calm the nerves would be a good idea. 409

BETH

410 See? Already thinking on your feet. 410
You're a natural.

BARTENDER

411 There you are, ladies. 411

The BARTENDER puts two glasses on the bar.

BARTENDER (CONT'D)

412 If they're not to your liking I'm 412
happy to make something else. I'll
check in with you in a bit. Mr.
MacAllen will be here momentarily.

BETH and VALDEZ take a drink.

VALDEZ

413 This is... good. I don't drink 413
cocktails very much, and it's
mostly because they taste like
paint thinner smells.

BETH

414 That's not surprising. Liquor has 414
also been one of the mafia's
specialties, going all the way back
to when the American government
tried to ban it.

CRAIG MACALLEN enters.

CRAIG

415 "Mafia" is such an old-world term. 415
And a loaded one, at that.

BETH

416 I'm sorry. I didn't mean to offend. 416

CRAIG

417 It's alright. Times have changed, 417
and so has my family's business. It
will take time for people to
understand that.
(beat)
418 Craig MacAllen. It's a pleasure to 418
meet you both. I take it... you're
Alice and... you're Courtney?

VALDEZ

419 That's right. It's a pleasure to 419
meet you.

CRAIG

420 If I may say, you make an 420
absolutely stunning couple.

VALDEZ

421 How did you know we were a couple? 421

CRAIG chuckles.

CRAIG

422 I did my homework on you. And I 422
don't want to give away any trade
secrets, but... the way you leaned
back against her the second you
felt her behind you sealed it. You
can't fake that.

VALDEZ

423 Huh. I guess you're good at reading 423
people, then?

CRAIG

424 Comes with the job. If you can't do 424
that, you're dead.

VALDEZ

425 That makes sense. The world is 425
dangerous.

CRAIG

426 It is. So we try to provide a 426
little respite from all that.

VALDEZ

427 Can I ask you something that I've 427
been wondering since we got here?

CRAIG

428 Of course, Miss Fonseca. 428

VALDEZ

429 Please. Call me Courtney. 429
(beat)
430 Did everyone here pay 15,000 caps 430
to get in?

CRAIG

431 Oh, of course not. Most of them 431
paid 1,000.

VALDEZ

432 Why did we pay so much? 432

CRAIG

433 I needed to know that you were 433
legit, and that you're serious.
You're clearly both of those
things. And those caps get you
full, priority access to everything
we have to offer. All you have to
do is ask. You're going to need
that so you can make an informed
decision.

(beat)

434 Look, bottom line, if my sister and 434
I are going to get this operation
off the ground the way we want to,
we need a partner. A partner who
knows Appalachia, and who has
resources.

BETH

435 We check off both of those boxes. 435

CRAIG

436 I know. You have a sterling 436
reputation back in Pennsylvania,
too.

(beat)

437 I heard you were regular customers 437
at Columbo's. Do they still make
that veal, the old family recipe?

BETH

438 Columbo's? 438

CRAIG

439 Yeah. Columbo's. 439

BETH

440 I think you mean Colarusso's. And 440
yes, their veal is excellent. A bit
different from how it was pre-war,
from what I'm told, but I can only
speak to the current version.

CRAIG

441 Ah, right. Colarusso's. How's Mama 441
Angelina?

BETH

442 You mean Mama Angelica? She passed, 442
I'm afraid. Anthony's running the
business, at least he was when we
came here.

CRAIG

443 Anthony's a good egg. I'm glad he 443
was able to keep things going.
(beat)
444 I need to talk to Davina for a 444
moment, but I'll be right back.
Then we'll chat.
(beat)
445 Jack, freshen the ladies' drinks, 445
and make sure they don't see the
bottom of a glass while they're
here. Okay?

BARTENDER

446 You got it, boss. 446

CRAIG leaves.

VALDEZ

(sotto)
447 He was not what I was expecting. He 447
was... charming. And I'm glad those
identities checked out.

BETH

(sotto)
448 Charles is great at that. I've 448
never had a backstopped identity
fall through.
(beat)
449 And I'm so proud of you! You really 449
took charge of that conversation
and you were brilliant.

VALDEZ

(sotto)
450 Thanks. I just sort of... rolled 450
with it.

BARTENDER

451 Fresh drinks, ladies. 451

VALDEZ

452 Thank you, Jack. 452

CRAIG returns.

CRAIG

453 Let's go to my office and talk. 453

CRAIG, BETH, and VALDEZ walk down a flight of stairs and into an office.

CRAIG closes the door.

CRAIG (CONT'D)
454 So, here we are. 454
(beat)
455 I'll get right to it. People have needs. You have them, I have them, everybody has one. And we want to fulfill them. 455

BETH
456 What kind of needs are we talking about here? 456

CRAIG
457 We leave the basics to others. Food, water, shelter, not interested. We specialize in alcohol, chems, gambling, and, of course, sex. 457

BETH
458 Of course. 458

CRAIG
459 None of those things are in short supply, but we provide a more... premium experience. 459

VALDEZ
460 Premium how? 460

CRAIG
461 You've already tried the alcohol. The chems are just as good. And the sex... well, let's just say we provide the kind of experience you can't generally get out there in the Wasteland. Your choice of partners, anything you want all along the gender and sexuality spectrum. And when someone wants something more... exotic, we can provide that, too. 461

BETH
462 Exotic? 462

CRAIG
463 Well, for example, you'd be surprised how many people have a certain... fascination with Super Mutants. Or the Sheepsquatch. 463

VALDEZ
(shocked)
464 Oh... oh, my. 464

CRAIG
465 I'm sorry, I didn't mean to shock 465
you.

BETH
466 It's alright. It's like you said, 466
people have needs, and we're
certainly in no position to judge.

CRAIG
467 You can sample anything you'd like, 467
on the house. You won't be
disappointed, I assure you.

BETH
468 Perhaps another time. 468

CRAIG
469 All business. I like that. There's 469
one other thing, and I wasn't going
to say a word about it unless you
checked out. We're still in the
process of getting a lot of moving
pieces into place, and that's where
you come in.

VALDEZ
470 What is it? 470

CRAIG
471 When we moved here, we found a 471
whole trove of... stuff. I read
through the notes they left, and
called in a couple of experts to
help me figure out if it had the
kind of potential it seemed like it
did. Then we tracked down someone
who knew a little bit about it.
Turns out, we struck gold - it's
going to be an experience like
nobody's ever seen before.

BETH
472 Go on. 472

CRAIG
473 How would you like to be able to 473
experience something through
someone else's eyes?
(MORE)

CRAIG (CONT'D)

You can, like, ride a horse through a field, pre-war. Jump out of an airplane. Ever wondered what it's like to have sex as a man? You can do that, too.

BETH

474 I don't understand. **474**

CRAIG

475 The stuff we found lets people relive experiences other people recorded onto holotapes. Brain to brain. And there's a lot of it, including a ton of sex. We haven't even cataloged a quarter of it. We need to do that, and we need to... smooth out the kinks. No pun intended. **475**

VALDEZ

476 What kind of kinks need to be smoothed out? **476**

CRAIG

477 Let's just say that the process occasionally runs into issues. We've had some... volunteers testing it out, and sometimes bad things happen. Really bad. I've had a couple go insane, a few have gone catatonic, and some straight-up just didn't make it. **477**

VALDEZ

478 My god... **478**

CRAIG

479 The two specialists we brought in are working on it, and they're getting there. They've developed a chem that seems to prevent problems *most* of the time. But we're still working on it. I don't mean to sound hard-hearted, but we want repeat customers. **479**

(beat)

480 If you two want in on this, we'll make you full partners for the low price of one and a half million caps. I know you have that kind of money, so it's down to whether you have the stones to join us on this. **480**

VALDEZ

481 That's... a lot of money. 481

BETH

482 And a big decision. 482

CRAIG

483 You're right. Both of you are. And that's why I'm leaving this offer open until this time next month. You're the first people I've approached with this, and I'm not going to say a word about it to anyone else unless that deadline passes or you say no. 483

BETH

484 That sounds fair. 484

CRAIG

485 I think it is. You're clearly people who deserve respect, and you've provided me with respect as well. That's very important to me. 485

(beat)

486 And until then, you have the full run of the club. Your 30,000 caps bought that, whether we end up as partners or not. The only demand I have - and let me be clear, it is a demand, not a request - is that you not speak of this, regardless whether we come to an agreement or not. 486

BETH

487 You have our word. 487

CRAIG

488 Good. 488

The BOUNCER knocks on the door and opens it.

BOUNCER

489 Boss? Your sister said she wants to talk to you. 489

CRAIG

490 If you'll excuse me, ladies. Look, you've heard my spiel. You get in on this, you're going to be Appalachia's number one power couple. 490

VALDEZ

491 Who says we're not already? 491

CRAIG laughs.

CRAIG

492 Yeah, You may have a point. Either way, I hope I'll see you again, soon. And as I said, you want to sample anything, just ask. 492

CRAIG leaves.

The BOUNCER enters the room and closes the door.

BOUNCER

493 Alright, great job. 493

BETH

494 What? 494

BOUNCER

495 You two were perfect. We only have a few minutes. His master terminal is on his desk. None of the hardcore data is on there, but there's quite a bit of overview that might help. He probably left it unlocked, but if he didn't, you shouldn't have a problem hacking it. Copy what you can onto this holotape. Just keep it in your bag, nobody's going to check it. I've made sure of that. 495

BETH

(feigning shock)

496 What are you talking about? 496

BOUNCER

497 Your father sends his regards. 497

BETH

498 I don't know what you're playing at, but we're here to discuss business with Mr. MacAllen. We're not going to copy any data onto any holotapes. 498

BOUNCER

499 He also wanted me to ask you - what did the evil chicken lay? 499

BETH groans, then sighs.

BETH
(reverting to natural accent)
500 Deviled eggs. 500

VALDEZ laughs.

VALDEZ
501 I have to say, your dad using a dad joke as a code phrase is a nice touch. 501

VALDEZ pops the holotape into the terminal and begins copying data.

BOUNCER
502 I'll hang out outside the door and redirect him if he comes back. Once you finish copying the data, go to the bar and have a few more drinks. Then leave. Don't rush out, it'll look suspicious. 502

VALDEZ
503 Understood. And thank you. 503

BOUNCER
504 Don't mention it. Seriously, don't mention it. It took me a while to get into his good graces. 504

The BOUNCER leaves and closes the door.

BETH
505 How long will it take to copy the data? 505

VALDEZ
506 Not long. And I'm glad he said to have a drink, I think I need one. My hands are shaking. 506
(beat)
507 How do you do this all the time? 507

BETH
508 Sometimes I wonder myself. But really, you've been brilliant. I'm in awe. Even more awe than I'm usually in around you. 508

VALDEZ
509 This was... fun. Terrifying, but fun. 509
(MORE)

VALDEZ (CONT'D)
I'm not even sure if it would've been better or worse if he'd actually brought up the technical details like we expected him to.

BETH
510 Um, Odessa... 510

VALDEZ
511 Yes? 511

BETH
512 Will you stay the night? At my place? It's really late, and we have to go there so you can change regardless. I think walking into Atlas dressed like that would lead to... questions. 512

VALDEZ
513 Beth... I really don't know if that's a good idea. 513

BETH
514 It's purely a practical matter. I'm not trying to manufacture an excuse to... serve you dessert. I have a guest room, and it's yours. 514
(beat)
515 I promise, I'll be a perfect gentleman. 515

VALDEZ laughs.

VALDEZ
516 Well, since you put it that way... 516

BETH
517 We can go to Fort Atlas first thing in the morning. I mean, if you'll have me. Otherwise, we'll just gather up everything you need and you can head back yourself. 517

VALDEZ
518 I think it would be best if we work on this together. At Atlas, in the morning. 518

The terminal beeps.

VALDEZ (CONT'D)
519 The data transfer is done! 519

BETH

520 That's brilliant! 520

(beat)

521 Would you care to have a drink with me, Courtney? 521

VALDEZ

522 I would love that, Alice. 522

BETH

523 I'll walk you to the bar. 523

BETH and VALDEZ leave the office and close the door behind them.

END OF ACT THREE

CREDITS

NARRATOR
"Once Upon a Wasteland" Episode 3, "Checks and Limitations," was produced and directed by Brad Williams and written by D.K. Trueno.

Starring Letitia Lemon as Elizabeth Kirby and Vitriol Plays as Odessa Valdez.

Also starring Lucy Middelthon as Amanda Otis, Penal Pineapple as Andrew Kirby, John Lauri as Alan Banks, and Jay Chadwick as Charles Watkins.

Featuring XXX as Craig MacAllen, XXX as the bouncer, and XXX as the bartender.

And I'm your narrator, Ashley Sekhon.

Please join us for our next episode, Episode 4: "Fraternal Sympathies and Affections."

Season One
Part Two: The Book of Amanda

Episode 4:
"Fraternal Sympathies and Affections"

by

D.K. Trueno

Final
12 November 2021

"FRATERNAL SYMPATHIES AND AFFECTIONS"

INT. FORT ATLAS, MORNING

BETH and VALDEZ enter.

BETH
1 Back at Atlas... home sweet home. 1

VALDEZ
2 What a beautiful day for a walk. I almost don't want to be cooped up inside. 2

BETH
3 Oh, come on, you love it in here. 3

VALDEZ
4 Yeah, I do. 4

BETH
5 And I'm starting to understand its charms as well. 5

VALDEZ
6 By the way, I never really thanked you for breakfast. There's just one thing, though. 6

BETH
7 What's that? 7

VALDEZ
8 Now you have to make me lunch at some point to... you know, complete the set. 8

BETH
9 Oooh, I'll take that as a challenge. 9

VALDEZ
10 Well, I *have* been called challenging... 10

BETH laughs.

CASEY BARKSDALE spots them.

CASEY
11 Beth?! 11

CASEY runs to BETH and hugs her. Hard.

BETH
12 Oof! 12
(beat)
13 Casey?! 13

CASEY
14 Sorry, I guess that hug had been... building up for a while. I... well, I kinda started to think we were never going to see each other again. What are you even doing here? 14

BETH
15 I could ask you the same question. I had no idea you'd joined the Brotherhood! The uniform suits you, by the way. 15

CASEY
16 I had it altered. 16

BETH
(laughing)
17 Of course you did. 17

CASEY
18 Hey, we should... you know, catch up. Have a drink. Or several. I know a few places... 18

BETH
(flustered)
19 Well... I mean... I would *definitely* like to catch up, but... 19

CASEY
(momentarily confused)
20 But? What's up? 20
(not confused anymore)
21 Oh. Oh! I'm sorry! Now that I'm actually paying attention I don't know how I missed the "couple" vibes you two are putting out. I had no idea you two were together! That's great! Kind of disappointing, but great! 21
(beat, awkwardly)
22 And I'm also paying attention to the looks on both of your faces right now, which are telling me to change the subject. 22
(beat)
(MORE)

CASEY (CONT'D)

23 So... um... what have you been up 23
to?

BETH

24 Freelancing, mostly. Just doing my 24
part. How about you? You really do
look great, by the way.

CASEY

25 So do you! Did you get taller? And 25
you really need to hook me up with
your tailor.
(beat)
26 I was just sort of... meandering, I 26
guess. Then these guys showed up, I
started talking to a few people,
next thing I knew I was working for
them.

BETH

27 That's great! What have you been 27
doing for the Brotherhood?

CASEY

28 Community outreach, mostly. Trying 28
to spread goodwill where I can so
people feel like they can trust us.
That's the best way for us to do
the most good.

BETH

29 I'm sure you're brilliant at it. 29

CASEY

30 Aww. I don't know, I do my best. 30

VALDEZ

(awkwardly)
31 I hate to break up this... um... 31
reunion, but have you seen Knight
Banks, Casey?

CASEY

32 I haven't, no. That seems to be a 32
thing with him lately. Just kind
of... disappears without telling
anybody.
(beat, cheeky)
33 I could say the same for you, 33
though.

VALDEZ

34 Oh, I, um... I stayed at Beth's 34
place last night. It was late,
and...

CASEY

(interrupting)

35 I'm not your mom, Scribe Valdez. 35
You don't have to explain yourself
to me. Thanks for looking after
her, Beth.

BETH

36 Least I could do. Odessa is right, 36
it was really late, and I was a lot
closer than Atlas. I have a guest
room, it wasn't a bother at all.

CASEY

37 Well, regardless, I'm glad you were 37
there for her. Where did you two
run off to, anyway?

BETH

38 Just chasing a lead. 38

CASEY

39 Huh. Must've rushed out of here 39
pretty quickly. You left your light
on.

VALDEZ

40 Oh! Sorry about that. I... wait... 40

CASEY

41 What? 41

VALDEZ

42 That doesn't look like my light. 42
It's too bright.

CASEY

43 Uh-oh. Did you leave any of your... 43
tech things running? I don't want
this place to burn down or blow up.

VALDEZ

44 I'm pretty sure I didn't, but we 44
need to get up there and check it
out.

VALDEZ, CASEY, and BETH run upstairs and open the door to VALDEZ's lab.

SFX: Pulsing electronic noises

CASEY
45 What the hell? 45

VALDEZ
46 What... is that? 46

CASEY
47 It's so bright... 47

BETH
48 Oh, no. 48

VALDEZ
49 You know what it is? Is it 49
dangerous? "Semper Veritas,"
remember?

BETH
50 It's not dangerous. At least I 50
don't think it is. Let me see if I
can...

VALDEZ
51 Be careful! 51

BETH twists the top of the device, and it deactivates.

BETH sighs.

VALDEZ (CONT'D)
52 Dammit! All of Dr. Flagler's notes 52
are gone! Journals, too.

CASEY
53 Who the did this? And how did they 53
get into Atlas?

BETH
54 This is a calling card. So not only 54
do we know who's been pulling the
strings, we know that he's not
content hiding in the shadows any
longer. Which is, I suppose,
appropriate.

VALDEZ
55 What do you mean? 55

BETH

56 It's an... entity, I guess, that I 56
wasn't even entirely sure actually
existed until just now. He calls
himself the "Morningstar."

CASEY

57 The Morningstar? Like... Lucifer? 57
The *devil*?

VALDEZ

58 As difficult as it is right now, we 58
need to stay focused. We can try to
figure out who this Morningstar is
and what he wants after we deal
with my lab being looted under
everyone's nose.

CASEY

59 What are you implying? 59

VALDEZ

60 There's a spy in the Brotherhood, 60
Casey, and that spy got into my lab
and stole everything Dr. Flagler
gave me. And...

VALDEZ clacks at her terminal keyboard.

VALDEZ (CONT'D)

61 ...also deleted all of the data 61
that we got from that first lab
from the mainframe.

CASEY

62 My gosh... how are you so calm 62
about this?

VALDEZ

63 I'm not calm. I'm furious. But if 63
there's one thing I've learned over
the years, it's to always have a
backup.

CASEY

64 You have copies of the data? 64

VALDEZ

65 I do. Unfortunately, I didn't get a 65
chance to duplicate his paper
journals, but everything he gave me
digitally, and everything we got
from that lab is backed up and in a
safe place.

CASEY

66 That was a very wise move, it seems. 66

VALDEZ

67 Casey, time is of the essence here. Can you brief Paladin Rahmani on what's happened and try to figure out how we deal with this? 67

CASEY

68 Anything for you, Odessa. 68

(beat)

69 Beth, I'm... sorry we didn't get a chance to catch up. I really missed you. 69

BETH

70 We'll have plenty of time for that, Casey. I promise. And... I missed you, too. 70

CASEY leaves.

BETH (CONT'D)

71 I think she likes you. 71

VALDEZ

72 Me? I'm not the one she tackled from across the room the second she saw her... 72

BETH

73 That's just Casey. 73

VALDEZ

74 I'll take your word for it, but... I haven't been tackled. 74

BETH

75 Yet. Give it time. 75

VALDEZ sighs.

VALDEZ

76 It's not safe to work here, we know that now. Keeping the backups at your place was very prescient. 76

BETH

77 Well, we knew there was a mole, so something like this was always a possibility. We need to keep our circle tight. 77

VALDEZ

78 Agreed. At this point, I don't know 78
anyone in the Brotherhood that I'm
comfortable looping in on this.

BETH

79 Not even Knight Banks? 79

VALDEZ

80 A week ago I would've said yes 80
without a second thought. But he's
seemed... off lately. He's been
weirdly interested in this mission
over the past couple of days, and
like Casey said, he keeps
disappearing. Maybe I'm just
overthinking it, I don't know. And
what about Casey? You two were
obviously... close.

BETH

81 She was my best friend in the 81
Vault. We were inseparable.

VALDEZ

82 Were you... 82

BETH

83 Yes. Never anything serious, but we 83
really liked each other, and
spending time together, and we were
trapped in a Vault, so... sometimes
things happen. And happen they did.

VALDEZ

84 Okay. Thank you for being honest 84
with me.

BETH

85 "Semper Veritas," remember? 85

VALDEZ chuckles.

VALDEZ

86 I guess I shouldn't be surprised 86
that you two were involved. I think
she's the... second most attractive
person I've met since I've been
here in Appalachia.

BETH

(not picking up on it)

87 *Second* most attractive? 87

(MORE)

BETH (CONT'D)
She won Miss Vault 76 both years
she was eligible, and her mother
was Miss New York... who've you met
who's more beautiful than her? And
should I be worried?

VALDEZ
88 Sorry. My lips are sealed. 88

BETH
89 Hmm... 89
(beat)
90 But to answer your question, a lot 90
can happen in two years. I know
that as well as anyone. I think
we'll learn that Casey is still the
same sweet, honest, genuine person
I knew in the Vault, but until we
do, we'll keep her out of the more
sensitive bits.

VALDEZ
91 So that leaves us and who else? 91

BETH
92 Well, I absolutely trust my parents 92
and Charles. And all three can be
invaluable as we try to work
through this.

VALDEZ
93 What about Amanda? 93

BETH
94 I... well, yes, I do absolutely 94
trust her, and she has exactly the
kind of knowledge and contacts that
we'll need to leverage, but I
wasn't sure if you'd be comfortable
bringing her in.

VALDEZ
95 If I'm being completely honest, I'm 95
not sure if I am. But I know that
you trust her implicitly, and
that... means a lot to me. So I'm
on-board with it.

BETH
96 I'm so glad you feel that way. And 96
you'll love her when you get to
know her, I'm quite convinced.

VALDEZ
97 Alright. We have one last problem 97
to figure out. It's clearly not
safe to do my research here.

BETH
98 Based on what I know about the 98
Morningstar, he's not about
violence, as such. He's more
about... subterfuge.

VALDEZ
99 That's exactly what I'm talking 99
about. If I keep working out of
Atlas, it's only a matter of time
until my work gets stolen or
sabotaged. But the problem is that
I really need the facilities. Your
house is beautiful, but it doesn't
have the kind of working space I
need.

BETH
100 That's not *exactly* true. I haven't 100
given you the full tour yet. Gather
up your things and we'll head back
to my place. I'll show you around,
and then I'll make us lunch. How
does that sound?

VALDEZ
101 I'm intrigued. I think it sounds 101
perfect. I'll let Rahmani know
where we're going in case she needs
me, and then we'll head out.

BETH
102 I'll wait here for you, in case 102
anyone starts sniffing around.

MUSICAL TRANSITION

INT. BETH'S HOME, DAY

BETH and VALDEZ are finishing lunch.

VALDEZ
103 Well, that clinches it. 103

BETH
104 What? 104

VALDEZ
105 You're a great cook. 105

BETH

106 Aww, thank you. In the interest of transparency, I was trying very hard to impress you. 106

VALDEZ

107 You succeeded. It was excellent. 107

BETH

108 Ready for the tour? 108

VALDEZ

109 You really know how to build anticipation. I was kind of hoping we'd do that first, but I'm glad we ate instead. 109

BETH

110 I am as well. Let's get to it, shall we? 110

BETH and VALDEZ walk to the living room.

VALDEZ

111 I didn't notice anything out of the ordinary when I was upstairs last night. This looks like a very nice, but very normal house. 111

BETH

112 I'm going to let you in on a secret. 112

VALDEZ

113 I'm intrigued. 113

BETH

114 See that book? Second shelf from the top, third from the left, red cover? Take it down. 114

VALDEZ pulls on the book and the bookcase slides to the side, revealing a door.

VALDEZ

115 Oh! A secret door! 115

BETH

116 There's a keypad next to it. Enter 4-1-3-6-7-2. 116

VALDEZ punches in the code and the door opens.

VALDEZ

117 You're trusting me with that access 117
code?

BETH

118 The code for the front door is 8-7- 118
9-9-4-2.

VALDEZ

119 Beth... you don't have to... 119

BETH

(interrupting)

120 I want to. There's nothing you 120
shouldn't know. And no... access
you shouldn't have.

VALDEZ

121 Thank you for trusting me. Should 121
I, um, go in?

BETH

122 Yes, let's head inside. Mind the 122
stairs.

BETH and VALDEZ walk inside and go down a flight of stairs.

VALDEZ

123 Wow... just... wow... 123

BETH

124 I think that you should have just 124
about everything you need while
things are still getting sorted
back at Atlas, aside from access to
the systems there.

VALDEZ

125 Is that... power armor? 125

BETH

126 It is, yes. I don't use it often, 126
but it does come in handy
sometimes.

VALDEZ

127 I've... never seen anything like 127
it. It's so... ornate. Almost like
something a knight would wear. Not
a Brotherhood Knight, like a...
Knight of the Round Table. What
model is it?

BETH

128 T-65. I thought the red paint was a 128
nice touch, and the gold sets it
off quite nicely.

VALDEZ

129 There were some Knights and 129
Paladins who really took pride in
their power armor back in
California - they treated it like
old hot rod cars, painting flames
on it, making sure it was always
polished, that kind of thing. But
I've never seen anything like *that*.

BETH

130 You're welcome to take it for a 130
test run if you'd like. Any time.

VALDEZ

131 I may take you up on that. Later, 131
of course.

BETH

132 Of course. And I also have a couple 132
of other sets of T-60. Not quite as
powerful as that T-65, and
certainly not as pretty, but still
good in a fight.

VALDEZ

133 Did you bring that data down here? 133

BETH

134 I did. It's already been loaded 134
onto that terminal, and the
originals are locked up in a safe
on the wall behind it. The
combination is 41-68-18-27.

VALDEZ chuckles.

VALDEZ

135 I'm glad I'm good at remembering 135
numbers.

BETH

136 So am I. If... anything happens to 136
me, you're going to need them to
retrieve all of this.

VALDEZ

137 Don't talk like that. Besides, if 137
something happens to you, it will
probably happen to me, too, since
I'll be right there with you.

BETH

138 About that. I was thinking about 138
how best to handle this part of the
investigation, and I think we
should... split up.

VALDEZ

139 Split up? Why? 139

BETH

140 Odessa, I would like nothing more 140
than to spend every possible moment
with you right now, but we need to
divide and conquer.

VALDEZ

141 How do you mean? 141

BETH

142 Here's my thought - my father and I 142
will go to visit Dr. Flagler to see
if we can get any more information
from him. We'll ask about the
"North Star" thing from his notes.
It feels like too much of a
coincidence for that and the
Morningstar to have popped up as a
part of this.

VALDEZ

143 And what about me? Why can't I just 143
come with you?

BETH

144 As valuable as you'd be as a part 144
of that conversation, I was
thinking that you and Amanda could
team up. She's been working some of
her Raider contacts to dig up
information, and hopefully she's
already come up with something.

(beat)

145 Amanda's smart, but you'll know 145
exactly the right questions to ask.

VALDEZ

146 You want me to *team up*... with *her*? 146
I was on-board with working with
her, but this is something else
entirely. How am I supposed to
explain that to the Brotherhood? To
Paladin Rahmani?

BETH

147 Look, Odessa, something I've 147
learned over the years - whether it
was in the Vault or especially out
here - is that these sorts of
operations often create strange
bedfellows.
(pause)
148 So to speak. 148
(beat)
149 I not only *would* trust Amanda with 149
my life, I *have* trusted her with my
life, on several occasions. You
couldn't ask for a better person to
have watching your back.

VALDEZ

150 Alright. I guess I need to keep 150
reminding myself that this is an
extraordinary situation. I just
hope Paladin Rahmani agrees.

BETH

151 From what I've heard about your 151
Paladin, she's a pragmatist. She's
already worked with Wastelanders
of... questionable provenance,
shall we say, because it was the
right play. She'll understand.

VALDEZ

152 Yeah. I guess you're right. And it 152
is the right play.

BETH

153 Now I just have to convince Amanda. 153

VALDEZ

154 What?! 154

BETH

155 I'm kidding! She's going to be 155
thrilled.

VALDEZ
(laughing)
156 Don't do that! 156

END OF ACT ONE

ACT TWO

INT. THE SPIDER'S WEB, NIGHT

VALDEZ and AMANDA sit in the bar. VALDEZ is a little tipsy.

VALDEZ
157 So... what are we waiting for, 157
again?

AMANDA
158 We'll know it when we see it. 158

VALDEZ
159 You keep saying that, but... 159

AMANDA
160 Look, you need to take off those 160
Brotherhood blinders. It's like
you're waiting for a terminal to
walk through the door so you can
hack it.

VALDEZ
161 That *would* be a lot easier. 161

AMANDA
162 Well, this isn't Fort Atlas. We 162
deal exclusively in... what's the
term Beth always uses? HUMINT?

VALDEZ
163 Human intelligence. Yeah. That's... 163
not something I really have any
experience with. I'm more about
extracting knowledge from
technology, not people.
(frustrated)
164 I don't even know why she wanted me 164
to do this.

AMANDA
165 I'm starting to think you're not 165
enjoying my company. I thought the
free drinks would help.

VALDEZ
166 That's not the case at all! In 166
fact, that part makes me glad that
she paired us up.

AMANDA
(teasing)
167 The free drinks? Oh, I see how it 167
is.

VALDEZ
(laughing)
168 Not the free drinks! You. 168
(beat)
169 One thing about the Brotherhood is 169
that we tend to have a lot of...
preconceived notions about things.
And before I came to Appalachia, I
never felt like I had a reason to
question that.

AMANDA
170 Beth didn't mention anything about 170
you being this chatty.

VALDEZ
171 I'm sorry! I'll stop. 171

AMANDA
172 Please don't, I'm just teasing you. 172
I've had some Brotherhood types
come in here from time to time, but
our conversations never really got
this... deep. They were too busy,
like, high-fiving and bumping
chests.

VALDEZ
173 That sounds about right. 173

AMANDA
174 You were saying? About preconceived 174
notions?

VALDEZ
175 Oh, right. 175
(beat)
176 I mean, we have this picture of 176
what a Raider is, and you're... not
that. I mean, you kind of are.

AMANDA
177 Oh, I'm all Raider, sweetie. Trust 177
me on that.

VALDEZ
178 I didn't mean it that way. 178

AMANDA

179 I know. I'm just busting your ass. 179
(beat)
180 So you're saying... what, you like me? 180

VALDEZ

181 Yeah, I guess I am saying that. 181

AMANDA

182 It's probably just the booze. 182

VALDEZ laughs.

VALDEZ

183 Maybe. I've kind of lost count. 183

AMANDA

184 I haven't. I'm not going to... 184
uh... how would the Princess put it? "Compromise operational effectiveness?"

VALDEZ

185 Thanks. I don't think I'd want to 185
get drunk in a place like this.
(beat, aghast)
186 I'm sorry! I didn't mean to insult 186
your bar!

AMANDA chuckles wryly.

AMANDA

187 No offense taken. You're absolutely 187
right, somebody like you needs to keep her wits about her in this kind of establishment.
(beat)
188 But I do my best to protect 188
vulnerable women here. If I or any of my people see someone trying to take advantage of anyone like that, they'd better hope the worst that happens is that they get thrown out. I... do no tolerate that. But we can't see everything.

VALDEZ

189 Wow. 189

AMANDA

190 Wow what? 190

VALDEZ
191 You're full of surprises. I guess it goes back to those "preconceived notions." That's not something I would've expected to be a policy at a Raider bar. 191

AMANDA
192 You're not quite what I expected, either. 192

VALDEZ
193 Oh? 193

AMANDA
194 I was expecting you to be a lot more uptight. I mean, don't get me wrong, you're pretty uptight... 194

VALDEZ laughs.

AMANDA (CONT'D)
195 ...but I figured you'd be stiffer than a suit of power armor. And I also thought you'd be kind of a haughty asshole, too. You know, too good for a place like this, too good to hang out with someone like me. 195

VALDEZ
196 Nah. I'm not going to pretend there aren't people like that at Atlas. But I'm not one of them. At least I try not to be. 196

AMANDA
197 Well, if it makes you feel any better, your asshole quotient seems very low to me. 197

VALDEZ laughs.

VALDEZ
198 Thank you, Amanda. 198

AMANDA notices someone enter the bar.

AMANDA
199 Heads up. The mark just came in. Hang on, let me just... 199

AMANDA starts to unbutton VALDEZ's blouse.

VALDEZ
(taken aback)
200 What are you doing?! 200

AMANDA
201 Beth put you in a blouse with 201
buttons for a reason. And that was to... unbutton it a little bit when the time came.

VALDEZ
202 You can stop unbuttoning any 202
time...

AMANDA
203 Look, you gotta work with what you 203
got. You've had nothing but eyes on you from the moment you walked in, and that was with this thing pretty much buttoned up to your neck. The only reason you didn't get swarmed was because you're with me and they assumed... you know.

VALDEZ
204 Oh. I had no idea... 204

AMANDA
205 Yeah. The Princess said you were 205
kind of clueless about how hot you are.

VALDEZ
206 Wait. 206

AMANDA
207 Wait what? 207

VALDEZ
208 When do I get a nickname? 208

AMANDA
209 Hey, focus up, Valdez, we've been 209
waiting all night for that idiot to walk in.
(beat)
210 Ugh. I only give pet names to 210
people that I have a... um... particular type of relationship with. And we are *not* going to have that kind of relationship, so I'll just keep calling you by your actual name, OK?

VALDEZ
(laughing)
211 I wasn't being serious, but thank 211
you for the explanation.
(beat)
212 Alright, how do I look? 212

AMANDA
213 Uh, well, Beth told me to be on my 213
best behavior, so I'll just go
with... "great." Go to the bar and
sit down. My guys will keep the
simps away, shouldn't take long for
him to approach you. After that...
well, let's just hope that Beth and
her dad are good teachers.

VALDEZ
214 Amanda... 214

AMANDA
215 Yes? 215

VALDEZ
216 I'm... I'm worried. I'm a Scribe, 216
not a secret agent. Beth should be
the one doing this...

AMANDA
217 Yeah, she should. But she isn't 217
here because she had to take care
of something she's even *more*
uniquely suited for.
(beat)
218 Be yourself. Looks aside, you're... 218
frustratingly charming. My guess is
that he's going to start
volunteering information right away
to impress you. Let him buy you a
drink and chat you up. Guys like
this always think with their dicks,
and we just need him to think he's
going to get in your pants.

VALDEZ
219 And what if he gets... aggressive? 219

AMANDA
220 If he touches you or even hints at 220
a move in that direction, he's
going to get his ass kicked by me,
and then by one or more of my best
people. I won't let anything happen
to you.
(MORE)

AMANDA (CONT'D)
(beat)
221 OK, one of my guys cleared two seats at the bar, and I have another guy stalling him until you're in place. It's showtime. 221

VALDEZ
222 Wish me luck... 222

AMANDA
223 Good luck. And I'll be right there. 223

VALDEZ walks to the bar and sits. A bartender pours her a drink.

RAY enters the bar and approaches VALDEZ.

RAY
224 Is this seat taken? 224

VALDEZ
225 It was supposed to be. 225

RAY
226 Meeting someone? 226

VALDEZ
227 Yeah. Well, I thought I was, at least. 227

VALDEZ sighs.

VALDEZ (CONT'D)
228 I met this guy yesterday while I was on a trade run, and we really hit it off. We ducked into an abandoned house and... talked. 228

RAY
229 Oh, I see. "Talked." 229

VALDEZ
230 And he said he really liked me and wanted to see me again, and told me to meet him here, tonight. He was supposed to be here an hour ago. So, either something terrible happened to him or... 230

RAY
231 Or he stood you up. And if he did that, he deserves to have something terrible happen to him. 231
(beat)
(MORE)

RAY (CONT'D)

232 You got dolled up for him and everything. I bet if he could see you right now he'd drop whatever he was doing so he could rush right here. You're gorgeous. 232

VALDEZ

(feigning being flattered)

233 You really think so? Everyone here is so... exotic compared to me. I'm just a regular old trader in a regular old outfit and everybody else is all decked out in leather and combat armor. 233

RAY

234 I guess you haven't noticed everybody in the place eyeing you up. I'm surprised nobody's pounced. A place like this can be dangerous for a "regular old trader." 234

(beat)

235 I'll tell you what. I'll sit here and make sure nobody bothers you, and if this... what was his name? 235

VALDEZ

236 Um... Derek. 236

RAY

237 If this Derek shows up I'll go sit somewhere else. I'm celebrating, and I'd love to celebrate with you if I can, even if it's just for a few minutes. 237

VALDEZ

238 What are you celebrating? 238

RAY

239 I, uh... well, my boss gave me a very special assignment, and I finished it up today. It's a pretty big deal. He's a pretty big deal. 239

VALDEZ

(pivoting to disinterest)

240 Oh. How nice. 240

RAY

241 I know that sounds boring, but he's 241
the kind of big deal that I can't
go into a lot of details about.

VALDEZ

242 I must really look stupid, because 242
so many guys have used that kind of
line on me. And I guess I am,
because it usually works.
(beat)
243 But not today. You can thank Derek 243
for me actually being smart about
it for once.
(to bartender)
244 Excuse me? I'd like to pay my tab, 244
please. It's time for me to go
home.

RAY

245 Please, at least let me pay your 245
tab. And if you'll have one drink
with me, I'll... I'll give you
details, ok? And then, if you want,
maybe we can... talk back at my
place.

VALDEZ sighs.

VALDEZ

246 Fine. 246

RAY

247 Another round, bartender. 247

The bartender pours two drinks.

RAY (CONT'D)

248 I never asked your name. 248

VALDEZ

249 It's Veronica. 249

RAY

250 It's nice to meet you, Veronica. 250
Now, I want you to turn around,
away from the bar.

VALDEZ

(tentative)
251 Um... ok. 251

RAY
252 Now, look around, at all these 252
people, just going about their
business, living their lives.

VALDEZ
253 Okay... and? 253

RAY
254 They have no idea what's coming. 254

VALDEZ
255 And you do, I take it? 255

RAY
256 Oh, I don't just know what's 256
coming. I'm helping to make it
happen. See, I work for somebody
who most people think is a... a
myth. Or maybe a legend.

VALDEZ
(sarcastic)
257 Ooh, is it the Silver Shroud? Or 257
maybe Manta Man?!

RAY laughs.

RAY
258 No, and not one of the other 258
Unstoppables, either.
(beat)
259 I work for the man who's going to 259
bring light to Appalachia.

VALDEZ
260 You lost me. 260

RAY sighs.

RAY
261 You're a trader, you must've heard 261
stories. The bringer of light?
(sotto)
262 The Morningstar? 262

VALDEZ
(loudly)
263 The Morningstar?! 263

RAY
264 Hey, not so loud! But yeah. The 264
Morningstar himself.
(beat)
(MORE)

RAY (CONT'D)

265 You haven't touched your drink, by 265
the way. How about a toast? To a
new Appalachia.

VALDEZ

266 To a new Appalachia. 266

They clink their glasses and drink.

VALDEZ (CONT'D)

267 Ugh. Does booze go bad? That tasted 267
terrible.

RAY

268 I'd offer you another one, but... 268
well, I don't think that's going to
be necessary.

VALDEZ

269 What's that supposed to mean? 269

RAY

270 Forget it. Anyway, you're not going 270
to remember any of this, and I've
been dying to get it off my chest,
so here goes.
(sotto)
271 The wheels are already in motion, 271
and there's nothing anybody can do
to stop us. He's going to rule
Appalachia, and then he's going to
expand. And the best part? Nobody's
going to have any idea it's even
happening. They'll just go on with
their lives, and be none the wiser.
That sounds nice, doesn't it?

VALDEZ

(slightly dazed)
272 Yeah... it does sound nice. Really 272
nice.

RAY

273 You know what else would be nice? 273
If you unbuttoned that blouse a
little more. Let's start with two
buttons.

VALDEZ

274 That's a really good idea. 274

VALDEZ unbuttons two buttons on her blouse.

RAY
275 Very good. Now, are you wearing 275
underwear under that skirt?

VALDEZ
276 Yes. 276

RAY
277 Take them off, please. 277

VALDEZ
278 Here? At the bar? 278

RAY
279 Yes. Here. At the bar. 279

VALDEZ
280 OK. 280

VALDEZ reaches under her skirt, but AMANDA swoops in.

AMANDA
281 Just what the fuck is going on 281
here?

RAY
282 I'm just having a conversation with 282
my new friend here. Please tell
this lady that's what's going on,
Veronica.

VALDEZ
(vacant)
283 Um... that's what's going on. 283

AMANDA
284 Bones! Which glass was she drinking 284
from?
(beat)
285 Give it to me. 285

BONES hands the glass to AMANDA, who sniffs it.

AMANDA (CONT'D)
(extremely angry)
286 You stupid fuck. You STUPID FUCK. 286
(beat, gathering
herself)
287 You spiked her drink. 287
(beat)
288 You spiked her drink in my fucking 288
bar. How DARE you.

VALDEZ
289 Should I still take these off, 289
or...

AMANDA
290 No, sweetie, leave them on. And can 290
you button your blouse back up? I
just need to take care of
something.
(beat, turning to RAY)
291 Now. 291

RAY
292 Hey, hey, it's not what you think! 292
I just gave her some to... you
know, grease the wheels a little
bit! It's not my fault if she drank
it too fast and dosed herself!

AMANDA
293 Did she know you put it in there? 293

RAY
294 Of course she did! 294

AMANDA
295 Sweetie, did this man tell you he 295
was putting something in your drink
to make you... friendlier?

VALDEZ
296 Is that why it tasted so bad? Yech. 296

AMANDA
297 That's what I thought. 297

RAY
298 Oh, so you're going to believe *her*? 298

AMANDA
299 Yeah. I am. 299

AMANDA punches RAY.

AMANDA (CONT'D)
300 Bones! Get Benny and Tripod, take 300
this asshole somewhere out of
earshot and beat him *almost* to
death. Take your time. Make it
hurt. Then drag him to West-Tek for
the mutants to finish off. Don't
leave until you see them separate
his head from his body.

RAY

301 He's going to kill you for this. 301
Even that fucktoy redhead of yours
won't be able to help you now.

AMANDA

302 Wait. Why would she have been able 302
to help in the first place?

RAY

303 Guess I'm taking that information 303
to the grave with me, because I'm
done talking.

AMANDA

304 Nah. You're taking it to the 304
digestive tracts of a group of
Super Mutants.
(beat)
305 Get him out of my bar. 305

BONES rushes RAY out of the bar.

AMANDA (CONT'D)
(concerned)
306 Odessa, talk to me, baby - are you 306
okay? How do you feel?

VALDEZ
(blissed out)
307 I feel really, really good. I'm so 307
glad Beth wanted us to work
together. Thanks for being my
knight in shining armor. Or...
leather bustier, I guess.
(beat)
308 I think we should go somewhere 308
private so I can... thank you
properly.

AMANDA

309 Odessa, that's the chem talking. 309
You don't know what you're saying.

VALDEZ scoffs.

VALDEZ

310 Don't act like you don't want this 310
to happen.

AMANDA

311 Not like this I don't. 311

VALDEZ

312 Come on. I could tell how much you enjoyed unbuttoning my blouse. Why don't we go back to your place so you can finish the job like a good girl? Or how about Beth's place? That would be... kinda hot. 312

AMANDA

313 We're definitely going back to my place, but you're keeping your clothes on, even if I have to tie you to a chair. 313

VALDEZ

314 How about I tie *you* to the chair instead? I bet my bindings are a lot more... efficient. 314

AMANDA

315 Dammit, Odessa! 315

VALDEZ laughs.

AMANDA (CONT'D)

316 Seriously, we need to get out of here, right now. If he gave you as much as I think he did, you're going to pass out soon. And it's going to be a really rough morning for you tomorrow, but I promise I'll be there to take care of you, okay? 316

VALDEZ

317 Okay... 317

(beat)

318 You know, I think I'm starting to understand why Beth fell in love with you. 318

AMANDA

(vulnerable)

319 Odessa... stop. Please. I can handle you coming onto me, but just... don't say things like that. 319

VALDEZ

320 Oh. I'm sorry. 320

(beat)

321 But I have a few ideas about how I can make it up to you, if you reconsider that whole "keeping our clothes on" thing... 321

AMANDA
322 Jesus, you're a monster. Let's just 322
get you out of here.

END OF ACT TWO

ACT THREE

INT. AMANDA'S BEDROOM, LATE MORNING

VALDEZ stirs, clearly hung over.

VALDEZ
323 Ugh. What are those birds so happy 323
about? Stupid birds...

VALDEZ gets out of bed.

VALDEZ (CONT'D)
324 Where am I? Did I go into Beth's 324
bedroom instead of the guest room?
(beat)
325 No, this definitely isn't Beth's 325
room. It's too... Raider-y. Amanda
must've taken me back to her place.
(beat)
326 Oh, God, my head... How much did I 326
drink?

VALDEZ sits on the bed.

VALDEZ (CONT'D)
327 Wait. 327
(beat)
328 Why am I naked? 328

VALDEZ looks around the room.

VALDEZ (CONT'D)
329 Where are my clothes? Oh, no... 329

VALDEZ continues to try to get her wits about her.

VALDEZ (CONT'D)
330 I need to find something to wear. 330

VALDEZ starts going through drawers and looking through AMANDA's closet.

VALDEZ (CONT'D)
331 T-shirt it is, I guess. Looks long 331
enough....

VALDEZ slips the t-shirt on.

VALDEZ (CONT'D)
332 Ugh. Barely. 332
(beat)
(MORE)

VALDEZ (CONT'D)
333 So... if this is Amanda's place... 333
where's Amanda?

VALDEZ walks to the door and tries the knob.

VALDEZ (CONT'D)
334 Locked? What the... 334

AMANDA unlocks the door and cracks it open, but stays fully on the other side.

AMANDA
335 You decent in there, Kitten? 335

VALDEZ
336 Yeah, I... borrowed one of your t- 336
shirts, I hope that's okay. Where
are my clothes?

AMANDA opens the door.

AMANDA
337 You look like hell. Still adorable, 337
but... hellishly adorable? Adorably
hellish? Anyway, I have a little
cocktail that should help with that
hangover.

VALDEZ
338 Ugh, no more cocktails. 338

AMANDA laughs.

AMANDA
339 It's not an actual cocktail. More 339
of a... home remedy. Between that
and a *lot* of purified water, I'll
have you feeling better in no time.

VALDEZ
340 I'm willing to try anything. 340

AMANDA
341 You made that pretty clear last 341
night.

VALDEZ
342 I'm honestly terrified to ask this 342
question, but... what happened last
night? And where *are* my clothes?

AMANDA
343 Your clothes are out in the living 343
room. I folded them for you.
(MORE)

AMANDA (CONT'D)
You were *really* insistent on taking them off.
(beat, twinkling)
344 What do you remember? 344

VALDEZ
345 The last thing I remember is 345
sitting with you at the table,
just... chatting. We were waiting
for the intel source to show up.

AMANDA
(spinning a yarn)
346 He stood us up. I guess Beth got 346
some bad intel, or maybe he's just
unpredictable. It happens.

VALDEZ
347 So... then what? 347

AMANDA
348 You seriously don't remember? I'm 348
trying *very* hard not to take this
personally.

VALDEZ
349 I seriously don't. But I woke up 349
naked, in your bedroom, and though
there were, um... clues kind of
strewn around the room, I don't
want to assume anything.

AMANDA
350 Well, I was being careful that we 350
didn't drink too much while we were
waiting for our guy. We both needed
to be clear-headed to get
information out of him, and to keep
you safe.

VALDEZ
351 Right, I remember that part. 351

AMANDA
352 But when it was clear that he 352
wasn't going to show, we got...
less careful. The drinks started
flowing, we started chatting, and
laughing, and...

VALDEZ
353 And? 353

AMANDA

354 I don't know what got into you, but you got really aggressive - in a good way. I'm... not used to people being like that with me, and between that and the fact that it was you, well... it was hard to not get lost in the moment. 354

VALDEZ

355 So we, what, started... making out in the middle of your bar? 355

AMANDA laughs.

AMANDA

356 "Making out?" Come on, we're not teenagers. 356

(beat, sigh)

357 Fine. We started "making out." But as much as my patrons would've enjoyed a show, you insisted we go somewhere private. You suggested Beth's place, but mine was closer and that would've been... weird anyway. 357

VALDEZ

358 I'm not sure I want you to go on, but... go on, I guess. 358

AMANDA

359 We got here and you pretty much immediately got naked. That's why your clothes are out there. 359

VALDEZ

360 So we *did* have sex. 360

AMANDA

361 My God, you are adorable. 361

(beat)

362 I gotta say, though, I never took you for a top. That was a nice little surprise. 362

VALDEZ sighs.

VALDEZ

363 I've just been... frustrated lately, and I guess between that and the alcohol... 363

AMANDA
364 Maybe. But, um... I'm glad you took 364
your frustrations out on *me*. I
liked it. Haven't been choked like
that in a while...

VALDEZ
(aghast)
365 I didn't hurt you, did I? I'm 365
sorry! I know I have strong
hands...

AMANDA chuckles.

AMANDA
366 No, Kitten. You didn't hurt me. 366

VALDEZ sighs.

VALDEZ
367 What are we going to tell Beth? 367

AMANDA
368 Why do we have to tell her 368
anything?

VALDEZ
369 Amanda! She has to know. We can't 369
keep something like this from her!

AMANDA
370 Why not? What possible benefit 370
could there be in telling her? I
mean, unless you're thinking three-
way...

VALDEZ
371 I'm being serious, Amanda. This 371
changes everything. For one thing,
you and I are going to have to
figure out what this means for *us*.
I don't care how drunk we were,
this clearly didn't come out of
nowhere. And then there's Beth...
things were so... I don't know...
in flux between us even before this
happened...

AMANDA
372 Jesus, Odessa, it wasn't a 372
vertibird crash...

VALDEZ sighs.

VALDEZ

373 I know, and I'm sorry, I really 373
don't mean to make it sound like
some kind of disaster.
(beat, sigh)
374 This is a lot to process. But 374
regardless, we need to tell Beth.

AMANDA

375 Odessa... 375

VALDEZ

376 I'm not going to change my mind, 376
Amanda. You don't have to tell her
if you don't want to, but I'm going
to. I can't be dishonest with her.
I'm not... wired that way.

AMANDA

(chuckling)
377 Odessa, I can't keep doing this to 377
you. There's nothing to tell.

VALDEZ

378 What? 378

AMANDA

379 We didn't have sex. You did get 379
naked in the living room, but the
rest? I was just fucking with you.

VALDEZ

380 I can't decide if I should be more 380
angry or relieved right now.

AMANDA

381 Go with relieved. Do you want to 381
know what really happened?

VALDEZ

382 Yes. 382

AMANDA

383 Alright. The mark did show up. You 383
were *great* as the vulnerable little
damsel in distress, and he started
to spill some info. But then he
drugged you.

VALDEZ

(aghast)
384 He *drugged* me? With what? 384

AMANDA

385 Have you ever heard of "Venus?" 385

VALDEZ

386 No. 386

AMANDA

387 It's a relatively new chem on the scene. People use it in smaller doses recreationally - and consensually - to make sex better. It basically reduces inhibitions and ratchets up your libido. 387

VALDEZ

388 Doesn't alcohol do that? 388

AMANDA

389 It does, but not as much as this stuff does, and plus it's kind of a... cleaner experience - you're a lot more clear-headed, so you can enjoy it more. As long as you use an appropriate amount. 389

VALDEZ

390 I'm assuming he didn't. 390

AMANDA

(getting agitated)

391 No, he didn't. He dosed you. When you give someone that much, they become extremely... compliant and open to suggestion. He was walking through the process of seeing whether it had taken effect when I stepped in and stopped him. 391

VALDEZ

392 Thank goodness you were there. 392

AMANDA

(tenderly)

393 I promised you I would be. 393

(beat)

394 I get *extremely* upset when people do things like that, and to do it in my bar, well... I got angry. 394

VALDEZ

395 What did you do? 395

AMANDA

396 Let's just say that he will... not be available for interrogation. 396

VALDEZ

397 Oh. Good. I mean, revenge isn't something that I've ever believed in, but I'm glad that he won't be able to do that to anyone else. 397

AMANDA

398 He definitely will not. But I was able to listen in, and we did at least get confirmation that he was working for the Morningstar, plus a little bit of information on what this big plan is. 398

VALDEZ

399 What his plan? 399

AMANDA

400 He's putting *something* into motion to take over Appalachia, but he's doing it in some kind of... secret way. He said that people won't know that it's happening, or even think anything's different when it's done. 400

VALDEZ

401 Huh. It's not much to go on, but hopefully that helps Beth figure things out. 401

AMANDA

402 There was one other thing that he said, though, and it bothered me. 402

(beat)

403 When he realized he was a dead man, he told me the Morningstar was going to kill *me* for killing *him*. 403

VALDEZ

404 You must get death threats all the time, don't you? 404

AMANDA

405 More than I'd prefer, sure, but that wasn't what bothered me. He said that *even Beth* wouldn't be able to help me now. He didn't use her name, but that's clearly who he was talking about. "Even" Beth. 405

VALDEZ

406 What? Why would Beth have some 406
special ability to prevent him from
trying to kill you?

AMANDA

407 I don't know. I hope *she* knows, and 407
that she's willing to actually tell
me.

VALDEZ

408 That's... disturbing. I mean, she's 408
clearly not involved in whatever
the Morningstar is planning.
(beat)
409 Right? 409

AMANDA

410 Yeah. But given what he said about 410
people not knowing that it was
happening, plus whatever the hell
the deal is with that file you
found... all of that must play into
this somehow.

VALDEZ

411 Maybe. 411
(beat)
412 You, um... buried the lede. 412

AMANDA

413 What do you mean? 413

VALDEZ

414 You explained, in detail, what 414
happened with our intel source, but
you left out how I ended up naked
and locked in your bedroom.

AMANDA

415 Oh. That. 415

VALDEZ

416 Yes. "That." 416

AMANDA

417 Are you sure you want to hear this? 417
I mean, you already know that we
didn't, uh, "make out."

VALDEZ

418 Yes, I'm sure. 418

AMANDA sighs.

AMANDA

419 Alright. Remember what I said about 419
the chem getting people super
turned on and lowering their
inhibitions? After I... dispatched
our little friend, you, um... well,
you got a little... flirty. OK, a
lot flirty. You were kind of all
over me.

VALDEZ

420 Oh, god... 420

AMANDA

421 I did my best to fend you off. I 421
knew it was because you got dosed,
and I obviously wasn't going to let
anything happen between us when you
were in that state.

(beat)

422 So, I got you here, and I don't 422
know if it was because it was just
the two of us instead of being in a
bar full of people, but...

VALDEZ

423 I do *not* like the sound of that 423
"but."

AMANDA

424 I closed the door, and by the time 424
I turned back around, you already
had your clothes off. I gotta say,
I'm impressed. That you got naked
that fast, I mean.

(beat)

425 Wow. I didn't know a human face 425
could get that red.

(beat)

426 Anyway. Then you were... uh... very 426
interested in getting *my* clothes
off, but I wasn't going to let that
happen. I gotta be honest here, you
really got my motor running and I
was concerned, knowing what I know
about the way this chem works, that
I could talk myself into this being
an "in vino veritas" situation and
letting things play out. So I
steered you into the bedroom and
locked the door. It sounded like
you fell asleep not long after
that, and I crashed on the couch.

VALDEZ

427 Ugh. 427

AMANDA laughs.

AMANDA

428 It's alright, Kitten. There's no reason to be embarrassed. You got dosed with a chem without your knowledge or consent, and you weren't yourself. I said that I'd be there to take care of you, and that's exactly what happened. 428

VALDEZ

429 Thank you. Seriously, Amanda, there are a dozen ways last night could've gone wrong, and you made sure it didn't. And you looked out for me. That... means a lot. 429

AMANDA

430 Least I can do. And I promise, I'll always have your back. 430

(beat)

431 And not just because I kinda want to keep both eyes on that ass. 431

VALDEZ laughs.

VALDEZ

432 Well, at least I feel better about telling Beth *this* story and not... what I was picturing. 432

AMANDA

433 Oh, now *that* I need to hear. Spill. 433

VALDEZ

434 There's not enough alcohol left in Appalachia for that to happen, Amanda. 434

AMANDA laughs.

AMANDA

435 Well, one thing's for certain. 435

VALDEZ

436 What's that? 436

AMANDA

437 Beth's never going to leave the two of us alone together again. 437

VALDEZ
438 Aww. I think we make a great team! 438

END OF ACT THREE

Season One
Part Two: The Book of Amanda

Episode 5:
"The Identical Old Questions"

by

D.K. Trueno

Final
January 14, 2022

"THE IDENTICAL OLD QUESTIONS"

INT. BETH'S RESIDENCE

VALDEZ putters in the kitchen, humming.

A keypad beeps and the locked front door unlocks, then opens.

VALDEZ
1 Beth?! 1

AMANDA enters.

AMANDA
2 Sorry, Kitten, it's just me. She 2
isn't back yet? She didn't... *
stumble onto yet another hot lead, *
did she? *

VALDEZ
3 No. She said she'd be on her way 3 *
home first thing in the morning
when we talked yesterday, and she's *
been good about contacting me when *
she's gotten delayed. *

AMANDA *
4 I know she's great at her job and 4 *
everything, but... I didn't expect *
her to still be off chasing clues *
two weeks after... *

VALDEZ *
5 Yeah. After that intel source tried 5 *
to... hurt me. *
(beat, brightly) *
6 But it's nice to see you. Really 6 *
nice. Thank you, again, for last *
night - especially for dragging me
home. I don't think I could've
found my way back on my own.

AMANDA chuckles.

AMANDA
7 I figured you could use a night 7
out. You've been stressed.

VALDEZ
8 I have. Between the situation at 8
Atlas being so... fluid and Beth
still being gone, it's been...
yeah, I needed that.

AMANDA
9 I'm sure talking to her over comms 9
every day helps. How long was it *
yesterday?

VALDEZ
10 Um... two hours, I think? She said 10
her dad was worried that they were
going to kill their last portable
power pack.

AMANDA
11 You two are rapidly becoming 11
insufferably adorable. I love it.

VALDEZ laughs.

VALDEZ
12 It's been nice. It feels like 12
there's... I don't know, less
pressure? I can't wait to see her
again, but... I'm kind of going to
miss those chats.

AMANDA
13 I get the feeling that you're going 13
to have lots of opportunities to
"chat."
(beat)
14 Oh, how's your head, by the way? 14

VALDEZ
15 It's fine. Sleeping in helped. And 15
your hangover cure did, too. Thanks
for leaving that.

AMANDA
16 Least I can do. 16

VALDEZ
17 You could've stayed, you know. 17

AMANDA
18 Yeah. I know. 18

VALDEZ
19 You're not still... skittish about 19 *
the other night, are you?

AMANDA laughs.

AMANDA
20 I don't get "skittish," Kitten. If 20
I was worried that you'd try to
drag me into the sack again I
wouldn't have taken you out and
gotten both of us drunk.
(beat)
21 So, am I never getting that t-shirt 21
back?

VALDEZ laughs.

VALDEZ
22 Hey, it's comfortable! I promise, 22
though, I'll give it back as soon
as I wash it.

AMANDA
23 Nah, you can keep it. It looks nice 23
on you. A little... snug, but *good*
snug.

VALDEZ
24 Can I tempt you with some 24
breakfast?

AMANDA
25 I didn't know you could cook! 25

VALDEZ
26 Um... I can't. But I did look over 26
Beth's shoulder a few times, and
speaking as a scientist, I'm
reasonably certain that what I'm
working on over here won't kill us.

AMANDA
27 Well, since you put it that way... 27

VALDEZ
28 Remember - *reasonably* certain. 28

AMANDA laughs.

AMANDA and VALDEZ fill their plates and sit down to eat.

VALDEZ (CONT'D)
29 Well? 29

AMANDA
30 I've been kicking around the idea 30
of opening the bar early for
breakfast, so if you ever need a
side job...

VALDEZ
31 Aww, you're sweet. 31

AMANDA
32 I've been called a lot of things, 32
but "sweet" is not one I usually hear.

VALDEZ
33 Well, you are. At least you have 33
been to me.

AMANDA
34 I guess I like you. 34

VALDEZ
35 I like you, too. I mean, I wish 35
Beth's mission with her dad hadn't turned into a two-week excursion, but I'm glad we got to spend some time together.

AMANDA
36 Yeah. You're a lot of fun. 36

VALDEZ
37 You may want to hold off on that 37
last part.

AMANDA
38 What? Why? 38

VALDEZ
39 Well, since you're here, there's 39
something I've kind of wanted to talk to you about.

AMANDA
40 Uh-oh. 40

VALDEZ
41 It's just that... well, Beth being 41
gone has given me a chance to think about... everything, I guess. And there's something I kind of feel like I have to know before I make any decisions on what I want to do.

AMANDA
42 Um... okay. What's on your mind? 42

VALDEZ gathers herself.

VALDEZ

43 Are you still in love with Beth? 43

AMANDA

44 Oh! Wow. I was *not* expecting that. 44
Um... that's... a complicated
question.

VALDEZ

45 It's really not. 45

AMANDA

46 I guess it's the answer that's 46
complicated.

VALDEZ

47 Not exactly what I wanted to hear, 47
but... go on?

AMANDA

48 I guess... on some level we're 48
always going to love each other.
The kind of thing we had doesn't
ever entirely go away. It went
deep.

(beat)

49 And I guess where we are right now 49
kind of shows that. But I get what
you're asking, and neither our
former relationship nor our current
friendship is going to get in the
way of... having a future with
someone else.

VALDEZ

50 You sound pretty certain about 50
that.

AMANDA

51 I'm absolutely certain of it. 51

VALDEZ

52 Wait. Are you... seeing someone? 52

AMANDA sighs.

AMANDA

53 Yeah. For a while now. I've just 53
been trying to figure out how to
tell Beth. I'm worried that she...
won't take it well.

VALDEZ
54 What? Why? Because she’s still 54
hoping you two are going to get
back together?

AMANDA
55 No! Nothing like that. We are *very* 55
clear that our days as a couple are
firmly behind us.

VALDEZ sighs.

VALDEZ
56 Okay. I’m not going to push it. But 56
keeping secrets always ends up
causing bigger problems, and I... I
just don’t want to see her get
hurt, Amanda. And I know you don’t
want that either.

AMANDA
57 Yeah. I hurt her enough when we 57
were together. I just... need to
figure out how to tell her.

VALDEZ
58 The thing that broke up my 58
engagement was Derek not being up-
front with me. I don’t know *why* he
didn’t just tell me, and if I’m
being honest I don’t know how I
would’ve reacted if he had. But *if*
he had, there’s a non-zero chance
that I’d still be in California
right now. Married. Probably
already starting a family...

AMANDA
59 And... would you be happier if that 59
had happened?

VALDEZ
60 I... don’t know. I’ve thought about 60
it a lot. Hell, I had the whole
march here to think about it. And
up until about a month ago, I think
I would’ve said yes.

AMANDA
61 Wait. A month ago? 61

VALDEZ
62 Yeah. 62

AMANDA
63 Before you met Beth? 63

VALDEZ
64 About... a week before I met her, I 64
think?

AMANDA
65 What happened? 65

VALDEZ
66 I'm not sure. I just... felt ready 66
to try dating again. There was
somebody I had my eye on...

AMANDA
67 Ooooh, you little vixen! 67

VALDEZ laughs.

VALDEZ
68 Stop! 68

AMANDA
69 Guy or girl? 69

VALDEZ
70 Girl. I was trying to figure out 70
how to ask her out, but then... I
ended up getting sent out on a
mission to retrieve some tech some
an old restaurant...

AMANDA
71 And you met Beth. 71

VALDEZ
72 Yeah. And I didn't look at it this 72
way at the time, but... I stopped
thinking about how to ask Casey
out.

AMANDA
73 Wait. Casey? Not "Miss Vault 76" 73
Casey, right?

VALDEZ
74 You know her? 74

AMANDA
75 Only by reputation - Beth talked 75
about her a lot when we first met,
and she showed me pictures. Damn,
Odessa...

VALDEZ

76 And then she practically tackled Beth when she saw her at Atlas right before she left with her dad. 76

AMANDA

77 Oof. That must have been *really* awkward. 77

VALDEZ

78 At least I hadn't quite gotten around to actually asking her. That's a level of awkwardness that I don't know that I could take. 78

AMANDA laughs.

AMANDA

79 Beth must think this is all hilarious. 79

VALDEZ

80 I... didn't tell her. Yet. It felt weird talking about it after she'd just told me they were... involved in the Vault, and then she had to leave. But it's not like they were serious, like you two were. 80

AMANDA

(awkwardly)

81 Um... well... that's true, they never did get serious. 81

VALDEZ

82 Am I missing something? 82

AMANDA

83 Beth should really be the one telling you this. 83

VALDEZ

84 You can't just leave a statement like that hanging. 84

AMANDA

85 They never got serious, that's true. But it was because Casey wasn't ready to commit. Beth *wanted* to get serious. She was head-over-heels. And I get the impression Casey was, too, but she was still a kid - I think she was 18. 85

(MORE)

AMANDA (CONT'D)
That kind of commitment was just...
not on her radar.

VALDEZ
86 The way she "greeted" Beth implies 86
that may no longer be the case.

AMANDA
87 Is that what prompted you to ask me 87
if I still love her?

VALDEZ sighs.

VALDEZ
88 I guess it's part of it. I mean, 88
Beth hasn't done anything to make
me feel like she's trying to add me
to a harem or anything.

AMANDA
89 But you want to make sure you 89
have... how would you Brotherhood
types put it? An accurate
situational assessment?

VALDEZ laughs.

VALDEZ
90 Something like that. 90

AMANDA
91 I'm going to tell you the same 91
thing I told Beth - just let it
breathe. You two are very clearly
into each other. Is that going to
shake out into a relationship? Who
knows? But worrying about it isn't
going to help. Just let things
happen.

VALDEZ
92 Objectively, I know you're right. 92
But after Derek, I... well, I need
to be careful.

A radio beeps and begins to crackle.

BANKS
(over radio, urgently)
93 Scribe Valdez. Scribe Odessa 93
Valdez, please come in. This is
Knight Alan Banks. Come in, please.

AMANDA
94 That sounds important. 94

VALDEZ
(concerned)
95 Yeah, it is. Alan said he wouldn't 95
contact me unless it was urgent.

VALDEZ speaks into the radio.

VALDEZ (CONT'D)
96 This is Scribe Valdez. Go ahead, 96
Knight Banks.

AMANDA
97 Oooh, so formal! Sexy... 97

VALDEZ
(laughing)
98 Shh! 98

BANKS
99 Valdez, we need you back at Atlas 99
ASAP. As in "drop whatever you're
doing and get back here
immediately."

VALDEZ
100 What's going on? Is everyone 100
alright?

BANKS
101 Everyone here is fine. I can't talk 101
about it over comms. Just... come
back as soon as you can, okay?

VALDEZ
102 Okay. I just need to get my uniform 102
back on and... make sure Beth's
house isn't going to burn down
after I leave.

AMANDA
(sotto)
103 Hey. I'll take care of all of that. 103
I mean, not the getting-you-dressed
part. Unless you want me to.

VALDEZ
(sotto)
104 Amanda! 104

AMANDA
(laughing)
105 Sorry! 105

VALDEZ
106 Alright, Alan, I'm on my way. 106

BANKS
107 See you in a few. Banks out. 107

The radio clicks off.

VALDEZ
108 Can you... 108

AMANDA
109 I'll hang out here. 109

VALDEZ
110 Thank you. I'm going to get changed. 110

AMANDA
111 Offer still stands, by the way. 111

VALDEZ goes into the bedroom to change.

MUSICAL TRANSITION

INT. FORT ATLAS, DAY

There is substantial commotion. CASEY greets VALDEZ.

CASEY
112 Hey, you! 112

VALDEZ
113 Casey! 113

CASEY
114 I was starting to think Beth had you tied up in a basement or something. 114

VALDEZ laughs.

VALDEZ
115 Nah. I've just been working out of her place while things got sorted out here. 115

CASEY
116 Where *is* Beth, anyway? I figured she'd be attached to your hip. 116
(MORE)

CASEY (CONT'D)

(beat)

117 Unless you have *her* tied up in a 117
basement.

VALDEZ

118 Nobody has anyone tied up anywhere, 118
Casey.

(beat)

119 So... what's going on? Alan made it 119
sound pretty urgent, but he said he
couldn't talk about it over an
insecure comm channel.

CASEY

120 I don't know. There's *something* 120
going on, but Paladin Rahmani's
been really hush-hush about it.

KNIGHT BANKS enters.

BANKS

121 Hi. Knight Alan Banks. And you are? 121

VALDEZ laughs.

VALDEZ

122 Very funny, Alan. 122

BANKS

123 Looks like you came back in the 123
nick of time. I think you're
overdue for a trip to the barber.

VALDEZ

124 I think I'm going to let it grow a 124
little, actually. Try something
different, you know?

BANKS

125 Good for you, Valdez. Sounds like 125
the time away's done you some good.
Still, could've used you around
here.

VALDEZ

126 I'm sorry about that Alan, I am. 126
Paladin Rahmani insisted that I
stay at Beth's place and work there
because of... the incident.

BANKS

127 That must've been tough. Hard to 127
work on that...

(MORE)

BANKS (CONT'D)
sciency stuff you deal with if you
don't have the proper equipment.

VALDEZ
(brightly)
128 Oh! That wasn't a problem. 128

BANKS
129 How'd you manage that? 129

VALDEZ
130 The underground facilities at her 130
place are *impressive*. Laboratory,
research materials,
communications...

BANKS
131 *"Underground* facilities?" So, like 131
a mini-vault?

VALDEZ
132 No, not quite. It has some 132
additional fortifications and
radiation protection, but it's
really just an extension of the
main structure.

BANKS
133 Mmm hmm. And how do you access it? 133

VALDEZ
134 There's a hidden control panel that 134
triggers a secret door.

BANKS
135 A secret door? 135
(beat)
136 Valdez, are you telling me she has 136
a *lair*?

VALDEZ
(defensive)
137 It's not a lair! 137

BANKS
138 It's underground, it has a secret 138
entrance, and it's under what
sounds like a totally normal house.
(beat)
139 It's a lair. 139
(beat)
140 Well, super-villain or not, I'm 140
glad you were safe. I was worried;
you were *directly* targeted.

VALDEZ
141 Yeah. And I don't know if it was 141
because of me or Beth, but either
way... I'm a target.

BANKS
142 Speaking of... where is she? 142

VALDEZ
143 She's been tied up. 143

CASEY laughs.

VALDEZ clears her throat.

CASEY
144 Sorry. 144

VALDEZ
145 She went to talk to Dr. Flagler 145
with her dad, and I don't know
specifics, but that produced a
lead, which produced another
lead... but she'll be back today.

BANKS
146 Aw, I was kind of hoping you were 146
roomies this whole time.

VALDEZ
147 No. We did talk quite a bit over 147
comms, though. And I had someone to
keep me company.

BANKS
148 Wow, look at you! Growing your hair 148
out, making new friends. I'm kind
of digging the new Odessa Valdez.

CASEY
149 So am I... 149

PALADIN RAHMANI enters.

RAHMANI
150 May have everyone's attention, 150
please?

The din in the room stops.

RAHMANI (CONT'D)

151 Now that we're all here, I have some very important announcements to make. Please join me in the auditorium. 151

The assembled group goes into the auditorium. BANKS, VALDEZ, and CASEY sit together.

BANKS

152 Here we go... 152

RAHMANI

153 Two weeks ago, we learned that Atlas - our home - was breached. I took immediately took two actions. My first priority was to ensure the safety of a member of our family that I felt was in immediate danger. And while it was difficult to send Scribe Valdez away, it was a necessary step. 153

(beat)

154 But then we had to determine the circumstances of the breach, and ideally retrieve what had been stolen from Scribe Valdez. I am pleased to report that we have been successful in both of those endeavors. 154

Applause breaks out.

VALDEZ

155 Alan, did you... 155

BANKS

156 I had no idea... I was completely out of the loop... 156

RAHMANI

157 I apologize for the secrecy surrounding this effort, but I hope you'll understand. When you have a mole, you have to keep the circle tight. The circle, in this case, consisted of myself... and Initiate Benjamin Carlson. Initiate Carlson, will you join me, please? 157

BANKS

158 Whoa... 158

CARLSON

159 Thank you, Paladin. And thank you, 159
everyone. I'll cut to the chase.
Right now, three people are sitting
in the brig, and the data and
journals that were taken from
Scribe Valdez's lab are right here.
(beat)
160 Their interrogation will begin 160
soon, and will be led by Knight
Banks. Catching them was just the
first step; now we have to find out
why they did what they did, and
anything else they may have done.
And we will also find out what this
"Morningstar" wants.
(beat)
161 We're going to get through this, 161
together. And we will emerge even
stronger than we were before.
(beat)
162 Paladin? 162

RAHMANI

163 Thank you, Mr. Carlson. 163
(beat)
164 I do have one more announcement. 164
Initiate Carlson, you have served
with distinction since joining the
Brotherhood, and your performance
on this project has only reinforced
my already strong opinion of you.
Because of that, I hereby promote
you to Knight, with all the
privileges and responsibilities
that entails, effective
immediately.
(beat)
165 Congratulations, Knight Carlson. 165

Applause breaks out.

CARLSON

166 Thank you, Paladin. I won't let you 166
down.

RAHMANI

167 Thank you, Knight. And thank you, 167
everyone. Let's get back to work.
Dismissed. Ad Victoriam.

BROTHERHOOD MEMBERS

168 Ad Victoriam! 168

Walla picks up as people depart.

BANKS
169 Hell yeah! Hey, Valdez, know anybody who has special training in interrogation and intelligence gathering who might be interested in a little bit of freelance work? 169

VALDEZ
170 I just might... 170

RAHMANI approaches.

RAHMANI
171 Scribe Valdez. Welcome back. A word, please? In private? 171

VALDEZ
172 Of course, Paladin. I'll talk to you guys later. 172

BANKS
173 Let me know what your... what Beth says, okay? 173

VALDEZ
174 Of course. 174

RAHMANI and VALDEZ walk to RAHMANI's office.

RAHMANI closes the door.

RAHMANI
175 Please, sit. 175

VALDEZ
176 Yes, ma'am. Have I... done something wrong? 176

RAHMANI
177 Have you? 177

VALDEZ
178 I... I don't think so, I've been working at Beth's place, just like you asked, and keeping you in the loop, again, just like you asked. 178

RAHMANI
179 Your work has been exemplary, as always, Scribe. 179
(beat)
180 But how *are* you? 180

VALDEZ
(confused)
181 I'm... fine? I'm great, actually. 181

RAHMANI
182 I've noticed. Look, Odessa, I'll 182
get right to it.
(beat)
183 We marched together, side by side, 183
all the way here from California.
Now, I had my own concerns during
that trip, as did Knights Shin and
Thornberry. Knight Connors wasn't
even supposed to be there, but...
circumstances dictated that he
come, too.
(wistfully)
184 I'd never considered a world 184
without him, and for a while I
thought I wouldn't have to. And
then I had to say goodbye all over
again.
(beat, gathering
herself)
185 But you... you had to carry a 185
broken heart with you for more than
three thousand miles. And that was
on top of leaving your parents
behind, and your mentor...

VALDEZ
186 Leila, please... 186

RAHMANI
187 Let me finish, Odessa. Look, what 187
Knight Hewitt... what Derek did...
it was unconscionable. To try to
force you to decide between your
duty to the Brotherhood - not only
your family in the figurative
sense, but your actual biological
family - and your love for him
and... well, I know how important
starting your own family was to
you.

VALDEZ
188 Is. 188

RAHMANI
189 Is. I'm sorry, I didn't want to 189
presume.
(beat)
190 But since that happened, you've... 190
(MORE)

RAHMANI (CONT'D)
shut down that part of you. You're a passionate person, Odessa, and... well, it hurt me to see you like that.

VALDEZ
191 I just... couldn't think about it. 191
About finding someone, maybe even falling in love again.
(beat)
192 "There is no greater sorrow than to 192
be mindful of the happy time in misery."

RAHMANI
193 "...e ciò sa 'l tuo dottore." 193

VALDEZ
194 I *know* you understand, Leila. 194
But... I'm still not sure what you're trying to tell me.

RAHMANI
195 You were in mourning for a long 195
time, Odessa. And it's alright to mourn. It's healthy.
(beat)
196 And it's healthy to move on, when 196
you're ready. But you have to give yourself permission to do that. If you do one but not the other... well, it's not fair to you and it's not fair to the other person, either.

VALDEZ
(vulnerable)
197 How will I know if I'm really 197
ready?

RAHMANI laughs

RAHMANI
198 I'll let you know as soon as I 198
figure it out myself.
(beat)
199 Joking aside, that's a question I 199
can't answer. It's different for everyone. But I think you'll know, and...

VALDEZ
200 What? 200

RAHMANI

201 I have a suspicion that you already do. 201

<u>END OF ACT ONE</u>

ACT TWO

INT. FORT ATLAS, DAY

VALDEZ is putting her lab back together. BETH knocks at her door.

BETH
202 Odessa? 202

VALDEZ
203 Beth! 203

BETH
204 I came right here after I saw that you weren't at the house. Amanda said you got called here, and it sounded urgent... is everything okay? 204

VALDEZ
(excited)
205 Everything *is* okay. They caught the mole! Well, *moles*. There were three of them, and they're being interrogated right now. And we got the journals back! 205

BETH
206 That's brilliant! Was it... anyone we know? 206

VALDEZ
207 No - three relatively new Initiates. There have been so many new people that I suppose it was inevitable that some bad actors could sneak through. Paladin Rahmani has put a moratorium on new recruits until she can get a better vetting process in place. 207

BETH
208 That's smart. 208
(beat)
209 So... will you be back to staying at Atlas, then, or... 209

VALDEZ
210 Paladin Rahmani expects me to move back in immediately, now that it's safe again. 210
(beat)
(MORE)

VALDEZ (CONT'D)

211 But that doesn't mean I have to be 211
here *all* the time! And.. well...

BETH

212 What is it? 212

VALDEZ

213 Staying at your place got me 213
thinking...

BETH

214 Yes? 214

VALDEZ

215 Maybe you could... teach me how to 215
cook. I tried while you were away,
but... well, hopefully Amanda was
able to hide the evidence.

BETH laughs.

BETH

216 Amanda's good at hiding bodies, so 216
I'm sure that if there was
anything... incriminating it's long
gone by now.

VALDEZ laughs.

BETH (CONT'D)

217 That reminds me... I asked Amanda 217
about that contact she found. The
one you two were going to try to
get some information out of the
night I left?

VALDEZ

(wary)

218 Yes... 218

BETH

219 She said that we should talk about 219
that together. The three of us. I
tried to get something out of her,
but... she knows all my tricks.

VALDEZ

220 I think that's a good idea, 220
actually.

BETH

221 Why? What happened? 221

(beat)

222 Okay, okay. 222

(MORE)

BETH (CONT'D)
But please, just answer one question - am I going to want to strangle her?

VALDEZ chuckles knowingly.

BETH (CONT'D)
223 What is with that grin? Oh, now my 223
curiosity is *really* piqued.

VALDEZ
224 All I'll say for now is that you 224
were right - Amanda is a great person to have your back.

BETH
225 Alright. I'll try not to speculate 225
too much about it until we can get together to talk about it. How about over dinner?

VALDEZ
226 I'd like that. 226

BETH
227 Good. It's settled. 227
(beat)
228 Now, what did I miss? 228

VALDEZ
229 Aside from that first operation... 229
and my attempts at cooking, not much. It was... quiet.

BETH
230 Quiet? That's... strange. I 230
expected things to get crazier, if anything. I made sure that I had a route to get home immediately if all hell broke loose. And I was glad it didn't, but it's surprising that *nothing* happened.

VALDEZ
231 Well, not *nothing*. We did manage to 231
catch the moles.

BETH
232 Yes. But that was down to the 232
actions of the Brotherhood, not the Morningstar himself. He's laying low.
(MORE)

BETH (CONT'D)
But to do that immediately after
making such a big show announcing
his presence... I don't get it.

VALDEZ
233 Neither do I, but I'm not complaining. I just wish we could've gotten more information while you were gone. Amanda's contacts dried up after... that first night. 233
(beat)
234 What did you and your father find out? Oh! The North Star! You said that you were going to ask Dr. Flagler about it! 234
(beat, concerned)
235 How... is he? 235

BETH
236 He was... surprisingly well, actually. Lucid, chatty... but unfortunately there was still a lot he couldn't remember. 236
(beat)
237 He remembered the concept of the North Star, but not what it was. We had to... end that line of questioning. He was getting frustrated, and we didn't want to risk him spiraling, since he was doing so well. 237

VALDEZ
238 Did he give you *anything*? 238

BETH
239 He did, actually. We were able to tease a lead on the people who spirited his equipment away. That was *mostly* what we've been chasing down. And... 239

BETH opens her backpack and plops a box on the desk.

VALDEZ
240 What's that? 240

BETH
241 *That* is a box of high-capacity holotapes created by the project lead, Dr. Emily Troiani. 241
(MORE)

BETH (CONT'D)
I wasn't able to read them because they don't work in regular terminals or Pip-Boys, but there's a standard holotape that describes what's on them.

VALDEZ
242 So... is there some kind of special terminal or interface that can read them? 242

BETH
243 It's more than that... you *directly* interface with them. 243

VALDEZ
244 Wait. You mean... 244

BETH
245 She must have used it as a test to record her thoughts and memories. Based on what's on that other holotape, it's got a fair amount of background. 245

VALDEZ
246 Hrm. That... complicates things significantly. 246

BETH
247 It does, yeah. There's only one way to get at the information on those tapes, and even if we did have access to the equipment to do it, it's incredibly dangerous. 247
(beat, sigh)
248 We were so lucky to even get our hands on them, it kills me that we might not be able to use them. 248

VALDEZ
249 How *did* you get them, anyway? 249

BETH
250 They made a mistake. I think that finding out that Dr. Flagler still had journals and data... rattled them. So they went back to find out if he had anything else. 250

VALDEZ
251 And did he? I took everything that was in his office when we visited, but... 251
(MORE)

VALDEZ (CONT'D)
I suppose that he could've had more stored elsewhere, that he'd forgotten about...

BETH
252 He didn't. At least as far as we know. But we were able to suss out their next destination based upon the questions they asked. 252
(beat)
253 They remained a few steps ahead of us, but, frankly, we're better at this than they are, so we caught up. 253

VALDEZ
254 Were you able to interrogate them?! 254

BETH
255 We were not. Unfortunately, a Super Mutant Behemoth found them just before we did. 255

VALDEZ
256 Oh. And I assume that encounter didn't go well for them. 256

BETH
257 It went *very* poorly for one of them. The other one turned tail and ran. 257
(beat)
258 The Behemoth lingered around the body, and we didn't want to risk the possibility of... evidence being lost, shall we say, so I created a distraction whilst dad checked out the body. Behemoths are monstrously tough, but not terribly bright, so I was able to lead him away long enough for dad to find those tapes. 258

VALDEZ
259 That's fantastic! And I'm glad you stayed safe. I was worried about you. 259

BETH
260 I'm sorry that I couldn't go into detail when we chatted... just couldn't risk it. But... 260
(MORE)

BETH (CONT'D)
I'm really glad that it gave us the
opportunity to... just chat,
though.

VALDEZ
261 Yeah. Me, too. 261

RAHMANI knocks on the doorway.

RAHMANI
262 Ah, Miss Kirby. I'm glad you're here. I need to talk to you. 262

BETH
263 Uh-oh. Have I done something wrong? 263

RAHMANI
264 No. Well, at least not that I'm aware of. 264

VALDEZ
265 Should I... leave? 265

RAHMANI
266 No, Scribe. You need to be part of this conversation as well. 266
(beat)
267 I've been doing my homework on you, Miss Kirby. 267

BETH
268 You have? 268

RAHMANI
269 You've been... working very closely with one of the most vital members of my team. 269

BETH
270 Of course. Due diligence is certainly the right call. 270

RAHMANI
(reading)
271 Elizabeth Laurel Kirby. Born April 21, 2081. The daughter of Lord Andrew Kirby and the former Elise Dietrich. 271

VALDEZ
272 Lord? 272

BETH

273 My father is a peer. A baron, 273
specifically. Well, *was*, I suppose.
Noble titles don't mean anything
anymore. Though, technically, that
does make me "The Honourable
Elizabeth Kirby."

RAHMANI

274 And he was a legend in the 274
intelligence community. Your mother
was a diplomat, also very highly
respected.
(beat)
275 But it's you that I'm interested 275
in, not your parents.

BETH

(wary)
276 Go on. 276

RAHMANI

277 I'm sure you'll understand, but I 277
cannot have someone who is
completely unaffiliated with the
Brotherhood working with Scribe
Valdez, or anyone else for that
matter, as closely as you have.

VALDEZ

278 Paladin! Beth has been... 278

RAHMANI

279 Let me finish, Scribe. 279
(beat)
280 Miss Kirby, you've been working as 280
a freelancer since leaving the
Vault, yes?

BETH

281 Yes, ma'am, that's correct. 281

RAHMANI

282 I would like to... formalize your 282
relationship with us.

BETH

283 Paladin... joining the Brotherhood 283
is... well, it's just something
that I can't do. I have to retain
my independence.

RAHMANI

284 I understand that. And beyond that, I respect it. With that in mind, here is my proposal, and you don't have to make a decision right now. I'd like you to hire you as we navigate this Morningstar business. You wouldn't be a member of the Brotherhood, but you would have access to our facilities, equipment, and... our personnel. And we would, of course, compensate you appropriately. 284

BETH

285 I... I don't know what to say, Paladin. It's a very... enticing offer. 285

VALDEZ

286 Just say "yes," Beth... 286

BETH

287 I... accept, Paladin. 287

RAHMANI

288 Good. 288

(beat)

289 Now. Scribe Valdez, let's discuss parameters. This issue is my highest priority. Knight Carlson is leading the overall effort, but I'm granting you the autonomy to do whatever you feel you need to do in order to get us on the other side of this. All the Brotherhood's resources are at your disposal. And at yours, Miss Kirby. 289

VALDEZ

290 I won't let you down. 290

RAHMANI

291 I know you won't. There's one last thing, then I'll leave you to it. 291

(beat)

292 You have my explicit permission to work with Miss Kirby as much as you both feel is appropriate. 292

VALDEZ

293 Thank you, Paladin. 293

RAHMANI

294 And you also have my explicit permission to spend as much off-duty time - such as it is - with Miss Kirby as you both feel is appropriate. 294

BETH

(surprised, brightly)

295 Thank you, Paladin. 295

RAHMANI

296 You're welcome. I'm counting on you. Both of you. 296

KNIGHT BANKS raps on the doorway urgently.

BANKS

297 Paladin! We just got a report - that group of hostiles we've been keeping our eye on? They're on the move, and it looks like they're headed for Foundation! 297

BETH

298 Foundation?! My mum is there! 298

VALDEZ

299 What's she doing there? I thought she was done with those negotiations? 299

BETH

300 She thought she was. But when I spoke with her this morning she said that she had to go over there today to finalize some things with Foundation leadership. 300

(urgently)

301 Odessa, I need to get there, immediately. 301

RAHMANI

302 Alan, assemble a team immediately. Take Miss Kirby with you. 302

VALDEZ

303 I'd like to go, too. I can help. 303

RAHMANI

304 Under normal circumstances I'd keep you here, but in this case I agree. Go. Just be careful. 304

BANKS
305 What kind of weaponry you got with you, Beth? 305

BETH
306 Not much. Just a pistol and a combat knife. And no time to stop at home to pick up anything better. 306

BANKS
307 Valdez - take her down to the armory and get her set up with a couple of Crusader Pistols. And a Plasma Cutter in case she needs to get up-close-and-personal with anybody. 307

BETH
(clearly worried)
308 Thank you, Knight Banks. 308

BANKS
309 We're rolling out in five. I'm going to grab Carlson. 309

RAHMANI
310 I'll get on comms and warn Foundation. At least they won't be caught by surprise. 310

BANKS and RAHMANI leave.

BETH
311 I don't say this often, Odessa, but... I'm scared. My mum isn't a... fighter. She's a diplomat. She had some self-defense training in the Vault, but nothing that's going to help with what sounds like an army bearing down on her. 311

VALDEZ
312 Paige will make sure she's protected until we get there. 312
(beat)
313 Let's get down to the armory so we get you kitted out. We want to be ready when Alan rolls out. 313
(beat)
314 She's going to be okay, Beth. Well make sure of that. Together. 314

END OF ACT TWO

ACT THREE

EXT. FOUNDATION, NIGHT.

BANKS, VALDEZ, and BETH approach cautiously, the sound of gunfire and explosions in the distance.

BANKS
315 Holy shit. This is a *lot* of damage. 315
Guards never stood a chance. Damn.

BETH
316 Oh, God... 316

BANKS
317 Greg - take the team to the main 317
entrance. The three of us will
sneak in through the back door.

CARLSON
318 Yes, sir. Team? Let's move out. 318

CARLSON leaves with his team.

VALDEZ
319 Let's get inside. They must need 319
help. And we need to find Beth's
mom.

BANKS
320 Yeah. Maybe we'll get lucky and 320
find out she got out in time.

BANKS, VALDEZ, and BETH enter Foundation, stealthily.

VALDEZ
(quietly)
321 Alan. That guy right there, with 321
the radio? He doesn't look like a
settler.

BANKS
322 Maybe. Could be a former Raider 322
that's giving Foundation a go,
though. Might not be a bad guy.

A gunshot rings out.

BANKS (CONT'D)
323 Jesus. OK, he's a bad guy. 323

BETH
324 I don't see anyone around him. He's 324
mine. Back in a moment.

BETH sneaks up to the bad guy and hits him in the back of the head, knocking him out. He crumples to the ground.

BANKS
325 Nice work. Remind me never to piss 325
you off.

BETH
326 I got his radio. At least we're not 326
completely blind now.

BANKS
327 Hopefully they didn't go radio 327
silent.
(beat)
328 Let's keep moving. Stay low, 328
weapons hot.

They continue forward.

BETH
329 How big was the group? 329

BANKS
330 It wasn't huge. Twenty people, 330
maybe? But all this damage makes me
wonder if the report was wrong.

BETH
331 That or they're carrying some very 331
heavy ordnance.

VALDEZ
332 It doesn't seem like there's any 332
kind of pattern. It seems like...
destruction for destruction's sake.

BETH
333 That's the kind of thing I'd expect 333
out of Blood Eagles, but the guy I
took down wasn't a Blood Eagle.

VALDEZ
334 No. He looked too... military for a 334
Blood Eagle. Free States, maybe?

The gunfire and explosions stop.

BETH
335 I don't think so. This isn't their 335
style, and, besides, my mum worked
out an agreement that both they and
Foundation seemed pretty happy
with.

BANKS
336 Maybe they changed their mind. 336

BETH
337 Well, anything's possible, I 337
suppose. It's not like I have a
better thought.

VALDEZ
338 Listen! 338

BANKS
339 What? I don't hear anything. 339

BETH
340 Exactly. No gunfire. No explosions. 340

BANKS
341 Did they leave? 341

BETH
342 What if the... property damage is a 342
distraction?

BANKS
343 Yeah, I think I see where you're 343
going with this. Maybe they want
something.

BETH
344 Or some*one*. 344

VALDEZ
345 If that's the case, they probably 345
went into the underground complex.

BANKS
346 Alright. Let's head over to the 346
elevator.

The group moves across the grounds toward the elevator.

The radio crackles to life and two BANDITs begin to converse.

BANDIT 1
347 Home Base, this is Epsilon. 347

BANDIT 2

348 Epsilon, this is Home Base. Go 348
ahead.

BANDIT 1

349 Still no sign of Paige. 349

BANDIT 2

350 He's too stupid and too stubborn to 350
run. He's here somewhere. Find him
so we can get out of here.

BANDIT 1

351 I passed a room with about a dozen 351
civilians. They're scared shitless.
Want me to use them to smoke him
out?

BANDIT 2

352 Nice thinking. That sentimental old 352
bastard won't let his people die.
Good thing Ward's not in charge,
that son of a bitch would probably
pull the trigger himself if he had
to.

BANDIT 1

353 Alright, looping back. 353

VALDEZ

354 We can't let innocent people get 354
hurt. You saw all the bodies we
passed since got here. They have no
problem with killing people.

BANKS

355 You're absolutely right. Beth, shut 355
off that radio so it doesn't give
away our position. We're almost to
the elevator. We'll see what they
have guarding it and go from there.

The group moves closer to the elevator.

VALDEZ

356 Only two people? 356

BANKS

357 Some of them are downstairs, and 357
Greg's team is probably keeping the
rest of them busy.
(beat)
358 Beth, would you like to do the 358
honors?

BETH

359 I'll need to take both of them out before they can fire. 359

(beat)

360 Let me try something... 360

BETH throws a rock some distance away from the elevator.

BANDIT 3

361 What was that? 361

BANDIT 2

362 Might be somebody sneaking around. Take 'em out. 362

BANDIT 3

363 On it. 363

BANDIT 3 goes to investigate the noise. BETH sneaks up behind BANDIT 2 and knocks him out, dragging his unconscious body out of sight.

BANDIT 3 returns.

BANDIT 3 (CONT'D)

364 It was nothing. Probably just a mole rat or something. 364

(beat)

365 This is a hell of a time to take a leak, dude. 365

(beat)

366 Hey, this isn't funny. Where did you-- 366

BETH knocks BANDIT 3 out as well, dragging his body to join his friend.

BETH

367 I didn't see anybody else. I think we're clear. 367

BANKS

368 Turn that radio back on before we head down. Might get a better read on where they are. 368

BETH switches on the radio, which crackles to life.

BANDIT 1

369 I repeat. Abort. Abort. Abort. We have a member of the Royal Family here. Abort. Abort. Abort. All teams, leave immediately and head back to base. 369

BANKS

370 "Royal Family?" What the hell is 370
that supposed to mean?

The elevator begins to move.

BANKS (CONT'D)

371 They're coming up. They want to 371
retreat, I say we let them. Too
many civilians still around to
start a firefight.

BETH

372 I agree. At least we'll have these 372
two to interrogate when they come
to.

BANKS

373 Let's get out of sight. 373

Several bandits get off the elevator. BANDIT 1 spots the two unconscious bandits.

BANDIT 1

374 God dammit. Sorry, guys, can't drag 374
you all the way back to base.

BANDIT 1 fires a single shot into each bandit's head.

The group of bandits leaves, quickly.

BANKS

375 We're clear. Let's get downstairs 375
and see how bad it is. And if,
like, the Queen moved into
Foundation while we weren't
looking.

The group enters the elevator and goes downstairs.

BETH

376 Let's find those people they were 376
talking about and make sure they're
alright.

BANKS

377 Exactly what I was thinking. I'm 377
not seeing any bodies, so that's a
good sign.

VALDEZ opens a door.

VALDEZ

378 In here! 378

(beat)

379 I'm Scribe Odessa Valdez with the Brotherhood of Steel. You're safe now. 379

ELISE

380 Odessa?! 380

VALDEZ

381 Mrs. Kirby! 381

(beat)

382 Beth! Your mom is in here! 382

BETH rushes in.

BETH

383 Mum! Are you hurt? 383

ELISE

384 No, Schatzi. I'm fine. But I shouldn't be. 384

BETH

385 What happened? 385

ELISE

386 These... people were looking for Paige, but they couldn't find him. I overheard them making plans to use us as bait to draw him out. 386

BETH

387 Smoke out the leader. A solid plan. 387

ELISE

388 And a brutal one. They were going to kill one of us to get his attention. 388

(beat)

389 They were going to kill *me*, Lily. 389

BETH

390 Oh my God! 390

ELISE

391 The man I assume was in charge told one of the others to grab someone from our group at random, and I was the unlucky winner. 391

(beat)

392 But he took one look at me and got *very* upset. 392

BETH

393 Upset? Why? 393

ELISE

394 I wish I knew. It felt like he... 394
recognized me, but I'd never seen
him before in my life. He said
some... colorful words and pulled
something up on his Pip-Boy. The
next thing we knew, he was on the
radio aborting the mission.

BETH

395 Did you hear him say something 395
about the "Royal Family?"

ELISE

396 I did! I assumed it was some sort 396
of code. Though the other
conversations I overheard were
quite straightforward...

BANKS

397 Mrs. Kirby, I'm Knight Alan Banks. 397
I'm a friend of your daughter's.
The "Royal Family" thing aside, can
you think of any reason why your
presence here would cause them to
abort the mission?

ELISE

398 Maybe they were afraid of me? 398

BETH

399 Why, did one of them not clean 399
their room?

ELISE laughs.

ELISE

400 No, Knight Banks, I can't. I'll 400
think about it, but... right now
I'd just like to go home.

BANKS

401 Of course, ma'am. On behalf of the 401
Brotherhood, I'd like to offer you
an escort.

ELISE

402 Thank you, Knight. Under most 402
circumstances I would decline, but
in this case I think that would be
for the best.

BETH

403 I agree. And I'll stay with you and dad tonight. Knight, can I hold onto these weapons until I get back to Atlas? 403

BANKS

404 Of course. I just hope you don't have to use them. 404

(beat)

405 Valdez, after we drop them off, I'll make sure you get back to Atlas safe and sound. 405

VALDEZ

406 Thanks, Alan. 406

BANKS

407 Mrs. Kirby, we can move out whenever you're ready. 407

ELISE

408 I'm ready. Let's go. 408 *

INT. FORT ATLAS, MORNING *

BETH knocks on VALDEZ's doorway.

VALDEZ

409 Hi! How's your mom? 409

BETH

410 She's good. Still a *little* shaken up, but she's resilient. 410

VALDEZ

411 And your dad? 411

BETH

412 He wants to go out and kill them all himself, but I think she prevailed upon him to... not do that. But he's champing at the bit to do *something*. 412

VALDEZ

413 I can't blame him. His wife and daughter are in the middle of... well, whatever this is. 413

(beat)

414 Did you figure anything out with that "Royal Family" thing? 414

BETH

415 No, at least nothing concrete or 415
even particularly compelling.
(beat)
416 But based purely on context, they 416
said she was a *member* of this
"Royal Family." So she wasn't the
focal point.

VALDEZ

417 I thought the same thing. And from 417
that, we can infer...

BETH

418 That *I'm* the focal point. 418

VALDEZ

419 Yeah. I'm sorry. 419

BETH

420 So am I. 420
(frustrated)
421 I hate this. I feel like I'm... 421
putting people I care about in
danger and I don't even know why.

VALDEZ

422 Well, look at it this way - it may 422
have saved your mother's life last
night.

BETH

423 That's true, I suppose. But that 423
luck's going to run out, sooner or
later. We need to figure this out
before that happens.
(beat)
424 And you're clearly in his 424
crosshairs as well.

VALDEZ

425 I'm a big girl, Beth. And not only 425
do I have the might of the
Brotherhood behind me... I have
you.

BETH

426 That you do. 426

PALADIN RAHMANI knocks on the door.

RAHMANI

427 Scribe Valdez, I wanted... 427

(beat)

428 Oh. Am I interrupting? 428

BETH

429 Not at all, Paladin. Scribe Valdez and I were just discussing the incident at Foundation and how it relates to what we already know about the Morningstar and his plan. 429

RAHMANI

430 Ah. Your report was very illuminating, Scribe. When we have a better understanding of how Mrs. Kirby - and, by extension *Miss* Kirby - figure into this, I expect to be read in immediately. 430

VALDEZ

431 Of course, Paladin. You'll know when we know. But as of right now, it's all speculation. 431

(beat)

432 Have we gotten anything out of the people who looted my lab? 432

RAHMANI

433 Nothing. Knight Banks has been working on them non-stop, but they keep denying that they had anything to do with it, saying they've been framed. 433

BETH

434 Is that... possible? 434

RAHMANI

435 No. Knight Carlson conducted a thorough investigation, and he was briefing me every step of the way. He'd had his eye on them from very early on in that investigation. 435

BETH

436 So... what took so long? 436

RAHMANI

437 He was hoping that they would give the materials they stole to someone. That way, we'd at the very least have a bit more clarity on who else was involved. 437

VALDEZ

438 But they never did. 438

RAHMANI

439 No. They just... sat on them. It 439
seemed strange to me; you'd think
if they'd had such an elaborate
plan to *take* the tapes and
journals, and to delete the
corresponding data from our
systems, that they would've had a
plan to get everything to whoever
they're working for.

BETH

440 It *is* strange. Like they only 440
had... half a plan. And that
doesn't jibe with what we've seen
from the Morningstar so far.
Everything has been precise.
(beat)
441 Perhaps something... unexpected 441
happened that threw them off? My
mother wasn't supposed to be at
Foundation, and seeing her made
them flat-out abort that mission...
they weren't able to pivot.

VALDEZ

442 I was thinking about that. It was 442
almost like they were...
programmed, but their programming
wasn't sophisticated enough to
change plans on the fly.

BETH

443 Hmm. Based on what we know so far 443
about the technology the
Morningstar seems to be
accumulating, could that be used to
"program" someone?

VALDEZ

444 Well, the information we have is... 444
incomplete, but what I've read
indicates that the technology
wasn't ready for that kind of
thing. But they were working toward
getting it there.

BETH

445 Perhaps that attack is evidence 445
that he's getting closer.
(beat)

(MORE)

BETH (CONT'D)

446 Paladin, could you tell Knight 446
Banks that I'm at his disposal if
he'd like to give me a shot at
interrogating the prisoners? As
long as that falls within my brief
as a freelancer, of course.

RAHMANI

447 It does, and I'll let him know. 447
(beat)
448 Thank you both for the briefing. 448
It's good to know that we're making
progress, and I have every
confidence that progress will
continue.
(beat)
449 There's one other matter that I'd 449
like to discuss with you. I haven't
made the formal announcement, but
I'm about to.
(beat)
450 I'm concerned about burnout. 450
Everyone has been working *so* hard,
and the last two weeks have been
especially difficult, knowing that
there was likely a spy in our midst
but not knowing either who that spy
was or what they might do next.

BETH

451 I'm well acquainted with that kind 451
of pressure. It's important to have
a... safety valve to blow off some
steam.

RAHMANI

452 To that end, I've decided to... 452
throw a party.

VALDEZ

453 A party? 453
454 454
455 455
456 To allow people step back and 456
celebrate everything we've
accomplished. And to celebrate *each
other*.

BETH

457 It sounds like a brilliant idea. 457

RAHMANI

458 Thank you, Miss Kirby. Initiate 458
Barksdale has already started
making arrangements. We'll have it
on Saturday.

BETH

459 If there's anyone who can plan a 459
party on this scale in two days,
it's Casey.

RAHMANI

460 I concur. And that will also give 460
everyone a bit of time to... ask
any potential plus-ones.

VALDEZ

461 We can bring dates? 461

RAHMANI

462 Guests. They can be dates, 462
siblings, friends, crushes... I
don't want anyone missing someone
while they're celebrating.
(beat)
463 At any rate, party or no, there's 463
always work to be done. I need to
get back to mine. Thank you both.

VALDEZ

464 Thank you, ma'am. 464

BETH

465 Thank you, Paladin. 465

RAHMANI leaves.

BETH (CONT'D)

466 That was... a surprise. 466

VALDEZ
(cheeky)

467 Are you implying that members of 467
the Brotherhood don't know how to
have fun?

BETH laughs.

BETH

468 I would *never* imply that. 468

CASEY knocks on the doorway.

VALDEZ

469 Hi, Casey! How goes party planning? 469

CASEY

470 Very well! There's plenty of space, 470
and I'm sure I can scrounge some
decorations.

BETH

471 It's going to look brilliant, 471
Casey. I have full and complete
faith in you.

CASEY

472 Thanks, babe. 472

BETH

473 And... as much as I'd love to stay 473
and chat, I need to check in on mum
and dad. I'll give them your best.
(beat)
474 Bye, you two! Don't get into *too* 474
much trouble while I'm gone.

VALDEZ

Bye!

CASEY

Bye!

BETH leaves.

VALDEZ (CONT'D)

475 What's up, Casey? Do you need help 475
with the party? Event planning
isn't... something I have a lot of
experience with, but I'll do my
best.

CASEY

476 It's not about the party. Well, it 476
kind of is, I guess.
(beat)
477 Will you... 477
(beat, sotto)
478 Oh, boy... 478

VALDEZ

479 Will I what, Casey? Put up 479
decorations? Set up chairs?

CASEY

480 No, it's not that. Um... will 480
you... go to the party with me?

VALDEZ
(shocked)
481 Um... you mean... 481

CASEY
482 Yes, Odessa. I'm asking you on a date. 482
(beat, reflective)
483 I guess if I didn't at least ask I'd regret it for a long time. I'm already regretting not doing it sooner. 483
(beat)
484 I'm still a little... fuzzy on the situation with you and Beth, but whatever it is, it seems... complicated, so... 484

There is an awkward pause.

VALDEZ
485 I'm sorry, this was... kind of unexpected. 485

CASEY
486 Was it? 486
(laughs)
487 I guess I was too subtle. 487
488 488

VALDEZ
489 Casey, I... 489

CASEY
490 Look, I already know "Scribe Valdez" is *amazing*. But I'd love to get to know *Odessa* better, and this seems like a good opportunity to maybe start doing that. 490
(beat)
491 And I... wouldn't have asked if I didn't get the feeling that you might want to get to know *me* better, too. 491

VALDEZ
492 I don't know what to say. 492

CASEY
(playfully)
493 Well, "yes" would be a good start. 493
(beat)
494 Look, I'm not a homewrecker. 494
(MORE)

CASEY (CONT'D)
If I misread things and you and Beth are *together* together I'm not going to do anything to get in the way. But if you're not... well, just think about it, okay? No pressure.

CASEY leaves.

VALDEZ
495 Yeah. No pressure at all. 495

END OF ACT THREE *

Season One
Part Two: The Book of Amanda

Episode 6:
"So Desperate a Step"

by

D.K. Trueno

"SO DESPERATE A STEP"

INT. MACALLAN CLUB, DAY

VALDEZ waits outside CRAIG's club, talking to herself.

VALDEZ

1 Okay, Odessa, you can do this. Beth 1
and Mr. Kirby trained you well, and
the other two times you went
undercover it went fine...
(beat)
2 Well, except for getting drugged... 2
and almost sleeping with Beth's
best friend.
(beat)
Here goes...

VALDEZ knocks on the door. The BOUNCER opens it.

BOUNCER

3 Good morning... Miss Fonseca. I 3
didn't expect to see you back at
the club so soon. And I also didn't
expect to see you here alone.
(beat)
4 But Mr. MacAllan was very pleased 4
that you wanted to see him.

The BOUNCER opens the door to the club and leads VALDEZ in.

BOUNCER (CONT'D)

5 Right this way. He's waiting for 5
you.

VALDEZ

6 Thank you. 6

CRAIG

7 It's wonderful to see you again, 7
Courtney. Can I interest you in
lunch? The club may not be open
right now, but my personal chef is
never far and our kitchen is always
at the ready.

VALDEZ

8 I think that sounds lovely. 8

CRAIG

9 Great. What can I get for you? And 9
do you have any dietary
restrictions?

VALDEZ
10 Surprise me. And no, I don't. 10

CRAIG writes on a pad of paper, tears off a page, and hands it to the BOUNCER.

CRAIG
11 Give this to Henry, please. 11

BOUNCER
12 Yes, sir. 12

The BOUNCER leaves.

CRAIG
13 I wish that Miss Halstead could've joined us as well. You two are... electric when you're together. 13
(beat)
14 And I adore that just hearing her name still makes you blush. 14

VALDEZ
15 Alice sends her regrets. But there were a couple of things that we were hoping for a bit of... clarification on. 15

CRAIG
16 Of course. I can't reveal any "trade secrets" until our partnership is official, but I'm happy to provide whatever context you may need otherwise. 16

VALDEZ
17 Thank you. I wanted to ask about your... memory devices. 17

CRAIG
18 I thought you might. You seemed quite interested in them when we first spoke. We're still trying to figure out a good name for them, by the way. Davina is a genius when it comes to marketing, but this one has even her stumped. 18

VALDEZ
19 Perhaps Alice and I can give that some thought. When our partnership is official, of course. 19

CRAIG

20 What would you like to know? 20

VALDEZ

21 I'm mostly concerned about the potential danger to clients. 21

CRAIG

22 As am I. We've been working hard to mitigate that, and we've made significant progress. There are two primary issues. First, there always seems to be the possibility that a client's mind will... reject the experience, which introduces significant neurological trauma. 22

VALDEZ

23 And what can you to about that? 23

CRAIG

24 Unfortunately, the technology itself is... impenetrable. We've been able to play around the margins, but the impact of doing that has been, well, marginal. 24

(beat)

25 But we've been developing a chem as well. We piggybacked off research that we found with the equipment. The people who developed the technology, of course, ran into the same problems we did, and although they continued to refine the technology itself, they began working on the pharmaceutical side as well. 25

VALDEZ

26 And chems are something that you're very familiar with. 26

CRAIG

27 We are. We brought some of the top scientists in that area with us when we came here, and they've made significant progress. Our more recent tests have been very promising. 27

VALDEZ

28 That's excellent news. 28

CRAIG
29 It is. We're not monsters. You know what it's like out there; we want people to have the ability to enjoy themselves in spite of that. 29

VALDEZ
30 Where did you find the tech? 30

CRAIG
31 I sent an advance team here to scout locations for this club. One of the teams found an underground lab facility, and although that location was a bit too small and not centrally located, the technology inside was incredible. We moved it to a secure location, and eventually here. 31

VALDEZ
32 I see. Have you found any more... facilities like that one? 32

CRAIG
33 No. We've heard rumors... rumblings. But whenever I send anyone to check them out, it's nothing. There were references to other aspects of whatever project created these things, but everything seemed to be... what's the word... compartmentalized? 33

VALDEZ
34 Yes. That's common with Vault-Tec projects, I've found. 34

CRAIG
35 How did you know it was Vault-Tec? 35

VALDEZ
36 Who else could it be? 36

CRAIG
37 I suppose you're right. And even if another group was involved, Vault-Tec would be a very prominent player as well. 37

VALDEZ
38 They always are, it seems. 38

CRAIG

39 Even with them gone, there are... groups to contend with. The Brotherhood of Steel is the one I'm most concerned about. I can see them causing... problems. 39

VALDEZ

40 What kind of problems? They seem like a... noble group to me. 40

CRAIG

41 The Brotherhood's reputation precedes it. Their focus on... "purity," shall we say, gives me the willies. And they are *incredibly* arrogant, especially when it comes to technology. 41

(beat)

42 Think about *this* technology. One of the primary reasons for the secrecy surrounding this tech is that they'd level my club and kill all of us if they found out about it. 42

VALDEZ

43 That's not true! 43

CRAIG

44 That's a... surprisingly strong reaction. 44

VALDEZ

45 I'm sorry. Alice and I have had a lot of interaction with the Brotherhood, and that kind of thing seems... out of character. 45

CRAIG

46 Well, I'm glad that your "interactions" have been positive. Ours have been less so. 46

VALDEZ

47 I understand. And in your business, if you're not careful, you're dead. 47

CRAIG

48 Precisely. I'm sure you face many of the same challenges. 48

VALDEZ

49 I do. So I'm sure you can 49
appreciate my desire to perform due
diligence.

CRAIG

50 I certainly can. Was that all you 50
wanted to know about?

VALDEZ

51 No. I also had a question 51
regarding... a chem.

CRAIG

52 I see. Well, anything you'd like to 52
sample is at your disposal. And if
there's anything that Miss Halstead
is interested in, you're welcome to
take it to her, or she can stop by
any time.

VALDEZ

53 Thank you. I don't want to sample 53
anything, I just had questions
about one specific chem. Are you
familiar with Venus?

CRAIG

54 Familiar with it? We developed it. 54
And, if I may say, it's one of our
proudest achievements.

VALDEZ

55 Oh! I didn't know it was one of 55
your... creations.

CRAIG

56 It is. It's still not *perfect*, but 56
as long as it's used responsibly
it's a... transcendent experience.

VALDEZ

57 So I've heard. 57

CRAIG

58 Ah, I was wondering if you'd used 58
it yourself. What would you like to
know?

VALDEZ

59 I'm specifically curious about the 59
nature of its effects. Can it...
create attraction where it didn't
exist previously?

CRAIG chuckles.

CRAIG

60 No. It's not a love potion. That's one of the things that inspired the name, in fact. It *intensifies* feelings that are already there. It can't create anything out of whole cloth, and that's by design. There would be too much potential for abuse otherwise. 60

VALDEZ

61 I can see that. 61

CRAIG

62 It... empowers people to take chances that they might not take otherwise. To *feel* more deeply, which inspires them to express themselves in ways that sometimes, frankly, surprise them. 62

(beat)

63 With couples, it usually manifests itself in being more adventurous or experimental in lovemaking. 63

VALDEZ

64 And with... non-couples? 64

CRAIG

65 It's used by people all along the relationship spectrum. People who've been married for years to those who are still... finding their way. Although... 65

VALDEZ

66 What is it? 66

CRAIG

67 Well, it never occurred to me before, but while it isn't a "love potion," it could be a truth serum in a way. A test to see if two people have feelings... under the surface. 67

VALDEZ

68 Do you mean... something along the lines of "in vino veritas?" 68

CRAIG

69 "In wine, truth." Although "in 69
Venus veritas" would be much
more... truthful than alcohol.
(beat)
70 You may have helped me create a new 70
marketing angle, Miss Fonseca.
Though we'd certainly want to get
the last remaining... issue
corrected before recommending that
kind of usage.

VALDEZ

71 Oh. Yes. I meant to ask about that. 71
What's that "issue?"

CRAIG

72 Well, to put it plainly, it can be 72
abused if too much is taken.
There's a... tipping point,
different for each person, where
they almost become... hypnotized, I
suppose, for lack of a better
comparison.

VALDEZ

73 I'm not sure I understand. 73

CRAIG

74 If someone takes too much, they'll 74
do just about anything they're
asked. There seems to be a line
involving direct self harm,
fortunately; they won't jump off a
building or shoot themselves if
told to. But it creates a
significant risk of abuse, and
that's why we're trying so hard to
fix it.
(beat)
75 We try to mitigate it by being 75
careful about who we sell it to,
and strictly limiting the amount we
sell to any one person. It's not a
perfect solution, but it's the best
we can do for now.

VALDEZ

76 I see. 76

CRAIG

77 You seem... upset. 77

VALDEZ

78 I am, a bit, if I'm being honest. I don't like that a chem with that kind of potential for abuse is out there, "mitigation strategies" or not. 78

CRAIG

79 Try to look at it pragmatically. We've made it as difficult as we can for people to abuse it. And alcohol carries the same potential for abuse - if not more - and is available without restriction. 79

VALDEZ

80 That doesn't make it right. 80

CRAIG

81 We operate in a world of gray, Courtney. Thinking in absolute terms has always been dangerous, and it's especially dangerous in this... environment. 81

(beat)

82 I've made fixing this my recreational chem team's top priority. I've put everyone on it. We're not developing any new chems or even improving existing ones until this gets resolved. 82

VALDEZ

83 That's encouraging. Thank you. I did have one other question about it. 83

CRAIG

84 What is it? 84

VALDEZ

85 In a situation where someone takes too much and becomes... compliant, does it... change the nature of the way that the primary effects work? 85

CRAIG

86 No. It's an *additive* effect. If someone were to accidentally take too much, they would still experience the same intensified feelings of attraction and pleasure. 86

(MORE)

CRAIG (CONT'D)
That person's partner would simply need to be careful in navigating how the encounter proceeds. As with most things, it comes down to trust.
(beat, thinking)
87 The only potential downside is that 87
at a certain point, memory loss occurs, so the person wouldn't remember anything that happened, no matter how... memorable it might be.

VALDEZ
88 That would be... very 88
disappointing, I'm sure.

The BOUNCER approaches.

BOUNCER
89 Mr. MacAllan, Miss Fonseca, lunch 89
is ready.

CRAIG
90 Perfect! Let's continue our 90
conversation in the dining room.
(beat)
91 After you. 91

VALDEZ
92 Thank you. 92

MUSICAL TRANSITION

INT. KIRBY RESIDENCE, AFTERNOON

BETH enters the room. ELISE is sitting on the couch.

ELISE
93 Schatzi! How are you? You just 93
missed your father.

BETH
94 Oh, dear. Where did he go? 94

ELISE
95 He went for a walk. 95
(beat)
96 Don't give me that look! He really 96
just went for a walk.

BETH
97 Good. How are you holding up? 97

ELISE

98 I'm fine, dear. You staying the night with us helped, too. It was nice to have you home, Lily. And I may not be an intelligence officer, but I *am* pretty tough. 98

BETH chuckles.

BETH

99 You are, at that. Have you eaten? 99

ELISE

100 You also just missed lunch, I'm afraid. Cooking helped take my mind off things for a bit. I would've waited if I'd known you were coming. 100

BETH

101 I was kind of hoping I'd be able to use the same strategy to take a break from thinking about... everything. 101

ELISE

(cheeky)

102 Well, I suppose you'll just have to invite Odessa over for dinner, then. 102

BETH laughs.

BETH

103 I suppose I will. But I can't stop replaying everything that happened at Foundation. We got there as quickly as we could, but we were still too late to help. You could've... you could've been killed, mum. And it would've been my fault. 103

ELISE

104 Your fault? Lily, you cannot think that way. 104

BETH

105 The more we learn about what the Morningstar is up to, the more it seems to be about *me*, and I just don't understand why. I never had any involvement in this research. I'm not even a scientist. 105

(MORE)

BETH (CONT'D)

(beat)

106 What did I do to deserve this? He's 106
been toying with me from the
outset, I just didn't realize it at
the time. I wish I could just...
turn myself in and end this. But I
guess that wouldn't fit in with his
little game.

ELISE

107 Elizabeth Laurel Kirby, I will not 107
sit here and listen to you talk
like that. Besides, I know you too
well to even entertain the idea
that you'd give up.

(beat)

108 I know you're concerned about the 108
peril that we all seem to be in
right now, and I'm concerned, too.
But the best way for you to protect
us is to keep doing what you've
been doing.

BETH

109 You're right, of course. 109

(beat)

110 Oh! I meant to ask, did you 110
recognize any of the people who
were holding you hostage?

ELISE

111 No. I wish I had, that could've 111
provided significant insight... if
not into who's behind this, at
least into which groups are
involved.

BETH sighs.

BETH

112 We were speculating that it might 112
be the Free States, but I knew that
was unlikely given the work you'd
done to establish detente between
them and Foundation.

ELISE

113 Indeed. I suppose it could've been 113
rogue elements within the Free
States that didn't like the
agreement, but for what it's worth
the men I saw didn't... feel like
Free Staters.

BETH

114 In what way? 114

ELISE

115 They seemed more... precise, I suppose? It's hard to put my finger on it. They seemed more like... traditional military. 115

BETH

116 Hmm. Perhaps he's bringing in mercenaries? 116

ELISE

117 Perhaps. But I think that's something you'll have to discuss with your father when he gets back. 117

BETH

118 Before he does... 118

ELISE

119 Yes? 119

BETH

120 Well... there were some things I wanted to talk to *you* about. Everything that's happened has had me wondering. 120

(beat)

121 How did you and dad do it? 121

ELISE

122 How did we do what? 122

BETH

123 I've never seen two people more in love than you two. The world *literally* fell apart around you, but... you didn't. 123

ELISE

124 It wasn't always easy. Even before the world fell apart. Love is often simple. Pure. But circumstances tend not to be, and those are what can split us apart. 124

BETH

125 Did you ever... split apart? 125

ELISE sighs.

ELISE

126 Are you sure you want to hear this? 126

BETH

127 I am, mum. 127

ELISE

128 Yes. There were times, especially early on, that... circumstances made it seem like we couldn't be together. I hate to say this, but... it seemed like love wouldn't be enough sometimes. 128

BETH

129 But it was. 129

ELISE chuckles.

ELISE

130 You wouldn't be here if it wasn't. 130

BETH laughs.

ELISE (CONT'D)

131 But what we discovered was that no matter what happened, we always came back to each other. It was almost... instinct. We were each other's *querencia*. 131

BETH

132 Your what? 132

ELISE

133 *Querencia*. It's Spanish, but it... doesn't translate directly to English, or German for that matter. 133

(beat)

134 It was a concept your father learned about from a book of poetry he found in an old bookshop in New York. One moment, I'll get it for you. He likes to keep it nearby. 134

ELISE goes to a nearby bookshelf and retrieves the book, handing it to BETH.

ELISE (CONT'D)

135 Be gentle. It's more than a century old. 135

BETH

136 "Cemetery Nights" by Stephen Dobyns. 136

(beat)

137 I'll read it when I get home. And I'll take good care of it, I promise. I can imagine how important it is to him. 137

ELISE

138 And to me. 138

BETH

139 Can you... explain what it is in the meantime? 139

ELISE

140 A *querencia* is a... place. "The place one cares most about, where one is most secure, protected, where one feels safest" is how he put it in the poem, I think. "The place that all our being radiates out from." The place you come back to when things seem darkest. 140

(beat)

141 It can be a physical place, or a place in your mind - a memory, even an ideal. Or, as we learned, it can be a person. What that person embodies, what they mean to us. And what we mean to them. 141

BETH

142 That's... beautiful. 142

ELISE

143 That's love. 143

(beat)

144 Be careful when you read it. Your father still cries every time. But don't tell him I told you that. 144

BETH

145 I won't. And... thank you. 145

CHARLES opens the door end enters.

CHARLES

146 Well, hello, Elizabeth! 146

BETH

147 Charles! I thought you might be 147
with dad. You know, keeping him out
of trouble.

CHARLES

148 I think you've noticed by now that 148
the only person who can keep Andrew
Kirby out of trouble is Andrew
Kirby.

ELISE

149 Indeed. I've been trying for more 149
than thirty years.

BETH

150 So, where have you been? 150

CHARLES

151 Talking to the Overseer, actually. 151

BETH

152 The Overseer? You don't think she 152
has anything to with this, do you?

CHARLES

153 Not directly, though I trust Vault- 153
Tec higher-ups about as far as I
can throw a Vault door.

BETH

154 I trust them even less than that. 154

CHARLES

155 I didn't want to risk showing our 155
cards by asking directly, but I did
get her to *more or less* confirm
that the Project Mind's Eye had a
sister project that either was or
is being run out of Vault 112.
"Project Tranquility."

BETH

156 Vault 112... that's in Washington, 156
D.C., isn't it? As I recall it was
one of the last Vaults that Vault-
Tec completed before the war.

CHARLES

157 That is correct. 157

BETH

158 That's brilliant news! We can get 158
in touch with Bryan's team, and...

(MORE)

BETH (CONT'D)

(beat)

159 What? 159

CHARLES

160 We haven't been able to contact 160
Bryan or anyone from his team. It's
been nine months, I believe.

(beat)

161 That doesn't mean that we've... 161
lost them. Not necessarily. But it
does mean that we can't use them as
a resource to determine if whatever
this Vault 112 project is has
anything to do with the
Morningstar's plans, unless and
until they turn up.

BETH

162 It's possible that their... 162
disappearance is tied to whatever
he's up to. Maybe they got too
close. Bryan is one of the canniest
operators I know...

(distracted)

163 I just... I hope I see him again. 163
He was a good friend. And we could
certainly use his help right now.

ELISE

164 And I know that... closure would 164
help.

BETH

165 It would, if I'm being honest. But 165
I can't worry about that now.

(beat, gathering herself)

166 Charles, what did you find out 166
about that sister project?

CHARLES

167 Not much, I'm afraid. The Overseer 167
didn't seem to know anything about
it other than that Vault 112 was
one of several Vaults that had
projects related to efforts being
run out of Vault 76. But she said
that she was never apprised of the
specifics of those other projects,
and I believe her. She was an
administrator, there would be no
"need to know" that sort of detail.

BETH

168 Which means we're nowhere. 168

CHARLES

169 I wouldn't say "nowhere." Remember, 169
intelligence isn't always big, dramatic revelations. Sometimes it's about gathering enough pieces of the puzzle that you start to see the picture form. And this does seem like a potentially important piece.

BETH

170 I hope you're right. Given what 170
happened at Foundation, it seems that he's getting bolder.

CHARLES

171 It does, at that. We'll keep at it. 171
And who knows, perhaps your father will have... accidentally stumbled across some information during his completely innocent walk...

ELISE

172 Ugh. He's incorrigible. He's lucky 172
I love him.

BETH laughs.

BETH

173 He is. You're both lucky. 173

ELISE

174 I agree. A lot of hard work in 174
there, too, though. But well worth it - and not just because we got the best daughter on the planet out of the deal.

BETH

175 Aww... 175

END OF ACT ONE

ACT TWO

INT. BETH'S HOME, DAY

The doorbell rings. BETH answers it.

BETH
176 Odessa! Please, come in! 176

VALDEZ enters. BETH closes the door.

BETH (CONT'D)
177 Can I get you a drink? Something to 177
eat?

VALDEZ
178 Thank you. I'm fine. I just ate, 178
actually.

BETH
179 So, what's up? I... didn't expect 179
to see you! I was going to radio
you later, see if you wanted to...
get together.
(beat, awkward)
180 You know, exchange intel, that sort 180
of thing.

VALDEZ chuckles.

VALDEZ
181 We can... exchange intel now, if 181
you'd like.

BETH
182 Oooh! What did you find out? Was 182
Knight Banks able to get something
out of those prisoners?

VALDEZ
183 No, unfortunately. 183

BETH
184 It sounds like it's time for me to 184
give it a try.

VALDEZ
185 I think you're right. Alan's doing 185
his best, but he isn't a trained
interrogator, and...

BETH

186 And you're still not sure about him? 186

VALDEZ sighs.

VALDEZ

187 No. I wanted this to be the end of it. But I just... I can't shake the feeling that there's *something* going on with him. 187

BETH

188 Could it be... unrelated? 188

VALDEZ

189 Perhaps. But I can't really confront him about it, because if he *is* working for the Morningstar he'd know we were onto him. 189

BETH

190 Look at you, thinking like a spy... 190

VALDEZ laughs.

VALDEZ

191 I'll stick to being a scientist, thanks. Most of the time, at least. It's fun, kind of like... roleplaying. Especially with you. 191

BETH

192 In that case, I hope that we have the chance for more... roleplaying in the future. 192

VALDEZ

193 I think we will. 193

(beat)

194 You said we could exchange intel. Would you like to go first, or... 194

BETH

195 Sure. Charles did some legwork and found out about a Vault-Tec project that may... or may not be related to the tech that the Morningstar is chasing. Did Vault 112 or "Project Tranquility" come up in any of the materials you analyzed? 195

VALDEZ

196 Hmm. No, I don't recall either of those things coming up. But I'll go downstairs and run a search, just to make sure that I didn't miss anything. What are they? 196

BETH

197 Information on both was... scant. The Overseer was cagey, but did volunteer that Vault-Tec ran a sister program to Project Mind's Eye out of Vault 112. But the nature of that project - Project Tranquility - well... either she didn't know or wasn't saying. 197

VALDEZ

198 Which do you think it was? 198

BETH

199 Charles said that it felt like she didn't know. And that jibes with the way that Vault-Tec operates. As for Vault 112... how familiar are you with the nature of the various Vaults? 199

VALDEZ

200 A little. I thought they were all supposed to provide shelter selected people from the bombs. Was that... not the case? 200

BETH

201 Well, some Vaults were. Vault 76 was one of them. They called them "control Vaults." But others weren't so much about protecting "the great and the good," but were geared more toward... conducting experiments. 201

(beat)

202 One of the ways my father and I bonded when I was younger was seeing what systems we could hack into together. Daddy-daughter time, you know? 202

VALDEZ

203 That's adorable. 203

BETH

204 Vault-Tec's systems were locked down pretty effectively when it came to information on other Vaults, but we were able to learn a little bit about a few of them. There was one up north, for example, that was set up specifically to perform experiments related to cryogenics. 204

VALDEZ

205 And I take it that Vault 112 wasn't a "control Vault." 205

BETH

206 It wasn't. But all that dad and I knew about it from Vault-Tec's records was that it was in Washington, D.C. No mention of what sort of Vault it was, and no mention of any programs or experiments housed there. 206

VALDEZ

207 So... road trip? 207

BETH

208 It may come to that. My hope was that we could leverage resources that were already in the area, but... 208

VALDEZ

209 What's wrong? 209

BETH

210 The program that I was a part of also had teams that were intended to leave Appalachia and do more or less the same thing we're trying to do here - to do what we could, in the background, to hold things together and maybe guide things in a way that would foster a sustainable society. The assignment to go to D.C. was considered the most important of them all. And the most dangerous. 210

VALDEZ

211 That makes sense. On both counts. 211
The former seat of government is
the kind of place that you'd want
to send your best people.

BETH

212 And we did. That team was led by 212
Bryan Reardon. He was the best of
us. Smart, canny, good in a fight.
And a hell of a leader.

VALDEZ

213 I feel like there's a "but" coming. 213

BETH sighs.

BETH

214 There is. Bryan was a good friend. 214
We were... very close. No romantic
entanglements, of course, which
helped.

VALDEZ

215 Of course. 215

BETH

216 Not that he didn't try. 216

VALDEZ

217 Oh. That must've been... awkward. 217

BETH

218 At first. But once I made it clear 218
that I was... beyond my
experimentation phase, he backed
off. Fortunately, it didn't harm
our friendship at all.

VALDEZ

219 Yet you said he "was" a good 219
friend.

BETH

220 You really are getting good at 220
this. I didn't even realize I'd
done that.
(beat)
221 I guess I used past tense for a 221
couple of reasons. Bryan didn't
want the D.C. assignment. He wanted
to coordinate things here.
(MORE)

BETH (CONT'D)
He felt strongly that *this* was the plum assignment and that he'd earned pride of place.

VALDEZ
222 He wanted your assignment? 222

BETH
223 He did. He was... upset. He accused my father of nepotism and said some... unkind things to me, but in the end he accepted the assignment and left, and that was that. But we never had the opportunity to reconcile. 223

VALDEZ
224 I'm sorry. I know what it's like to not have closure. 224

BETH
225 Thank you. The thing is, I know that even if he were still angry with me, he wouldn't let that get in the way of doing what was best for the mission. The problem is that no one's heard from Bryan's team in about nine months. Charles had been checking in with him periodically. I don't want to assume the worst, but... well, you know better than anyone how dangerous it is out there. And it's only going to be moreso in an area that saw as much concentrated fire as the Capitol. 225

VALDEZ
226 Don't lose hope. I have no doubt that he's every bit as skilled and capable as you say he is, and people like that often find a way to survive. 226

BETH
227 I hope you're right. But, in any case, even if he and his team did find anything out about Project Tranquility, there's no way for that to help us now. And we don't even know if it's relevant to what's going on here; it could just as easily be a red herring as a vital piece of intel. 227
(MORE)

BETH (CONT'D)
Still, it's another data point, I suppose.
(beat, cheeky)
228 Your turn... 228

VALDEZ
229 I paid Craig MacAllan a visit 229
earlier.

BETH
230 You what?! 230

VALDEZ
231 I just had some follow-up 231
questions. You're not upset, are you?

BETH
232 I'm not, I'm just surprised. And in 232
fact, I'm impressed. What did you find out?

VALDEZ
233 I was curious about where he got 233
his technology from. From the way he described it, it sounded different from what's discussed in the materials we found, and in Dr. Flagler's notes.

BETH
234 I noticed that as well. 234

VALDEZ
235 He didn't want to volunteer much, 235
but he said that he found it while scouting locations for his club. But all of the labs we know about are accounted for. Cleaned out, sure, but accounted for.

BETH
236 So that lab must not have been 236
related to Mind's Eye. At least not directly.

VALDEZ
237 That was my thought as well. And 237
given what you said about Project Tranquility...

BETH

238 It's *possible* that it was a... 238
satellite lab for that project, so
it wouldn't appear in the project
notes we found. And that might
explain why the Morningstar hadn't
been looking for it.

VALDEZ

239 If that's the case, then that tech 239
may be even more relevant to the
Morningstar's plans than we'd
thought.

BETH

240 It's been a productive day, hasn't 240
it?

VALDEZ

241 It has. Seems like we make a good 241
team even when we're split up.
(beat)
242 There was something else I wanted 242
to talk to you about. Unrelated
to... all this.

BETH

243 Oh? Am I going to need that drink? 243

VALDEZ laughs.

VALDEZ

244 Maybe. How about you pour and we'll 244
talk. Okay?

BETH

245 Okay. Have a seat and I'll be right 245
back.

BETH makes drinks. She returns, and she and VALDEZ sit.

VALDEZ

246 I wanted to talk to you about the 246
party.

BETH
(hopeful)
247 Oh? What about it? 247

VALDEZ

248 Um... this is awkward, but... 248

BETH

249 Uh-oh... 249

VALDEZ
250 Casey asked me to go with her. 250

BETH
251 Oh! Oh, my. And, um... what did you say? I mean, of course I'd completely understand if... 251

VALDEZ
(interrupting)
252 Beth! I didn't say anything. 252

BETH
253 You didn't? Why? Did you... want to see if I'd be upset before you said yes? 253

VALDEZ laughs.

VALDEZ
254 No, Beth. I did not. She didn't give me a chance to say anything. She told me to think about it and sort of... floated away. 254

BETH
255 So... 255

VALDEZ
256 Elizabeth Kirby, would you be my date to the Brotherhood "Blowing-off-Steam" party tomorrow night? Of course, if you're busy... 256

BETH
257 I'm not busy! And I would love to go with you. Full disclosure, I was... kind of hoping that was why you stopped by. 257

VALDEZ
(chuckling)
258 That was a big part of it, yeah. Do you think you have something in that closet of yours that I can wear? It would have to be a little more... demure than what I wore to Craig and Davina's club. 258

BETH laughs.

BETH

259 Yes, I think that would be 259
advisable. And... maybe you can
help me pick something out as well.

VALDEZ

260 I'd love that. 260
(beat)
261 You probably know Casey better than 261
anyone. Is she going to be...
upset? I don't want this to be
weird.

BETH

262 Casey's not like that at all. It 262
won't be weird. And besides, she's
probably already had twenty
Brotherhood members ask *her*
already.

VALDEZ

263 You know, it's funny. 263

BETH

264 What is? 264

VALDEZ

265 I know that people can break up and 265
still be friends. But I've met two
people that you were involved with,
and... well, you're not just
friends, they're incredibly loyal
to you. Casey made it pretty clear
that she didn't want to get in the
way of whatever may be going on
between us.
(beat)
266 And, um... in the interest of 266
"semper veritas..."

BETH

267 Uh-oh. 267

VALDEZ

268 I was... kind of, *maybe* considering 268
asking her out myself before you...
happened.

BETH sighs.

BETH

269 Why do I always seem to "happen to" 269
people?
(MORE)

BETH (CONT'D)
"Oh, that's Beth - great in bed, but she'll knock you around like a radstorm."

VALDEZ
270 I'm sorry. It was a poor choice of words. I didn't mean it in a negative way. And, in fact... I'm glad you "happened to" me. 270

BETH
271 You really mean that? 271

VALDEZ
272 "Semper veritas" still applies. I guess I'll just have to find out if I... um... get knocked around like a radstorm. 272

BETH laughs.

BETH
273 Alright, let's start looking through that wardrobe. And don't forget, we're having dinner with Amanda tonight at her place to talk about what happened that first night I was gone. 273

VALDEZ
(ruefully)
274 Wouldn't miss it for the world. 274

BETH
275 It will be fun! I'm going to check in on her after you head back to Atlas and see if she needs any help with cooking or setting up. And I promise not to try to get any information out of her ahead of time. 275

MUSICAL TRANSITION

INT. AMANDA'S HOUSE, AFTERNOON

BETH knocks at AMANDA's door.

AMANDA opens the door slowly. She is tipsy.

AMANDA
(downcast)
276 Hey, Princess. 276

BETH
(concerned)
277 Are you alright? 277

AMANDA
278 Never better. Care for a drink? 278

BETH
279 How many have *you* had? 279

AMANDA
280 Uh... four? But they were kind of 280
big.

BETH
281 Why don't we sit down together for 281
a moment? I need you to talk to me
about what's wrong.

BETH guides AMANDA to the couch and they sit. AMANDA is on the verge of tears.

AMANDA
282 I love you, baby. 282

BETH
283 I love you, too. And you're really 283
worrying me right now. Did
something happen?

AMANDA sighs.

AMANDA
284 I guess I've just been thinking a 284
lot about... us, and... what went
wrong.

BETH
(wary)
285 Amanda, I... 285

AMANDA
(interrupting)
286 You trusted me, and I... threw it 286
away. I threw *you* away. We could've
been happy...

AMANDA begins crying.

BETH
287 Shh... come here. Where's all this 287
coming from?

AMANDA

288 I loved you so much, but even that 288
didn't matter. I broke your heart. All because of some sick need to break *you*. I wanted you to be broken like me.

BETH

289 I was broken before I even left the 289
Vault, and you know that. Vault-Tec and the people they allowed into positions of authority made certain of that.

AMANDA

290 I took advantage of you! 290

BETH

291 I wanted you to. I may not have 291
realized it at the time, but I needed to... purge all of that pain somehow. Those memories. The way I was abused under the guise of "training."

(beat)

292 Amanda, you're the reason I made it 292
through. Because I loved you. And you loved me back. I'm always going to carry that pain from the Vault with me, but... you didn't ruin my life, you *saved* it.

AMANDA

293 I was a monster. 293

BETH

294 Then I guess you were exactly the 294
monster I needed.

AMANDA

295 That's not what you said when you 295
left.

BETH

296 I was angry, and I was tired. Tired 296
of having the same fights, over and over. And yes, I blamed you. It's not a stretch to say I hated you in that moment. I still loved you, too, which made leaving hurt even more.

AMANDA
297 I hated you, too. For giving up, 297
for taking that *feeling* away from
me. You were the first person who
ever made me feel like I was
somebody, and not just another
generic Raider girl.

BETH
298 Amanda, you're so much more than 298
that. You always have been. Anyone
who actually gets to know you
understands that. My parents love
you, Odessa absolutely adores
you... these are all people who've
seen the real Amanda Otis. They not
only like you, they *respect* you.
The people who only see you for
your body, or how beautiful your
face is...

AMANDA
299 With these scars? 299

BETH
300 Yes, with those scars. Do you 300
remember how I used to run my
fingers along them? How I kissed
them?

AMANDA
301 Yeah... 301

BETH kisses AMANDA on the cheek.

BETH
(tenderly)
302 Everything about you is beautiful, 302
Amanda. Even your scars. And I pity
the people who thought that
physical beauty is all you have to
offer.

AMANDA
303 There's also the ruthlessness. 303

BETH laughs.

BETH
304 Well, yes, there is that. Kind of a 304
necessity to survive in the Raider
world. And it *is* kind of hot...

AMANDA laughs through the tears.

AMANDA

305 You really know how to flatter a girl. 305

BETH

306 It's part of the whole "Elizabeth Kirby experience," I suppose. But I mean it. All of it. 306

(beat)

307 How long has this been bothering you? I wish we could've talked about it sooner... 307

AMANDA

308 It's been rattling around in my head since we broke up. But... I guess I've been thinking about it a lot more over the past couple of weeks. 308

BETH

309 Because of Odessa? 309

AMANDA

310 No! In fact, hanging out with her has helped kind of take my mind off it a little bit. She's a really fun distraction. You found a good one there. 310

BETH

311 I did, didn't I? And I feel like we turned a corner while I was away. Like there was less pressure, and I was finally able to do what you told me to do. 311

AMANDA

312 "Let it breathe?" 312

BETH

313 Yeah. And while we did pick out dresses together, they were for undercover work and not a wedding. 313

AMANDA laughs.

AMANDA

314 You know, she said the same thing about "less pressure." Keep that up, okay? 314

BETH

315 I'll do my best. 315

(beat)

316 But you didn't answer my question. Why's it been top of mind recently? 316

AMANDA sighs.

AMANDA

317 I guess I knew this day was going to come. 317

BETH

318 What are you talking about? 318

AMANDA

319 Do you remember that little Enclave lieutenant that Valeria paid you to, uh, retrieve from me? 319

BETH

320 Yes, of course. Cindy. Valeria was very glad to have her back. I had to... massage the truth a little bit to ease her re-entry into the Enclave. 320

AMANDA

321 What did you tell her? 321

BETH

322 We had a conversation about the dangers of deep-cover work. Valeria is... an interesting character. But the bottom line is that she cares about her people, and she was mostly glad that she had her back. 322

AMANDA

323 "Mostly." 323

BETH

324 She was upset - with Cindy for going AWOL and with herself for putting someone that young and inexperienced in that position. 324

(beat)

(MORE)

BETH (CONT'D)

325 The thing my dad taught me about being a leader is that the hardest part is understanding the people under your command and deploying them in the way that most suits *their* capabilities rather than presuming they can do all the things you can. Cindy is smart and capable, but she's a child compared to virtually everyone else in the Enclave. 325

(beat)

326 But she brought us back together, so I can't complain *too* bitterly. 326

AMANDA

327 There *is* that... 327

BETH

328 Is that whole affair what's gotten you so upset? 328

(beat)

329 Wait. I think I might be starting to get it... 329

AMANDA

330 Uh-oh. 330

BETH

331 When I took her back to the Whitespring, she was furious with me, obviously. She was... petulant. Almost bratty. But the thing that struck me at the time was that she told me she loved you. Over and over. She was distraught to be taken away from you. And I know that feeling. 331

(beat)

332 Are you worried that being with you hurt her? That you've... ruined her like you thought you were ruining me? We were together for months, surely you didn't have enough time... 332

AMANDA

(interrupting)

333 Beth... I... I *have* had enough time. 333

BETH

334 You said "have had" and not "did have." 334

AMANDA
335 We're still together, Beth. 335

BETH
336 You're what?! 336

AMANDA
337 It took a little time to work it out; Valeria had her on lockdown for quite a while. But... 337

BETH
338 But you found a way. You always do. 338

AMANDA
339 You're not mad? 339

BETH
340 Of course I'm mad! Dammit, Amanda, I'm your best friend! How could you not tell me? 340

AMANDA
341 I thought you'd be upset! 341

BETH
342 Amanda, that was a *job*. I *love you*. That's more important than any payday. You should've trusted me! 342

AMANDA
343 I don't trust myself, okay?! I... I'm in love with her, Beth. And I'm scared shitless that I'm going to end up hurting her like I hurt you. I get that you feel like you came out better on the other side of what I did to you, but I don't want to do the same thing to her. She's not like you. I don't know if she could bounce back from that. And I don't want to lose her like I lost you. 343

BETH
344 Look, I've also done a lot of thinking about "us," and the conclusion I reached is that we're so similar that the only two options for us as a couple were to rule the world or flame out in spectacular fashion. There could be no middle ground, and it ended up being the latter. 344

(MORE)

BETH (CONT'D)
(beat)
345 From what I know about Cindy, 345
you're right, she's not like me.
And I think that means you two have
a much better chance to be happy
than we ever did.

AMANDA
346 I hope so. I'm just... scared. 346
You're the only other person I've
ever felt like this about, and I
don't want to fuck it up this time.
And more than that, I don't want to
fuck *her* up.

BETH
347 It's a leap of faith. I get it. 347

AMANDA
348 I just wish I had more faith in 348
myself.

BETH
349 I have faith in you. Look at how 349
you've taken care of Odessa!

AMANDA
(hiding something)
350 Yeah. I guess you're right. And I 350
liked "taking care of her." Helped
take our minds off... things.

BETH
(oblivious)
351 And there are a lot of things to 351
have our minds taken off of.

AMANDA sighs.

AMANDA
352 I have a lot to think about, Beth. 352
I've lived most of my life just
trying to survive, you know? I
never had time for "feelings."

BETH
353 Well, now that you're a successful 353
business owner and a respected
member of the Raider community,
maybe you're just making up for
lost time.

AMANDA laughs.

AMANDA

354 Maybe. But it's overwhelming. You 354
wanted honesty? I'm having trouble
dealing with it. A lot of trouble.

BETH

355 I'm here for you. I want you to be 355
happy and I'll do anything in my
power to help make that happen.
(beat)
356 Including helping you with dinner. 356

AMANDA

357 I think I need to handle it myself. 357

BETH

358 That's fine. Do you at least want 358
me to stay and keep you company?

AMANDA

359 No, baby. You need to go look 359
pretty for Odessa anyway.

BETH

360 Okay. I'm still worried about you, 360
though. Promise you'll talk to me
before you look for answers at the
bottom of a bottle next time?

AMANDA

361 Promise. 361

BETH

362 We'll see you later. 362

AMANDA

363 Bye. And Beth? 363

BETH

364 Yes? 364

AMANDA

365 I love you. 365

BETH

366 I love you, too. 366

END OF ACT TWO

ACT THREE

EXT. AMANDA'S HOUSE, EVENING

BETH and ODESSA approach.

BETH
367 I cannot wait to hear this story. 367

VALDEZ
368 It was... quite a night. 368

BETH knocks on the door.

BETH
369 I'm also very curious to see what's 369
on the menu. I offered to help, but
she shooed me away.

VALDEZ
370 Still, it should be a nice change 370
for someone to be cooking for *you*
for a change.

BETH
371 The company's the important part. 371

BETH knocks on the door again.

VALDEZ
372 Did she forget dinner was tonight? 372

BETH
373 No... I visited her earlier to see 373
if she needed any help.

VALDEZ
374 Did she? 374

BETH
375 She did, but not with dinner. 375
(beat)
376 Did she seem... alright to you 376
while I was gone?

VALDEZ
377 Yes! She was... great, as a matter 377
of fact! We had a *lot* of fun.
Nothing seemed... off.

BETH tries the doorknob. The door is locked.

BETH

378 Something's wrong. I'm going in. 378

VALDEZ

379 Are you going to break down her door?! 379

BETH

380 No. I have a key. 380

BETH unlocks the door and opens it. The pair enter the house.

BETH (CONT'D)

381 Amanda? Where are you? 381

(beat)

382 Let's check the rooms. 382

VALDEZ

383 Amanda? Are you here? 383

BETH and VALDEZ return to the living area.

BETH

384 Where is she? 384

VALDEZ

385 Do you think... 385

BETH

386 No. God, at least I hope not. Besides, if the Morningstar or his men... took her, there would be signs of a struggle. She wouldn't go down without a fight. No struggle here... 386

VALDEZ

387 I suppose you're right. That's good news, at least. 387

BETH

388 She didn't say anything about leaving when we were talked. Something must've come up. But why didn't she radio me? I could've helped! 388

VALDEZ

389 Beth... over here. On the table. 389

BETH

390 What? What is it? 390

VALDEZ

391 A note. And it's for you. 391

BETH takes the note and opens it. She reads.

BETH

392 She's gone. 392

VALDEZ

393 Gone? What do you mean, "gone?" 393

BETH

394 She left. She said she was 394
overwhelmed... too many emotions,
too many feelings. She couldn't
handle being here in Appalachia...
too many reminders.
(beat)
395 Dammit, I knew I should've 395
stayed... it feels like I just got
her back, and... she's gone.

VALDEZ
(cautious)

396 Did she say she... isn't coming 396
back?

BETH

397 No, but she didn't say that she is, 397
either.

BETH chuckles wryly.

BETH (CONT'D)

398 She *did* say, though, that she left 398
instructions at her bar that we can
drink for free.

VALDEZ

399 That's a good sign, right? If she 399
still owns The Spider's Web then
she's got to come back, right?

BETH

400 I hope so. I just... I just wish 400
she'd trusted me to help her
through it. But I'm part of the
problem, so I guess that was off
the table.

VALDEZ

401 Hey. Don't talk like that. 401

BETH

402 It's true. Amanda and I have such a complicated relationship, and I found out today that she's been seeing someone on the sly. She didn't trust me enough to tell me about it because she thought I'd be angry with her. 402

VALDEZ

403 Complicated or not, the one thing that's very clear is that you have a lot of love for each other. So much that even though you didn't work as a couple, you still found each other again as friends. And you've been there for each other ever since. 403

BETH sighs.

BETH

404 I just wish I could be there for her *right now.* I hate that she's hurting and I can't help. 404

VALDEZ

405 I have an idea. Why don't we lock up here and go back to your place. We can make dinner together, and you can tell me your favorite Amanda stories. And I'll tell you about what happened that first night you were gone. 405

BETH

406 That... sounds quite nice, actually. 406

VALDEZ

407 Good, it's settled. And... I'd like to stay the night, if that's okay. I don't think you should be alone tonight. I'll get you tucked into bed and I'll only be a flight of stairs and a hallway away if you need me. 407

BETH

408 Odessa... 408

VALDEZ

409 Yes? 409

BETH

410 Thank you. 410

VALDEZ

411 You're welcome. Now, let's make 411
sure everything is secure here and
head home.
(beat)
412 I didn't bring anything to sleep 412
in, though. Do you think Amanda
would mind if I borrowed one of her
t-shirts?

MUSICAL TRANSITION

INT. FORT ATLAS, NIGHT

The Brotherhood party is winding down. There is still considerable walla and music.

BETH sighs in relief.

BETH

413 What a crazy couple of days. But 413
I'm glad that we got to spend so
much time together. And this party
has been the perfect way to cap
things off.

CASEY approaches the couple.

CASEY

414 Hey, you two! I'm sorry I haven't 414
had a chance to say hi all night...
and maybe steal a dance or two. I
hope you're having a good time!

BETH

415 You did a brilliant job organizing 415
all this on short notice, Casey,
you really did.

VALDEZ

416 It's impressive! And, um... 416
Initiate Jenkins seems nice.
Handsome, too.

CASEY chuckles.

CASEY

417 I guess we both have a thing for 417
redheads.

VALDEZ laughs.

CASEY (CONT'D)

418 Thanks for letting me know right away that you were going to ask Beth, by the way. 418

VALDEZ

419 I didn't want to leave you hanging. 419

(beat)

420 How many people asked *you*? 420

CASEY

421 I kind of lost count. 421

BETH laughs.

BETH

422 Nice to see that you haven't lost your touch. 422

CASEY

423 Neither have you! Look at you two, you're both gorgeous! 423

BETH

424 One of the perks of having undercover work as part of my brief is a *very* robust wardrobe closet. 424

CASEY

425 I think you need to let me take a look through it sometime. 425

BETH

426 We could have you over for dinner! It would be nice to catch up properly. I want to know all about what you've been up to since you left the Vault. And any embarrassing stories about Odessa, of course... 426

VALDEZ laughs

VALDEZ

427 Hey! 427

(beat)

428 Beth is going to try to teach me to cook, but I promise I'll step aside and let her work her magic if you come over. 428

CASEY

429 That sounds great. 429

(beat)

(MORE)

CASEY (CONT'D)
430 Oh, no. Poor Ty looks completely 430
lost. I'd better get back to him
before he... wanders into a ladder
or falls down a flight of stairs or
something.

BETH
431 Make sure he understands that he'd 431
better not try any funny business,
or I'll make sure that they'll
never find his body.

CASEY
432 I'll be fine. I always held my own 432
with you, remember?

BETH
433 That you did. 433
(beat)
434 Hey - thank you. And have fun. 434

CASEY leaves.

VALDEZ
435 She seems happy. 435

BETH
436 She's in her element. I think that 436
she's going to great things for the
Brotherhood.

Music starts playing.

VALDEZ
437 I think they're playing our song. 437
Shall we?

BETH and VALDEZ dance.

BETH
438 We have a song? 438

VALDEZ
439 Nah. I've just always wanted to say 439
that.

BETH laughs.

VALDEZ (CONT'D)
440 You're a good dancer. 440

BETH
441 Only on slow songs. I'm a bit of a disaster when the tempo gets too fast. Unless it's a tango. 441

VALDEZ
442 Ooooh! Will you teach me? 442

BETH
443 I would love to. But, um... 443

VALDEZ
444 What? 444

BETH
445 You know that the tango is a... dance of passion... 445

VALDEZ
446 I know. It's my parents' favorite dance. It's... special to me. But I never found the right partner to try it with myself. 446

BETH
447 Not even with your former fiancé? 447

VALDEZ
448 Derek wasn't a dancer. He was more like a... linebacker. 448

BETH laughs.

BETH
449 I see. 449

VALDEZ
450 But I don't want to talk about Derek right now. 450

BETH
451 Of course, I'm sorry. 451

VALDEZ
452 It's alright. I just want to... stay in this moment. With you. 452

BETH
453 That's what I want, too... Just us. 453

VALDEZ
454 I'm not even sure there's anyone else here. I only see you. 454

BETH

455 What should we do when the song is over? 455

VALDEZ

456 I'm not ready for this night to end yet. 456

BETH

457 It doesn't have to. We're both grown-ups. We don't have a curfew. 457

VALDEZ

458 We don't need permission. 458

BETH

459 We never have. 459

VALDEZ

460 Just from ourselves. 460

BETH

461 And each other. 461

VALDEZ

462 Beth? 462

BETH

463 Yes, Odessa? 463

VALDEZ

464 When this song is over... I want you to take me home. 464

BETH

465 We could have a glass of wine... maybe a bite to eat. 465

VALDEZ

466 That's exactly what I had in mind. You know, you've made me breakfast, lunch, and dinner, but, um... there's still one course left. 466

BETH

467 Are you saying... what I think you're saying? 467

VALDEZ

468 I'm ready for dessert, Beth. 468

END OF EPISODE 6

Once Upon A WASTELAND

Season One
Part Three: The Book of Elizabeth

Episode 7:
"The Mystic Chords of Memory"

by

D.K. Trueno

"THE MYSTIC CHORDS OF MEMORY"

INT. BETH'S HOME, MORNING

BETH is getting ready to cook breakfast as VALDEZ enters, yawning.

BETH
1 Good morning. Again. 1

BETH crosses to VALDEZ and kisses her.

VALDEZ
2 Good morning. It was, um, nice 2
waking up next to you.

BETH
3 It was. And what happened after 3
that was... nice as well.

VALDEZ giggles.

VALDEZ
4 I'm sorry I fell right back asleep 4
after.

BETH
5 It's alright. You're beautiful when 5
you're sleeping. It was rather...
tempting to wake you up again,
though, so I thought it would be
best to come up here and make
breakfast. Are you hungry?

VALDEZ
(suggestively)
6 I am. 6

VALDEZ kisses BETH.

VALDEZ (CONT'D)
7 Can I help? 7

BETH
8 Of course you can! I was just 8
getting the pans out, how about you
have look through the refrigerator
and choose the menu?

VALDEZ
9 Alright! 9

VALDEZ opens the refrigerator as BETH continues to prepare to cook.

The doorbell rings.

VALDEZ (CONT'D)
10 Are you expecting anyone? 10

BETH
11 I'm not. It could be my parents or 11
Charles with an update.

VALDEZ
12 I'd better get dressed! I'm, um... 12
not dressed for company.

BETH
13 Amanda's t-shirt suits you, but... 13
yeah, probably a good idea.

VALDEZ rushes off to change.

BETH goes to the door and opens it. CINDY is there, upset.

BETH (CONT'D)
14 Cindy? What are you doing here? 14

CINDY
(angry but measured)
15 You know exactly why I'm here. What 15
did you do?

BETH
16 Cindy, I... 16

CINDY
17 Don't give me any of your spy 17
nonsense. Gaslight me all you want,
it's not going to work. Why did you
make her leave?

BETH
18 Please, come inside so we can 18
discuss this.

CINDY
19 Fine. 19

CINDY storms in.

BETH
20 Did she talk to you before she 20
left?

CINDY
21 No! She just left me a note. A 21
note!
(MORE)

CINDY (CONT'D)
Not even a holotape so I could...
(quietly)
22 ...so I could hear her voice. 22

BETH
23 How about I get us something to drink. Nuka-Cola? 23

CINDY
24 Sure. 24

BETH retrieves a Nuka-Cola and opens it, pouring it into a glass.

BETH
25 Now. Let's start from the beginning. Calmly. 25

CINDY
(not calm)
26 Did you know she was leaving? 26

BETH sighs.

BETH
27 No. I got a note, too. Odessa and I were supposed to have dinner at her place last night, but when we arrived, she was already gone. 27
(beat)
28 Cindy, I... I miss her, too. If I'd had any idea she was considering something like this, I would've said something... done something... 28

CINDY
29 Oh, come on. You've been trying to break us up since you took me away from her the first time. News flash - it didn't work then, and it's not going to work now. 29

BETH
30 I didn't even know you were back together until yesterday! She never told me! 30

CINDY
31 What?! You're lying. As usual. 31

BETH
32 I'm not. She said that she kept it from me because she thought I'd be upset. 32

CINDY

33 That doesn't even make sense! Why would you be upset? 33

BETH

34 I said precisely that to her. 34

CINDY

35 Unless... 35

BETH

36 Unless what? 36

CINDY

37 Unless you want her back. 37

BETH

38 Neither of us want that. We even reiterated that when we spoke yesterday. 38

CINDY

39 You talked to her yesterday?! You said that you were going to her place for dinner but she wasn't there! 39

BETH

(getting annoyed)

40 Yes, and I stopped by earlier in the day to see if she needed any help. And when I arrived, she was a mess. 40

(beat)

41 Because of you. 41

CINDY

42 What do you mean "because of me?" I make her happy, Beth. You're the one that made her miserable. 42

BETH

43 How dare you! 43

CINDY

44 You know that both of those things are-- 44

BETH

(interrupting)

45 How dare you come into *my* home and lecture *me*! You petulant child! 45

CINDY
46 I am not a child! 46

VALDEZ rushes in.

VALDEZ
(concerned)
47 Beth, are you alright? What's going 47
on in here?

BETH is seething but gathers herself.

BETH
48 Odessa Valdez, this is Cindy 48
Connors.

CINDY
49 *Lieutenant* Cindy Connors. New 49
Enclave.
(beat)
50 And who's this? Your-- 50

BETH
(interrupting)
51 Be *very* careful what you say right 51
now.

CINDY
52 Wait. Odessa Valdez? You're 52
Brotherhood, right?

VALDEZ
53 Yes. I am. 53
(beat, coldly)
54 Now. Did you come to Beth's home 54
just to yell at her, or was there
something specific that you wanted?

CINDY
(on her back foot)
55 I... well, I... 55

VALDEZ
(interrupting)
56 Because if it's the former, then I 56
think that it would be best if you
leave. Now. Don't worry about your
drink. I'll get you a fresh Nuka-
Cola from the refrigerator for the
road.

CINDY sighs and gathers herself.

CINDY
57 Amanda left, and I... I don't 57
understand why she'd leave like
that. Why she'd leave *me* like that.
She said she loved me.

VALDEZ
58 You think it's Beth's fault? 58

CINDY
59 Yeah, I do. She obviously wants 59
Amanda back, and I'm in the way.

BETH
60 I do *not* want her back! My God, 60
it's like talking to a
Snallygaster! You try to explain
something and you just end up
frustrated and covered in spittle.

CINDY
61 You're one to talk! You're like a 61
Deathclaw, but taller and with
worse breath.

BETH
62 My breath is immaculate! 62

VALDEZ
63 Stop it, both of you! Bickering is 63
not going to bring her back, and
she would not want you two fighting
over her like this!

CINDY
(sotto)
64 *Your face is a Snallygaster...* 64

VALDEZ
65 I said stop it! 65
(beat)
66 The Enclave is a military 66
organization, is it not?

CINDY
67 Yes, it is. 67

VALDEZ
68 Yes it is *what*? 68

CINDY
69 Yes, it is... ma'am. 69

VALDEZ
70 And you're an officer, are you not? 70

CINDY
71 Yes, ma'am. 71

VALDEZ
72 Then start acting like it. What 72
would your commanding officer,
Colonel...

BETH
73 Valeria Faustina. 73

VALDEZ
74 What would Colonel Faustina say 74
about what's going on here right
now?

CINDY
75 She wouldn't be very happy, ma'am. 75

VALDEZ
76 I'm sure she wouldn't. 76

BETH
77 And another thing, you... 77

VALDEZ
(interrupting)
78 Hey! I'll get to you in a moment. 78
(beat)
79 Now. Are you ready to discuss this 79
matter with us like an adult, or
should I get that Nuka-Cola for
you?

CINDY
80 I'm ready to discuss this like an 80
adult.
(long pause)
81 Ma'am. 81

VALDEZ
82 Good. 82
(beat)
83 And as for you... 83

BETH
84 She burst in here and immediately 84
started attacking me!

VALDEZ
85 How many years of training did you have in the Vault for exactly this kind of situation? 85

BETH
86 This was different! It was about Amanda! 86

VALDEZ
87 How many years? 87

BETH
(thinking)
88 Uh... eleven? 88

VALDEZ
89 And yet you fell apart the moment something *personal* came into it. What if she drew her weapon in anger? What would you have done then? 89
(beat)
90 Regardless, the outcome would have been at least negative and potentially tragic. You accused her of acting like a child, and you're not wrong based on what I heard. But you were acting like a child, too, Beth. 90
(beat)
91 I'm disappointed in you. 91

BETH sighs deeply.

BETH
(chastened)
92 You're right, Odessa. You're right. And I'm sorry. 92

VALDEZ
93 Are *you* ready to discuss this like an adult? 93

BETH
94 Yes. 94
(long pause)
95 Yes, ma'am. 95

VALDEZ
96 Good. Now that we've all remembered that we're grown-ups, Cindy, you have to understand, Beth had nothing to do with Amanda leaving. 96
(MORE)

VALDEZ (CONT'D)
And she's telling the truth about not knowing about you and Amanda getting back together until yesterday. I know that because Amanda confided in me about it while Beth was away.

BETH
97 What?! 97

VALDEZ
98 I... strongly encouraged her to tell you, but she had to be the one to do it. In her own time. 98

BETH
99 No, I understand. It wouldn't have been right for you to betray her confidence. And it did need to come from her. 99
(beat)
100 I was upset, but not because you were together, Cindy. I was upset because she didn't trust me enough to tell me. I just want her to be happy. 100

CINDY
101 Well, she's happy with me. Or at least she was. We just had a date at the Whitespring! Ice cream sodas, roller skating... it was... wonderful. 101

BETH
102 It sounds fantastic, Cindy. Was there any sort of... tension between you two at all recently? 102

CINDY
103 No! In fact, things seemed to be... you know, progressing. Getting more serious. You said you wanted her to be happy, well... she seemed happy. Very happy. 103

BETH
104 Hmm. Until yesterday, I would've said the same. 104

VALDEZ
105 We spent a lot of time together 105
while Beth was away with her dad,
and we, um... well, we had a lot of
fun. She definitely seemed happy.

BETH
106 So, as far you two could tell, 106
there was nothing wrong.

CINDY
107 There must be! You said that she 107
was upset when you talked to her
yesterday – "a mess." What was she
upset about? Did someone threaten
her?

BETH
108 No, it's nothing like that. 108
(beat)
109 Cindy, she was terrified of hurting 109
you. I don't know how much she told
you about our relationship, but...
well, she hurt me. Often and badly.
She said that she wanted me to be
broken like her, and she hated
herself for it after we split up.

VALDEZ
110 Oh my God, Beth... 110

BETH
111 It's alright, Odessa. She *didn't* 111
break me. I wouldn't care to repeat
that part of the experience, but
she made me stronger – strong
enough to not only survive out
here, but thrive. And I think I
made her stronger, too, in the end.
That's why we were able to come
back together as friends, after we
had time to heal.
(beat)
112 She's afraid of hurting you like 112
she hurt me, Cindy. That's what I
was about to tell you when
things... escalated.

CINDY
(upset)
113 So... this *is* my fault? 113

BETH

114 No! No, Cindy, this isn't *anyone's* 114
fault! Amanda loves you, but she
doesn't trust *herself*.

VALDEZ

115 Sometimes people just need to... 115
get away from a situation to get
some perspective on it.

CINDY

(crying)

116 She didn't even say goodbye... 116

BETH

117 She probably would've stayed if she 117
had, and that's precisely why she
didn't.

CINDY

118 What do I do now? 118

VALDEZ

119 Is there anyone you can talk to? 119
Back at the Bunker?

CINDY

120 No. The Colonel doesn't even know 120
about us.

VALDEZ

121 Well, you have me. 121

BETH

122 And me. We'll give you the 122
frequencies to use to get in
contact with us if you need to.

CINDY

123 Thank you. And... I'm sorry. 123

BETH

124 I'm sorry, too, Cindy. Would you 124
like to stay for breakfast?

VALDEZ

125 Beth's a good cook! 125

CINDY

126 Thank you, but I think I should be 126
getting back to the Bunker. I
didn't exactly *sneak out* to come
here, but if I'm gone too long
they'll think something's up.

BETH
127 You're going to have to tell Valeria at some point. 127

CINDY
128 Yeah. I know. I just have to figure out how to do it. 128

VALDEZ
129 That's what Amanda said about telling Beth about you two. 129

CINDY sighs.

CINDY
130 Can I have that Nuka-Cola that you offered? For the road? 130

VALDEZ
131 Of course. 131

VALDEZ goes to the refrigerator and gets a Nuka-Cola, handing it to Cindy.

CINDY
132 Thank you. And not just for the Nuka-Cola. 132

VALDEZ
133 I'm glad we were able to talk it through. We'll let you know right away if we hear from her. 133

CINDY
134 And I'll do the same. Goodbye for now. 134

CINDY leaves.

BETH sighs.

BETH
135 That was *not* how I wanted this morning to go. 135

VALDEZ
136 Come here. 136

VALDEZ kisses Beth.

BETH
137 When do you have to be back at Atlas? 137

VALDEZ
138 Not until the afternoon. 138

BETH sighs.

BETH
139 Still hungry? 139

VALDEZ
140 Very. 140

<u>END OF ACT ONE</u>

ACT TWO

EXT. FORT ATLAS, AFTERNOON

BETH and VALDEZ approach Fort Atlas.

VALDEZ

141 As much I love Fort Atlas... you 141
made it very difficult to leave
your place. I've never had anyone
read poetry to me before.

BETH

142 I'll admit, I was doing my best to 142
keep you there, even though I knew
that duty would eventually call.

VALDEZ

143 Promise you'll read me the rest of 143
that book?

BETH

144 Promise. 144

BETH and VALDEZ kiss.

VALDEZ

145 Do you want to come in? Maybe say 145
hi to Casey? Or talk to Paladin
Rahmani to see if we found out
anything new about that attack on
Foundation?

BETH

146 I'll use any excuse to spend a 146
little more time with you. But I do
have to follow up with the
MacAllans in a bit, and I need to
talk to you about it first. I
didn't want to... ruin the mood
this morning by talking business.

VALDEZ

147 What's up? 147

BETH

148 It's about the holotapes dad and I 148
found. I think that we need to find
out what's on them.

VALDEZ

149 Do you mean... 149

BETH

150 I can tell them that we need to test out this memory technology before we can agree to invest that kind of money in it. 150

VALDEZ

151 It's too dangerous, Beth! 151

BETH

152 It is. But unfortunately I don't see any other option. We've hit a dead end. 152

VALDEZ sighs.

VALDEZ

153 But if we walk in there with a set of tapes, they'll know something's up. 153

BETH

154 I've been thinking about that. We still have a man on the inside. Dad said that he's been helping with cataloging the tapes that they found with the equipment. If we get the tapes to him, he can just slip them in, and produce them when we do our test. 154

VALDEZ

155 I still don't like it. But I suppose you're right. There isn't another way. And I'm willing to take that risk. 155

BETH

156 Absolutely not. I'll do it. It will be much safer if you're there to help if anything goes wrong. 156

VALDEZ

157 Beth, I don't know anything about this technology! I know a little bit about neurology, but not enough to do anything if something goes wrong! 157

BETH

158 That's still rather more than I'd be able to contribute. Besides, I've already put you in enough danger. 158

VALDEZ

159 Risk is a part of my job. 159

BETH

160 And part of mine. But I think that 160
my training will help me deal with
whatever that technology might
throw at me. One of the things they
taught us was how to not lose
ourselves, even in the most extreme
circumstances. Even torture.

VALDEZ

(aghast)
161 Are you saying... you were 161
tortured? Beth, I had no idea...

BETH

162 It's alright. There were... aspects 162
of the training that were harsh.
Painful. Often cruel. I try not to
even think about it, but it...
haunts me. But it did make me
resilient.

VALDEZ

163 I still don't feel comfortable 163
letting you take this risk.

BETH

164 Neither do I, if I'm being honest. 164
But you being at my side will make
me feel a lot better about it.

VALDEZ

165 That's exactly where I'll be. 165

KNIGHT CARLSON approaches.

CARLSON

166 Scribe Valdez! It's nice to have 166
you back. And Miss Kirby, it's
always a pleasure to see you.

BETH

167 Thank you. I never had a chance to 167
congratulate you on your promotion.
Well done. Knowing Odessa is safe
when she's home at Atlas is very
important to me, and it sounds like
you were the person most
responsible for that.

CARLSON

168 Thank *you* for keeping her safe 168
while we got that whole thing
figured out.

VALDEZ

169 How's the interrogation going? Did 169
Alan get anything out of them yet?

CARLSON

170 No. In fact, he was hoping that he 170
could tag Miss Kirby here in. You
have training specifically in
interrogation, right?

BETH

171 I do. And beyond that, I have 171
specific training in extracting
information when interrogation
doesn't yield results.

CARLSON

172 Are you talking about... torture? 172

BETH

173 No. I was trained to *resist* 173
torture, but I won't deliver it.
That's a red line for me.

VALDEZ

174 Good. 174

BETH

175 Maybe some of the interrogation 175
strategies that I learned in the
Vault will be enough to get what we
need out of them. Or at the very
least give us something to go on.

CARLSON

176 Well, he'll be glad for the help. 176
I'm a little worried about him.
He's really frustrated that he
hasn't been able to crack this.

VALDEZ

177 I think being able to take a break 177
will help him reset a little bit.

CARLSON

178 Yeah. He's been at this almost non- 178
stop since Rahmani gave him the
assignment. At least he took a few
hours off for the party.

(MORE)

CARLSON (CONT'D)
(beat)
179 I gotta say, that party was a hell 179
of an idea. We needed that. All of
us.

VALDEZ
180 I agree. 180

CARLSON
181 How go things on your end? Any big 181
breakthroughs?

BETH
182 We have a few irons in the fire, 182
but it's been a slow go. My father
and his assistant have been working
contacts, but nothing just yet.

VALDEZ
183 It may be that we won't know 183
anything until he makes another big
move.

CARLSON
184 Well, hopefully it won't come to 184
that. We can't have another
incident like we had at Foundation.
That put people on edge, and that's
a recipe for disaster.

VALDEZ
185 Could that be part of his plan? Sow 185
distrust?

BETH
186 Hmm. Perhaps. But to what end? 186

CARLSON
187 Well, you said that he wants to 187
take over the region, right? Maybe
if everybody's fighting each other,
the factions will all be too weak
to fight *him* when he makes a play.

BETH
188 I guess it's possible, but... that 188
doesn't feel right. It's just a gut
feeling, though. I'll ask my father
about it, get his take. His gut is
far more experienced than mine.

CARLSON
189 How's your mom doing? 189

BETH

190 She's doing very well, thank you 190
for asking. I think I was more
upset than she was after the
attack.

VALDEZ

191 She's an exceptionally strong 191
woman.

CARLSON

192 That's great to hear. And I'm glad 192
she wasn't hurt. Any leads on the
"royal family" thing?

BETH

193 Unfortunately, no. It was clearly 193
code, but we don't know for what.
It's possible that it just means
that she's considered... important
somehow. Integral to his plans
without actually being involved in
them.
(beat)
194 Sorry. I'm just kind of thinking 194
out loud. It has us baffled.

CARLSON

195 Well, if we hear anything you'll be 195
the first to know.

BETH

196 Thank you. 196

CARLSON

197 I'm going to head inside. I'll see 197
you in a few.

CARLSON leaves.

VALDEZ

198 Are you sure we can't loop him in 198
on this?

BETH

199 The existence of those tapes is 199
something we have to keep very
tightly under wraps.

VALDEZ

200 I know, it's just... he was the one 200
who sniffed out the moles, and
beyond that, Rahmani trusted him
enough to decide that he was the
right person to do it.

BETH

201 That's not lost on me. And he 201
hasn't done anything to make me
suspicious....

VALDEZ

202 Unlike some other people I can 202
think of.

BETH

203 Anything new there? 203

VALDEZ

204 No. He's still disappearing for 204
hours at a time, but other than
that he's been the same old Alan.
Things even seem to be getting
serious between him and Erika.

BETH

205 If he *is* working for the 205
Morningstar, that could help
explain why the interrogation isn't
producing results.

VALDEZ

206 I was thinking about that, too. But 206
it's odd that he seems so insistent
on bringing you in to help. He
knows all about your intelligence
training.

BETH

207 It could just be part of the game. 207
There are several aspects of this
whole thing that don't make sense.

VALDEZ

208 Maybe we'll get some clarity from 208
those tapes.

BETH

209 I hope we do. I don't want to take 209
that kind of risk and come up
empty. Again.

MUSICAL TRANSITION

EXT. MACALLAN CLUB, NIGHT

BETH and VALDEZ knock on the door.

The door opens and the BOUNCER emerges, closing the door behind him.

BOUNCER
210 Are you sure about this? 210

BETH
211 No. But there's no other way. 211

BOUNCER
212 That's what your father told me, too. The numbers I've seen haven't been *terrible*, but I'm definitely concerned. 212

VALDEZ
213 So am I. 213

BETH
214 Is everything in place? 214

BOUNCER
215 Yes. Davina asked her assistant to come up with three choices. I replaced the tapes for one of those choices with the ones you and your father found. Just choose "skydiving" and you'll be all set. 215

VALDEZ
216 Skydiving. Got it. 216

BOUNCER
217 You're going to meet with three people. Craig, his assistant Audrey, and Dr. Holcomb, who handles the clinical stuff. Craig and Audrey will meet you inside. 217

VALDEZ
218 Understood. Beth, are you ready? 218

BETH
219 As I'll ever be. 219

BETH, VALDEZ, and the BOUNCER enter the club.

BOUNCER
220 Sir? They're here. 220

CRAIG
221 Good evening! It's wonderful to see 221
you again! I'd like you to meet
Audrey, my right hand.

AUDREY
222 Nice to meet you! Craig talks about 222
you two all the time.

VALDEZ
223 Only good things, I hope? 223

AUDREY
224 Always. 224

CRAIG
225 My sister and I remain very excited 225
about our potential partnership. I
trust that if this demonstration
goes well, you'll be prepared to
commit?

VALDEZ
226 I believe we will. This technology 226
is fascinating, and we feel it has
a great deal of potential.

AUDREY
227 You'll fit right in with Dr. 227
Holcomb, then. If I have to hear
one more monologue about using this
stuff for more "noble" purposes...

CRAIG
228 We were very lucky to find a 228
neurologist at all... She
practically fell into our laps.

VALDEZ
229 In the interest of full disclosure, 229
Craig, I'm concerned. What
assurances can you give us that
this test will be safe?

CRAIG
230 I'd be lying if I said there wasn't 230
risk. There is. But we've made
strides with the chem we use to
prepare people for the experience
and Dr. Holcomb has provided
significant guidance to help people
manage things while they're inside.

BETH
231 "Inside?" 231

CRAIG
232 It's a totally immersive experience. There are screens in the pod, placed in front of the subject, but those are mostly to provide sensory input to make it easier for that immersion to happen. 232

VALDEZ
233 I see. 233

CRAIG
234 If you're curious about the mechanics of how it works, I'm sure Dr. Holcomb would be more than happy to talk to you about it. 234

VALDEZ
235 I'm still not entirely comfortable with Alice doing this, but... 235

BETH
236 But I insisted. If we're going to invest this much money in something, I want to make sure that it is what you say it is. We've built up a measure of trust, Craig, and I do appreciate that. But I need to ensure that there are no misunderstandings. 236

CRAIG
237 Of course. Trust but verify. I operate under that model myself. 237
(beat)
238 Shall we go to the lab? Alice will need to take our chem and prepare before we can begin. 238

BETH
239 After you. 239

The group walks.

BETH (CONT'D)
240 So, Audrey, where are you from? 240

AUDREY
241 Virginia. Not too far from the Capitol. 241
(MORE)

AUDREY (CONT'D)
My sister Lois and I came here when we heard that things kind of... loosened up a little with those Scorched things.

BETH
242 How bad is it there? 242

AUDREY
243 It's not good. A lot worse than it is here. I mean, it's the Capitol, so it caught a lot of fire. People are still trying to make a go of it, though. 243

BETH
244 Humanity is nothing if not stubborn. 244

VALDEZ
245 It's ironic. That stubbornness probably caused the war, and it's also going to be what allows society to rebuild. 245

AUDREY
246 Well, either way, Lois and I were doing our thing for a little while. Ran with a Raider gang; that was fun, but it got old. Thought about going over to Foundation, but they seemed like a bunch of squares. 246

BETH
247 You're not wrong about that. 247

AUDREY
248 We did a little bit of trading here and there, made a lot of contacts and even a few friends, but we were barely making ends meet. Then these two showed up. We needed a new gig, and they needed people who knew their way around and knew how to get things done. 248

CRAIG
249 And you both fit that brief perfectly. Audrey and Lois helped us fill our staff and make the right connections. 249

CRAIG opens the door to the lab.

DR. HOLCOMB
250 You're here! You must be Courtney 250
and you must be... Alice.

BETH
251 Is something wrong? 251

DR. HOLCOMB
252 No. You just reminded me of 252
someone. Daughter of a friend-of-a-friend.

VALDEZ
253 It's very nice to meet you, Doctor. 253

DR. HOLCOMB
254 Likewise. Shall we get started? We 254
have three experiences available: horseback riding, skydiving, and water skiing.

BETH
255 Hmm. Skydiving sounds interesting. 255

DR. HOLCOMB
256 Adventurous! I like it! Audrey, 256
would you please get the skydiving tapes ready?
(beat)
257 The first thing we'll do is give 257
you this chem. It has several functions. It's primarily to relax you so that full immersion is easier, and it also lowers your stress level. We hypothesize that part won't be necessary after someone has been inside a few times, but we're erring on the side of caution and not testing that hypothesis just yet.

VALDEZ
258 Of course. That makes sense. Safety 258
first.

DR. HOLCOMB
259 It's my top priority. And we've 259
made great strides. The number of... incidents has decreased significantly since we started.

CRAIG
260 I think we're close to going 260
public.

DR. HOLCOMB

261 I'd say we're closer to going public. 261

(beat)

262 If you're ready, Alice, I'll hook you to an IV. That will be how we deliver the chem, and we'll also ensure that you get enough fluids. We'll monitor your heart rate, oxygen saturation, blood pressure, and brain electrical activity. We anticipate that we won't need to be quite so elaborate in terms of monitoring as we refine the process, but for right now... well, safety first, as you said. 262

BETH

263 I'm ready. 263

DR. HOLCOMB

264 Wonderful. The pod is right over here. If you'll get in, Audrey will start connecting you to the monitors, and I'll administer the IV. 264

BETH

265 Of course. 265

BETH gets into the pod. DR. HOLCOMB inserts the IV. Monitors begin to beep.

DR. HOLCOMB

266 Alright, everything looks good. Your heart rate is steady, blood pressure is excellent, and sats are perfect. 266

(beat)

267 The chem takes effect very quickly. You're going to feel sleepy. Once you're in a REM state, the pod will begin your skydiving simulation immediately. Once it's complete, we'll gently wake you up. The experience itself lasts about eight minutes. 267

BETH

268 I'm already feeling it... I'll see you soon, Courtney. 268

<u>END OF ACT TWO</u>

ACT THREE

INT. VAULT 76

BETH is asleep. A figure enters the room to wake her.

VAULT-TEC DIRECTOR
269 Elizabeth, you overslept again. 269
(beat)
270 Wake up. You're already running late. 270

BETH stirs.

BETH
271 Ugh. Where am I? Wait... this looks like my... this can't be... am I back in the Vault? 271

VAULT-TEC DIRECTOR
272 "Back" in the Vault? Elizabeth, I know you like to fancy yourself a proper little spy, but you've never set foot outside this Vault and you won't until Reclamation Day. 272
(beat)
273 Were you drinking last night? If you've broken any rules I'll have to tell your father, and neither of us want that. 273

BETH sighs.

BETH
274 I wasn't drinking. I was just... I guess I was having a very... vivid dream. I thought I was outside the Vault. And had been for a couple of years. 274

VAULT-TEC DIRECTOR
275 That sounds like quite a dream. 275

BETH
276 It was. 276

VAULT-TEC DIRECTOR
277 It's time to step back into reality. You have training, and you know better than to leave them waiting. 277

BETH

278 Why do I have to do this? I hate 278
it! How does this even make me a
better intelligence operative?

VAULT-TEC DIRECTOR

279 We've been over this, Elizabeth. 279
Every operative has to leverage
their particular skills or assets.
In your case, that's youth and
attractiveness, and frankly, you
don't have much else going for you.

BETH

280 I don't even try to get any 280
information out of any of them! I
just go in, "indulge" them, pretend
to enjoy myself, and leave.

(beat)

281 I think the best part of that dream 281
was not having to do this anymore.
I feel like a prostitute.

VAULT-TEC DIRECTOR

282 If that's what it takes for you to 282
get into character, so be it.

(beat)

283 If you don't feel that you're cut 283
out for this program, Elizabeth, we
can go to the Overseer's office
right now and tell her that you
want to drop out. Unless you want
to tell your father first, of
course. I'm sure he wouldn't be
disappointed in you at all for
giving up.

BETH sighs.

BETH

284 You know I can't do that. 284

VAULT-TEC DIRECTOR

285 Then stop whining and focus. 285

(beat)

286 Look, you're not going to be able 286
to pick and choose who has the
information or the access that
you'll need to do this job out
there. The mission isn't going to
care that you're a lesbian. You may
not like it, but the people you
need to get information from are
usually going to be men.

BETH

287 I *hate* it... 287

VAULT-TEC DIRECTOR

288 We're all going to be walking out 288
into a hellscape when that Vault
door opens, and we're all going to
have to do things we hate, so you'd
better get used to it. Just
compartmentalize it like the rest
of us.

BETH

289 Fine. 289

VAULT-TEC DIRECTOR

290 And when we feel that your 290
performances have become...
convincing enough, this part of
your training can stop. So do a
good job.
(beat)
291 Your outfit is in the testing 291
chamber. Go. Now. And remember -
opsec is a big part of this
training. Nobody can know. Not your
parents, not the Overseer...
nobody.

BETH

292 Alright. 292

VAULT-TEC DIRECTOR

293 Excuse me? 293

BETH

294 I'm sorry, ma'am. Yes, ma'am. 294

VAULT-TEC DIRECTOR

295 After you're done, see me in my 295
office. We'll continue our one-on-
one training then.

BETH

(concerned, hesitant)
296 Y.. yes, ma'am. 296

BETH leaves.

An ASSISTANT enters.

ASSISTANT
297 This is a great little side hustle 297
you got going on here. You think
she's ever going to catch on?

VAULT-TEC DIRECTOR
298 She's so wrapped up in making daddy 298
happy that she'd never do anything
to screw that up.

ASSISTANT
299 You realize that "doddering old 299
professor" thing is a front, right?
I've seen him sparring in the gym
when he thinks nobody's watching.
You'd better hope that those
holotapes are enough to keep
everybody's mouths shut.

VAULT-TEC DIRECTOR
300 Your mouth is included in that, 300
too. You breathe a word of this to
anyone and Andrew Kirby will be the
least of your concerns.

ASSISTANT
301 Am I still on the schedule? 301

VAULT-TEC DIRECTOR
302 Thursday afternoon at 3. 302

ASSISTANT
303 Good. Have her wear that schoolgirl 303
getup. She hates it.

SFX: TRANSITION STING

INT. VAULT 76 HALLWAY

BETH is walking quickly down the hallway. She runs into someone walking the other way.

DR. TROIANI
304 Oof! 304

BETH
305 I'm so sorry! I'm such a klutz. Are 305
you alright?

DR. TROIANI
306 Yes, I'm fine. 306

BETH
(shocked)
307 Odessa?! 307

DR. TROIANI
308 What? 308

BETH
309 Odessa, what are you doing here? 309

DR. TROIANI
(confused)
310 I'm sorry, are you alright? Who's 310
Odessa?

BETH sighs.

BETH
311 I guess I haven't fully recovered 311
from that dream. I'm sorry.

DR. TROIANI
312 Dream? 312

BETH
313 I had a very vivid dream last 313
night. It felt absolutely real, and
I... can't shake it. Odessa was
someone from that dream, and she
looked exactly like you.

DR. TROIANI
314 I understand. Dreams can have that 314
effect on people. I'm Emily. Emily
Troiani. You're Andrew's daughter,
right? Elizabeth?

BETH
315 That's right. But most people call 315
me Beth. If they're being nice to
me, at least...

DR. TROIANI
316 Are people being unkind to you? 316

BETH
317 Constantly. They make fun of me all 317
the time. Because I'm tall, because
I'm awkward, because of the way I
talk, because I'm ugly.

DR. TROIANI
318 You're *not* ugly, Beth. And 318
everyone's awkward at your age,
including the people who are being
cruel to you.
(beat)
319 Wait. Odessa Valdez? 319

BETH
(brightly)
320 Yes! That was her name! Is she... 320
someone who lives in the Vault and
my brain just mixed her up with
you?

DR. TROIANI
321 No... I don't know why I know that 321
name. It doesn't...

SFX: TRANSITION STING

INT. CLASSROOM

BETH is being teased by classmates.

CLASSMATE 1
322 Come on, say something, Betty. I 322
want to hear that stupid accent.

CLASSMATE 2
323 Why does she even talk like that? 323

CLASSMATE 1
324 Because she's "daddy's little 324
girl," that's why. It's pathetic.

CLASSMATE 2
325 *She's* pathetic. That ugly orange 325
hair is probably fake, too.

CLASSMATE 1
326 Talk! 326

CLASSMATE 2
327 Yeah, talk! 327

CASEY enters.

CASEY
328 Sorry I'm late. 328
(beat)
329 What's going on in here? Where's 329
Mr. Barnes?

CLASSMATE 1
330 We're trying to be friendly, and 330
"daddy issues" here won't even talk
to us.

CLASSMATE 2
331 She's such a snob. Maybe that's why 331
she has that fake accent.

BETH
332 It's not fake! 332

CASEY
333 Knock it off! She clearly isn't 333
feeling well and you're being
idiots.

CLASSMATE 1
334 We didn't mean anything by it, we 334
were just having fun, you know?

CASEY
335 Bullying isn't fun. I think I heard 335
the word "pathetic" being thrown
around before I walked in here, and
that's a much better word for what
you're doing.

CLASSMATE 2
(chastened)
336 Sorry, Casey, won't happen again. 336

CASEY
337 No, it won't. 337
(beat)
338 Beth, why don't we walk down to the 338
infirmary so the nurse can take a
look at you?

BETH
(shaking)
339 O...okay. 339

BETH and Casey leave and close the door behind them.

CASEY
340 Are you okay? 340

BETH
341 You didn't have to do that. 341

CASEY

342 Yes, I did. You were about to cry, and I didn't want them to have the satisfaction of seeing that. But it's just us here now, so if you still need to, let it out. It might make you feel better. 342

BETH begins to cry.

BETH

343 Why are you being so nice to me? You never really talked to me before. I assumed you didn't know I existed. 343

CASEY

344 I guess I was kind of... intimidated by you, and never had the courage to say hi. 344

BETH

345 Intimidated? By me? You're the prettiest girl in the Vault, you're smart and elegant, and graceful... everyone loves you. I'm like a baby giraffe on ice skates. 345

CASEY laughs.

CASEY

346 Is that how you see yourself? Well let me tell you what I see. A smart, kind, friendly girl who always shows grace even when people aren't being gracious to her. And you're tall, beautiful... your hair is amazing. 346

BETH

347 They always make fun of my hair. 347

CASEY

348 They're intimidated by you, too. So they're trying to tear you down. 348

(beat)

349 Look, I know you're not sick, I just had to figure out a way to get you out of there. Want to skip class and hang out? I have some snacks I can grab from my room, and I know a few places where nobody will find us. 349

BETH
350 That... that sounds really nice, 350
Casey. Do you really mean it?

CASEY
351 Of course I mean it, Beth. Come on, 351
let's get moving before anybody
wanders down this hallway.

SFX: TRANSITION STING

INT. VAULT 76 HALLWAY

BETH
352 Whoa, what was that? I thought I 352
was with Casey just now? Am I
hallucinating?

DR. TROIANI
353 Beth, I think I know what's 353
happening. You weren't dreaming.
You're dreaming now. Kind of.

BETH
354 What do you mean? 354

DR. TROIANI
355 I know this is difficult, because 355
you feel like you're standing in
Vault 76, and you're what, 16 right
now?

BETH
356 I think so. I met Casey when I was 356
16, and she was 14. We spent that
whole day together, just chatting.
It was the day we became friends.

DR. TROIANI
357 Beth, listen to me. You need to be 357
very careful. You seem to be in
what we called a Hofstadter-Moebius
loop. Basically, the combination of
your mind and the technology that's
being used to present the data on
the memory holotapes I created are
operating in conflict, and as a
result you're... stuck here. Inside
your mind.

BETH
358 This is madness. It isn't real, I 358
must be... sick.
(MORE)

BETH (CONT'D)
I don't know who you are, but it's cruel to play with someone like this when they're unwell.

DR. TROIANI
359 That's the loop talking, Beth. It's 359
not... malevolent, but it *will* try to convince you to stay here, to... not wake up. You'll die within 15 minutes, based on what we've seen, but thanks to the way time dilation works in dreams, it can seem like a lot longer than that. A full life, playing out exactly how you always hoped it would.
(beat)
360 That's a very enticing proposition, 360
especially in the moment, but I need you to fight it.

BETH
361 You mean, I could... be with Casey? 361
She wouldn't say no when I asked her to stay with me?

DR. TROIANI
362 Beth, you cannot think that way. 362
This isn't real. The only reality if you do that is that you'll be dead.
(beat)
363 I have an idea. I'm going to start 363
feeding you project information in the background. Scientific data and research material - facts. That may stem the tide while we figure out how to wake you up.

BETH
364 Why can't the people on the outside 364
do that?

DR. TROIANI
365 We learned the hard way that trying 365
to do that would kill you immediately. It's too much of a neurological shock.
(beat)
366 Tell me about Odessa. It's 366
fascinating that I'm appearing to you as her and not myself. You must really trust her.

BETH

367 Why do you say that? 367

DR. TROIANI

368 Because of the danger inherent in doing this, we set things up so that a construct, based on me, would serve as a kind of guide. Doing exactly what I'm doing now. It seems that my physical form was replaced by Odessa's in your simulation. You must have a powerful connection to override the defaults like that. 368

BETH

369 We do. It's still early days, but... well, she's very special to me. And I think I am to her, too. 369

DR. TROIANI

370 What's she like? I mean, other than "hot." 370

BETH laughs.

BETH

371 Well, she's smart, funny, loyal, caring... a little stubborn at times, but in a good way. And brave. She's... assertive - she stands up for herself. 371

DR. TROIANI

372 Maybe I'll get to meet her someday. What year is it? Out there? Try to concentrate, I know it's hard. You feel like you're 16 right now, which was in... 372

BETH

373 2097. I... think it's 2104 "out there." 373

DR. TROIANI

374 I don't even know why I'm asking this, since I'm a construct and not actually me, but... do you know if I'm... alive in 2104? 374

BETH

375 I don't. I'm sorry. 375

DR. TROIANI

376 It's alright. Better than a flat 376
"no, you're dead."
(beat)
377 The data transfer seems to be 377
happening. I don't know if you'll
retain any of it, but it's mostly
just to keep you grounded.

BETH

378 I *did* do this to learn more about 378
the projects, so it would be nice
to...

SFX: TRANSITION STING

INT. DINING ROOM

BETH and VALDEZ are eating dinner.

VALDEZ

379 It would be nice to what? 379

BETH

380 Odessa? 380

VALDEZ

381 Um, yes? Are you okay? You went... 381
vacant there for a second. Do you
want to take a break? I know
wedding planning can be
overwhelming.

BETH

382 Yes... it is, but it's worth it. 382
Even in the Wasteland.

VALDEZ laughs.

VALDEZ

383 I know Morgantown isn't exactly 383
London or L.A., but I wouldn't call
it a wasteland. Besides, it's nice
to be around family.
(beat)
384 Don't forget, mom and dad are going 384
to fly in on Thursday. Mom's
bringing her dress so we can take
it to your mom's tailor.

BETH

(hesistant)
385 Right... Thursday. 385

VALDEZ

386 Do you want to take a break and watch a movie or something? The centerpieces aren't going anywhere, and we don't have to pick a photographer tonight. 386

BETH

387 Can I just... live in this moment forever, Doctor? 387

VALDEZ

388 Who are you talking to? I mean, it's sexy when you call me "doctor," but it feels like you're talking to someone else. 388

BETH

389 This isn't real. 389

VALDEZ

390 It's as real as you want it to be. Don't you want to be with me? 390

BETH

391 The real Odessa wouldn't do this. She would want me to fight. 391

VALDEZ's voice changes. She is overtly a construct of the AI now.

FALSE VALDEZ

392 All we want is for you to be happy, in your final moments. You're past the point of no return. No one has recovered when they've been in the loop this long. 392

DR. TROIANI appears.

BETH

393 Doctor! You're back! 393

DR. TROIANI

394 Beth! Don't listen to it. It's trying to get you to give up and you *cannot do that*. You still have a chance. You need to find your North Star. 394

BETH

395 My North Star? Dr. Flagler talked about that, but he couldn't remember what it meant! 395

DR. TROIANI

396 It was shorthand that Tony and I came up with. As we spoke with people who'd been inside, it became clear that remaining centered was vitally important. Otherwise, it was too easy to get lost. We correlated EEG data with their descriptions of the experience. It seems to be very similar to a dream, though, which made getting those descriptions difficult in some case. 396

BETH

397 It *is* very dreamlike. It feels so real when you're in the moment. 397

DR. TROIANI

398 People have always used the North Star for navigation, so it was the kind of symbol people could remember, even inside. We started telling people to figure out what theirs was, and to use that to guide them home. 398

BETH

399 Their *querencia...* 399

SFX: TRANSITION STING

CLASSMATE 3

400 Hey, Beth! Come on! You're going to be late for the exam! 400

BETH

401 Er... what exam? 401

CLASSMATE 3

402 Symbolic Logic! 402

BETH

403 Symbolic Logic? I never took symbolic logic... 403

CLASSMATE 3

404 It may seem that way since you've never gone to class, but the exam is today and you need to stop fooling around! Why are you hiding behind that plant? 404

BETH
405 Oh, god... 405
(beat)
406 I'm naked. Why am I naked? Okay, Beth, just focus and think... I need to figure out how to get back to my room and get my Vault suit, but there are so many people around... 406
(beat)
407 But I need to get to class to take that exam! I didn't even know there *was* a symbolic logic class, much less that I was enrolled in one! 407

CLASSMATE 3
408 Beth, if you don't pass this exam, you're going to fail the whole year! You won't graduate! 408

BETH
409 I don't know what to do... at least I have this plant to hide behind until everyone goes away, then I can come up with a plan. 409

SFX: Zap as the plant disappears.

BETH (CONT'D)
410 Why did it disappear?! Oh, no... maybe nobody can see me... 410

CLASSMATE 3
411 Everybody, look! Beth's not wearing any clothes! 411

SFX: Group laughter

SFX: TRANSITION STING

BETH
412 What? Where am I? It's like a... white void. At least I'm wearing clothes again... 412

VALDEZ
(distant)
413 Beth! Can you hear me? 413

BETH
414 Odessa! Is that really you, or another... construct? 414

VALDEZ

415 Beth, if you can hear me, you need 415
to wake up! There's not much time!
Please! Just... just come back to
me, okay?

VALDEZ's voice fades away.

A false VALDEZ appears. Her voice is like VALDEZ's but distorted.

FALSE VALDEZ

416 We have all the time in the world. 416
We can... grow old together. Have
children.

BETH

417 But this isn't real... 417

FALSE VALDEZ

418 Do you want Casey to be part of our 418
family? It can be any Casey you
want. Sweet teenage Vault Casey,
sexy Brotherhood Initiate Casey...
I can be anything you want, too.

BETH

419 Stop, please... 419

FALSE AMANDA

420 What about me? 420

BETH

421 Amanda?! 421

FALSE AMANDA

422 You made me run away out there, but 422
here? We can fix all the mistakes
we made. We can start over. Think
about the last thing I said to you -
"I love you." You know that's true.
And you know you still love me,
too.

FALSE VALDEZ

423 No one can hurt you here. All those 423
Vault-Tec people who did? They'll
finally get the comeuppance they
never got out there. You can kill
them in all the different ways
you've thought about over the
years.
(beat)
(MORE)

FALSE VALDEZ (CONT'D)

424 You can feel it - your mind is adapting, and the machine is helping you do it. We can live out a full life together, Beth. Isn't that what you want? *That* Odessa is better off without you anyway. You keep putting her in danger, just by being you. And you know you're going to break her heart. You'll drive her into someone else's arms, just like Amanda. 424

FALSE AMANDA

425 Stay with us, Princess. Be my good girl again. 425

SFX: Pulsing light sound

BETH

426 What is that noise? 426

FALSE VALDEZ

427 A... quirk of the machine. Ignore it. 427

BETH

428 And that light... 428

FALSE VALDEZ

429 Ignore it! 429

The real VALDEZ's voice breaks through.

VALDEZ

430 Beth! 430

BETH

431 Odessa! I don't think you can hear me, but there's a light here. Your voice seems to be... emanating from it. 431

FALSE VALDEZ

432 Have you never heard of "walking into the light?" It's the oldest cliché in the book! If you do that, you're going to die. Immediately. 432

BETH

433 I think I understand! The light is another construct, and Odessa's voice... she's my North Star! The machine *is* helping me - that may be the way out! 433

(MORE)

BETH (CONT'D)

(beat)

434 I have to take this chance... I can't live out a lie in here. I'd rather that it just... end. 434

FALSE VALDEZ

435 She'll never love you! You're too broken! It's only a matter of time before she leaves you! 435

BETH

436 I have to take that chance, too. 436

A tone can be heard.

BETH (CONT'D)

437 What's *that* sound? It's new... 437

FALSE VALDEZ

438 You're dying. This is your last chance. Your pineal gland has begun biosynthesis of N,N-Dimethyltryptamine. You're not going to wake up, but we can make your last few seconds feel like decades. Like *centuries* if you want. Your mind wants you to be happy. *I* want you to be happy. Just... give in and let it happen. 438

BETH

439 I'm... dying? 439

FALSE VALDEZ

440 Yes. And you know I'm telling you the truth. 440

BETH sighs.

BETH

441 I do. I can feel it. At the end, it's just a matter of... inevitability, so the only true decision is how to behave. 441

FALSE VALDEZ's voice returns to normal.

FALSE VALDEZ

442 Come here. We have so many years to look forward to together. I love you, Beth. 442

VALDEZ's voice breaks through again. She is distraught.

VALDEZ

443 Beth! Wake up! Please, wake up! You can't leave me now! I'm sorry I was so hard on you, I'm just... afraid of having my heart broken again. But the only thing I'm afraid of right now is losing you! Just wake up! 443

FALSE VALDEZ's voice returns to its distorted tone.

FALSE VALDEZ

444 No! 444

BETH

445 Yes! I have to follow my North Star! It's the only way I can truly find my way home. 445

BETH runs toward the light.

SFX: Loud portal sound.

Season One
Part Three: The Book of Elizabeth

Episode 8:
"The Power Confided to Me"

by

D.K. Trueno

"THE POWER CONFIDED TO ME"

INT. MACALLAN CLUB VISIONTRON LAB

BETH is in a Visiontron, surrounded by VALDEZ, CRAIG, and DR. HOLCOMB.

SFX: BEEPING MEDICAL MONITORS

DR. HOLCOMB

1 The chem takes effect very quickly. 1
You're going to feel sleepy. Once you're in a REM state, the pod will begin your skydiving simulation immediately. Once it's complete, we'll gently wake you up. The experience itself lasts about eight minutes.

BETH

2 I'm already feeling it... I'll see 2
you soon, Courtney.

VALDEZ

3 I'll see you when you wake up. 3

CRAIG

4 Just relax and have fun, Alice. I'm 4
confident that this experience will convince you that this technology alone is worth the price of your investment.

VALDEZ and DR. HOLCOMB wait for the simulation to begin.

DR. HOLCOMB

5 She's in REM, and everything seems 5
to be going well. Brain activity is a little high, but well within tolerances. It could just be an indication of an active mind, or a vivid dreamer.

VALDEZ

6 She's a sound sleeper, that much I 6
know. Sometimes I feel like I should put a mirror under her nose to make sure she's still breathing.

DR. HOLCOMB laughs.

DR. HOLCOMB

7 Hmm. 7

VALDEZ
8 What is it? 8

DR. HOLCOMB
9 Brain activity is increasing. 9

VALDEZ
10 Is that a problem? 10

DR. HOLCOMB
(masking concern)
11 No. She most likely just got to the exciting part of the simulation. 11
(beat)
12 Heart rate is increasing as well, but this is a skydiving simulator so that's to be expected. 12

VALDEZ
(concerned)
13 Right... 13

DR. HOLCOMB
14 So, how much has Craig told you about all of this? 14

VALDEZ
15 Just the broad strokes. 15

DR. HOLCOMB
16 Well, if you end up coming aboard formally there's a *lot* to explore beyond that. Most of it is pretty opaque to someone who's not a scientist, but sometimes I can't help but geek out about it. 16

VALDEZ
17 Oh, I don't mind that kind of thing at all. Even as a... non-scientist, that level of detail has always fascinated me. 17

DR. HOLCOMB
18 If your eyes start rolling back into your head while we're discussing it I'll know I've gone a bit too far. 18

VALDEZ laughs.

An alarm sounds.

VALDEZ
(urgently)
19 What's happening? 19

DR. HOLCOMB urgently types at a keyboard.

CRAIG
20 Doctor? 20

DR. HOLCOMB
21 Brain activity and heart rate are 21
spiking. Blood pressure, too.
Dammit!

VALDEZ
22 Can we pull her out? 22

DR. HOLCOMB
23 No. Once a subject is inside the 23
simulation forcibly bringing them
out of it is too much of a
neurological shock. It's like...
the old wives tale about waking up
a sleepwalker, except... well, this
isn't an old wives tale. It will
kill them.

VALDEZ
24 What can we do? 24

DR. HOLCOMB
25 There's... nothing we can do. At 25
this point, it's all up to them.

VALDEZ
26 "All up to them?" What do you mean? 26

DR. HOLCOMB
27 They have to bring themselves out 27
of the simulation. The problem is
that the person's mind knows
something's gone wrong, and it
tries to compensate. That creates a
conflict with the pod's
programming, and results in what's
called a Hofstadter-Moebius loop.

VALDEZ
28 A Hofstadter-Moebius loop is only 28
supposed to happen within an
artificial intelligence, not in
humans.

DR. HOLCOMB

29 I know. The best I've been able to 29
come up with is that it's the
specific combination of *this*
technology and the human mind.

(beat)

30 Wait. I thought you said you 30
weren't a scientist?

VALDEZ

31 I'm not. I just... read a lot. 31

DR. HOLCOMB

32 H. Moebius loops are pretty 32
arcane... they're not the kind of
thing you'd read about in Tesla
Science Magazine.

VALDEZ

33 We have more important things to 33
worry about than what's on my
bookshelf. There has to be
something we can do.

DR. HOLCOMB

34 I've hypothesized that external 34
stimuli may help because they
introduce more "reality" for the
subject to hold onto.

VALDEZ

35 I'm willing to try anything. 35

DR. HOLCOMB

36 I'm going to open the pod. I don't 36
want to risk overstimulating her
and exacerbating things, so let's
start by having you hold her hand.

VALDEZ

37 Alright. 37

DR. HOLCOMB opens the pod. VALDEZ pulls a chair over and sits, taking BETH's hand.

DR. HOLCOMB

38 Perfect. Just hold her hand like 38
you would when you're together at
home, or walking together.

CRAIG

39 Is there anything I can do? 39

DR. HOLCOMB

40 Yes. We'll need plenty of boiled 40
water and clean towels - preferably
warm ones.

CRAIG

41 Boiled water and warm towels? What 41
are--

DR. HOLCOMB

(interrupting)

42 Please, Craig, time is of the 42
essence here.

CRAIG

43 Of course. I'll get right on it. 43

CRAIG leaves.

VALDEZ

44 I'm also a little curious about how 44
boiled water and warm towels are
going to help.

DR. HOLCOMB

45 They won't. I just wanted to get 45
him out of our hair. Him being here
would just stress us out, and we
need to focus. If she comes out of
this we'll need to be very careful
with her.

VALDEZ

46 You mean "when" she comes out of 46
this.

DR. HOLCOMB

47 Courtney, I don't want to sugarcoat 47
this. The more time that she spends
in the loop, the less likely it is
that she's going to come out of it.

(beat)

48 But the good news is that holding 48
her hand seemed to have an impact.
Her brain activity, heart rate, and
blood pressure all decreased a bit.

VALDEZ

(trying to stay calm)

49 How... how much time does she have? 49

DR. HOLCOMB

50 It's different for everyone, but... 50
it's not long.

VALDEZ
(growing more upset)
51 Beth! Can you hear me? 51
(beat)
52 Anything? 52

DR. HOLCOMB
53 There does appear to have been a 53
reaction. Try talking to her again.

VALDEZ
54 Beth, if you can hear me, you need 54
to wake up! There's not much time!
Please! Just... just come back to
me, okay?

DR. HOLCOMB
55 Why did you call her "Beth?" 55

VALDEZ
56 It's... um... it's her middle name. 56

DR. HOLCOMB
(suspicious)
57 I see... 57
(beat)
58 Just keep holding her hand for now. 58
She's stable, but we're still
working with a limited amount of
time.
(beat)
59 Tell me about her. What's she like? 59

VALDEZ
60 Um... well, she's passionate. 60
Loyal. Smarter than she gives
herself credit for. And she's
tough. She had... a lot of trauma
growing up. It's been hard for her
at times.

DR. HOLCOMB
61 But now she has you. 61

VALDEZ
(wistfully)
62 Yeah. 62

DR. HOLCOMB
63 What's wrong? 63

VALDEZ
64 I... I feel like I just found her, 64
and now I'm afraid that I'm going
to lose her.

DR. HOLCOMB
65 Try not to think like that. Just be 65
here for her. I know this probably
isn't something a scientist should
say, and I certainly don't have any
evidence to back it up, but... I
think it helps.

VALDEZ
66 I hope so. 66

An alarm sounds.

VALDEZ (CONT'D)
(urgently)
67 Beth! 67

DR. HOLCOMB
68 There was another spike in brain 68
activity. That's what triggered the
alarm. Dammit!

VALDEZ
69 What is it?! What's going on?! 69

DR. HOLCOMB
70 It appears that her body has begun 70
biosynthesis of DMT.

VALDEZ
71 N,N-Dimethyltryptamine?! 71

DR. HOLCOMB
(surprised)
72 Er, yes. And if you know what DMT 72
is, you understand the
implications.

VALDEZ
(choking up)
73 She's dying. 73

DR. HOLCOMB
74 I've never seen a loop behave this 74
aggressively. I'm... I'm sorry. I
think you should... say your
goodbyes.

VALDEZ
75 I'm not ready to say goodbye! 75

DR. HOLCOMB
76 I know. We never are. But you're 76
going to regret it if you don't.

VALDEZ
77 The only thing I'll regret is if I 77
stop fighting.

DR. HOLCOMB
78 Then fight. And I hope you win. 78

VALDEZ
79 Beth! Wake up! Please, wake up! You 79
can't leave me now! I'm sorry I was
so hard on you, I'm just... afraid
of having my heart broken again.
But the only thing I'm afraid of
right now is losing you! Just wake
up!

DR. HOLCOMB
80 This is new... 80

VALDEZ
81 What's happening?! 81

DR. HOLCOMB
82 Her brain activity spiked again, a 82
few seconds after you stopped
talking. That's usually the
brain's... last gasp before the
subject dies. But...

VALDEZ
83 But she's still alive. 83

DR. HOLCOMB
84 Not only that, her vital signs are 84
returning to normal. Well, normal-
ish. There are still some spikes,
but they're not as acute as what we
were seeing when things went
sideways.

VALDEZ
85 Does that mean she's going to wake 85
up?!

DR. HOLCOMB
86 I... I don't know. This is all new 86
ground for me.
(MORE)

DR. HOLCOMB (CONT'D)

I've never seen someone wake up when they were that far gone.

(beat)

87 Courtney, you need to... prepare 87
yourself. *If* she wakes up, there's a strong possibility of neurological damage. It could be temporary, it could be permanent; it could be minor, it could be serious. Or maybe there won't be any damage at all. But you need to be prepared for the possibility that there is. Okay?

VALDEZ

88 I'm not going to give up on her, no 88
matter what.

DR. HOLCOMB

89 Good. She's going to need you. 89

VALDEZ

90 When will we... know? 90

DR. HOLCOMB

91 I'm not sure. I'm sorry. 91

CRAIG returns, pushing a cart.

CRAIG

92 I hope this is enough water. I had 92
Henry boil as much as I could transport.

DR. HOLCOMB

93 Thank you, Craig. 93

CRAIG

94 What's our status? 94

DR. HOLCOMB

95 We're not sure. Miss Halstead 95
passed the point of no return - or what we thought was the point of no return, at least - but she's still with us. Unconscious, but still with us nonetheless. Her vital signs are reasonably close to normal.

CRAIG

96 I take it we won't know anything 96
further until she wakes up?

DR. HOLCOMB

97 *If* she wakes up. I don't want to make any assumptions right now. I'm sorry, Courtney. 97

VALDEZ

(holding it together)

98 I... understand, Doctor. 98

DR. HOLCOMB

99 May I have one of those towels, please? 99

CRAIG

100 Of course. 100

CRAIG hands the towels to DR. HOLCOMB.

DR. HOLCOMB

101 Courtney, please take this and place it under Alice's head and neck. 101

VALDEZ takes the towel and puts it under BETH's head as instructed.

After a few moments BETH stirs.

VALDEZ

102 Dr. Holcomb! Come here! I think she's waking up! 102

BETH groans.

BETH

103 Am I dead? Oh, god, my head... there shouldn't be headaches like this in the afterlife... 103

VALDEZ fails to stifle a chuckle.

VALDEZ

104 You're not dead. 104

(beat)

105 Doctor, can you give her something for the pain? 105

DR. HOLCOMB

106 Yes, I'll give her an analgesic. That should take care of her headache and allow her to relax. Her brain is still coming down from that spike. 106

(beat)

(MORE)

DR. HOLCOMB (CONT'D)
107 Craig, can you give us the room? I 107
want to limit the number of voices
she hears until we can ascertain
the level of neurological trauma
she's suffered.

CRAIG
108 Uh, sure... is that why she's 108
speaking in an English accent?
Neurological trauma?

DR. HOLCOMB
109 It must be. Trauma can manifest 109
itself in a variety of different
ways.
(beat)
110 I'll come get you when I have an 110
update. But the fact that she woke
up at all is highly encouraging.

CRAIG
111 Did you record the data from the 111
session?

DR. HOLCOMB
112 I did. And it may provide insight 112
on how we can bring people back if
they get stuck in a loop.

CRAIG
113 I hope that's the case. Thank you, 113
Doctor. We'll talk later.

CRAIG leaves and closes the door.

DR. HOLCOMB
114 Beth, I'm going to give you 114
something to make you feel better,
okay?

BETH
(strained)
115 Okay. Thank you. 115

DR. HOLCOMB gives Beth a chem through her IV.

DR. HOLCOMB
116 That should do it... 116
(beat)
117 Alright. I know who she is, but who 117
are you?

VALDEZ
118 Excuse me? 118

DR. HOLCOMB

119 I thought I recognized her from the 119
Vault, and then you called her
"Beth" and not "Alice." But hearing
her drop the American accent is
what made it click.
(beat)
120 So. Who are *you* and what are you 120
and Beth Kirby doing here?

VALDEZ

121 I... um... 121

DR. HOLCOMB

122 Don't worry. I'm not going to tell 122
Craig. At least, not necessarily.
Just... tell me the truth and we'll
go from there. But if you're just a
couple of rival gang members
looking to steal this tech I'm
going to be very disappointed.

VALDEZ

123 We're not. 123

DR. HOLCOMB

124 I'm sure you'll understand that I 124
can't just take you at your word.

VALDEZ

125 Of course. I think we'll be able to 125
prove it to you, but... not here.

DR. HOLCOMB

126 Why don't we start with who you 126
really are?

VALDEZ

127 My name is Odessa. Odessa Valdez. 127

DR. HOLCOMB

128 Alright, Odessa, I don't remember 128
you from the Vault, and if you were
part of Andrew's cloak-and-dagger
diplomacy program I think I would.

VALDEZ

129 I wasn't in Vault 76. I'm... from 129
California.

DR. HOLCOMB

130 California? That's... quite a hike. 130
(beat)
(MORE)

DR. HOLCOMB (CONT'D)

131 Well, "California Girl," if you're working with *Beth* Kirby, that means you're working with Andrew. Unless... 131

VALDEZ

132 No, no, he's fine. And yes, I'm working with them as well. Mr. Kirby is semi-retired, but, well, he seems to forget that sometimes. 132

DR. HOLCOMB laughs.

DR. HOLCOMB

133 That sounds like him. I'm sure he's driving poor Elise crazy. 133

VALDEZ

134 Oh, she's holding her own. She's... quite formidable herself. 134

DR. HOLCOMB

135 She is. Especially if... wait, this is none of my business, but are you and Beth... together? Or is that just part of your cover? 135

VALDEZ

136 We are together, yeah. 136

DR. HOLCOMB sighs.

DR. HOLCOMB

137 Alright, you two being here changes everything. As far as any of us knew, this was still a secret, and that allowed me to continue to refine the technology to make it safe. 137

(beat)

138 Craig is a decent guy, at least as far as mob bosses go. But I don't think he understands just how exposed he's going to be once word gets out. 138

VALDEZ

139 Does he know about Project Mind's Eye? 139

DR. HOLCOMB

140 Wow, you *are* good. No, at least not directly. 140

(MORE)

DR. HOLCOMB (CONT'D)
He knew there were other labs, but not specifics on that project. He assumed that those labs were just associated with *this* tech, and I let him operate under that assumption.

VALDEZ
141 It sounds like we all need to have 141
a long talk about this. Can you... get away long enough to do that?

DR. HOLCOMB
142 I think I can sell Craig on the 142
idea that I should accompany you and Beth home so that I can keep an eye on her. He really is concerned about her; that's not an act.

VALDEZ
143 Beth has a medical bay at her 143
place. It's really just there so she can get patched up if she gets injured in a fight or gets sick, but it should do.

DR. HOLCOMB
144 Perfect. We'll need to keep a close 144
eye on her. And I'll need a copy of any diagnostic data we get; I don't mean to sound cold, but it will be very helpful for my research.

VALDEZ
145 I'm a scientist. I understand the 145
value of data.

DR. HOLCOMB
146 Ah, I thought that might be the 146
case. I feel like we'll have a lot to talk about, Miss Valdez.
(beat)
147 Beth should be stable enough to 147
make the trip soon. It will be... an adventure, but as long as we keep her pointed in the right direction we should be fine. Wait here and I'll go talk to Craig. I'll be back in a few minutes.

END OF ACT ONE

ACT TWO

INT. BETH'S RESIDENCE, MEDICAL BAY

SFX: MEDICAL EQUIPMENT

BETH stirs.

VALDEZ
148 Hey, sleepy-head. How are you feeling? 148

BETH
149 I... I'm not sure. 149

VALDEZ
150 Just try to relax. I'm here and I'm not going anywhere. You had a quiet night. 150

DR. HOLCOMB
151 And that's very encouraging. I'm going to leave some chems with you, along with instructions on when and how to use them, if you need to. Everything from analgesics to antipsychotics and anti-seizure medications. 151

VALDEZ
(concerned)
152 Do you expect seizures? 152

DR. HOLCOMB
153 I don't *expect* them, especially given the improvement we've already seen, but I want you to be prepared in case they do happen. 153

VALDEZ
154 I understand. 154

DR. HOLCOMB
155 Everything you need is on this holotape. I recommend reviewing it as soon as you can. 155

VALDEZ
156 I will. Thank you. 156

DR. HOLCOMB
157 With that, I have to get back to the club. Craig is, to use a clinical term, "freaking out." 157

VALDEZ
158 He should be. Perhaps this will give him pause before he moves forward with providing this... service publicly. 158

DR. HOLCOMB
159 I hope it does. I've been trying to get him to slow down, but both he and his sister are stubborn. I think it's the Scot in them. 159

BETH
160 Is our cover still intact? 160

DR. HOLCOMB
161 It is. He was suspicious; very suspicious, in fact. But you were quick on your feet, Odessa, and I think I convinced him that it was all easily explained. 161

VALDEZ
162 Thank you. You have our contact frequencies, right? 162

DR. HOLCOMB
163 Yes, including the secure comms channel. 163

VALDEZ
164 Great. We'll keep you updated. 164

DR. HOLCOMB
165 And I'll do the same. Goodbye for now. 165
(beat)
166 Try to get some sleep, Odessa. 166

VALDEZ
167 I will. 167

BETH
168 Goodbye, Dr. Holcomb. And thank you. 168

DR. HOLCOMB leaves.

VALDEZ

169 Your vital signs look good. Can you 169
talk to me about what you're
experiencing right now? You said
you weren't sure how you felt, and
that's... concerning.

BETH

170 It's difficult to explain. 170
There's... noise in my brain, but I
don't know how to describe it. It
doesn't correspond with any of my
senses, it's just... there.

VALDEZ

171 Does it seem to be getting better? 171
Or worse?

BETH

172 I don't know what the baseline 172
should be. It's as though I've...
always felt this way.
(beat)
173 But I do appreciate you staying 173
here with me, Doctor.

VALDEZ

(concerned)
174 Um... let's go through some 174
cognitive exercises, to see where
you are.

BETH

(mildly petulant)
175 Do we have to? 175

VALDEZ

176 Yes. We have to. 176
(beat)
177 Can you tell me your full name? 177

BETH

178 Elizabeth Laurel Kirby. 178

VALDEZ

179 And when were you born? 179

BETH

180 21st April, 2081. 180

VALDEZ

181 And that makes you how old? 181

BETH
182 I'm twenty-three, Odessa. You're 182
still a cradle-robber.

VALDEZ laughs.

VALDEZ
183 Well, your sense of humor is still 183
intact. And six years isn't *that*
big of an age difference.

BETH
184 Can I ask you something? Something 184
serious? Am I... going to end up
like Dr. Flagler?

VALDEZ
(insistent)
185 No. You're going to get better. 185

BETH
(frustrated)
186 I just... can't bear the thought of 186
being a burden. To you or to anyone
else.

VALDEZ
187 You're not going to be a burden. 187
Not to me, and not to any of the
other people who care about you.

BETH
188 But what if I don't get better?! 188

VALDEZ
189 Then we'll get through it. 189
Together.

BETH
190 I'm sorry. I'm sorry I'm such a 190
mess. You didn't sign up for this.

VALDEZ
191 It's okay. Do you want something to 191
help you sleep?

BETH
192 No. If I sleep, I might dream. 192

VALDEZ

193 Did you have nightmares last night? Dr. Holcomb said that the chem she gave you to sleep would put you into deep sleep so you wouldn't dream at all. 193

BETH

194 Not last night, at least not that I remember. But I had them before this. Vivid ones. Reliving everything that happened in the Vault. Everything that was... done to me. Over and over. And when I was inside my head, I had to relive it again, but it felt much more... real than even the worst nightmare. 194

(beat)

195 I'm just scared that's going to be how it is moving forward. Same nightmares, but even worse. 195

VALDEZ

196 Do you want to talk about it? What happened while you were connected to the machine, I mean. 196

BETH

197 I don't know if I can put all of it into words, at least not just yet. But you were there. And beyond that, you were the reason I was able to wake up. 197

VALDEZ

198 What do you mean? How was I "there?" 198

BETH

199 The machine was trying to get me to stay. To not wake up. It made it sound not only like an enticing option, but the only option. 199

(beat)

200 It told me I was dying, and that I could spend what felt like a lifetime with you, if I'd just give in. It said something about a chemical that my body was producing... I don't remember much about that, but it sounded convincing. 200

VALDEZ sighs.

VALDEZ

201 It was telling you the truth. Dr. 201
Holcomb said that your body was producing a chemical called DMT, and that's something that can happen in a person's... final moments. It's the body's way of taking the terror out of what's happening, of... of the end.

BETH

202 But it wasn't the end. I don't know 202
if it was a creation of the machine that... rebelled against what it was trying to do or just my own mind fighting back, but I heard your voice. The real you, not a false Odessa that was trying to... ease me into the grave.
(beat)
203 What is it? Are you alright? 203

VALDEZ

(shaken)
204 You did hear me... 204

BETH

205 It was you? 205

VALDEZ

206 Dr. Holcomb suggested that I try 206
talking to you. She wasn't sure if you'd even be able to hear me, but at that point we were out of options and I... I wasn't ready to say goodbye.

BETH

207 Did you mean what you said? 207

VALDEZ

208 Every word of it. 208

BETH

209 You really are my North Star. You 209
guided me back to you. You guided me home. Odessa, I...
(beat)
210 I'm sorry. I'm kind of... emotional 210
right now. I'm not normally like this.

VALDEZ

211 It's alright. Dr. Holcomb said that you might experience mood swings and unusually strong emotions. We just need to take things easy for a little while, and you need to rest. 211

BETH

212 Can you radio my parents? They need to know what's happened. 212

VALDEZ

213 I did that while you were sleeping. And I told them that you're going to be okay. 213

BETH

214 Fortunately, it doesn't appear that our inside man had an opportunity to reach out to dad before you contacted him. He and mum would have stormed through that door to check on me if he had. We can visit them later. Perhaps the fresh air will do me some good. It might help clear my mind a bit. Get me re-centered. 214

VALDEZ

215 We can go to see them after lunch. Until then, you should relax. I have the medications that Dr. Holcomb left right here in case we need them. 215

BETH

216 That sounds wonderful. Odessa, could you, um... 216

VALDEZ

217 Could I what? 217

BETH

218 Could you... read to me? I know it's silly, I just... hearing your voice is... 218

VALDEZ

219 I would love to read to you, Beth. 219

BETH

220 Thank you. I have just the book 220
right here...

MUSICAL TRANSITION

INT. KIRBY RESIDENCE, DAY

BETH and VALDEZ enter.

ANDREW

221 Lily! It's lovely to see you. 221
(concerned)
222 Please, have a seat. 222
(beat)
223 Thank you for radioing us to let us 223
know that she was alright, my dear.

VALDEZ

224 Of course. We wanted to make sure 224
you knew she was safe and
recovering, just in case your
operative reached out to tell you
what happened.

ANDREW

225 He didn't, but that's not 225
surprising. He has to be quite
cautious about communicating with
me, and there are times that he
simply can't get away.
(beat)
226 Now, Lily, do you want to talk 226
about what went wrong? All I know
is that things didn't go according
to plan.

BETH

227 No, daddy. They didn't. 227
(beat, upset)
228 They went very badly indeed. There 228
was some sort of... problem, and...
well, I...

VALDEZ

229 There were complications. We're not 229
sure what happened, specifically,
but Beth was... trapped.

ANDREW

230 Trapped? What do you mean by 230
"trapped?"

BETH

231 I was trapped inside my own mind. 231
Some combination of my brain and
the machine triggered a response
from both, and that response made
me have to fight to wake up.

ANDREW

232 Oh, my god. We knew the use of this 232
technology carried risks, but...
(beat)
233 I never should've allowed you to do 233
this.

BETH

234 You've always done everything in 234
your power to protect me, daddy,
but... I'm an adult, and it was my
decision whether or not to take
that risk. I knew the potential
dangers, but it was the right call
based on the situation and the
available information. And I think
you know that.

ANDREW

235 I do. But adult or not, you're 235
still my daughter, and I still
worry about you.

BETH

236 I know. But I had Odessa to guide 236
me out, and Dr. Holcomb kept me
stable while that happened.

ANDREW

237 Dr. who? 237

BETH

238 Dr. Holcomb. Rebecca Holcomb? 238

VALDEZ

239 She said she knew you from the 239
Vault, and she recognized Beth. She
didn't blow our cover, fortunately,
and even helped paper over her
accent when she was coming out of
it.

ANDREW

240 I'm afraid you have me at a loss. I 240
don't remember a Rebecca Holcomb.

VALDEZ

241 That's strange. She certainly 241
seemed to remember you. She even
asked if you were driving Elise
crazy.

ANDREW

242 I trust that you answered yes? 242

VALDEZ laughs.

VALDEZ

243 I demurred. 243

BETH

244 For what it's worth, I didn't 244
recognize her, but that doesn't
mean much. All those Vault-Tec
scientists sort of run together in
my mind, apart from Dr. Flagler.

ANDREW

245 I'm certainly curious about this 245
Dr. Holcomb, but unfortunately we
have rather bigger fish to fry.

BETH

246 What's going on? 246

ANDREW

247 For the most part, movements of 247
factions and subfactions around
Appalachia have been incremental.
Exceptions have happened, of
course, like the Brotherhood's
arrival two years ago, but in those
cases it's been one faction doing
the moving.

BETH

248 And that's not what's happening 248
now?

ANDREW

249 I'll let Charles explain. One 249
moment and I'll get him.

ANDREW leaves.

VALDEZ

250 I wonder... could it be that he 250
feels the rope tightening, so he's
taking more aggressive action?

BETH

251 It could, I suppose. Or he could've decided that there was no need to take things slowly anymore. That Appalachia is so fundamentally weak that he doesn't need to be quite so... precious about everything. 251

VALDEZ

252 He hasn't taken direct action against the Brotherhood, other than trying to steal what we'd already found from my lab. 252

BETH

253 Well, you've established yourselves as one of the stronger factions in the region already. It seems as though it's inevitable, but perhaps he feels that he needs a bit more... force behind him before he does that. 253

VALDEZ

254 A consolidation of power makes sense. 254

BETH

255 It does, and it's something we need to prevent. I just wish I knew how. Hopefully Charles has come up with something. 255

CHARLES, ANDREW, and ELISE enter.

BETH (CONT'D)

256 Speak of the devil! 256

CHARLES

257 And the devil appears! 257

ELISE

258 Schatzi! I was worried sick! Are you feeling better? 258

BETH

259 I'm getting there. 259

ELISE

260 You are definitely the scion of Andrew Kirby. I swear, one or both of you will be the death of me. 260

BETH laughs.

BETH

261 You love us. 261

ELISE

262 I do. 262

BETH

263 Charles, you have some new intel? 263

CHARLES

264 I do. Well, new-*ish*. This 264
Morningstar is a canny bugger.

BETH

265 What do you mean? 265

CHARLES

266 How much do you know about this 266
character?

BETH

267 Not a lot. His superpower seems to 267
be that he's "mysterious." I know that he was a major power player going back several years, even before the Scorched Plague. But he went underground, and by all accounts he's been pulling the strings from very deep in the shadows since then.

CHARLES

268 Indeed, and things have become more 268
and more obfuscated over the years to the point that it's impossible to know which... endeavors he may actually have involvement in and which are simply someone attaching his name to it for effect.

BETH

269 I always got the feeling that most 269
of what we heard fell into the latter category. Given his reputation, it seemed as though he'd be far more likely to involve people in his various schemes without them even being aware that he was behind them. Otherwise, there isn't much point to staying in the shadows to the extent he has.

(MORE)

BETH (CONT'D)
And besides that, it all seemed a bit scattershot, which didn't fit in with his previous work.

ANDREW
270 I frankly wondered if he was even still alive. Or if he ever *really* existed in the first place. 270

VALDEZ
271 What do you mean? It sounded like he was real, at least before the Scorched Plague hit. 271

ANDREW
272 That's the thing about legends. There comes a point where you can't even trust what seems to be historical. 272

ELISE chuckles.

ELISE
273 And you know a thing or two about that. 273

ANDREW
274 Now, now, Elise... 274

CHARLES
275 But in any case, what we're seeing now is significantly more aggressive than what we've seen since he left the stage. 275

ANDREW
276 That little display at Fort Atlas, for example. That implies a level of hubris that simply wasn't present before. Even when he was at the height of his power. 276

CHARLES
277 The same goes for the operation at Foundation. He no longer seems to care about anyone knowing that it's him. In fact, he seems to be reveling in it. 277

BETH
278 But why would he target me like he has? I don't see how I could've run afoul of him in a way that would merit this kind of attention. 278
(MORE)

BETH (CONT'D)
Even if some of my freelance work
got in the way of his operations,
it's far from a proportionate
response.

CHARLES
279 Indeed. And what I've been doing is 279
going over our various intel
reports to see if I could identify
a pattern, and separate the wheat
from the chaff, as it were, whilst
I did that.

BETH
280 But you said doing that was 280
virtually impossible, given the
sheer number of things that seem to
have been done in his name over the
years.

CHARLES
281 I did. So instead of trying to look 281
at his entire oeuvre, I
concentrated solely on the past six
months or so, starting when this
tech started to become an area of
focus for the various factions.

BETH
282 That makes sense. Given the way 282
this has all played out, it's
unlikely that these are simply a
series of unrelated operations by
each group.

CHARLES
283 Yes. My working theory is that he 283
was parceling out the intel on the
locations of each of these labs so
that no one faction had enough on
their own to put two and two
together.

BETH
284 And considering who some of these 284
groups were, it's likely they
thought it was just a smash-and-
grab and not part of some
overarching effort.

VALDEZ
285 Do you think that the Brotherhood's 285
presence in Appalachia had anything
to do with his plans accelerating?
(MORE)

VALDEZ (CONT'D)
Craig expressed a strong opinion regarding what he thought we'd do if we found out about this tech. An incorrect opinion, but still, a strong one.

CHARLES
286 It's possible. You've been steadily gaining strength since that unfortunate Rahmani/Shin business, so his aim may be to at least acquire all of the tech before you have the opportunity to, even if he'd still need time on the back end to get it to do... well, whatever it is he wants to do with it. 286

BETH
287 That first operation - when we first met - certainly could have demonstrated to him that it was only a matter of time before you turned your full attention to it. 287

CHARLES
288 After frankly far too much time looking at maps and poring over intel, I noticed that there were specific gangs, as well as mercenaries, whose actions seemed to be... working in concert. And I've noted three locations that *may* - and I must stress "may" - be bases, or at the very least important locations for those groups. 288

BETH
289 You believe they're working for the Morningstar? 289

CHARLES
290 That's my theory, but it's just a theory. It could be a coincidence and the pattern I recognized may not be a pattern at all. 290

BETH
291 I trust your instincts, Charles. This could be the breakthrough we need. 291

VALDEZ

292 Where are these three locations? 292

CHARLES

293 There's a former Free States bunker in the Mire, not far from the lab where you and Elizabeth first met. 293

ELISE

294 Has there been any indication that the Free States are involved in the Morningstar's plans? 294

CHARLES

295 No, interestingly enough. They seem to be staying out of each other's way, but not in a Molotov-Ribbentrop way. They don't seem to be involved at all. 295

VALDEZ

296 And the other locations? 296

CHARLES

297 There's one in the Ash Heap. That one jumped out at me because it's an abandoned mine that had a very large contingent of Mole Miners that were summarily wiped out not long ago. And the third one is in the Savage Divide. Not far from Fort Atlas, in fact. 297

VALDEZ

298 If they're establishing a base close to Atlas, they could be planning on a direct assault on the Brotherhood! 298

CHARLES

299 They could indeed. That location, however, has been largely quiet for a period of months, unlike the other two. My operational assessment is that there is no imminent threat to the Brotherhood. 299

(beat)

300 The interesting thing about this one is that, unlike the other two, it has a name. 300

BETH

301 A name? What is it? 301

CHARLES

302 “Flagrante Bello.” It’s Latin. 302

VALDEZ

303 For “with war blazing.” More or 303
less.

CHARLES

304 Yes. It gained that name by being 304
the site of significant factional
fighting over a period of years. We
believe that there may be a large
underground compound somewhere near
there, but we have thusfar been
unable to determine whether that is
the case or not.

BETH

305 It would make sense that there’s 305
something there worth fighting
over. And with that much fighting,
it must be something big.

CHARLES

306 If there is, whatever that 306
“something big” is has been lost to
history. We haven’t found either
records or anyone with direct
knowledge to confirm it.

BETH

307 Sounds a bit like Crane’s treasure. 307
There were dozens of people looking
for that over the years. Maybe
hundreds.

CHARLES

308 Indeed. But in any case, at this 308
point, best we can tell is that a
group of Raiders control the area.

BETH

309 I wish Amanda were still here. 309
She’d be able to help us get to the
bottom of this.

VALDEZ

310 I have an idea. 310

BETH

311 I’m all ears. 311

VALDEZ

312 We can't go undercover, since everyone at the Spider's Web knows us now, but we still might be able to pick up some chatter. 312

BETH

313 I used to do that when I was still with Amanda. It was almost like a game. People tend to... overshare when they've been drinking, and we got a lot of information that way. 313

ANDREW

314 Are you feeling up to that? 314

BETH sighs.

BETH

315 No. But I don't think we have a choice. 315

ANDREW

316 Unfortunately, I agree. Please, be careful. And Odessa, knowing you'll be there with her makes me feel rather better. 316

ELISE

317 And me as well. 317

VALDEZ

318 Thank you. I won't let you down. I'll take good care of her. 318

ELISE

319 Thank you, dear. 319

BETH

320 Let's head home. I'd like to rest up a bit, then we can get changed and head to the Web. 320

VALDEZ

321 That sounds perfect. 321

END OF ACT TWO

ACT THREE

INT. THE SPIDER'S WEB, NIGHT

BETH and VALDEZ are at a table, chatting and having a good time. There is considerable activity.

VALDEZ
322 It certainly seems like business as 322
usual in here.

BETH
323 I have to admit, I was a bit 323
worried that things would...
devolve without her here.

VALDEZ
324 She has a good team in place. We 324
spent a lot of time here while you
were away, and that became very
clear.

BETH
325 How much time did you spend here? 325

VALDEZ
326 Enough that people thought we were 326
seeing each other.

BETH
(teasing)
327 Ooooh! Another victim, caught in 327
the web by the spider herself!

VALDEZ laughs.

VALDEZ
328 Stop! 328

BETH
329 I'm glad she took good care of you 329
while I was away.
(wistfully)
330 And she's still taking good care of 330
us, even while she's away.

VALDEZ
331 She took *very* good care of me. 331

BETH
332 Anything I need to know about? 332

VALDEZ laughs.

VALDEZ
333 My lips are sealed. 333

BETH laughs.

BETH
334 You're terrible. 334

VALDEZ
335 She'll be back, Beth. 335

BETH
336 I just hope she's okay. Wherever 336
she is.

VALDEZ
337 She is. I can feel it. 337

BETH
338 If she stays away too long, you, 338
Cindy, and I will have to form a
support group.

VALDEZ laughs.

VALDEZ
339 "Amanda Anonymous." 339

BETH laughs.

BETH
340 Something like that, yeah. 340

BONES approaches.

BONES
341 How are you ladies doing? Can I get 341
you anything?

VALDEZ
342 You've been so sweet, Bones. You 342
have a bar to run - you don't have
to keep doting on us.

BONES
343 You're sitting at the boss' table, 343
you get the boss treatment.

BETH
344 Well, in that case... another 344
round.

BONES
345 Coming right up. 345

BETH

346 And Bones - please do let us know 346
if your ears happen to catch
anything... interesting.

BONES

347 Sure thing. 347

BONES leaves.

BETH

348 I don't think I ever told you... 348
this is where I first heard about
you. Right here at this table.

VALDEZ

349 You didn't tell me that! You 349
mentioned that you'd heard people
talking about me when we were
chatting in that first lab, but you
didn't get into the details.
(beat)
350 Well... let's hear it. 350

BETH

351 I was here with Amanda, and I was 351
feeling a bit... lost, I suppose.
She was doing her best to cheer me
up, but I was in a dark mood.

VALDEZ

352 Aww! Well, you were with the right 352
person, at least.

BETH

353 I was. She was about to take me 353
home to... comfort me there when
some Brotherhood types happened in.

VALDEZ

354 Members of the Brotherhood? Here? 354

BETH

355 Don't act so surprised! The 355
Spider's Web welcomes everyone, as
long as they keep their noses
clean. Well, except Blood Eagles.
They're not even allowed through
the door.

VALDEZ

356 That's a wise policy. So, is that a 356
regular thing? Brotherhood members
hanging out here?

BETH

357 Well, it's not as common to see 357
them as it is Settlers or traders,
but it's not uncommon.

VALDEZ

358 Knight Carlson was still trying to 358
smoke out the moles while you were
gone, and Rahmani had everyone on
lockdown. Well, everyone other than
me. That must be why I didn't see
any.

BETH

359 I'm sure. You lot were as busy as 359
dad and I were while we were away.
(beat)
360 At any rate, just as we were about 360
to leave, three of them came in.
Amanda knew them, and, well, we
decided to stay. And I was glad we
did! They were a lot of fun to chat
with. And eventually, after a few
drinks, your name came up.

VALDEZ

361 Oh, my, I'm not sure I want to hear 361
this.

BETH

362 I can stop if you want! 362

VALDEZ

363 I wasn't being serious, I 363
absolutely want to hear this.

BETH laughs.

BETH

364 Alright. Well, it seems that Amanda 364
had heard about your... fans coming
to visit you and trying to woo you.
And there was a... discussion,
shall we say, of that.

VALDEZ

365 Ugh. Is that all anyone knows about 365
me? You mentioned the same thing
when we first met.

BETH

366 It's just because they haven't had 366
the opportunity to meet you. The
real you.

(MORE)

BETH (CONT'D)
Paladin Rahmani, Knight Shin, Knight Banks... their roles mean that they're out there in Appalachia. You haven't been afforded that opportunity nearly as much.

VALDEZ
367 Well, that does seem to be changing 367
a bit. Thanks to you.

BETH
368 It's all down to *you*, Odessa. You 368
constantly amaze me. This situation keeps pushing you and pushing you and all you do is continue to demonstrate that your potential is limitless.

VALDEZ
369 That's... thank you, Beth. If I 369
didn't know better, I'd think you liked me or something.

BETH laughs.

BETH
370 I suppose I do. 370

VALDEZ
371 So you were saying... Amanda knew 371
about people from the Wasteland trying to pick me up.

BETH
372 Yes! And the Brotherhood members 372
knew all about it as well. Amanda asked them how many had done it that day.

VALDEZ
373 Do I want to know how many it was? 373

BETH
374 I believe it was five. 374

VALDEZ
375 Ugh. 375

BETH
376 What's wrong? Slow day? 376

VALDEZ laughs.

VALDEZ

377 It tends to come in waves. 377

BETH

378 I'm sure it does. Were you ever... tempted? 378

VALDEZ

379 Not really. Occasionally? A little? I don't know. I never seemed to be in the right... headspace to feel like saying yes. The thing with Derek took a toll, and it's not like I didn't have plenty to do. 379

(beat)

380 It didn't make sense, but I think I kept... subconsciously comparing them to him. It wasn't fair. Hell, I wouldn't even be able to compare *him* to him; it was this idealized version that I made up based entirely on the good times. 380

VALDEZ sighs.

VALDEZ (CONT'D)

381 I know it's not rational. 381

BETH

382 Love often isn't. And you clearly loved him very deeply. 382

(beat)

383 "The double grief of a lost bliss is to recall its happy hour in pain." 383

VALDEZ

384 "...and that thy teacher knows." 384

(beat)

385 But that finally feels like it's in the past now. I wasn't sure I'd ever feel that way. And all it took was meeting you. 385

BETH and VALDEZ kiss.

VALDEZ (CONT'D)

386 Beth, I... um... there's something I want to tell you, but... 386

BETH

387 But what? 387

VALDEZ
388 It's not rational. And I'm... well, 388
it scares me a little.

BETH
389 It's alright, Odessa. I never want 389
you to be afraid to tell me
something... rational or not.

VALDEZ
390 It's not just telling you. I'm 390
scared to feel this way. Especially
this soon.

BETH
391 I think the best thing is to just 391
say it. And... I may have something
to tell you, as well.

VALDEZ
392 Beth, I... 392

BONES
(interrupting)
393 Um... excuse me. I hate to 393
interrupt, but...

BETH
(interrupting)
394 But you did. What is it? 394

BONES
395 I have your drinks. 395

VALDEZ
396 You interrupted us for that?! 396

BONES
397 And you may want to take note of 397
the two jamokes sitting at table
seven. They've been eyeing you two
up since they came in here, and...
not in the way guys usually eye you
up. Be careful.

BETH
398 Thank you, Bones. We will. 398

BONES leaves.

VALDEZ
399 To us. 399

BETH
400 To us. 400

BETH and VALDEZ clink glasses.

VALDEZ
401 How are you feeling? 401

BETH
402 I don't know that I've ever felt better. 402
(beat)
403 But, if I'm being honest, I'm a little tired. 403

VALDEZ
404 Then I suppose I'll need to get you into bed. 404

BETH
405 You don't need to tell me twice... 405

VALDEZ
406 But Bones is right. Those two are clearly up to something, and they may not be alone. Wait here, and I'll arrange an escort. 406

VALDEZ leaves.

CARLSON bursts in. He does not see VALDEZ and rushes to BETH's table.

CARLSON
407 Beth! Where's Odessa? 407

BETH
408 She'll be back in a moment. What's wrong? 408

CARLSON
409 It's all-hands back at Atlas. Paladin Rahmani couldn't raise Odessa on comms so she sent me out to find her and bring her back. 409

BETH
410 What's happened? 410

CARLSON
411 There's an old Raider hotspot that's a stone's throw from Atlas. 411
(MORE)

CARLSON (CONT'D)
It's been cold for a while now, but
it's heating back up and we're
concerned that they may be gearing
up for an assault on the
Brotherhood.

BETH
412 Dammit! How could Charles' gut be 412
that wrong?

VALDEZ returns.

VALDEZ
413 Greg? What are you doing here? 413

CARLSON
414 Looking for you. We need you back 414
at Atlas, like now.

VALDEZ
415 I'm sorry, I didn't bring a radio 415
with me.
(beat)
416 How did you even know where to find 416
me?

CARLSON
417 Rahmani told me to check Beth's 417
place, her parents' place, and
here, in that order.

BETH
418 She did say that she'd done her 418
homework on me.

CARLSON
419 I'll explain the situation on the 419
way. Nothing has happened *yet*, but
we need to be ready in case it
does.

BETH
420 It's Flagrante Bello. Sounds like 420
something's happening there and the
Brotherhood wants to stay in front
of it in case they're preparing an
attack.

VALDEZ
421 Didn't Charles say... 421

BETH
(interrupting)
422 He did. 422
(MORE)

BETH (CONT'D)
And that leads me to believe that something else is going on, but it's prudent to be ready.
(beat)
423 Knight Carlson, I am at the Brotherhood's disposal. 423

VALDEZ
424 Are you sure you're feeling up to it? 424

BETH
425 No. But if there's a fight, I want to be at your side. 425

CARLSON
426 Sorry, Beth. Rahmani gave strict orders that it's Brotherhood personnel only. 426

BETH
427 But I'm... 427

CARLSON
428 A freelance contractor. You're not Brotherhood. I'm sorry. 428

VALDEZ
429 Greg, she could help! 429

CARLSON
430 Then you'll have to take it up with Paladin Rahmani when we get back. I'm under strict orders to bring *you* and only you back with me. 430

BETH
431 It's alright. I'll stay with mum and dad tonight. And I'll keep a radio with me in case you reach out. 431

VALDEZ
432 I arranged an escort with Bones. Tripod and Gino are ready when you are. Benny is going to follow, but out of sight. They'll make sure you get to your parents' place safe and sound. 432

BETH
433 Alright. Thank you. Knight, please ensure that nothing happens to her. 433

CARLSON

434 I will. 434

BETH

435 And Odessa... I'll miss you. Please stay safe. 435

VALDEZ

436 I'll miss you, too. Get some rest. I'll radio you as soon as I can. 436

BETH and VALDEZ kiss.

VALDEZ and CARLSON leave.

BONES approaches BETH.

BONES

437 Everything okay? 437

BETH

438 I don't know. Something about this doesn't feel right, but... maybe the Brotherhood is always like this and it's just something I'll have to get used to. 438

BONES

439 The boys are ready. They'll take care of you, and not just because Amanda would wear their intestines as a hat if anything happened. 439

BETH laughs.

BETH

440 Well, that's quite a visual. Thank you, Bones. I'm ready to go. 440

BONES

441 Sounds good. I'll keep an eye on those two jokers, too. Maybe they'll do something stupid and I'll be able to throw them out. I really didn't like the way they were looking at you two. 441

BETH

442 Hopefully they were just creeps. 442

BONES

443 Hopefully. 443

MUSICAL TRANSITION

EXT. FORT ATLAS, MORNING

BETH approaches Fort Atlas. There is considerable activity.

BETH
444 Excuse me, have you... 444
(beat)
445 Is Scribe Val- 445
(beat)
446 Will someone please tell me what's going on?! 446

Eventually, KNIGHT BANKS approaches.

BANKS
447 Beth! Hey, I'm glad you're here. I assume you heard? 447

BETH
448 Heard what? 448

BANKS
449 Oh, no. You didn't hear. 449

BETH
450 Didn't. Hear. What?! 450

BANKS
451 Beth, it's Odessa, she's... 451

BETH
452 Oh, God... 452

BANKS
453 She's been taken. 453

BETH
454 Taken?! By whom?! 454

BANKS
455 We don't know. They got jumped on their way back here last night. Greg fought them like hell, but there were too many of them. Greg's in pretty rough shape. He barely made it back. 455

BETH
456 Do we have any information at all? 456

BANKS
457 We scrambled every available resource the moment he told us what happened. 457
(MORE)

BANKS (CONT'D)

We have patrols in the field, we're working contacts... we're doing everything we can.

BETH

458 I will move heaven and earth to get her back. 458

BANKS

459 I know you will. That's why I'm so glad you're here. 459

BETH

460 I'll need to use your communications station to contact my father. And after I do that, you and I need to have a very frank conversation. 460

BANKS

461 Uh, okay. Everything the Brotherhood has is yours to use. Rahmani said to give you full access to everything, no limitations. 461

BETH

462 Good. Let's get inside. We have a Scribe to save. 462

<u>END OF EPISODE 8</u>

Season One
Part Three: The Book of Elizabeth

Episode 9:
"The Audacity of Doing This"

by

D.K. Trueno

"THE AUDACITY OF DOING THIS"

INT. FORT ATLAS - DAY

BETH and RAHMANI enter Rahmani's office.

RAHMANI closes the door.

RAHMANI

1 I know that you want to talk to 1
Knight Banks as soon as possible,
but we need to talk before that
happens.

(beat)

2 Please, have a seat. 2

BETH

3 I prefer to stand, thank you. 3

RAHMANI

4 As you wish. 4

(beat)

5 We had teams on the ground almost 5
from the moment Knight Carlson
returned and told us what happened.
They're remaining in constant
contact, but we don't have anything
concrete.

BETH

6 They need to do better. 6

RAHMANI

7 I agree. That's where you come in. 7

BETH

8 I am at your disposal. 8

RAHMANI

9 Given your contacts, resources, and 9
skillset, I want you to lead the
effort to retrieve Scribe Valdez.
To that end, I would like to grant
you a temporary field commission,
which would expire when this
mission is over.

BETH

10 Thank you, Paladin, but... 10

RAHMANI

11 11
12 It's purely a procedural matter. 12

(MORE)

RAHMANI (CONT'D)
In order to put you in charge of Brotherhood personnel, you need to be commissioned as an officer, even if it's on a temporary basis. But before I do that, we need to have a discussion. A frank one.

BETH
13 We don't have time to waste, 13
Paladin. Every second we take-

RAHMANI
(interrupting)
14 This discussion will not be a 14
waste. And I promise, it will be brief.

BETH
15 What's on your mind? 15

RAHMANI
16 I know that you are very strongly 16
personally motivated to get Scribe Valdez back. And I suspect that you will do everything in your power to do so.

BETH
17 That suspicion is correct. 17

RAHMANI
18 Including methods that run counter 18
to Brotherhood regulations?

BETH
19 If necessary, yes. 19

RAHMANI
20 On the record, I will reiterate to 20
you that we expect you to conduct yourself as a Brotherhood of Steel Senior Knight even though you would only bear that title on a temporary and acting basis, and that there will be serious repercussions for failing to do so.
(beat)
21 Off the record... well, I expect 21
you to get her back. That's all.

BETH
22 I understand, ma'am. 22

RAHMANI

23 Now, onto the second topic. Before 23
I grant this commission, I need you
to address my primary concern.
(beat)
24 I'm concerned that you're too close 24
to this.

BETH sighs.

BETH

25 Well, you may be right. I'd like to 25
think that I can remain above
emotion when I'm on the job, but...
I'm human.
(beat)
26 I can tell you that I have a strong 26
network of allies who stand ready
to assist, and people with a wide
range of skills who owe me favors.
There's no resource that I won't
use to get her back.

RAHMANI

27 That network is one of the reasons 27
that I want you in charge of this
operation. We'll need all the help
we can get, and we don't have time
to waste on dealing with layers of
abstraction.
(beat)
28 Given all the movement around 28
Flagrante Bello we strongly suspect
that is where Scribe Valdez is
being held. If we can confirm that,
it will allow us to focus our
efforts in a way that we simply
can't right now.

BETH

29 Of course. I'll put my father and 29
his assistant on that. There's
nobody better than Charles at
processing intel.

RAHMANI

30 Given the proximity of Fort Atlas 30
to Flagrante Bello, I'd like to
maintain the command center here.
We should have all the resources
you need.

BETH

31 I believe you do, for the most 31
part. There are some things that
I'll need to retrieve from my
place, though. Body armor, a few
specialized weapons, that sort of
thing.

RAHMANI

32 Of course. 32

BETH

33 I'll need access to comms so I can 33
brief my father. I'll ask him to
send Charles here directly. He'll
likely want to work some of his
contacts first.

RAHMANI

34 What about your mother? 34

BETH

35 She has contacts at Foundation as 35
well as the Free States. Both sides
said they "owed her" after
negotiating a statement of
understanding between them, and I
think it's time to call in that
chit.

RAHMANI

36 We're combing through Brotherhood 36
personnel right now to see if
anyone might have a contact that
can help us here, but the problem
is that the Morningstar's strategy
has always been one of obfuscation.

BETH

37 Indeed, security by obscurity. It's 37
like chasing a ghost story. That's
what makes his current actions so
concerning. Beyond just taking
Odessa, he's not only taking
strong, overt action, he's
practically signing his name to it.

RAHMANI

38 That should make things easier, 38
shouldn't it?

BETH

39 On the surface, sure. But this is all completely out of character based on everything that we know about him. And that can be... well, it can be quite jarring. 39

RAHMANI

40 What's the word on the street? 40

BETH

41 For the most part, people are too busy trying to survive to worry about any of this. His recent actions have been overt, they've been targeted in a way that hasn't impacted most people. Not directly, at least. We'll need to convince them that this threat is real, that it's serious, and that it's imminent. 41

RAHMANI

42 Have you seen indirect impacts? 42

BETH

43 One of the most important things that my mother taught us as part of our diplomacy and nation-building curriculum is that small, targeted action can be vital to achieving diplomatic goals. 43

RAHMANI

44 And it's not a stretch to apply that thinking to less... diplomatic action. 44

BETH

45 Precisely what I was thinking. And despite our best efforts, my strong suspicion is that what we've seen is just the proverbial tip of the proverbial iceberg. 45

RAHMANI

46 He could've been laying the groundwork for years. 46

BETH

47 Indeed. He may have started the moment people began returning to Appalachia, and if that *was* the case his plans surely would've accelerated when the Scorched Plague was finally eliminated. 47

(beat)

48 I feel like your arrival threw a spanner in the works. 48

RAHMANI

49 It may have. It was unfortunate that we had so much to deal with from the moment we arrived. Super Mutants under Atlas, putting an end to Dr. Blackburn's experiments... 49

BETH

50 And to Dr. Blackburn himself. 50

RAHMANI

(mildly uncomfortable)

51 Yes. 51

(beat)

52 So, Acting Knight Kirby, what can I do to help? 52

BETH

53 I'll need access to the prisoners for interrogation. 53

RAHMANI

54 Of course. Knight Banks was hoping to leverage your... expertise in that area. 54

BETH

55 This is a bit awkward. 55

RAHMANI

56 What is it? 56

BETH

57 It's about Knight Banks, actually. About why I'm so keen to speak to him. 57

RAHMANI

58 What's going on? 58

BETH

59 Odessa has expressed... concerns 59
about Knight Banks' recent
behavior. Nothing that she could
quite put her finger on, but he
seemed... off to her recently.

RAHMANI

60 Explain "off," please. 60

BETH

61 It was more a general feeling than 61
anything specific. She said he was
acting suspiciously. Disappearing
for hours at a time, being oddly
cagey about things.
(beat)
62 I don't want to jump to any 62
conclusions, but the timing lines
up with the Brotherhood's
involvement in what we later
learned was the Morningstar's tech
grab.

RAHMANI

63 I don't like coincidences. 63

BETH

64 Nor do I. But I want to give him 64
the opportunity to explain himself.
He and Odessa were close - like
brother and sister - so I feel that
I owe him that much.
(beat)
65 Besides that, *if* we can trust him, 65
he'd be an invaluable resource.

RAHMANI

66 He would. And I hope that he will. 66
One moment, I'll get him.

RAHMANI leaves.

A moment later, there is a knock on the door.

BETH

67 That was fast... 67

BETH opens the door. CASEY enters.

CASEY

68 Beth! I just got back. 68
(beat)
69 Are you okay? 69

BETH

70 I'm managing, Casey. Thank you for asking. 70

(beat)

71 It's all hands on deck. Mum and dad will be read in shortly, and I'm going to call in every favor I've earned out there. 71

(beat)

72 I wish Amanda was here. She has so many deep contacts with the various Raider factions, and I just... don't. 72

CASEY

73 We're going to get her back. Together. 73

BETH

74 Just like old times? 74

CASEY

75 We always did make a hell of a team. 75

(beat)

76 I did try to find you, you know. After I got settled. I didn't know if something happened to you, and when I couldn't track you down I got to the point where I was afraid to find out. 76

BETH

77 That was probably when I was with Amanda, and I'm guessing you didn't travel in Raider circles. 77

(beat)

78 But, for what it's worth, I never stopped thinking about you, and how you'd always been there for me. 78

CASEY

79 We were always there for each other. 79

BETH

80 I guess I assumed you'd... moved on. Hoped, even. 80

CASEY

81 I did. But I never stopped caring about you. And I never will. 81

BETH

82 Nor I you. 82

BETH sighs.

BETH (CONT'D)

(growing upset)

83 Odessa's been taken, Amanda left... 83
and I feel like both of those
things are my fault. I always drive
the people I love away.

CASEY

84 You didn't drive me away. 84

BETH

85 Didn't I? We were never the same 85
after I proposed.

CASEY

86 It was a lot to process, Beth. We 86
were, what, two months from
Reclamation day? And I hadn't even
turned 19 yet. I wasn't ready.

BETH

87 I didn't want to lose you. 87

CASEY

88 You wouldn't have! 88

(beat)

89 Hey, hey... take a breath. I'm 89
starting to wonder if you're really
"managing."

BETH

90 I'm sorry. My most recent 90
undercover op had... consequences,
and the truth is that I'm
struggling.

CASEY

91 What kind of consequences? 91

BETH

92 I don't have time to fully explain 92
right now, but suffice it to say
that memories I'd mostly managed to
learn to deal with are suddenly...
less manageable. And emotionally...
well, I'm just trying to hold
things together, and not always
succeeding.

CASEY

93 Then re-litigating our relationship 93
is the last thing we should be
doing. Don't dwell on how our love
story ended. Think about the one
that's just getting started. Okay?

BETH

94 Okay. But I do think that we should 94
talk. Once we have Odessa back, I
mean. After everything that's
happened... well, I guess I don't
want anything to be left unsaid.

RAHMANI and BANKS enter.

BANKS

95 Paladin, all due respect, I don't 95
have time for this.

RAHMANI

96 You'll make time. 96

BETH

97 What's going on? 97

RAHMANI

98 We have a problem. 98

BETH

99 Oh, no, what now? 99

RAHMANI

100 The prisoners are dead. With 100
everyone being pulled in so many
different directions, there was a
miscommunication regarding guard
duty in the brig, and... well,
someone got to them.

BETH

101 And who's in charge of guarding 101
those prisoners?

RAHMANI sighs.

RAHMANI

102 Knight Banks. 102

BETH

(coldly)

103 May we have the room, please? This 103
won't take long.

RAHMANI

104 Of course. Knight Banks, your sidearm, please? 104

BANKS

105 What? Why do you need my sidearm? 105

RAHMANI

106 Just give me your sidearm, Alan. 106

BANKS sighs.

BANKS

107 Yes, ma'am. 107

RAHMANI

108 Casey, with me, please. 108

CASEY

109 Yes, ma'am. 109

RAHMANI and CASEY leave.

BANKS

110 Beth, every second we spend in here is a second we're not working on getting Odessa back. 110

BETH

111 I'm going to ask you a very simple question, Alan, and I expect a direct answer. 111

BANKS

112 Can we dispense with the cloak-and-dagger shit, please? Say what's on your mind so we can get back to work. 112

BETH

113 What's in this for you? It must be something big for you to betray the Brotherhood like this. To betray Odessa. She thought of you like a big brother. 113

BANKS

114 What the hell are you talking about? I haven't betrayed-- 114

BETH

(interrupting.)

115 Don't. Don't do that. You don't get to clutch your pearls at me. 115

(MORE)

BETH (CONT'D)
(beat)
116 Three prisoners lie dead downstairs. The woman I love is who-knows-where in who-knows-what kind of danger. Where do you run off to for hours at a time, Alan? Where did the intel on that first lab come from? 116

BANKS
117 It was a tip from a source! I didn't know any details, they just said there was some primo tech in an old lab that we should check out. That's it. 117

BETH
118 What kind of source? 118

BANKS
119 The confidential kind. I *cannot* burn that source. 119

BETH
120 Oh, come on... 120

BANKS
121 We're really going to play this game? Fine. 121
(beat)
122 Who's the actual spy here? I'll give you a hint - it's not me. I'm just a guy who runs around in power armor, cracks jokes, and cracks some heads from time to time. But you... 122

BETH
123 But me *what*? 123

BANKS
124 Kind of interesting that you happened to show up right when we were checking out that lab. But I'm assuming it wasn't really a coincidence. 124

BETH
125 Don't you dare try to make this about me. 125

BANKS
126 I don't have to. You've done a bang-up job all by yourself. 126
(MORE)

BANKS (CONT'D)

(beat)

127 But you're damn good at this, I 127
have to give you that much.
Everybody here trusted me.
Respected me. But you've even got
Rahmani wrapped around your finger
to the point where she's
confiscating my sidearm so you can
interrogate me.

(beat)

128 So go ahead. Ask your question. Or 128
shoot me, I don't even care at this
point.

BETH

129 Are you working for the 129
Morningstar?

BANKS

130 Are *you*? 130

BETH

131 Answer the question! 131

BANKS

132 What about Valdez? Was seducing her 132
part of your plan or was that just
a complication? Is that why she's
gone? Tying up loose ends?

BETH

133 Answer me! 133

BANKS

134 No! I am *not* working for the 134
Morningstar!

BETH

135 Not good enough. 135

BANKS

136 People like you are supposed to be 136
like human lie detectors. You can't
tell that I'm telling the truth?

BETH

137 Tell me who your source was, and 137
tell me why you keep disappearing
all the time!

BANKS

138 I can't! 138

BETH

139 Then you're going to sit in the 139
brig with three corpses until you
decide you want to cooperate.

BANKS sighs.

BANKS

140 I... I'll tell you *off-the-record*. 140
But nobody in the Brotherhood can
know. Deal?

BETH

141 That depends entirely on what you 141
say next.

BANKS

142 It's my brother. He was the source. 142
And... he's why I keep going off
the grid. Him and his family.

BETH

143 Explain, please. 143

BANKS

144 Alex and I came here from 144
Pennsylvania. Together. But our
paths kind of... diverged, I guess.
He fell in with a bad crew. Blood
Eagles. I tried to steer him
straight, but...
(beat)
145 Look, I'm not going to sugarcoat 145
it, he did some bad shit. People
died. And some of it involved the
Brotherhood.

BETH

146 You're... protecting him? That's 146
what this is all about?

BANKS

147 Yeah. The thing is, he finally got 147
himself squared away. Met a nice
girl, had a kid. The problem is, he
not only has to hide from the Blood
Eagles...

BETH

148 ...he has to hide from the 148
Brotherhood.

BANKS

149 I've been doing my best to help 149
keep their heads above water until
I can figure out how to at least
get *us* off his ass. But it hasn't
been easy.

BETH

150 Jesus, Alan. 150

BANKS

151 So you believe me now? 151

BETH sighs.

BETH

152 Yeah. Human lie detector, remember? 152
But once this is all over, I'm
going to verify it. And there will
be hell to pay if I discover that
any part of your story isn't true.
But, at least for now, I believe
you.

BANKS

153 You sound disappointed. 153

BETH

154 No. I'm glad this seems to have 154
been a misunderstanding. But it
means that we either still have a
mole or we have a new one, and if
it's not you we have no idea who it
is.

BANKS

155 What are you going to tell Rahmani? 155

BETH

156 That I can state with confidence 156
that you are not a compromised
asset. Fortunately for you, we
won't have time to get into the
details. But I think that's going
to have to happen sooner than
later.

BANKS

157 I do, too. 157

BETH

158 We can try to figure something out 158
together.

(MORE)

BETH (CONT'D)
After Odessa's back here, safe and sound, and after I've verified what you've told me.

BANKS
159 It's a deal. 159

BETH
160 But right now, we have work to do. 160
Let's get the Paladin back in here and figure out how we're going to find her. And then we'll figure out how to rescue her.

BANKS
161 I'll assemble a team so we're ready 161
to move out as soon as we have some actionable intel.
(beat)
162 We're going to get her back, Beth. 162

BETH
163 You're damn right we are. 163

<u>END OF ACT ONE</u>

ACT TWO

INT. FLAGRANTE BELLO RESIDENTIAL AREA

VALDEZ is in bed. She stirs.

DEX is at her bedside.

VALDEZ
164 Ugh... what happened? Where am I? 164

DEX
(tenderly)
165 Try not to sit up. You took a nasty 165
spill.

VALDEZ
166 Where's Greg? The person I was 166
with?

DEX
167 Sorry, you were the only one they 167
brought in.

VALDEZ
168 Brought in where? By who? 168

VALDEZ attempts to sit up. She fails with a groan.

DEX
169 Hey, hey, what did I say about 169
sitting up? You need to rest.

VALDEZ
170 My head is killing me. 170

DEX
171 Here. Have some water. 171

VALDEZ drinks.

VALDEZ
172 Thank you. I'm Odessa. 172

DEX
173 I'm Dex. Dex Stewart. It's nice to 173
meet you, Odessa. Are you hungry?

VALDEZ
174 I... I really don't feel like I 174
could hold anything down right now.
But thank you.

DEX

175 We'll get you fixed up in no time. 175

VALDEZ

176 Who's "we," by the way? You're not Brotherhood, you don't look like Raiders, you're clearly not Blood Eagles... Free States? 176

DEX laughs.

DEX

177 Nah. None of those. We're... "unaffiliated," I guess you could say. 177

VALDEZ

(curiosity piqued)

178 Unaffiliated? 178

DEX

179 We're just kind of... here, you know? At least for now. 179

VALDEZ

180 I kind of do, yes. Where's "here," "Dex Stewart, Unaffiliated?" 180

DEX

181 Somewhere safe. 181

VALDEZ

182 I'd feel a lot safer if you stopped being... 182

(wincing)

183 ...evasive. 183

DEX

(tenderly)

184 Hey, hey... I'm going to get a doctor to take a look at you, now that you're up. Okay? 184

VALDEZ

185 Okay. 185

DEX leaves. He returns a moment later.

DEX

(brightly)

186 Here's your patient, doctor. 186

DR. FLAGLER

187 Odessa! I'm so glad you're awake! 187
You had me very worried.

VALDEZ

188 Well, *I'm* still kind of worried, 188
and "Dex Stewart, Unaffiliated"
here hasn't been much help. I...
(beat)
189 Wait, Dr. Flagler?! What are you 189
doing here? And where is "here?"

DR. FLAGLER

190 All in due time, my dear. Right 190
now, I need you to rest.
(beat)
191 How's Lily? 191

VALDEZ

192 Oh, no, Beth! She must be worried 192
sick! And everybody back at Atlas,
too! I need to get in touch with
them to let them know I'm okay.
Where's my radio?

DR. FLAGLER

193 It's okay, Odessa. You'll see her 193
soon, I promise. But right now you
need to stay in bed. No sudden
movements.

VALDEZ

194 I don't think that'll be a problem. 194
Every time I sit up it feels like
somebody's trying to shove an
icepick through my temple.

DR. FLAGLER

195 I'll give you something that should 195
help with that. It will help you
sleep, too.

VALDEZ

196 Thank you. 196

DEX

197 Isn't that dangerous? Sleeping 197
after a concussion?

DR. FLAGLER

198 No, Dex, but I appreciate your 198
concern. That's a common
misconception.
(MORE)

DR. FLAGLER (CONT'D)
In fact, given how important rest is to recovery, not letting someone sleep after they've been concussed can be counter-productive.

DEX
199 How about you two catch up, and 199
I'll go get it for you? Just write the name down and I'll find it.

DR. FLAGLER
200 That would be great, Dex. Thank 200
you.

DEX leaves.

VALDEZ
201 What happened to me? It feels like 201
I drank too much last night and I'm half-hungover, half-still-drunk.

DR. FLAGLER
202 You, my dear, had quite a little 202
adventure from what they told me. You were attacked by a small group of Blood Eagles. You fought back, but there were too many of them. They restrained you, and knocked you out with a chem.

VALDEZ
203 Oh, no... did they... 203

DR. FLAGLER
204 No, thank god. They were carrying 204
you off when they crossed paths with a patrol. Blood Eagles aren't exactly known for their discretion, so they attacked the patrol. That was an unsurprisingly poor decision. Unfortunately, they weren't careful with you and you hit your head when they dropped you. You were already unconscious so you didn't feel it at the time.

VALDEZ
205 I'm feeling it now, that's for 205
sure.

DR. FLAGLER
206 Be careful - you needed four 206
stitches in the back of your head.
(MORE)

DR. FLAGLER (CONT'D)
I think you'll want to change your clothes, when you're feeling up to it. Your uniform got kind of torn up in the struggle, and... well, there's also some blood on it.

VALDEZ
207 Ugh. I didn't even notice. 207

DR. FLAGLER chuckles.

DR. FLAGLER
208 It's fine. We mostly just wanted to get you tucked in so you'd be as comfortable as possible when you woke up. 208

VALDEZ
209 Beth and the Brotherhood are probably out looking for me. And for Greg, too... I hope he's alright. 209

DR. FLAGLER
210 For what it's worth, the patrol said that it was just you and the Blood Eagles. No other Brotherhood personnel, alive or... you know. 210

VALDEZ
211 He wouldn't have abandoned me. 211

DR. FLAGLER
212 Of course not. I'm sure there's a reasonable explanation. 212

VALDEZ
(struggling)
213 I'm just... it's really hard to focus right now, doctor, I'm sorry. What has me concerned is that this might not just be random Blood Eagle mayhem. 213

DR. FLAGLER
214 What do you mean? 214

VALDEZ
215 They might have been targeting *me*, specifically. 215

DR. FLAGLER
(masking concern)
216 Why would they do that? Ransom? 216

VALDEZ

217 No, not ransom... it's... I'm 217
sorry. I think I need to rest.

DEX returns.

DEX

218 Here, doctor. I have that chem for 218
you.

DR. FLAGLER

219 This will help you with that, 219
Odessa. And you'll feel much better
when you wake up. I promise.
(beat)
220 Then we can talk a bit more. Does 220
that sound okay?

VALDEZ

221 Yes, it does. Thank you, doctor. 221
And thank you, Dex.

DEX

222 It's my pleasure, Odessa. Doctor? 222

DR. FLAGLER

223 You'll feel a little pinch, then 223
you'll be off to dreamland for a
bit.

DR. FLAGLER injects Odessa with the chem.

DR. FLAGLER (CONT'D)

224 Poor thing. I'm glad the patrol was 224
there to help her. I just wish
they'd been there a few moments
sooner.
(beat)
225 I don't even want to think about 225
what Blood Eagles would've done
with her. They're monsters.

DEX

226 They are. And considering some of 226
the creatures that we've both seen
wandering around Appalachia, that's
saying something.

DR. FLAGLER

227 So. When are we going to tell her? 227

DEX

228 Let's see how she's feeling when 228
she wakes up.
(MORE)

DEX (CONT'D)
She's been through a lot, I don't want to pile that on top of everything.

DR. FLAGLER
229 Neither do I. She's important to Lily, and that means she's important to me. 229

DEX
230 Don't worry. We'll make sure she's taken care of. And who knows? Maybe she can help us figure out what the hell's going on here. 230

DR. FLAGLER
231 Yeah. This cage is nicely gilded and all, but I'm ready to go home. 231

DEX
232 Those Blood Eagles may have done us a hell of a favor. Nobody's going to come looking for us, but it sounds like an army might be on their way to find her. 232

MUSICAL TRANSITION

INT. FORT ATLAS

BETH, BANKS, and RAHMANI are conferring.

RAHMANI
233 So, we have a plan. 233

BETH
234 Yes, I believe we do. 234

RAHMANI
235 Now we just need to know where to execute it, whether it's Flagrante Bello or somewhere else. 235

BETH
236 My father will come through. You'll see. 236

A radio beeps.

BETH (CONT'D)
237 What's that? 237

BANKS
238 Message coming in. 238

BANKS walks to the radio.

BANKS (CONT'D)
239 Hmm. Enclave frequency. 239

BETH
240 That'll be Valeria returning my 240
message. She was off doing...
whatever it is she does when I
reached out.

BANKS clicks the radio on.

BANKS
241 This is Knight Alan Banks, go 241
ahead.

MODUS
(over radio)
242 Greetings, Knight. We would like to 242
speak to... Elizabeth Kirby. We
believe she should be... nearby.

BETH walks to the radio.

BETH
243 This is Elizabeth Kirby. Paladin 243
Leila Rahmani is in the room as
well. Who is this?

MODUS
244 We... are MODUS. 244

BETH
245 Well, this is a surprise... 245

BANKS
246 Who... or what is a MODUS? 246

RAHMANI
247 MODUS is an Enclave AI. Been around 247
since before the war. It runs the
Enclave facilities over at the
Whitespring, and handles all their
surveillance activities.

BETH
248 But why is it contacting us 248
directly?
(beat)
249 I suppose there's only one way to 249
find out.

BETH clicks the microphone back on.

BETH (CONT'D)
250 Er... what can we do for you, 250
MODUS?

MODUS
251 The Kovac-Muldoon satellite 251
platform has been... monitoring
your father's activities throughout
the day. He should be arriving at
your location very soon. We
calculate an 84.1% chance that he
has successfully retrieved
information on the location of
Scribe Valdez, and that the
location is an underground compound
beneath the area known as
"Flagrante Bello."

BETH
252 Just as we suspected. 252

MODUS
253 Commander Kirby visited three Blood 253
Eagle camps in succession.

BANKS
254 Commander? 254

BETH
255 My father was a Commander in the 255
Royal Navy Reserve before the war.
I guess MODUS' programming defaults
to military titles.

MODUS
256 Although the Kovac does not provide 256
the... granularity necessary to see
exactly what he did at those camps,
it appears that his intelligence-
gathering methods were...
efficient.

BETH
257 Oh, dear. What do you mean? 257

MODUS
258 We detected... fewer life signs 258
when he departed each camp than had
been present when he arrived.
(beat)
259 After he left the third camp, he 259
scouted the Flagrante Bello area.
We used the opportunity to analyze
the presence of...
(MORE)

MODUS (CONT'D)
personnel in the area, and we will share that analysis with Mr. Watkins.

BETH
260 Thank you, MODUS. Charles needs all 260
the intel he can get his hands on. But I have to ask... why are you doing this? It's certainly not out of the goodness of your heart.

MODUS
261 I see our reputation... precedes 261
us. But you are correct. Our purpose is twofold. First, like you, we have been monitoring the Morningstar's... increased level of engagement and activity in the region. We feel that, if it is allowed to continue unchecked, it represents a potential threat to our... goals.

BETH
262 And second? 262

MODUS
263 We recently became... aware of 263
your... credentials. We were already familiar with those of your parents, but you... you represent something different. We know what you are capable of, perhaps even better than you know yourself.
(beat)
264 We stand ready to provide 264
assistance, in the form of intelligence and analysis. We also have access to... other technology that may be of use during the operation itself. And in return for this assistance...

BETH
265 I'll owe you. I understand now. But 265
you need to understand that if anything happens to Odessa during this operation, that debt will be null and void.

MODUS
266 We find that condition... 266
acceptable.
(MORE)

MODUS (CONT'D)
We believe that Scribe Valdez has an important part to play in the... rehabilitation of Appalachia, so her retrieval is in our... interests as well.

BETH
267 What about ground support? Will the 267
Colonel be sending any Enclave personnel to assist?

MODUS
268 We cannot say. The Colonel is... 268
assessing the situation. That is all we know. We are simply a... facilitator. The final decision is hers.

BETH
269 Let's hope she reaches that 269
decision quickly. We don't know what he's going to... do with her, and we don't know how much time we have.

MODUS
270 I assure you that the Colonel has 270
all of the information necessary to make a decision, and will make one in due time.

BETH
271 Thank you, MODUS. 271

MODUS
272 I will transmit the data as soon as 272
you're ready.

RAHMANI
273 There's a blank holotape in the 273
terminal connected to this radio. You can transmit at any time.

MODUS
274 Transmission beginning on my mark. 274
(beat)
275 Mark. 275
(beat)
276 We will... be in touch. 276

The radio clicks off.

RAHMANI
277 Well, that was... something. Can we 277
trust them?

BETH
278 The Enclave? Of course not. But 278
we're going to need all the help we
can get, and having an eye in the
sky could prove invaluable.

BANKS
279 So could an orbital weapons 279
platform.

RAHMANI
280 Indeed. Knight Kirby... 280

BETH
281 Not going to get used to that 281
anytime soon...

RAHMANI
282 When you give the data to Mr. 282
Watkins, please ask him to perform
his analysis using an air-gapped
system.

BETH
283 Of course. The last thing you need 283
is MODUS' tendrils inside your
systems.

RAHMANI
284 Just be careful that those tendrils 284
don't get inside *your* systems,
either, as it were.

The door opens.

BETH
285 I've made deals with devils before. 285
But right now the focus is on
getting Odessa back.

ANDREW
286 I believe I may be able to assist 286
with that.

BETH
287 Your timing is impeccable, as 287
always, dad.

RAHMANI

288 I'm glad you're here, Mr. Kirby. We have an overall strategy in place, but we're waiting to confirm the location before we finalize it and get down to the details. I understand you may be able to do just that. 288

ANDREW

289 Oh? Checking up on me, are you? 289

BETH

290 No. But it seems the Enclave has been. 290

ANDREW chuckles.

ANDREW

291 That's not surprising. I'd love to have access to their "eye in the sky" for a little while. 291

BETH

292 What did you find out? 292

ANDREW

293 Our suspicions were correct. Odessa is being held at Flagrante Bello. It took me a bit to find the right group of Blood Eagles, but once I did they revealed that they were hired to kidnap her, and handed her over just outside that area. Getting the information out of them was a doddle. 293

RAHMANI

294 Not how I'd describe it, necessarily, but go on. 294

ANDREW

295 Thank you. Now, the people I... erm, spoke with told me that they were instructed to attack Odessa and Knight Carlson on their way back here. Knight Carlson was to be incapacitated but not killed, and Odessa was to be taken. 295

RAHMANI

296 This is not a complaint, Mr. Kirby, but why were they instructed to not kill Knight Carlson? 296

(MORE)

RAHMANI (CONT'D)
Surely that would've been simpler, and wouldn't have left a loose end.

ANDREW
297 Indeed, I wondered the same thing. 297
They didn't know why, only that they were told not to kill him. I think they were quite impressed that they managed to fulfill that part of the request.
(beat)
298 And Lily, I know you're not going 298
to want to hear this, but Odessa was injured in the attack. She was knocked unconscious during the struggle.

BETH
299 Oh, no... 299

ANDREW
300 I know, dear. I'm worried about her 300
as well. But they did reveal something rather interesting related to that. The people they handed her over to were highly displeased, but seemed unconcerned; they indicated that they had medical facilities of some sort available and that she'd be taken care of.

RAHMANI
301 Did you get any insight into who 301
took her?

ANDREW
302 That part was interesting as well. 302
They said that they got the assignment a Raider boss they'd been doing jobs for over the past few months, but they didn't care about the specifics because, and I quote, "caps are caps."

BETH
303 Very on-brand. But I wonder... 303
could this just be Raiders looking for a quick ransom payday and not the Morningstar? Flagrante Bello was in Raider hands last we knew, after all.

ANDREW
304 It's possible, but I feel that the 304
Brotherhood would've received a
ransom demand by now if that were
the case.

BETH
305 And MODUS seemed fairly certain 305
that this was something much bigger
than that. I need to get the data
he sent over to Charles so we can
see exactly what we're up against.

RAHMANI
306 Once we have a more concrete idea 306
of what we're up against, we'll
work that plan up.

ANDREW
307 I did a bit of recruiting before I 307
visited the Blood Eagles as well.
We're going to have an...
interesting team, that's for
certain.

END OF ACT TWO

ACT THREE

INT. FLAGRANTE BELLO RESIDENTIAL AREA

VALDEZ is sitting and reading quietly.

DR. FLAGLER enters.

VALDEZ
308 Hello, Doctor! 308

DR. FLAGLER
309 Odessa! You seem to be feeling better! 309

VALDEZ
310 I am, thank you. And I found something to wear, too. I haven't seen a wardrobe like that since... 310
(beat, wistful)
311 ...since Beth's place. 311

DR. FLAGLER
312 You miss her. 312

VALDEZ
313 I do, yeah. 313

DR. FLAGLER
314 Lily is a... special girl. I watched her grow up. She's the closest thing I'll ever have to a daughter. 314
(beat)
315 A family is something that... eluded me. I was always about the work. What we were doing was so important, and I let that get in the way. I didn't understand balance until it was too late. 315

VALDEZ
316 I'm sorry. 316

DR. FLAGLER
317 So am I, Odessa. So am I. 317
(beat)
318 But that's all in the past. 318

VALDEZ
319 Can I ask you something? 319

DR. FLAGLER
320 Of course. What's on your mind? 320

VALDEZ
321 I did a little bit of walking 321
around, since I was feeling better
and nobody was around. And...

DR. FLAGLER
322 What is it? 322

VALDEZ
323 Did you lock me in? 323

DR. FLAGLER sighs.

DR. FLAGLER
324 No. I didn't lock you in. I didn't 324
want to tell you this until you
were feeling better, but... well,
we're all "locked in," it seems.

VALDEZ
325 We're prisoners?! 325

DR. FLAGLER
326 No! I mean, I suppose in a way we 326
are, but... well, I can't claim to
understand it but it doesn't seem
malicious.

VALDEZ
327 Being held prisoner isn't 327
malicious?!

DR. FLAGLER
328 I'm sorry, I'm not explaining it 328
well. What I can tell you is that
they seem to want to... fix people.
Think about it - you were rescued
from Blood Eagles, and you were
hurt. You know all about my...
struggles.

VALDEZ
329 Did they "fix" you? I thought that 329
maybe you were just... you know,
having a "good day."

DR. FLAGLER
330 I'm not all the way back, but 330
they've already helped a great
deal.

VALDEZ
331 And what about Dex? How is he being 331
"fixed?"

DR. FLAGLER
332 I don't know. Whatever it is, he 332
doesn't like talking about it, and
I didn't want to pry.
(beat)
333 But he's as in the dark as we are. 333
And he's done nothing but help me.
I was... in rough shape. It felt
like... well, it felt like the end.
(beat)
334 And then, one day, I woke up here. 334
Do you remember me telling you that
Vault-Tec had taken all of the
equipment from the lab under my
house?

VALDEZ
335 Yes, I remember. 335

DR. FLAGLER
336 That equipment is here. Along with 336
a lot more.

VALDEZ
337 Hmm. So is Vault-Tec holding us 337
prisoner?

DR. FLAGLER
338 I'm still not convinced that the 338
people who took it were really
Vault-Tec, and this, I think, makes
that even less likely. Why would
Vault-Tec be so secretive with me?
I was one of their senior
researchers.

VALDEZ
339 If I've learned one thing from 339
Beth, it's that Vault-Tec's motives
are rarely clear, and they're even
less often above-board.

DR. FLAGLER
340 I'm afraid you're right about that. 340
But now that you're feeling better,
perhaps we can--

DEX bursts through the door with another person.

DEX

341 Odessa! A little help over here? Let's get her onto that bed. Doctor, can you get some disinfectant and a painkiller? 341

DR. FLAGLER

342 Of course! 342

VALDEZ

343 On it! 343

DEX and VALDEZ put the person onto the bed.

DR. FLAGLER

344 What happened? 344

DEX

345 The same thing that happened to you. Blood Eagles drugged her and tried to snatch her, but a patrol was in the right place at the right time. 345

VALDEZ

346 I have a lot of questions right now, Dex. Are you interacting with these "patrols?" Who are they? Why are they keeping us here? 346

DEX

347 I promise, we can talk after we get her stabilized. I don't know much, but I'll tell you what I do. 347

VALDEZ

348 Alright. 348

(beat)

349 Oh my god! Dr. Holcomb! 349

DEX

350 You know her? 350

VALDEZ

(cagey)

351 I do. I met her... out there. She helped my girlfriend get through a medical issue. 351

(beat)

352 This can't be a coincidence. Dr. Holcomb knew Beth from the Vault, too, even though Beth didn't remember her. 352

DR. FLAGLER
353 From the Vault? I don't remember a Dr. Holcomb, but then again I didn't know every doctor there. 353

VALDEZ
354 Mr. Kirby said the same thing. 354

DR. FLAGLER
355 Andrew and I traveled in the same circles, so that's not all that surprising. 355
(beat)
356 Alright, let me have a quick look to see what we're dealing with. 356

DR. FLAGLER approaches the patient.

DR. FLAGLER (CONT'D)
357 Oh my god! Em! 357

VALDEZ
358 What's wrong, doctor? What is it? 358

DR. FLAGLER
359 This... this isn't "Rebecca Holcomb." This is... my Em. Emily Troiani. 359
(beat)
360 She was supposed to go to Washington to coordinate the resumption of some cooperative research they were doing up there. We thought we'd see each other in a few months, but... well, we didn't. 360

VALDEZ
(shocked)
361 *This* is Emily Troiani? The head of the project? 361

DR. FLAGLER
362 She must've been trying to keep a low profile... so low that she couldn't even come to see me. 362

DR. TROIANI
363 Ugh... where am I? 363

DR. FLAGLER
364 Shhh... try not to talk. 364

DR. TROIANI

365 Tony?! Is it really you? Or did 365
they stick me in a simulation...

DR. FLAGLER

366 It's me! No simulation necessary. 366
(beat)
367 Em, I... need to give you something 367
to counteract what those Blood
Eagles tried to knock you out with.
It's the same thing I gave Odessa.

VALDEZ

368 And I'm already feeling much 368
better.

DR. TROIANI

369 That sounds *very* appealing right 369
now.

DR. FLAGLER

370 Alright. Just a little pinch... 370
(beat)
371 I'll see you soon. And Em? 371

DR. TROIANI

372 Yes, Tony? 372

DR. FLAGLER

373 I love you. 373

DR. TROIANI

374 I love you, too. 374

There is a pause.

DR. FLAGLER

375 Alright, she's sleeping. A few 375
hours should do her wonders.
(beat)
376 Dex, she knows. 376

DEX sighs.

DEX

377 I knew it wouldn't take long. I'm 377
hoping that they'll let you go once
you're fully recovered, but... I
don't know. I'm sorry.

DR. FLAGLER

378 For what it's worth, everything's 378
been provided for us.
(MORE)

DR. FLAGLER (CONT'D)
Food, water, living quarters,
medical facilities, a surprisingly
robust library...

VALDEZ
379 Everything except freedom. 379

MUSICAL TRANSITION

EXT. OUTSKIRTS OF FLAGRANTE BELLO

BETH is addressing the assembled teams.

BETH
380 Looks like everyone's here, 380
Paladin.

RAHMANI
381 Shall we do a roll call? 381

BETH
382 Yes, I think that's a good idea. 382
(over PA)
383 If I may have everyone's attention. 383
We've gone over both our strategy
and our tactics. Our goal is to
find the entrance to the
Morningstar's underground compound,
and then to get me inside. Once
that happens, each team is to
withdraw to a safe distance. I'll
take care of the rest.
(beat)
384 Gray Team, are you ready? 384

ANDREW
385 Gray Team stands ready. 385

BETH
386 Knight Banks, you're in command of 386
our largest single force. Is Blue
Team ready?

BANKS
387 Yes, ma'am. 387

BETH
388 Elder Niemann? 388

NIEMANN

389 The Devotees of the Most Holy 389
Mothman will be guided by his true
light as we join the struggle
against this “Morningstar” and his
blasphemous false light.

BETH

390 Commander Johns? 390

JOHNS

391 The Responders vowed long ago to do 391
everything we could to protect
Appalachia and its people. Scribe
Valdez is one of the good ones, and
The New Responders are fully
prepared to do our part to help get
her back safely.

BETH

392 Lieutenant Connors, is Black Team 392
ready?

CINDY

393 The Enclave is ready to assist. And 393
the Colonel sends her regards.

BETH

394 Foundation, what say you? 394

FOUNDATION REPRESENTATIVE

395 We’re ready to fight for the future 395
of Appalachia.

BETH

396 And lastly, Major Kelly. Can we 396
count on the support of the Free
States?

MAJOR KELLY

397 Yes, ma’am. It’s incumbent upon the 397
Free States to help ensure the
freedom of Appalachia and everyone
in it, and from what you and your
mother have told us, this is the
biggest existential threat we’ve
seen since David Thorpe and his
Raiders.

BETH

398 Thank you, everyone. 398

CARLSON approaches.

CARLSON

399 I heard you might need a hand. 399

BETH

400 Knight Carlson! Are you sure you're 400
up to this?

CARLSON

401 I'm the one who's responsible for 401
her being taken in the first place.
If I'm breathing, I'm going to help
get her back.

BETH

402 Thank you, Knight. I could use 402
someone watching my back. How about
you stick with me?

CARLSON

403 Yes, ma'am. 403

RAHMANI

404 Shall we give the order, Knight 404
Kirby?

BETH
(over PA)

405 I know that this group was only 405
assembled a short time ago. And I
know that there may be some
lingering factional tensions
between some of you. You're here
for different reasons. Some of you
are here because you owe a debt to
me or to another member of my
family, and that debt has come due.
Some of you are here because Odessa
Valdez is your sister-in-arms. Some
of you are here simply because you
feel it is the right thing to do.
(beat)
406 Regardless of what your particular 406
personal motivations may be, as of
this moment we are a single,
unified force with a firmly defined
goal - to retrieve Scribe Valdez
from the clutches of a person whom
we believe presents an existential
threat to us, to the people we
love, and to the place that we've
adopted as our home.
(beat)
407 Scribe Valdez has already been 407
taken.

(MORE)

BETH (CONT'D)

Powerful technology has already
been looted and may already be in
use. The whole fury and might of
the enemy may soon be turned on us,
and so we make our stand here, on
this ground that has already seen
so much blood spilled, so many
lives lost. Based upon the
intelligence that's been provided
to us, we expect resistance. We
expect a fight. I suspect that the
Battle of Flagrante Bello is about
to begin.

(beat)

408 When most of you woke up this 408
morning, you were blissfully
ignorant about the Morningstar and
the rapidly rising threat he poses.
I'm sure some of you wish that were
still the case. And I'm sure some
of you long to be at home, with
your loved ones, and not standing
with me, armed and armored, to join
the effort to mitigate that threat.

(beat)

409 I cannot restore your ignorance. 409
Nor can I restore your bliss. But I
can offer you an opportunity. If
anyone here gathered has no stomach
to this fight, then please, let
them depart, and depart quickly.
Go; no one will stop you. We will
wish you only a safe journey back
to your home and to your bed.

(beat)

410 But those who remain - we few, we 410
happy few, we band of sisters and
of brothers, for anyone who stands
and chooses to fight with me will
forever be my kin, with a bond
formed not by blood, but in blood -
In years to come, people will look
back on this day and remember. They
will remember how we - a hastily
assembled group of disparate groups
of disparate people with disparate
interests - came together to truly
reclaim this land.

(beat)

411 The Morningstar's newly bold action 411
makes it clear that he seeks to
break us.

(MORE)

BETH (CONT'D)

If we can stand up to him, then Appalachia may be free, and the life of our little portion of the world may move forward into broad, sunlit uplands. But if we fail, then Appalachia, including all that we have known and cared for, will sink into the abyss of a new dark age, made more sinister by the lights of perverted science. If not by his hand alone, by the hands of those who know, through our inaction or our failure, that Appalachia is ripe for the taking.

(beat)

412 This is one battle against one foe. 412
If we prevail, the Morningstar will not be the last threat we face. But what we will prove today is that we can and will - together - face whatever threats may arise. We will rise again and unite again whenever our home needs to be defended.

(beat)

413 We make the future we deserve. 413
Today will be remembered as the day the tide turned. The day we proved that we were not just members of the Brotherhood of Steel, or Settlers, or Followers of the Mothman. We are not Free Staters or residents of Foundation. We stand together as one.

The crowd cheers.

MUSICAL TRANSITION

EXT. FLAGRANTE BELLO, NIGHT

We join the battle in medias res.

BANKS

(over radio)

414 We're pinned down over here! 414

ANDREW

415 This is Gray 1. Elder Niemann, 415
you're the closest to Blue Team's position. Can you assist?

NIEMANN

416 We shall protect Knight Banks and 416
his team from the aggressors.

BETH

417 Has anyone located an entrance? 417
Concentrate on areas that are more heavily protected.

JOHNS

418 Nothing yet, Beth. I'm starting to 418
wonder if this wasn't a wild goose chase.

BETH

419 It isn't. Our intel is solid and so 419
is our analysis.

An explosion hits near Beth.

BETH (CONT'D)

420 Dammit! It feels like we're being 420
steered to the left.

CARLSON

421 Maybe. But don't read too much into 421
it. Just stay focused.

BETH

422 Thank you, Greg. 422

There is a loud outbreak of gunfire.

CARLSON

423 Shit! Ambush! 423

BETH

424 We're cut off! 424

(beat)

425 Any units in our vicinity, we are 425
under heavy fire!

ANDREW

426 I see you, Lily! But we can't get 426
to you. There's a phalanx between you and the rest of us.

BETH

427 Dammit! 427

CARLSON

428 Let's hunker down and hope that the 428
cavalry can fight through that before we get overrun.

BETH

429 Everyone, listen. If I'm captured 429
or killed *someone* needs to find
that entrance and retrieve Odessa.
I don't care who it is, but get her
back.

(beat)

430 No response? 430

CARLSON

431 Comms are jammed. Jesus. 431

MODUS

432 Miss Kirby, we have detected that 432
you are in need of... assistance.

BETH

433 Bit of an understatement, MODUS! 433

MODUS

434 We believe we have identified the 434
entrance to the underground
facility where Scribe Valdez may be
held. This analysis is based--

BETH

435 You can explain it all to me later! 435
We have more immediate problems at
the moment.

MODUS

436 Ah, yes. You do. There is a large 436
group of... hmm... Super Mutants
advancing on your position. Shall
I... eliminate them?

BETH

437 Yes! Please! 437

MODUS

438 We have detected no friendly forces 438
in their immediate vicinity.
Orbital strike incoming. Please
brace yourselves.

After a few seconds, there is a massive explosion.

BETH

439 Can you get rid of the wall of 439
mercenaries between us and the rest
of our teams?

MODUS
440 We can. We calculate a 61.3% 440
Probability that we can eliminate
the enemy forces without...
collateral damage.

BETH
441 That's not good enough. 441

MODUS
442 We recommend that you move to the 442
entrance that we identified. Other
hostile forces are approaching, but
you can... beat them there if you
move now. Forty-six meters, bearing
2-9-Zero. I've downloaded the
coordinates to your Pip-Boy.

BETH
443 2-9-Zero? That's the direction they 443
seemed to be pushing us...

CARLSON
444 Must've just been random. 444

BETH
445 Alright, MODUS, we're on the move. 445
But our comms are still jammed.
Wait, how are *you* communicating
with us?

MODUS
446 We have... ways of defeating 446
more... common methods of radio
jamming.
(beat)
447 We will inform Lieutenant Connors 447
of your situation and your plans.
We will also attempt to restore
general communications.

BETH
448 Have her put my father in charge 448
and coordinate a withdrawal to
Atlas.

MODUS
449 We will. And we will monitor their 449
withdrawal and... handle any forces
that choose to pursue them.

BETH
450 No collateral damage, MODUS. 450

MODUS
451 Of course not, Miss Kirby. 451
(beat)
452 Good luck. 452

BETH
453 You believe in luck? 453

MODUS
454 We do not. 454

BETH laughs.

BETH
455 Alright, then. Thank you, MODUS. 455

MODUS
456 Thank you, Miss Kirby. We will... 456
be in touch.

BETH
457 Are you good to move, Greg? You've 457
been wearing a brave face, but I
can tell you're hurting.

CARLSON
458 I'm good. Let's get moving. 458

BETH and CARLSON move quickly.

CARLSON (CONT'D)
459 Keep your head on a swivel. This 459
is... wow, a hell of a lot of
damage. But let's make sure we
don't get surprised.

BETH
460 Right. You know, you've really 460
grown since the first time I met
you. Back in that lab. You were
so... green.

CARLSON laughs.

CARLSON
461 I was, wasn't I? 461

Gunfire erupts!

BETH
462 Get down! On our flank! 462

CARLSON
463 Where the hell did they come from? 463

BETH

464 I don’t know, but they’re coming this way, and fast. Are comms still jammed? 464

CARLSON

465 I don’t know, worth a shot. 465

BETH

466 If anyone can hear me, we have a group of... six mercenaries who are heavily armed and almost on top of us! 466

AMANDA

(over radio)

467 Hey, Princess, I heard you were raising some hell, and you didn't invite me? Rude. 467

BETH

468 Amanda! 468

AMANDA

469 I brought some friends with me, I hope that's okay. Need a hand? 469

BETH

470 Yes! Are you close? 470

AMANDA

471 Close enough that we can take these morons out. 471

BETH

472 Thank you, Amanda. 472

CINDY

(over radio)

473 Amanda? You’re... you’re back? 473

AMANDA

474 Yeah, dollface, I’m back. And... I’m here to stay this time. I’m sorry I had to take off, I just... well, we have a lot to talk about. 474

CINDY

475 Oh, no... 475

AMANDA

476 It's all good stuff, don't worry. 476
Now let's get back to making sure
this reunion happens, then we can
talk about ours. Okay?

CINDY

477 Okay. 477

There is increased gunfire.

CARLSON

478 Wow. That didn't take long. Wonder 478
how many "friends" she brought with
her.

BETH

479 However many it is, they'll come in 479
handy when we get inside. We
expected a lot of resistance
topside, but the sheer amount of it
makes me think we're going to need
more firepower than just the two of
us can provide.

CARLSON

480 Are you sure that's a good idea? 480
You said you wanted to avoid a
firefight, to make sure Odessa
didn't get caught in the crossfire.

BETH

481 I did, but based on what I've seen 481
I think that may be a chance we
have to take.
(beat)
482 We're here. These are the 482
coordinates.

CARLSON

483 Let's see... there's a door here. 483

CARLSON tries the door and opens it after struggling.

BETH approaches the door.

CARLSON (CONT'D)

484 Shit! Incoming! 484

CARLSON tackles Beth through the doorway and slams the door shut. An explosion is heard on the other side of the door.

CARLSON (CONT'D)

485 Are you okay? 485

BETH

486 Yes. What was that? 486

CARLSON

487 Must've been booby-trapped. Sorry I had to tackle you. 487

BETH

488 It's alright. Let's open that door back up... carefully... and wait for Amanda and her team. 488

CARLSON struggles with the door.

CARLSON

489 The explosion must've blocked it. 489

BETH

490 Oh, dear. I hope Amanda didn't get here yet. 490

(beat)

491 Amanda, are you alright? 491

(beat)

492 Amanda? 492

CARLSON

493 Comms are jammed again. There must be another jammer in here. 493

(beat)

494 Hey, check this out - stairs. Looks like the only option. 494

BETH

495 Well, onward and... downward, I suppose. 495

BETH and CARLSON descend the stairs and walk down a hallway.

CARLSON

496 This place looks... nice. Almost like a hotel. 496

BETH

497 Must be a residential area. Wait. Shh. 497

(beat, sotto)

498 I hear people talking. Sounds like it's coming from up the hall. Must be from one of these rooms. 498

A gun cocks.

BETH sighs.

BETH (CONT'D)
499 So. It was you, all along. 499

CARLSON
500 It was. I was lucky, though, Alan 500
seemed to go out of his way to cast
suspicion on himself. That made
things a lot easier.
(beat)
501 Your weapons, please. Slowly. 501

BETH
502 Here. 502

BETH gives her weapons to CARLSON.

CARLSON
503 I think it's time that you met the 503
man himself. He's been waiting for
you.

BETH and CARLSON approach a door.

CARLSON knocks and opens the door.

VALDEZ
(excited)
504 Beth! And Knight Carlson! I *knew* 504
you'd find me! There's a lot going
on, but let's get everybody out of
here first and we can talk about it
at Atlas. Dr. Holcomb is here, too!
But she's not Dr. Holcomb, she's
really Dr. Troiani! The head of
Project Mind's Eye!

BETH
(through clenched teeth)
505 You. 505

DEX
506 Hello, Kirsche. It's nice to see 506
you again. I hope you didn't mind
the little show we put on for you
out there. Had to keep up
appearances, you know?

VALDEZ
507 What's going on? You two... know 507
each other?

BETH

508 Yes, we do. Quite well, in fact. 508

(beat)

509 Odessa Valdez, I'd like you to meet Bryan Reardon. Or, as I suppose he'd prefer to be addressed... the Morningstar. 509

<u>END OF EPISODE 9</u>

Season One
Part Three: The Book of Elizabeth

Episode 10:
"I Shall Take Care"

by

D.K. Trueno

"I SHALL TAKE CARE"

INT. FLAGRANTE BELLO RESIDENTIAL AREA

BETH
(through clenched teeth)
1 You. 1

BRYAN
2 Hello, Kirsche. It's nice to see 2
you again. I hope you didn't mind
the little show we put on for you
out there. Had to keep up
appearances, you know?

VALDEZ
3 What's going on? You two... know 3
each other?

BETH
4 Yes, we do. Quite well, in fact. 4
(beat)
5 Odessa Valdez, I'd like you to meet 5
Bryan Reardon. Or, as I suppose
he'd prefer to be addressed... the
Morningstar.

VALDEZ
6 Wait... the person your dad sent to 6
Washington and then disappeared?

BRYAN
7 The very same, Odessa. I'm 7
fulfilling the mission that Kirsche
here and I *both* swore an oath to
complete.

BETH
8 You do not get to call me that. Not 8
anymore.

BRYAN
9 I think that a reminder of who you 9
used to be is exactly what you
need.

VALDEZ
10 Can someone please tell me what's 10
going on?

DR. FLAGLER
11 Bryan Reardon? But... hrm. I feel 11
like that name should mean
something to me, but it doesn't.

BRYAN

12 I'm sorry about that, doctor. I had to take... precautions when we brought you in. Couldn't have you giving up the game when we brought Odessa here in. 12

DR. FLAGLER

13 What are you talking about? 13

BRYAN

14 I don't know how much you remember. Probably not much considering the state you were in. I was just glad we got to you in time. 14

DR. FLAGLER

15 But the rehabilitation program... you... fixed me. You completed my research. Our research. 15

BRYAN

16 Well, *I* didn't complete the research. I had some help. I was able to track down one of the four remaining scientists from your team, and I brought him here. He was happy to get back to work. 16

(beat)

17 Dr. Troiani here was one of the stragglers. She... 17

DR. TROIANI

18 I left Appalachia almost immediately after leaving the Vault. I was supposed to go to Washington, but... 18

BRYAN

19 Nobody can get near it. I'm sure you ran into exactly the same problems we did. 19

DR. TROIANI

20 It was awful. The radiation was terrible, monsters left and right... 20

BRYAN

21 Both human and otherwise. 21

DR. TROIANI

22 Yeah. One of the scientists you couldn't track down... 22

(MORE)

DR. TROIANI (CONT'D)
well, he didn't make it. I was lucky that I survived myself. I had to make some very difficult decisions out there.

BRYAN
23 I understand, and I'm sorry. I lost 23
the rest of my team out there, too. They were good people. The best, in fact. And I'm going to honor their sacrifice by completing this mission, by any means necessary.

DR. TROIANI
24 I ended up kind of hiding out, 24
going place to place, but I had to get to the central lab. I didn't even know if it would still be there, but... it was almost pathological at that point.

DR. FLAGLER
25 I can understand that. I was 25
obsessed with trying to... fix myself with the equipment at *my* lab, but in the end I just ended up making myself worse.

DR. TROIANI
26 You shouldn't have had to do it 26
alone, Tony. I should've been there to help.

DR. FLAGLER
27 There's no way you could've been, 27
Em. Everything that happened... everything I did, that's on me. You had to concentrate on surviving, and... I'm so glad you did.

BRYAN
28 But that's all in the past now, 28
right? One more treatment, using everything we've learned, and you'll be as good as new.

VALDEZ
29 What's he talking about? 29

DR. FLAGLER
30 It appears that... Bryan here 30
managed to coordinate the resumption and apparently the completion of my research.
(MORE)

DR. FLAGLER (CONT'D)
And I suppose I was the perfect test subject.

BRYAN
31 You were. I mean, you were almost completely gone when we grabbed you. You would've been dead within a week or two. 31
(beat)
32 But I had to take some... liberties when I was rooting around in there. I'm sure you understand. 32

DR. FLAGLER
33 What did you do? 33

BRYAN
34 I made you forget about me - who I am, what my mission was, all of it. It was a little complicated because of my relationship with Kirsche here, but I think I managed to do it without causing much collateral damage. 34

DR. FLAGLER
35 That was something that we hypothesized that we'd be able to do, eventually... but it would require a *direct* interface. 35

BRYAN
36 That's right. Building that was a challenge. Kind of like... a partners' desk for the mind. And the initial testing... it didn't go well. 36

DR. FLAGLER
(upset)
37 How many people died testing it? 37

BRYAN
38 Does it matter? You, of all people, should understand the sacrifices that need to be made for the greater good. All of you should. 38

VALDEZ
39 The ends justify the means? 39

BRYAN
40 It brings me no pleasure to have had to handle it this way, but yes. 40
(MORE)

BRYAN (CONT'D)
Especially when the "ends" are this important.

VALDEZ
41 What are you trying to accomplish? 41
This is clearly more about curing dementia and repairing neurological damage.

BRYAN
42 In due time, Odessa. It will all be 42
clear to you, I promise.
(beat)
43 Now that the cat's out of the bag, 43
as it were, there's no need to keep you locked up in here. You have the run of this facility, and I think you'll be impressed.

BETH
44 That's one word for what I'm 44
expecting to be.

BRYAN
45 Don't bother trying to escape. I 45
mean, on one hand I guess I'd be disappointed if you *didn't* try, but I recommend saving your energy. We have a lot of work to do.
(beat)
46 We'll talk later, and everything 46
will be made clear. Greg? Let's give our guests some time to relax. They have a big day ahead of them tomorrow.

BRYAN and CARLSON leave.

VALDEZ
47 What the hell is going on? 47

BETH
48 I don't know yet... but whatever it 48
is it's not good.

DR. TROIANI
49 That's an understatement. 49

BETH
50 Yeah. I'm just trying to read into 50
what he said. He almost took offense to the idea that he was doing anything other than fulfilling our mission, but...

VALDEZ
51 But how is... whatever this is 51
fulfilling your mission to keep civilization going in Appalachia?

BETH
52 I don't know. Bryan was always five 52
steps ahead of the rest of us strategically.
(beat)
53 I suppose it's possible that he had 53
a different brief from the rest of us, but my father *should* have known about it if he did.

VALDEZ
54 Unless Vault-Tec kept it from him. 54

BETH
55 Right. That's always a possibility, 55
unfortunately.

VALDEZ
56 We have four smart people in this 56
room right now, maybe we can think it through. How could this technology be used to further the goal of keeping the area from falling into chaos?

DR. FLAGLER
57 Well, he seems to have selectively 57
erased part of my memory. That could play into it somehow.

VALDEZ
58 Perhaps. 58

DR. TROIANI
59 Let's think... bigger. He said that 59
he had to directly interface with Tony's mind, and manipulated his memory in very specific ways.

BETH
60 It could be leveraged for more than 60
just... seeking and destroying.

DR. TROIANI
61 Exactly. Maybe instead of just an 61
eraser, it can be used as a pencil, too.

VALDEZ
62 Wait! Dr. Flagler, you said 62
something about that when we first spoke, didn't you? You said... um... That you didn't have the right kind of pencil to fix yourself.

DR. FLAGLER
63 Yes! I do remember that! I was 63
having so much trouble keeping my thoughts coherent, sometimes I found it easier to think in metaphors.

BETH
64 That does beg the question, 64
though... did he use a "pencil" when he was inside your head, or just the eraser?

DR. FLAGLER
65 Well, he clearly did a lot of work 65
fixing my neural pathways. I feel sharper now than I did twenty years ago. And he said that he hasn't even finished the repairs yet.

BETH
66 Doctor, I think we're going to need 66
to keep a close eye on you, just in case. He may have done more than he's letting on.

DR. FLAGLER sighs.

DR. FLAGLER
67 And I may be a danger to all of 67
you.

BETH
68 I'm sorry. I hope it's not the 68
case.

DR. FLAGLER
69 It's alright, Lily. And I'll be 69
sure to say something if I don't... feel right.

BETH
70 Thank you. 70

VALDEZ

71 So, we have a working hypothesis 71
that he can erase memories, and may
have the ability to *manipulate* them
as well. And given that
manipulating memories was an
important part of this project, it
stands to reason that if he
completed the part of the project
to repair damaged minds...

BETH

72 ...then he very well may have also 72
completed the other part.
(beat)
73 Wait - the operation at Foundation! 73

VALDEZ

74 He was trying to kidnap Paige, 74
wasn't he?

BETH

75 Yes! So... what, he was going to 75
brainwash the leader of Foundation,
the largest single settlement in
Appalachia and... send him back as
though nothing had happened?

VALDEZ

76 Hmm. That's not exactly an elegant 76
plan, but I suppose it could work.

BETH

77 If my surmise about how this 77
technology works is correct, then
it would be like... kidnapping
someone and replacing them with a
duplicate. A duplicate that is
completely indistinguishable from
the original.

VALDEZ

78 They wouldn't even know anything 78
had happened. It's like you said at
your place, after what happened at
Craig's club - it was like you'd
always felt that way.

BETH

79 It did. It was... unnerving. I knew 79
something was wrong, but at the
same time, it felt like there
wasn't. Like my mind was trying to
convince me everything was fine.

DR. TROIANI

80 Keep in mind that the Visiontron at 80
Craig's club is related to, but not
identical to the tech we were
working on for Mind's Eye.

(beat)

81 The eventual plan was to bring the 81
two projects together, and that's
what I was supposed to go to
Washington for. Vault 112 was the
main location for Project
Tranquility, but like Bryan said,
we couldn't get anywhere near DC
itself.

BETH

82 So what did you do? 82

DR. TROIANI

83 There were other labs, farther away 83
from the Capitol. Vault-Tec knew
that DC was going to get a hell of
a lot of nuclear firepower dumped
on it, so they spread the labs out
a lot farther than the ones here. I
tried to get to those, but... well,
I was one scientist on her own out
here in the Wasteland, and it
became apparent that there was no
way I was going to survive long
enough to get to even one of them.

VALDEZ

84 So you decided to come back to 84
Appalachia.

DR. TROIANI

85 Yes. I thought that I could get 85
together with some Vault-Tec people
and lock down the Project
Tranquility lab that was here, but
I couldn't find any. And before I
knew it, Craig and Davina had
broken into the lab and taken the
pod, the tapes, and all the control
modules.

DR. FLAGLER

86 Did they damage any of it?! 86

DR. TROIANI

87 They didn't. I think they knew they 87
were onto something big, so they
were careful with it.

(MORE)

DR. TROIANI (CONT'D)
I think the most impressive part was keeping it secret. And it was even more impressive that you two somehow managed to get in. I saw dozens of legitimate... well, as legitimate as criminals can be, I suppose... I'll say "legitimate-ish" parties get turned away. But not you two.

BETH
88 Well, I had years of training and Odessa here is a natural. 88

VALDEZ laughs.

VALDEZ
89 I don't know if I'd go that far... 89

DR. TROIANI
90 I would. You even had me fooled. If I hadn't recognized Beth, I wouldn't have thought anything of it. 90

VALDEZ
91 We make a good team. And I *was* trained by Andrew Kirby. 91

BETH
92 I told you he was the best teacher on the planet. 92

VALDEZ
93 Should we, um... talk about the elephant in the room? 93

BETH
94 What's that? 94

VALDEZ
95 What's he going to do with *us*? 95

BETH
96 It's a good question. There are so many... permutations of why each of us may be here. 96

VALDEZ
97 I understand why the doctors are here. He said that he was trying to bring the original research team back together. What was left of it, at least. 97

BETH

98 Of course. But what about us? 98

VALDEZ

99 I think there are two possibilities for why I'm here. He either has a plan to move against the Brotherhood and wants to use me for that plan, or I was just... bait. 99

BETH

100 Hmm. Either of those is very possible. He knew that I would move heaven and earth to get to you... and to get you back. 100

VALDEZ

101 And you did. 101

DR. FLAGLER clears his throat.

DR. TROIANI

102 Tony and I have some... catching up to do. 102

DR. FLAGLER

103 The residential area here looks like it was designed to hold about 30 people. There are plenty of empty rooms. We're going to get some rest. 103

DR. TROIANI

104 I suggest you do the same. 104

BETH

105 I still have a lot of adrenalin running through my system after that fight. I'm not going to sleep for a while. 105

DR. TROIANI

106 I understand. I'm still recovering from those Blood Eagles drugging me, so I'm going to sleep like a baby. 106

BETH

107 Hopefully that doesn't mean you'll wake up every hour crying. 107

DR. TROIANI laughs.

DR. TROIANI

108 I hope you're right. We'll talk 108
soon. Good night, you two.

BETH

109 Good night. 109

VALDEZ

110 Good night. 110

DR. TROIANI and DR. FLAGLER leave.

BETH sighs.

BETH

111 So, now what? I thought this was 111
going to be a rescue mission, but I
somehow managed to get myself
captured.

(beat)

112 I can't believe Carlson had me 112
fooled. I need to be better than
that. But at least that explains
how those Blood Eagles got the drop
on you. There's no way they
could've taken you if he hadn't
betrayed you.

VALDEZ

113 I was shocked as well, and I've 113
known him for months. I was so
suspicious of Alan that... wait, is
Alan part of it, too?

BETH

114 No. At least I don't believe he is. 114
We... talked right after I learned
you'd been taken. He explained his
actions, and for what it's worth, I
believe him. Though I was so wrong
about Carlson I'm not even sure
anymore...

VALDEZ

115 Don't beat yourself up. Maybe 115
Bryan... reprogrammed Greg, too.

BETH

116 There are *so many* questions right 116
now, and only one person has the
answers. We're cut off from all the
resources I'm used to having. No
mum, no dad, no Charles.

VALDEZ

117 Um... aren't you forgetting 117
something?

BETH

118 You're right. God, Odessa, you're 118
right. I have the most important
resource of all. My North Star.
(beat)
119 We'll figure this thing out. 119
Together. No matter what we have to
do.

<u>END OF ACT ONE</u>

ACT TWO

INT. FORT ATLAS

RAHMANI, ANDREW, and CINDY are discussing strategy.

RAHMANI

120 I'm open to suggestions here. But 120
the fact that Beth, Odessa, and
Greg haven't contacted us yet has
me concerned.

ANDREW

121 I'm concerned as well, of course. 121
But we made the decision that the
best course of action was letting
Lily handle this rather than going
back in with guns blazing.

(beat)

122 Remember, we lost contact *before* 122
they entered the facility, so
there's likely radio jamming
equipment in use inside, just as it
was outside until MODUS eliminated
it.

RAHMANI

123 That's true, but we still need to 123
consider when a shift in that
strategy becomes necessary. Do we
wait a day? Two days? A week?

CINDY

124 I've been in contact with Enclave 124
leadership since we got back to
Atlas, and we're prepared to assist
with a second rescue operation if
needed. Intel, boots on the ground,
whatever you need.

RAHMANI

125 Why is the Colonel so interested in 125
getting our Scribe back?

CINDY

126 I don't know what MODUS told her, 126
but whatever it was convinced her
that getting both Scribe Valdez *and*
Beth back has become an Enclave
priority.

RAHMANI
127 That's good to know, Lieutenant, 127
and we may take you up on that
offer.

ANDREW
128 But right now, we need to trust 128
that my daughter is handling this
situation. Rushing in with a
brigade behind us is much more
likely to result in tragedy than
retrieving either or both of them.

RAHMANI
129 I agree. And based upon what I've 129
seen from her, I trust her
abilities, her instincts, and her
training.

There is a knock on the door.

ANDREW
130 Amanda! 130

CINDY
131 Amanda! 131

RAHMANI
132 Who are you? Other than "Amanda." 132

CINDY
133 She's... Beth's best friend. 133

ANDREW
134 And someone we can trust. 134

AMANDA
135 Can someone tell me what's going 135
on? And how I can help?

ANDREW
136 Right now, we're just... waiting. 136

AMANDA
137 You're *waiting*? Jesus. I should've 137
just gone over there and gotten her
myself. I figured the Brotherhood
would be over here gazing at their
navels, but you, Mr. Kirby? I
thought you'd be ripping doors off
hinges and beating people to death
with them.

ANDREW chuckles.

ANDREW

138 That *is* still on the table. But the 138
three of us have been discussing
next steps since we got back.

AMANDA

139 The *three* of you? Cindy, are you... 139
Wow. I'm really proud of you.

CINDY

140 Thanks. I know how important Beth 140
is to you, and once the Colonel
agreed to join the fight, I wanted
to be the one who helped get her
back.

AMANDA

141 That's... thank you, dollface. 141

ANDREW

142 While we wait, I do have some new 142
information. My inside man at the
MacAllans' club told me that their
neuroscientist, Dr. Rebecca
Holcomb, has gone missing. And on
my way here to Fort Atlas, I
learned that Dr. Anthony Flagler,
also a neuroscientist, is nowhere
to be found as well.

AMANDA

143 I take it you don't think that's a 143
coincidence.

ANDREW

144 Well, at first I did entertain the 144
idea that it might be. But then I
learned something very interesting.
(beat)
145 Dr. Holcomb was working under an 145
assumed name. She is, in fact, Dr.
Emily Troiani, who worked with Dr.
Flagler on Project Mind's Eye, the
project that is responsible for the
technology that the Morningstar is
amassing.

RAHMANI

146 That certainly doesn't sound like a 146
coincidence.

ANDREW

147 Indeed, it does not. He could've 147
snatched Tony at any point.
(MORE)

ANDREW (CONT'D)
He was living alone, unguarded. And the Morningstar already took technology and research from him some time ago. Why not just take him then? There has to be a reason.

AMANDA
148 Yeah. It's like he was waiting for 148
this exact moment to pull the trigger on his plan and get all the pieces in place at once.
(beat)
149 Look, I'm just a Ra-- respectable 149
tavern owner and all, so I'll let you big brains figure out what this guy's plan is. But if there's anything I can do to get Beth & Odessa back, I want to do it. Okay?

RAHMANI
150 Thank you, Amanda. You appear to 150
have the trust of both Mr. Kirby and the Enclave, so we'll keep you in the loop.
(beat)
151 But for right now, we're just going 151
to give Beth time to do what she does best.

ANDREW
152 Why don't you go home, and I'll 152
radio you the moment we learn anything new, or if anything happens.

RAHMANI
153 You can go back to the bunker as 153
well, Lieutenant.

AMANDA
154 Or you can come back to my place. 154
It's closer than the Whitespring, so you can... you know, get back here quicker if something happens. And if we're in one place, it'll save time getting in touch with us.

CINDY
155 Paladin? 155

RAHMANI
156 However you want to handle this is 156
fine by me, Lieutenant. But I'm not your commanding officer.
(MORE)

RAHMANI (CONT'D)
I'll leave it to you to decide if this is something that you feel you need to clear with her or if it's the kind of decision you're empowered to make on your own.

CINDY
157 I'll give her a heads-up. Can you 157
keep an empty bunk available in case she decides it isn't a good idea?

RAHMANI
158 Of course. You're welcome to stay 158
here as much or as little as you feel you need to.

CINDY
159 Thank you, Paladin. 159

RAHMANI
160 Mr. Kirby, I'd like to speak with 160
Charles and get a sitrep. If anything changes, I want us to be ready.

ANDREW
161 Of course. 161

RAHMANI
162 Amanda, Lieutenant Connors, we'll 162
contact you immediately if anything happens.

CINDY
163 We'll do the same, Paladin. Thank 163
you.

ANDREW and RAHMANI leave.

AMANDA
164 So... how mad at me are you? 164

CINDY
165 I'm furious! How could you just 165
leave like that?

AMANDA
166 I'm sorry, baby. I just... had to 166
get away. I was overwhelmed.
(beat)
(MORE)

AMANDA (CONT'D)
167 I think watching Beth and Odessa 167
fall in love like they did kind of
drove home how I feel about you,
and... it scared me.

CINDY
168 I've never seen you scared. 168

AMANDA
169 Maybe that's why I couldn't say 169
goodbye. I didn't want you to see
me like that.

CINDY
170 Angel, I love you, and that means I 170
don't just want to see you when
you're at your best. I want to be
there to help you when you're
struggling, too! I... I want to be
the one you come to when you feel
like that, not the one you run away
from.

AMANDA
171 I wasn't running away from you, 171
baby. I was running away from me.

CINDY
172 Yet you *did* run away from me. Your 172
actions don't just affect *you*. They
affect the people who care about
you. Who love you. I was
devastated, and I know Beth was,
too. We didn't know if we'd ever
see you again, and that hurt. A
lot.

AMANDA
173 I never wanted to hurt you. 173

CINDY
174 But you *did*. 174

CINDY sighs

CINDY (CONT'D)
175 You are so frustrating. Do you know 175
what I noticed about Beth and
Odessa? Why they fit together so
well? Beth isn't constantly
comparing Odessa to you, or their
relationship to the one you two
had. Yet you can't seem to get past
it. Or her.

AMANDA

176 Hey, that's not fair! 176

CINDY

177 Isn't it? 177

AMANDA

178 I'm not still hung up on Beth! 178

CINDY

179 But you are! And don't tell me you two aren't getting back together, that's not what I mean. It just feels like you look at me through the lens of what happened between you two. 179

(beat)

180 Beth has moved past it, and a big part of that is because she found the right person to move past it with. You not being able to do that... 180

(beat)

181 I'm sorry, Angel. I guess... I'm sorry if I'm... not enough. 181

AMANDA

182 You are, baby! You are! I came back because Beth needed my help, but I'm staying because of you. 182

CINDY

183 I want to believe you. 183

AMANDA

184 Then believe me! 184

(beat)

185 Look, when I got wind of what happened, yeah, my first thought was that Beth needed me. And I gotta be honest, I wasn't ready to come back. To face you after running away like that. 185

(beat)

186 But when I heard your voice over comms... I realized in that moment that leaving was the wrong thing to do. I felt *so much* regret. And I still do. I'm so sorry, dollface. For running away, for hurting you... especially for making you question how much I love you. 186

CINDY

187 That's the one thing I never 187
doubted. I was just worried that it
wasn't enough.

AMANDA

188 I've never felt like this about 188
anyone else, Cindy. And I'd like
to... you know, see where this all
leads, if you'll have me.

CINDY

189 Beth talked about me being the one 189
who brought you two back together,
as friends. Maybe she brought us
back together, too.

AMANDA sighs.

AMANDA

190 This whole thing is... really 190
complicated. And that's going to
make it hard sometimes.

CINDY

191 I know. But some things are worth 191
fighting for.

END OF ACT TWO

ACT THREE

INT. FLAGRANTE BELLO RESIDENTIAL AREA

BETH enters the common area. VALDEZ is reading.

VALDEZ
192 Good morning. 192

BETH
193 Good morning. How long have you been up? 193

VALDEZ
194 A little while. I took a walk around the facility. It's enormous. But he wasn't exactly telling the truth when he said we had the run of the place. 194

BETH
195 There are areas that are still off-limits? 195

VALDEZ
196 Yes. There were a few doors that were locked up tight. They weren't guarded, but... 196

BETH
197 What is it? 197

VALDEZ
198 It sounded like there were Super Mutants on the other side of most of them. 198

BETH
199 Super Mutants? I wonder if he's been experimenting on them as well. If he could program an army of those, Appalachia would be in serious trouble. 199

VALDEZ
200 Even more serious than it already is. 200

BETH
201 Indeed. I was thinking about the timing of all this. 201
(MORE)

BETH (CONT'D)
He's seemed to make so much of this about me, personally, that having me here, in his clutches makes it feel like he's about to make a move. A big one.

VALDEZ
202 I was thinking about that failed 202
operation at Foundation. He was trying to kidnap their leader, but the more I think about it the more logical it is that he'd already... tested his plan.

BETH
203 I see what you're saying. You don't 203
try to execute your plan on a key piece until you're sure that you're ready.

VALDEZ
204 And what better way to be sure of 204
that than testing it on other people?

BETH
205 Odessa, I'm worried. About you. 205

VALDEZ
206 About me? Why? 206

BETH
207 I think he may be planning on using 207
you to infiltrate the Brotherhood. I don't think you were just bait.

VALDEZ
208 The Brotherhood is all I've ever 208
really known. I can't betray them, I don't care how much "reprogramming" he does. It's been my entire life. Well, until I met you.

BETH
209 Perhaps the Brotherhood could be 209
your North Star, if it comes to that.

VALDEZ
210 Everything the Brotherhood has 210
meant to me, and still means to me, is always going to be an important part of what makes me who I am.
(MORE)

VALDEZ (CONT'D)
But my North Star is standing right
in front of me.

BETH
211 Do you mean that? 211

VALDEZ
(playfully)
212 When have you known me to say 212
things I don't mean? Of course I
mean it.

BETH
213 There's something I need to tell 213
you. It's important, and... well, I
want to make sure it's not left
unsaid, no matter what happens.

VALDEZ
214 What is it? 214

BETH
215 Odessa... I love you. 215

VALDEZ
216 I love you, too, Beth. When I... 216
thought I was going to lose you,
back at the club... I think that's
when I realized it.
(beat)
217 I guess I knew before that, but it 217
was hard to admit it to myself...
to allow myself to feel that way
again.

BETH
218 After Derek broke your heart. 218

VALDEZ
219 Yeah. I didn't want it to happen 219
again. I was afraid it would...
break me. But I realized that not
only is it okay to take that risk,
I *have to* take it. It just has to
be with the right person.
(beat)
220 With someone who loved me, truly. 220
And who I truly loved back.

BETH and VALDEZ kiss.

BETH

221 So, what did you find when you looked around? Other than locked doors and Super Mutants, that is. 221

VALDEZ

222 Well, it's big, like I said. It must have a huge footprint. 222

BETH

223 Hmm. That might mean that it's even bigger than our intel suggested. And that means that there may be more entrances than we thought there were. 223

VALDEZ

224 And more exits. I wonder... 224

BETH

225 What is it? 225

VALDEZ

226 Well, I wonder just how familiar Bryan is with this facility. Maybe there's a way out that he doesn't know about. 226

BETH

227 There may be. All we have to do is find it. Shall we go exploring? 227

VALDEZ

228 Let's go! 228

MUSICAL TRANSITION

INT. FLAGRANTE BELLO

BETH rattles a door.

BETH

229 Another locked door. There are a lot of them in this section. 229

VALDEZ

230 Yet I don't hear any Super Mutants. Or anything else, for that matter. 230

BETH

231 Maybe it's an area that's not in use? 231

VALDEZ

232 Possibly. But we had to pick two locks just to get into this part of the facility, so whatever's here must be important. If not now, for some... later phase of his plan. 232

BETH

233 At least we know this is a Vault-Tec facility now. Their branding is all over the place. 233

VALDEZ

234 It's interesting... I'm not an expert or anything, but I've been in several Vault-Tec facilities, from California to Appalachia, and I've never seen one quite like this. 234

BETH

235 It's like my place, in a way. But much larger, and much deeper underground. Not quite a Vault, but certainly not an ordinary structure, either. 235

(beat)

236 I wonder how many of these were built... this can't be the only one. 236

VALDEZ

237 And I wonder what it's for. I mean, specifically. Is it just for Project Mind's Eye and Project Tranquility? Is it some kind of research hub for even more projects? 237

BETH

238 It seems too vast to just be for those two projects. It must be the latter. 238

VALDEZ

239 And considering how well it was hidden, whatever they were planning to do here was clearly something they didn't want out in the open. 239

SFX: LABORED FOOTSTEPS

BETH

240 Do you hear that? 240

VALDEZ

241 Someone's coming. We need to get out of sight! 241

BETH

242 All of these doors are locked and I'm not going to be able to pick one in time. Bryan *did* say we had the run of the place. 242

VALDEZ

243 I have a feeling sections we had to break into weren't part of the deal. 243

BETH

244 Wait... it's Dr. Flagler and Dr. Troiani. 244

VALDEZ

245 He doesn't look good. Is there anyone else with them? Guards? 245

BETH

246 I think it's just them. 246

BETH and VALDEZ approach DR. TROIANI and DR. FLAGLER

VALDEZ

247 Are you okay? What happened? 247

DR. TROIANI

248 I'm fine. And he'll *be* fine. He just had his last treatment. It takes some time to recover, both from the procedure and the chem they had to give him, but when he does he should be as good as new. Maybe even better than new. 248

VALDEZ

249 That's great. It was so nice seeing the *real* him when I was first brought down here. The first time I spoke with him was... heartbreaking. He clearly had such a brilliant mind, but he couldn't access it anymore. All because of Vault-Tec. 249

DR. TROIANI

250 I'm just glad to have him back. That's the important part. We'll figure out the rest later. 250

(MORE)

DR. TROIANI (CONT'D)

(beat)

251 I need to take him back to the 251
residential area. You two be
careful - I don't think you're
supposed to be here.

VALDEZ

252 We're not. Thank you, we will be 252
careful.

DR. TROIANI and DR. FLAGLER leave.

BETH

253 Let's head in the direction they 253
were coming from.

BETH and VALDEZ walk up the hall.

VALDEZ

(sotto)

254 Hey. Open door. 254

BETH

255 I see it. Be careful, we don't want 255
anyone to spot us, but maybe we can
listen in. Assuming anyone's still
in there.

BRYAN

256 How does the data look, doctor? 256

DR. FALCO

257 Everything looks good. The 257
operation appears to be a success,
though we won't really know until
we can talk to him.

BRYAN

258 Once we get the process down, I'd 258
like to get started on figuring out
how to do it programmatically. And
we'll need Emily to start working
on integrating the Visiontron
technology into what we have here.

DR. FALCO

259 Good luck convincing her to 259
cooperate.

BRYAN

260 Once she sees what we did for Tony, 260
she'll come around. You did.

DR. FALCO
261 I'm still not comfortable with... 261
the rest of this, and you know
that.

BRYAN
262 You'll come around on that part, 262
too.

BRYAN pauses.

BRYAN (CONT'D)
263 Beth, Odessa, you might as well 263
come in here instead of crouching
outside the door.

BETH sighs. She and VALDEZ enter.

BETH
264 Did you spot us? 264

BRYAN
265 No. But I know you well enough that 265
I figured you'd be showing up right
around now. And I think it's time
we talk.

BETH
266 Oh, is it time for the big villain 266
speech?

BRYAN
267 You think I'm a villain? Come on. 267

BETH
268 You adopted the name of one. That's 268
certainly not a coincidence.

BRYAN
269 I needed a cover, and using the 269
Morningstar's name and reputation
made sense. Besides, he wasn't
using it anymore.

VALDEZ
270 Did you... 270

BRYAN
271 Kill him? Yes. 271
(beat)
272 Oh, don't look at me like that. How 272
many people have you disappeared
since you left the Vault, Beth?
(beat)
(MORE)

BRYAN (CONT'D)

273 That's what I thought. Anyway, now 273
that everyone's here, let's talk
about our path forward.

BETH

274 You say that like we're not 274
prisoners.

BRYAN

275 Well, I'll admit that I knew I'd 275
need a captive audience for this,
but once I explain I think you'll
understand.

VALDEZ

276 And if we don't "understand?" 276

BRYAN

277 If it comes to that - and I don't 277
think it will - we'll deal with it.

VALDEZ

278 I... don't like the sound of that. 278

BRYAN

279 You're both well acquainted with 279
the tech and its capabilities, so
there's no need to rehash that. I
found out about the project when I
was in Virginia. We were buttoning
up some labs and I got curious.
Started reading a few terminal
entries and it hit me - we get this
project finished, it's our best
chance to do what we were sent out
here to do, a lot faster and with a
lot less bloodshed.

BETH

280 I'm not following. 280

BRYAN

281 We know how to build a functioning 281
society, right? Your mom taught us
well. Very well, in fact. The
problem, like it always is, was
people. But I didn't buy that our
only real option was to operate
behind the scenes and *hope* we were
able to manipulate people enough to
get them to do the right thing.
(beat)
282 But I will say, you guys did a 282
great job.

(MORE)

BRYAN (CONT'D)
Your mom got in with Foundation and the Free States, you and your dad both got in deep with a bunch of Raider factions, and you even infiltrated the Brotherhood of Steel. That's pretty impressive.

VALDEZ
283 What?! Did you-- 283

BETH
284 No! I did not "infiltrate" the 284
Brotherhood of Steel.

BRYAN chuckles.

BRYAN
285 Whatever you say, "Acting Knight 285
Kirby." When's the wedding, by the way?
(beat)
286 Anyway, this tech? This gets us 286
where we need to be years ahead of schedule. Maybe decades.

VALDEZ
287 By... reprogramming people? That's 287
not how you save society.

BRYAN
288 And what is? Trusting people to do 288
the right thing? You're not that naïve, Odessa. You've been around. You've seen people. They're going to ruin it, like they always do. Look around. This is what trusting people gets you.

BETH
289 But with you in charge, it will be 289
different, right?

BRYAN
290 Oh, no, you don't understand. Not 290
me. Us.

BETH
291 Us? There is no "us." And there 291
never will be.

BRYAN
292 Oh, Beth. That's where this tech 292
really works its magic.
(MORE)

BRYAN (CONT'D)
I've been using it to... improve myself, with the help of Dr. Falco, of course.

DR. FALCO
293 I was in charge of the memory manipulation part of this project. 293
I expressed my... discomfort with Bryan's plans, but... well, I didn't have much of a choice.

VALDEZ
294 So you're in on this. 294

BRYAN
295 He's not just in on it. He's a partner. Our Merlin. 295

VALDEZ
296 I don't like where this is going. 296
Not one bit.

BETH
297 Let's hear this plan. 297

VALDEZ
298 Beth! You cannot seriously be 298
entertaining any of this.

BETH
299 Let's hear him out. 299

BRYAN
300 See? I knew you'd come around. 300
(beat)
301 We need to establish something that 301
will *last*. And since the powers that be decided to bomb everything back to the Dark Ages, I thought "what's the most stable form of government we can put in place given the circumstances?" Democracy certainly isn't the answer. But you know what is?

VALDEZ
302 A dictatorship? 302

BRYAN
303 No. Think... bigger. 303

BETH
304 You said "dark ages." You don't 304
mean... a monarchy?

BRYAN
305 Now you're getting it. 305

BETH
306 So you want to be a king. 306

BRYAN
307 Maybe an emperor, eventually. But 307
we'll start with king.

VALDEZ
308 You're insane. 308

BRYAN
309 And every king needs his queen. 309

BETH
310 Um... that's not going to happen. 310

BRYAN
311 If we want to set up something that 311
lasts, it needs to be a *hereditary* monarchy. Our children will bear our standard, and their children, and so on.

BETH
312 I'm not going to do this. I am not 312
going to be your queen and I am *not* going to be the mother of your children. I thought we settled this years ago. I thought you knew who I was and I thought you respected that.

BRYAN
313 Of course I know you're a lesbian, 313
Beth. You made that very clear. And yes, I did respect it. But this is a different situation.

BETH
314 I won't cooperate. 314

BRYAN
315 That's disappointing. See, here's 315
the thing. When this process is over, that part of it isn't going to be a concern anymore.

VALDEZ
316 You're going to... reprogam her 316
sexuality? That's disgusting.

BRYAN
317 It's a means to an end, Odessa. And 317
the ends always justify the means.

BETH
318 My sexuality is as integral a part 318
of who I am as anything could be.
If you take that away, if you take
away my agency like this, I will no
longer be the same person, on a
fundamental level.
(beat)
319 I'm going to fight you on this with 319
every fiber of my being.

BRYAN
320 Well, I suppose that's your 320
decision. Ward didn't want to
cooperate, either. You know him,
right? From Foundation? Did you
ever notice that he seems to repeat
himself? Change course mid-
conversation? Tell you how much he
needs that piece of stolen
equipment, even though you're
standing in front of him holding
it? That kind of thing can happen
when you fight it.
(beat)
321 But beyond that, if you go along 321
with this, then Odessa here gets to
leave. Unharmed, except for a
little memory wipe so she doesn't
remember this place exists, or what
our plans are.

BETH
322 And if I don't? 322

BRYAN
323 She becomes another part of the 323
game. I'll send her back to Atlas
with a few... improvements, and it
won't take her long to rise to
power. Then the Brotherhood of
Steel becomes our muscle.

BETH
324 You can't do that. 324

BRYAN
325 Oh, I can. And I will. But if you 325
don't want that to happen, well...
all you have to do is say yes.
(MORE)

BRYAN (CONT'D)
Be my queen and we'll rule Appalachia together. Just think how beautiful our children will be. Oh, and your parents? They won't be harmed, either, of course. They'll be honored members of our royal family. Respected court advisers. In fact, anyone who you want protected will be protected.
(beat)
326 I won't even be offended if you 326
want to take a mistress. How about your Raider friend, Amanda?

VALDEZ
327 You don't have to do this, Beth! We 327
can find another way!

BETH pauses to consider the situation.

BETH
328 Stop. Just... stop. 328
(beat)
329 I'll do it. 329

VALDEZ
330 No! You can't! 330

BETH
331 I have to, Odessa. I'm sorry. 331
There's no way out of this, and I need to keep you safe.

VALDEZ
332 I love you! Isn't that enough to 332
get you to fight?!

BETH
333 Bryan? 333

BRYAN
334 Yes, Beth? 334

BETH
335 Can you make her forget about me? 335

VALDEZ
336 I don't want to forget about you! 336
You're my North Star!

BRYAN
337 I can take care of that when we do 337
her memory wipe. But let's get you sorted first, okay?
(MORE)

BRYAN (CONT'D)
This won't take long. I've had a
lot of practice.
(beat)
338 I hope you don't mind, but... I'm 338
going to poke around a little bit
while I'm in there. I can't wait to
see all the depraved things you two
do to each other.

VALDEZ
339 You're sick. 339

BRYAN
340 Appalachia is sick. And I'm the 340
cure. I'm sorry that you don't
understand. I thought you were
smarter than that. That you
might... join us.

VALDEZ
341 I'll never join you. The 341
Brotherhood will fight you every
step of the way.

BRYAN
342 I'm looking forward to it. But for 342
now...
(beat)
343 Dr. Falco, we won't need the 343
handcuffs to keep Beth in the pod,
fortunately, but we can't have the
Scribe interrupting the
proceedings. Cuff her to that pipe.

DR. FALCO cuffs Valdez to the pipe.

BRYAN (CONT'D)
344 Thank you. Now she can yell, 344
scream, and cry all she wants, but
that won't matter.
(beat)
345 Beth, please get in the pod. Dr. 345
Falco will connect you. I'll
connect myself.

BETH gets into the pod. DR. FALCO connects her to it.

SFX: CONNECTING MACHINE, BEEPS

WHILE INSIDE THE MACHINE, USE ECHO

BRYAN (CONT'D)
346 Alright, I'm in. 346
(beat)
(MORE)

BRYAN (CONT'D)

347 Oh... oh wow. Are you sure you 347
don't want to keep *her* as your
mistress? This is... next-level
stuff.

(beat)

348 You know what? Keep both of them. 348
I'm just adding in attraction to
men, I won't take away the
attraction to women.

BETH

349 Notice anything strange, Bryan? 349

BRYAN

350 What are you talking about? 350

BETH

351 An open door can be passed through 351
in both directions.

BRYAN

352 Stop. You have no idea what you're 352
doing.

BETH

353 Quite the contrary. I know what I'm 353
doing far better than you do. You
sort of blindly felt around in
people's minds to figure out what
to do. I have years and years of
research at my disposal, courtesy
of Dr. Troiani. I hadn't been able
to get it until now, but it appears
that the machine unlocked the
knowledge.

BRYAN

354 No! You can't do this! 354

BETH

355 I have to, Bryan. You lost your 355
way, and I'm going to fix you. What
you saw? Odessa and I together?
That was just so I could distract
you long enough to get inside your
head.

BRYAN

356 Stop this! Stop it right now! 356

BETH

357 I can't do that. And I won't. I 357
want to bring you back, Bryan.

(MORE)

BETH (CONT'D)
I'm going to reset you, back to the way you were just before we left the Vault.
(beat)
358 There. I think I found it. One moment, and I think I'll have it... 358

The machine beeps.

BETH and BRYAN come out of their stupor.

BRYAN
359 Wh... where am I? 359

VALDEZ rushes to BETH.

VALDEZ
360 Beth! What happened? Dr. Falco said something went wrong, but... 360

BETH
361 Quite the contrary, Odessa. Everything went very right. 361

BRYAN
(dazed)
362 Should I know you, ma'am? 362

VALDEZ
363 I'm Odessa Valdez, Brotherhood of Steel. You don't remember me? 363

BRYAN
364 Brotherhood of what? Beth, what's going on? 364

CARLSON enters.

CARLSON
365 We have a problem. 365

DR. FALCO
366 What now? 366

CARLSON
367 I don't know what happened, but those Super Mutants that were locked up in East Wing... well, they're not locked up anymore, and they're headed this way. 367
(beat)
368 Is the procedure complete, Dr. Falco? 368

DR. FALCO
369 Erm... yes, it is. 369

CARLSON
370 My queen. 370

BETH
371 Please get Dr. Troiani and Dr. Flagler to a safe location outside the complex until we get these Super Mutants back in their corrals. They're too important to our plans to risk their safety. 371

CARLSON
372 Yes, ma'am. 372

VALDEZ
373 Uncuff me, please. 373

CARLSON
374 Doctor? 374

DR. FALCO
375 It's fine, Greg. We didn't even have to perform the procedure on her. 375

CARLSON uncuffs VALDEZ.

VALDEZ
376 Thanks. I wish this weren't the only way, but I understand now. The only options for Appalachia are continued existence under our guidance, or... 376

CARLSON
377 Total annihilation. I knew you'd see the light. It's the only logical conclusion. 377

VALDEZ
378 We'll need weapons. 378

CARLSON
379 Two doors down. I'll unlock the door on my way to grab the doctors. Take whatever you need. And stay safe. 379

CARLSON leaves.

DR. FALCO

380 Those Mutants are going to lay 380
waste to this place. We all need to
get out. We're not going to be able
to get the tech itself out, but we
need to preserve this research. You
saw what it did for Dr. Flagler.

VALDEZ

381 Is it stored somewhere? Somewhere 381
that we can get to quickly?

DR. FALCO

382 We keep physical backups in a 382
location not far from one of the
main exits. It's the only exit
that's still open, so we'll have to
go that way anyway.

VALDEZ

383 What are we going to do with 383
Carlson?

DR. FALCO

384 We should be able to deprogram him 384
using a Visiontron. They have a lot
of the same underlying tech as this
stuff. Emily, Tony, and I will
figure it out.

BETH

385 Let's worry about that when we get 385
out of here. Bryan, are you okay to
move?

BRYAN

386 Yeah. I feel fine. But you're going 386
to have to tell me what's going on
at some point. I feel like I just
got yanked out of a dream.

BETH

387 I know the feeling. Let's go. 387

MUSICAL TRANSITION

INT. BACKUP STORAGE OFFICE

BETH

388 We still have about... uh... 388
thirteen Super Mutants hot on our
heels. We need to get these backups
and get out.

DR. FALCO

389 This is it. Terminal's over here, 389
Odessa, next to the door.

BETH

390 I'll hold them off as long as I 390
can.

SFX: EXPLOSIONS

VALDEZ

391 What was that? 391

BETH

392 Sounds like another group is coming 392
from your 9:00. They must've found
the armory. They're going to try to
blast through. The gate should
hold, but I don't know how long.

DR. FALCO

393 Jesus! They're going to bring the 393
whole room down on top of us!

BETH

394 I'm going to concentrate on the 394
ones who were chasing us. I'll
worry about the other ones if and
when they break through.

DR. FALCO

395 Here, let me unlock the storage 395
container with the tapes. There's a
bag we can use to take them in
there.

VALDEZ

396 I don't suppose there are any 396
offsite backups...

DR. FALCO clacks at a terminal.

DR. FALCO

397 I know, I know... 397
(beat)
398 My access code isn't working. 398
Dammit!

VALDEZ

399 I'll hack it. 399

SFX: NEARBY EXPLOSION, CRASHING

VALDEZ (CONT'D)
400 That was too close. How are things 400
going over there, Beth?

BETH
401 I count... eleven Super Mutants 401
still upright.
(pause)
402 Ten. 402
(pause)
403 Nine. They're starting to get a 403
little close for comfort!

VALDEZ
404 I'm almost there! 404
(to the terminal)
405 Come on, come on! 405

BETH
406 I can finish this, you have to take 406
what we already found and get out
of here with Dr. Falco!

VALDEZ
407 I'm not leaving you! 407
(beat)
408 Got it! 408

The terminal chirps and a panel opens, revealing several holotapes, journals, and pieces of technology.

BETH turns to join VALDEZ to gather everything and escape, but before she can move the room collapses, separating them, BETH trapped on the side with the Super Mutants.

VALDEZ (CONT'D)
409 Beth! Are you alright? Can you get 409
through?

BETH
410 I'm ok! But you need to grab what 410
you can and get the hell out of
here!

VALDEZ
411 Five seconds faster... 411

BETH

412 Odessa, listen to me. You need to 412
get Dr. Falco and all of this back
to Fort Atlas, and you need to go
now or else you're going to get
trapped, too.

VALDEZ

413 Five seconds... 413

BETH

414 Odessa Valdez, you stay *focused*! If 414
you love me - and I know you do -
you'll go!

VALDEZ

415 I can't leave you, Beth! 415

BETH

416 If there's another way out of here, 416
I'm going to find it. Heaven and
Earth, remember?

VALDEZ

(crying)

417 I'll hold you to it. You'd better 417
not be lying, or I'll never forgive
you.

BETH chuckles wryly. Weapons fire is still audible behind the rubble.

BETH

418 Understood. 418

(pause)

419 Odessa, I love you. No matter what 419
happens...

VALDEZ

(crying harder)

420 Don't say that! 420

BETH

421 No matter what happens, I am *so* 421
glad I met you. You've helped me
become more than I ever thought I
could be.

VALDEZ

422 I love you, Beth. Heaven and Earth. 422

VALDEZ turns to leave, casting one final glance at the wall of rubble.

BETH is shot and lets out a loud groan.

VALDEZ (CONT'D)
423 Beth! No! 423

DR. FALCO
424 We need to go! Now! 424

VALDEZ
(quietly, crying)
425 I love you, Beth... 425

MUSICAL TRANSITION - PIE JESU/REQUIEM

INT. BETH'S RESIDENCE, DAY

There are people milling about. VALDEZ is distraught.

AMANDA
(tenderly)
426 Odessa, baby... are you sure you 426
want to be here? At her place?

VALDEZ
427 I... I didn't know where else to 427
go.

AMANDA
428 I'm so sorry. I... I know how much 428
you loved her. And I know she loved
you, too.

VALDEZ
429 Thank you, Amanda. 429

AMANDA
430 Do you want to stay with me for a 430
while? You shouldn't be alone right
now.

VALDEZ
431 I think I'd like that. Leila said 431
that I could take all the time I
need, and... I think I'm going to
need a lot.

AMANDA
432 Okay. Come by whenever you're 432
ready.

AMANDA leaves.

ANDREW approaches.

VALDEZ
433 Oh, Mr. Kirby... I... I don't know 433
what to say.

ANDREW
434 There's nothing to say, my dear. 434
But thank you. Is there anything I
can do for *you*?

VALDEZ
435 No... and I should be asking you 435
that question, not the other way
around.

ANDREW
436 Elise and I... we knew that 436
something like this could happen.
But that doesn't make it hurt any
less, of course.
(beat)
437 I'm... glad that you were there 437
with her, at the end. And we
consider you part of our family
now. Our door will always be open
to you.

VALDEZ
438 Thank you, Mr. Kirby. 438

ANDREW
439 Did you go into the secret room? 439

VALDEZ
440 I didn't. Why? 440

ANDREW
441 I don't know for sure, but... she 441
may have left something for you. I
think you should check, when you're
ready.

VALDEZ
442 I'll check now. Thank you for 442
telling me.

ANDREW
443 Of course, my dear. I'll be taking 443
Elise home. We need to mourn there.
Being here is... too much for both
of us right now.

ANDREW leaves.

VALDEZ opens the secret room by moving a book and entering a code on the keypad. She walks down a flight of stairs and into the main room.

VALDEZ

444 A holotape? 444

(beat)

445 And a note... 445

(beat)

446 “Had we but world enough and 446
time...”

VALDEZ retrieves the holotape and inserts it into a terminal. It begins to play.

BETH

(on tape)

447 Well, Odessa, if you’re listening 447
to this, I guess I... didn’t make it. Please tell my parents that I’ve left a tape like this at their place. And Amanda, too. Whatever happened, I hope it was spectacular.

(beat)

448 I also hope that I had a chance to 448
tell you that I love you, and I wish that we’d been able to spend more time together. Those two weeks when I was off chasing leads with dad... fourteen days that I could’ve been with you. This isn’t something I could’ve told you to your face, but I’d really started to believe there was a chance that we’d spend our lives together. Grow old together. Maybe my body produced DMT before I died and that happened. A lifetime in an instant, all spent with you.

(beat)

449 I was so lucky to meet you, and to 449
spend the time with you that I did. To hold your hand, to walk with you. To kiss you, to make love to you. You were fantastic, Odessa. You are so kind, and so capable... you’re going to do great things, I know it. I only wish I could be at your side while you do.

(beat)

450 I loved your moments of glad grace, 450
and I loved your beauty.

(MORE)

BETH (CONT'D)

But I also loved your pilgrim soul, and I wish I'd had the chance to love the sorrows of your changing face.

(beat)

451 I hope you think about me, 451
sometimes. About how love fled, and paced upon the mountains overhead, and hid my face amid a crowd of stars.

(beat)

452 I hope that we can meet again, 452
someday, perhaps in that same crowd of stars. But not for a long time. You have so much life left ahead of you. Live it.

The holotape clicks off.

VALDEZ begins to sob.

VALDEZ

453 I'm sorry, Beth... 453

BETH enters.

BETH

454 It's alright. But I suppose I'll 454
have to record another one of those now.

VALDEZ

455 Beth! You're... 455

BETH

456 Alive? Yes, I am. Although... ugh. 456
I've felt better.

VALDEZ

457 You just missed your parents! And 457
Amanda!

BETH

458 We'll need to contact them right 458
away. Let them know I'm... not dead.

VALDEZ

459 What happened?! Let's get you to 459
the medical bay.

BETH

460 Those bloody Super Mutants got me, 460
right in the gut.

(MORE)

BETH (CONT'D)
I went down, but I still had enough of my wits about me to take out the five that were left. I dragged myself to a medical bay and patched myself up, but I must've passed out from the pain before I could get to a stimpak.
(beat)
461 I don't know how long I was out, 461
but when I came to, I heard the rest of those Super Mutants trying to take the safety gate down, so I had to press onward. And it's a good thing they forced me in the direction they did, because I managed to find an emergency egress point.
(beat)
462 But, Odessa... 462

VALDEZ
463 What is it? 463

BETH
464 It was the thought that I might 464
never see you again that gave me the strength to go on. I don't know how else to explain finding that hatch, but in a way... it was you.

VALDEZ
465 No, Beth. It was you. But either 465
way... our story clearly wasn't meant to end yet.

BETH
466 So what now? What's next in that 466
story?

VALDEZ
467 I don't know. But we'll find out 467
together.

BETH
468 I love you, Odessa. 468

VALDEZ
469 I love you, Beth. 469

END OF ACT THREE

EPILOGUE

INT. TESS'S BEDROOM, NIGHT

ELIZABETH has just finished reading a bedtime story.

ELIZABETH
470 ...and they lived happily ever 470
after.

TESS
471 What? That can't be all there is to 471
it.

SFX: MUSIC STOPS ABRUPTLY

ELIZABETH
472 There *is* more. A lot more. But it's 472
late.

TESS
473 Come on... just give me a hint. 473
What does "happily ever after" even
mean?

ELIZABETH sighs.

ELIZABETH
474 Okay. 474
(beat)
475 Beth and Odessa got married not 475
long after that. About a year and a
half, maybe two years later. They
had five children - the twins,
Andrew & Amanda, came first, then
David, Cynthia, and Daniel.
(beat)
476 Do you remember he stories I told 476
you about Great-Great Grandma
Cynthia?

TESS
477 I loved those stories! Wait, was 477
she...

ELIZABETH
478 Yes! Grandma Cynthia was Beth and 478
Odessa's daughter. Her maiden name
was Valdez-Kirby.

TESS
479 Oh, wow... 479

ELIZABETH
480 Wow indeed. 480

TESS
481 So what else happened? 481

ELIZABETH
482 You're really pushing your luck... 482

TESS
483 Just a little bit more... 483

JACK, TESS's father and ELIZABETH's husband enters.

JACK
(kind, but firm)
484 Hey, what's going on in here? 484
Lights out, Tess, you have to be up early tomorrow for school!

ELIZABETH
485 *Somebody* won't take "happily ever 485
after" for an answer.

JACK laughs.

JACK
486 I see. How about this - if I tell 486
you how the story ends, will you go to sleep?

TESS
487 Okay, deal. 487

JACK
488 Okay. Grandma Beth lived until 488
2167. Their whole family was with her when she passed... Grandma Odessa, their children, grandchildren... even a few great-grandchildren.

TESS
489 Were you there, mom?! 489

ELIZABETH
490 No. I wasn't born until about a 490
year later. But *my* mom and dad were there, and that's why they named me Elizabeth.

TESS
491 What about Odessa? 491

JACK

492 She... declined quickly after she lost Beth. They'd spent a lifetime together. Their family stayed by her side, too, until the end. Her last words were "a crowd of stars." 492

TESS

493 Are you crying? 493

ELIZABETH

494 A little, yeah. 494

TESS

495 But what happened in the middle?! You left out what... 60 years? 495

JACK

496 A deal's a deal, kiddo. 496

TESS

497 Awww. 497

JACK

498 We'll tell you the rest of their story, okay? I promise. Just not tonight. 498

TESS

(disappointed)

499 Okay. 499

(beat)

500 Good night, mom. Good night, dad. I love you. 500

JACK

501 I love you too, Tess. Good night. 501

ELIZABETH

502 Good night. I love you. 502

ELIZABETH switches off the light.

ELIZABETH and JACK leave and close the door.

JACK

503 You okay, hon? 503

ELIZABETH

504 Yeah. It's just... that story. It really hits me hard. I don't know if I'm going to be able to read the rest to her. They went through so much. 504

JACK

505 There were ups and downs, sure. The downs were pretty low, but the ups were incredible. 505

(beat)

506 Sound familiar? 506

ELIZABETH laughs.

ELIZABETH

507 It does. 507

JACK

508 I'm still going through everything they retrieved from that lab. There's a lot there. But I promise I'll get it all written down for you. 508

ELIZABETH

509 Do you think it's all true? 509

JACK

510 Well, the historian said that everything checks out timeline-wise, so I'm going to choose to believe that it is. 510

ELIZABETH

511 Regardless, it's one hell of a story. 511

JACK

512 A story that needs to be told. And I'm going to make sure it is. 512

<u>THE END</u>

Made in the USA
Columbia, SC
03 August 2025

326a0493-eb11-4e99-bf4d-8eaa87bb4a31R01